"But as for an exact reckoning of days, after I had once lost it I could never recover it again."
— Robinson Crusoe

Part One
Chapter One

The evening launches were famously beautiful. The sprinters dashed across the black sky like flaming arrows. The interstellar arks gave a blue light so bright that it showed all the boats in the nighttime harbor. Colonel Endling liked to buy roasted peanuts and eat them at the seawall above the beach. From there, he could watch the departures and arrivals. After all these years of retirement, the grand movements in the sky still got to him. The ocean breeze was strong. It mussed his white hair and tickled his illustrious, white mustache.

"Storm coming," he said to his companion. "Bad one. Feel it in my whiskers, always feel it in my whiskers."

"Forecast agrees with you, Colonel."

Colonel Endling's assistant Sleeper was always with him. Sleeper was creepy. He had an ageless face. Could vanish into any crowd. And to the never-ending amazement of his boss, he chewed the peanut shells and threw away the nuts. A pair of rock pigeons wobbled over to nibble them. The birds were chummy. They had necks of sheeny purple and green. A stranger approached Sleeper at the wall and asked if he had the *true time*. Sleeper looked at his watch, but Colonel Endling shooed the man away.

As a rule, Sleeper stayed away from the beach. He broke that rule a few times every year. The sad fact is that's where he could buy some of the things outlawed in the city limits: rums over 90-proof, banned digital devices, a certain kind of companionship. Colonel Endling was the first person to lie to Sleeper about the shore. He wasn't the last, but since his early days on Triste, more than a decade now, Sleeper had come to know, if not the key to the shore's mysteries, then, as a consolation, what you could and couldn't get from the beach community.

The Colonel looked out at the sand. Their spot was very near the midpoint of the beach's enormous crescent. Cut into that mid-point like a single bite from a sandwich, there was a shallow tidal pool. It was surrounded by palm trees. The makers of Ocean Boulevard had built a wide, slow curve to preserve this oasis of green. Tonight, in the dark after second dusk, brave, young lovers swam there with the tiny, bioluminescent turtles that made it glow. A few hundred yards off-shore, around a rapidly-disappearing sandbar, a massive flamboyance of pink flamingos (many hundreds) stuffed themselves with algae ahead of the storm that was coming. As far as the Colonel could look, both left and right down the beach, people were taking down tents and packing to move inland.

"See the police?" Sleeper asked.

He hadn't, so he was impressed that Sleeper had seen them, moving from cluster to cluster of tents, encouraging the packing that was already under way. The Colonel touched his gun in its shoulder holster. Still there, always good to know it was there.

Sleeper wasn't the brightest, the Colonel thought, but he was loyal, and he noticed things the Colonel had started to miss as he grew older.

A military ark launched at eight on the dot and blasted out on an Earth-bound trajectory. The white tents on the beach went blue. So, did the faces that turned to look. The Colonel checked the trajectory. He didn't see any other vessels. There would be no near-miss this time. He felt relieved.

"Will we search tomorrow?" Sleeper asked.

"Depends upon the rain."

"Do you know where?"

"I'll decide. We'll hitch a ride with the Marines."

The Colonel kept all his maps in the Mission Building. The oldest map of Radium Beach looked to Sleeper like nothing more impressive than the water stains on the ceiling of his own apartment. Dark, geographical blobs looked like tranquil, dead lunar seas. Rumors long held that the Mission HQ was a massive Faraday cage, and, with its blue and black glass facades, it was thoroughly inscrutable from the outside. The world reflected in its surfaces looked more vivid than the world itself. Ever a puzzle, people looked at themselves in that glass and thought don't I look great, or why do I look so sad, or, amazingly, that looks nothing like me.

A cop walked up and grabbed Sleeper's shoulder. He pointed to an empty peanut carton on the ground.

"Pick that up," the cop said. He had an agitated face, as they all did when a storm was coming.

"It's not mine," Sleeper said.

"I saw you throw it there."

"You did not."

The cop's fingers dug into Sleeper's shoulder joint.

"Pick it up."

"Hey, this is bullshit," Sleeper said.

"All right, all right," the Colonel said. "Easy does it."

The old man bent to pick up the litter, and the cop glared at Sleeper before releasing his shoulder and walking away. They watched him move to the ramp leading off the beach where a line of men and women slowly walked off, shepherding their children. They had tired but acquiescent faces, as they dragged long tent poles behind them and all their worldly possessions. A quartet of children caught their attention. A fierce, Japanese adolescent with tall, black hair led three younger, white kids. They snuck furtively by the cop, and, once past him, sprinted full-tilt towards the tall buildings of the Radium Beach business district.

"Let's start early. We'll hitch a ride with the Marines."

The typhoon battered the city all night. When the fast sun came up, the beach people were already back, raking the sand level again, re-pitching their tents, starting the huge, communal breakfast that was tradition when they made it through another stormy night.

Chapter Two

They set out early to snag a ride on a Marine flight. Radium Beach used to be the murder capital of the galaxy. That was before the Marines moved in. Close to the same number of corpses ended up in the city morgue, but sanctioned kills changed the stats. Don't tell the Marines that. If you ask them, they're on edge twenty-four hours a day. If you ask them, they're being shot and bombed and ambushed all day long. Lieutenant Metzger met Colonel Endling and Sleeper at the gate. He let them into the base. He was the pilot for today's hyperotor flight. They'd flown with Metzger many times. He was competent. He knew how to maneuver if ground fire erupted.

The Lieutenant tried to take them on a path that turned away from an incoming landing, but Sleeper saw what Metzger didn't want them to see. A small band of soldiers trotted off the tarmac, carrying stretchers bearing the dead. The living looked as gray and horrible as the dead. The runners didn't look in their direction. They moved with grim, sacred purpose.

Metzger snorted when the Colonel said words like chopper and helicopter, habits from his childhood in Omaha. They got along like old friends. The storm had wound down. The Fast Sun was trying to break through. Six Marines piled in behind them. The rotor lifted off the pad, pointed its nose at Redemption Rock and hurtled forth at 400 knots.

"Okay, boys," Metzger said through the intercom. "You know the drill. Turn off your phones otherwise the pulse guns will break them."

Colonel Endling closed his eyes and drifted off to the hum of the huge Einhorn disc rotor above their heads. The Marines were all readiness. One grunt called Flowers whistled, as he adjusted the contrast on his helmet camera. They passed beyond the city limits and flew over miles of desert. All the vast space between landing zones was hostile to life. They saw the unknowable, stone sculptures at Daphne for just a few seconds before zipping past. There was nobody out there. On the approach to Redemption Rock, Metzger talked on the intercom again.

"We need to make a stop," he said. "There's a riot near the power district."

The rotor took a sharp turn right and slowed down. From a distance, the solar farm looked like black square pools for irrigation. They powered all three of the planet's large cities. Metzger circled twice to get eyes on the crowd near the farm's perimeter. When the rotor descended, parts of the crowd dispersed, but a majority stayed put and watched the landing. They touched down easy. The Marines jumped out. Many of the male civilians in the gathered crowd wore suits and ties. They were covered in dust. They looked at the Marines with contempt. Metzger shut down the rotor and talked on the PA system. His voice was genial but deep with authority.

He said, "Somebody tell these friendly Marines what is going on here."

"Stay here a minute, Colonel. I don't like the looks of this," he said through the com. And before he switched it off, Sleeper heard him say: "Drones to my position."

The drones arrived within a minute. There were two. They circled the area, sometimes low enough to threaten, other times stenciled against the high, stone mountains on the horizon. Sleeper felt himself pushing his own spine closer to the steel behind his back.

Flowers came walking back to the rotor and talked to Metzger in the cockpit. He examined the tight cables of muscle in his own forearm as he talked. Then, he looked at his own bald head in the shiny black side of the rotor. His head looked like a round, tan rock.

"They have a man over there," Flowers said. "The Guild tried to hang him, but the rope broke."

Sleeper looked over at the crowd, but they'd circled around whoever he meant.

"Fuck," Metzger said. "Shit. Are they gone now?"

"They left an hour ago."

"Police?"

"Police stopped by and then left without helping the guy. He's in bad shape."

"Let me talk to Command."

Flowers walked a few paces towards the crowd and bent over and did some stretches. His desert colored battledress had dark spots of sweat. Flowers adjusted his helmet camera. He looked at his watch. When he came back over, Sleeper asked what time did he have? Flowers looked at his watch again, but he caught himself, realizing what Sleeper was doing.

"I have the *true time*," he said. His smirk didn't quite acknowledge. It was close, but Sleeper was somewhere beneath his full recognition.

"Hey, orders from Command," Metzger said. "They want us to bring him in."

"Okay," Flowers said. "Done."

"Can you handle this?" Metzger asked. "Or do you need me to come out there and help?"

"We got this."

Metzger spoke again on the PA system. He sharpened his tone. The drones flashed overhead. Sleeper could not see much from his seat inside the rotor, but he could hear groans and rumbling from the people. Metzger said, "Attention, good people. The Marines are going to take this man into custody. Please make room for the Marines. Very good. Please make room. Good. Yes, that's good. Thank you."

Chapter Three

Colonel Endling became famous after he cracked the Case of the Big Brain. News clips loved the handsome, white-haired man standing by the table stacked with bars of gold. Every stolen ounce was returned. There was so much gold, the table collapsed. His sound bite went viral that year. "How'd you solve this case?" the woman with the microphone asked him. Colonel Endling played demure with his hand gestures, but then he tapped his own temple and said, "Bigger brain."

His fame continued a decade into retirement. In the landing zone's canteen, Marines came over to shake his hand. He froze. He wanted sugar for his wretched coffee, but he was too polite to brush off the admirers. He couldn't get near the table with the sugar packets. Sleeper watched him pull on his white whiskers. This happened everywhere they went, but today the Colonel was impatient.

"What the hell happened out there?" the Colonel whispered a few minutes later. They had followed Lieutenant Metzger to a quiet table. Metzger shoveled in chili like a machine designed to do only that.

"I can't tell you any details, Colonel, you're a civilian."

"I have highest clearance at the Mission."

"Shit, Colonel, that's like having a library card."

"Lieutenant, please."

"Clearance at the Mission isn't Military Ops."

The old man yanked at his white whiskers.

"The Guild is publicly hanging people," the Colonel said.

Metzger shrugged.

"That much we overheard. That's not their way."

Metzger shrugged again.

"It's some new way," Sleeper said.

It was last call on the chili pot, so a dozen Marines raced and laughed and swore at the far end of the canteen.

"This man you brought in today," Colonel Endling said. "Was he a scout on the ground for the drones?"

Metzger's eyebrow shot up. He nodded. Yes. Sleeper in his naiveté did not know that such a class of informant existed.

It was afternoon when they reached the Garden District. The well-to-do people of Redemption Rock went about their business in stores and restaurants. The Colonel and Sleeper sat beneath a red umbrella at an outdoor café. Sleeper sat with his back to the wall, so he could watch the street. The pink cobblestones and red bricks were charming despite his growing worry. It was the time of changing light between first dusk and second dawn. It grew dim but never full dark in that melancholy hour.

At a table nearby, three boys played with a xylophone. They ranged in age, the boys, from maybe six to nine, and they were great sharers. The mallet passed patiently among them, turn after turn, and they had all played it with some intention before, since there was no mad bang-bang-bang, but rather a sweet, improvised melody they built together. As he watched, Sleeper could not help his desire to protect them. One of the kids sat on his knees on his chair and leaned too far forward on his belly on the table, and Sleeper wanted to rush over and settle him safely, an emotion that surprised him.

The kids got up after a while and played hide and seek behind the imposing statues that ringed the square. The nearest was the angel atop the Explorers' Monument. He was so tall. The height of ten men, Sleeper guessed. He had enormous wings and a long sword. He looked like the angel that might point his sword and lead a young couple out of Eden and forever block their return. The kids didn't know that old story. Two boys climbed the angel and hung upside down from his shoulders until the Japanese teen they'd seen evacuating Radium Beach walked over and shouted at them. They climbed slowly down, then darted as soon as they hit the ground.

"Let's go for a stroll," the Colonel said. He put his hand on Sleeper's shoulder.

"All right."

Five blocks of walking brought them to a green lane they had scouted already. They passed under the ivy-covered arch that announced Embassy Row.

"You have a strong hunch about this neighborhood?"

"I do," the Colonel replied. "I'm almost certain."

Sleeper never believed in the legendary tunnel that the Colonel sought. He wasn't programmed for belief. But he loved the Colonel, so he always followed.

The Mission's interest in finding the tunnel was long dead, but it was too late to stop the Colonel. He was like an obsessed scholar. Sleeper didn't mind. Walks along the avenue of mansions were pleasant enough, he thought. He turned over in his mind the old story the Colonel liked to tell.

The first explorer to reach Triste was a French astronaut named Souci who landed solo and set up his camp wholly innocent of the fact that he would never return to Earth. The planet had only a Kepler number then. Souci's first transmissions describing the habitable planet brought wildly ecstatic celebrations to the Mission HQ in Colorado Springs. When his reports abruptly stopped, a follow team found his camp, his sprinter and all his records, but there was no Souci anywhere. Alive nor dead, he was never found.

Souci's journal, written in tiny engineer's block lettering, contained an eerie claim that could not be verified: Marvelous sign. Unexpected, unforeseen. I'm not the first. Today, I found a door that opens to a tunnel in the rock. Very old. At the end of the tunnel, small rooms with iron bars like a prison. I lost my breath in an attack of panic. Tomorrow I will take pictures.

It was natural for the Mission to assume they'd find Souci in the tunnel, but where was it? He didn't say. They had no idea. The mystery of the explorer's fate was eclipsed by the vital discovery of Earth's twin with her deep ocean and countless, pristine beaches. Settlers came, and some looked for the tunnel. It developed a legend. In the fourth year after settlement, eight million people moved to Triste. They built three cities and a sprawl of housing. That first generation multiplied, and with the children born on Triste, the myth of Souci took speculative twists. There was a city underground, some said, or a vast train system that led to untold parts of the world. Souci had been locked up in the prison, and his bones would be there today. It was a trap, the entrance to Hell.

The Colonel didn't care about those things. He cared about Souci's short journal entry, and he wanted the unknown eradicated from his brain. Over time, he developed a theory that the door was known to certain parties in Redemption Rock, and that it was hidden in one of the elaborate gardens on Embassy Row. He used friendly social engineering to gain access to the estates. As they strolled, the sidewalk meandered to follow a canal. Other walkers passed them. Women carried parasols to prepare for the bright explosion of the second dawn. When a bicycle cop began to pedal towards them, the Colonel stopped to sit on a stone bench.

"Let me do the talking," he said.

Chapter Four

If we saw the Trojan Horse coming, and we saw its true nature, we couldn't call it the Trojan Horse. That's what the Colonel told the judge about to hand down his sentence for espionage and treason. *Yes*, the judge retorted harshly, *and if the people you betrayed were not dead, they would still be alive.* The Colonel was nervous and bungled his point. This was later, during the trial for his life, and to say more would be to jump too far ahead in the story. It's enough to know the Colonel was talking about this day in Redemption Rock.

The bicycle cop put her foot on the stone bench. She steadied herself and politely asked for their passports. Her blue eyes were spellbinding. Captain Quince, her badge said. As the Slow Sun rose, the willows along the canal cast striped shadows all over. She was half in light, half in dark.

"I know a Captain Quince," the Colonel said.

"Oh yeah?"

"Is he your father?"

"Uncle," she said.

"He's the best sort of people."

She stared at the passports for a long time.

"Weren't you the Mayor over in Radium Beach?"

"No, no," the Colonel said. "Not the Mayor."

"Why do I remember you?" she asked.

"I have one of those faces."

"You do."

"How long have you had this patrol?"

"I'm only filling in today," she said. "But it sure is paradise over here. So green and so lovely."

She handed back the passports.

"Have you heard the Icelandic Singer?" Colonel Endling asked. "You must know his voice."

"Who?"

"The Icelandic Singer. Have you heard his garden songs?"

She laughed with genuine surprise.

"Come," the Colonel said. "Follow me."

She tensed at this, but, after considering, she followed. She pedaled slowly, as the old man led the way. The mania for formal gardens in Redemption Rock was a thing everyone assented to without love. The groundskeepers competed for prestige, and the gardener at Iceland's embassy was the greatest. He sang and whistled as he worked, not for joy but for mad, superstitious reasons. It was a wonder there was green life anywhere on Triste, a miracle almost. He sang to please it.

The footpath veered from the road to stick tighter with the canal's route. The Colonel stopped at a spot where the path was the high ground, and the embassy's land ran downhill. There, it could be viewed from a vantage. He walked to the black, wrought iron fence and motioned for Sleeper and Captain Quince to come too. The gardens looked as if some giant had embroidered patterns in the ground. There were acre-sized swirls and serpentine lines, perfect diamonds and sleeping tigers.

"Listen."

And the green grass grows all around and
around, and the green grass grows all around. Pause.
And the green grass grows all around and around, and
the green grass grows all around.

It was distant.

"I don't hear anything."

There was the spitting hiss of sprinklers, but, in
the distance, yes, a faint song.

And the green grass grows all around and
around, and the green grass grows all around. And the
green grass grows all around and around, and the green
grass grows all around.

It stopped abruptly, and they saw why. The
gardener bedeviled himself, as he tried to rid his hedge
maze of geese. He raised his arms above his head and
roared, but the blackheaded birds simply looked at him
and nibbled things on the ground or wobbled about on
their strange, webbed feet.

"Why does he rage like that?" Captain Quince
laughed.

"They shit everywhere," the Colonel said.

"Oh, ha ha ha."

"They do. They shit and shit."

Sleeper grabbed the fence. He poked his head
through the bars for a better peek at the madman, and
both men stood like that, their hands in identical
positions, like a father and son, it was too easy, almost
enough to break her heart, Piper thought, but only
almost. Her name was not Captain Quince--he was
bleeding out a mile away-—and she had never been an
officer of any police force. She removed a shiny, silver

vial from her pocket. When she pulled the seal off, tiny silver bots began to crawl on her hips. They looked like metallic fleas, and they could jump like those suckers, and jump they did. They landed on Sleeper's shirt and pants. They tucked into his sock. Others hid under the collar of the Colonel's blue shirt and in the white curls of his hair. They never suspected a thing.

Piper had tailed them from the café. She had not been hopeful, but as she watched them walk down Embassy Row, two miles at least, all the way up to the front door of the South American embassy (where they knocked), she pumped her first, because she could not have dreamed anything better.

Chapter Five

The South American Embassy was antique brick like much of Redemption Rock, not actually old, but designed to look that way. The entranceway was clear of the green ivy and vines that climbed the walls. Colonel Endling and Sleeper waited for the sentry to answer their knock. Sleeper ran his hands through his brown hair. He lacked patience. Gonna cut it all off, he said. Colonel Endling put a hand on his shoulder.

The heavy door opened.

"Colonel Endling to see Ambassador Hidalgo, please."

"One moment."

A few minutes later a tall figure in a black suit approached. It was the ambassador. Hugo Hidalgo was irresistible. He looked like a movie star who'd been a brawler in his youth. When he smiled, everybody smiled back. He won you to his side without a thought. That made him a great diplomat. Sleeper *hated* that smile, and he also hated Hugo's colder look that told you he was connected to power that could send you to prison or back to Earth.

"I'm so glad you've come."

"Can we talk?" the Colonel asked.

"We are just about to begin an important meeting," Hugo said. "But, yes. Perfect. You can join us."

They went up a flight of stairs to the Mezzanine. As they went up, some of the silver bots that had stowed their way into the building detached themselves from the visitors and slid down the escalator's handrails. No eye detected them. They dispersed.

The Mezzanine was immense. A small group of waiters hustled around, draping dozens of triangular tables with purple cloth. Hugo walked quickly to the kitchen with his guests behind him. His heels clicked on the immaculate floor. In the kitchen, his cook staff waited before a line of chocolate fountains.

"This is critical business," Hugo said. "Critical."

"This is the important meeting?" Sleeper asked. He snorted.

"You have no idea."

Hugo winked. He handed a bowl of bananas to the Colonel.

"We are in the final stages of planning a state dinner," Hugo said. "This is critical."

The cook staff wheeled the fountains out to the Mezzanine floor. Hugo dismissed them.

"We have all these varieties. Try them. Help me decide."

"Hugo, can we talk?" the Colonel asked.

"Yes. Talk."

"We hitched a ride on a Marine Corps flight today."

"Yes?"

"Very unofficial. I'm troubled by what we saw."

"You saw what?" Hugo asked, as he dipped a banana. "I like *this* one."

"The Guild is executing civilians in public."

"Ah, yes, the Guild, the loud-mouth The Guild. I would not worry, Colonel Endling."

"Why not?" the Colonel asked.

"They are glorious now," Hugo said. "They will not be glorious tomorrow."

"That's provocative," Sleeper said.

"I should not say more."

Hugo walked away with a dramatic turn on his heel and a strawberry held aloft. He headed to the dark chocolate bubbling and oozing at the end of the line. The man loved theater. How he and the Colonel ever became friends was bewildering to Sleeper.

"Please try this one."

Yes, the dark chocolate was the best, the Colonel declared.

"Did you find your tunnel today?" Hugo asked.

"No," the Colonel said. "But I am onto you, Hugo."

"You're too intense for me, my Colonel."

"You're too evasive. How do I get you to explain what you mean about the Guild?"

"You haven't asked me who I am hosting for dinner. Who loves chocolate?"

"All right," the Colonel said. "Who is it?"

"Gun Club."

The Colonel's face dropped.

"No."

"Yes."

"I've heard he does love chocolate."

"Yes," Hugo said. He rubbed his hands together.

"He's coming to Triste?"

"He's already here."

"Impossible."

Hugo shook his head.

Colonel Endling carried the bowl of bananas across the room and threw it into a trash barrel. It shattered loudly.

"I trust you both with this information. The news will be out soon enough, but keep this quiet. Don't tell anyone."

The Colonel had moved to a window. He stood looking out at the green world. Sleeper inserted himself into the talk.

"Gun Club has said he will never return to Triste."

"That is what he has said," Hugo replied.

"He says he will never leave his bunker in Boulder."

"Yes, that is what he says."

"It's not true?"

"He has been coming here in secret for years."

"You are blowing my mind."

"Look at me, Sebastian," Hugo said.

Sleeper looked him in the eye.

"You have to help. He is going to pick the wrong side. There's going to be a conflict. There is going to be a conflict, and our Colonel is going to pick the wrong side. I know him."

"Which side is the right side?"

"My side," Hugo said.

"Your side?" Sleeper repeated.

"Gun Club's side, the stronger side."

"I will help him."

"You have to help him. He's going to pick wrong."

Hugo pulled a blue envelope from his jacket pocket.

"Will you be flying back to Radium Beach?"

"Yes, tonight."

"I ask you to hand deliver this letter for me."

Sleeper looked over at his boss. The Colonel sulked, but he looked calm. The envelope had a name and address Sleeper recognized. Was it a love letter? Hugo did have a reputation.

"Do you know the address?"

"Yes," Sleeper replied. "You know her?"

"I know everyone."

Chapter Six

With darkness, the rotor lifted off and left Redemption Rock. Triste had no moons, so the nights were very dark. In the cabin with Sleeper and the Colonel sat four Marines and the incompletely hanged man. This man was cuffed to the seat harness. He looked half dead, but he was alert and agitated. In his frustration, he kept scratching his black beard. He scratched and scratched. Dozens of rotors flew in formation in the opposite direction. They flashed lights at each other, like winking fireflies, as they passed.

"Where are you taking me?" the hanged man asked.

"Safe house," the Marine called Flowers said.

"My Mum and Dad are back there. I've ruined them."

"They'll be okay. Stop talking now."

He was quiet for a while then began to mumble to himself. How could I be so stupid? For money? For money. How could I be so stupid? I'm dead.

"Stop talking now," Flowers repeated.

"It's quite possible your Mum and Dad are the ones who turned you in."

It was the Colonel who said this, and Sleeper couldn't believe it. The Colonel had an optimism that never failed him. This harsh realism was shocking. Sleeper heard everything the Colonel said in a new light. Hugo's warning had disturbed him.

"Wow," Flowers said. "At least somebody said it."

The hanged man turned a sad face to the Colonel.

"Do I know you, brother?" he asked. "Have we met?"

"No, we haven't met."

The Colonel had the kindest face in sight, so the hanged man turned to him with a look like a King in a tragedy who finds he has no friends left on the stage.

"My Mum and Dad wouldn't do that to me."

"In my experience, people have good instincts about things like this," the Colonel said. "They can surprise you."

"Things like what exactly?"

He coughed and rubbed his neck.

"Right and wrong," the Colonel said. "Life and death."

"I'm ready to stand behind what I did, but I can't believe they'd turn me in."

"You scouted for the drones. That's evil."

The Colonel closed his eyes as if he'd take a nap.

"Why are you talking to me like this?" the hanged man asked.

"Why is anyone talking at all?" (Flowers)

He scratched his black beard and looked from face to face before settling on the Colonel again.

"I know my story, old man, but how did *you* get tangled up with these killers?"

He said this as if under his breath, as if in an aside to an audience, but it was loud enough for all to hear. The Colonel did not open his eyes.

"Yes, avoid the question."

Sleeper was surprised the Colonel did not pepper the hanged man with questions.

"My poor Mum and Dad," the man went on. "They're just humble botanical importers. They have a modest greenhouse in Dreaming Back Lake, and they sell plants to the gardeners in Redemption Rock."

"Imports from Earth?" Sleeper could not help himself.

"Yeah. I was born here, but they are from the USA."

"Where?"

"Nebraska."

Sleeper looked at the Colonel, but, again, he did not open his eyes.

"Stop this talking now," Flowers said. "I'm serious. I will zap you."

The rotor flew the rest of the way in silence. Radium Beach did not allow high approach speeds, so the trip was long and slow. Sleeper always watched for the glow of the city's lights, and, just as he began to see that, Lieutenant Metzger in the cockpit did, too. He spoke on the radio.

"There's a big fire in the city," he said. "Really big."

As they closed in, they saw it. It was the new soccer stadium. The Atoms had just played their first game (before 50,000 spectators) in the last week. The stadium was a long cuboid with walls made of inflated ETFE plastic panels. These panels were burning. The fire was immense. The stadium was the largest thing in the city, so, when it was engulfed, fire became the largest thing in the city. A mile away, they felt the heat. The size was one thing, but that heat and the smell of the burning plastic scared Sleeper. He had a feeling the world was coming to an end.

"The parking lot is empty," the Colonel said. "Nobody there. That's a blessing."

"Amen."

Firefighting drones swarmed the flames. They moved too quickly to count, but there had to be sixty of them, Sleeper thought. The chemical retardants they dropped came down like the flakes in a snow globe, and the whole thing—the bright orange light, the grace of the machines in flight, the heat shimmer—the whole view was pretty, Sleeper had to admit, as he chewed the inside of his cheek and tried to beat down the dread that was growing inside him.

Metzger landed the rotor at the base. A Jeep load of Marines met them. Four of them jumped out of the vehicle, laughing and pointing at the hanged man. They looked in the mood for trouble. One sergeant shackled the man's cuffs to a bar that crossed the spare tire on the Jeep.

The Colonel must have noticed Sleeper was turning pale in the face. He touched his shoulder and got him walking towards the gatehouse, and just as quickly as the incompletely hanged man had entered the life of Sebastian Sleeper, he was out of it, never to be seen again.

Chapter Seven

Those four boys we saw leaving the beach, climbing the statue, we must pick up their story now. They were orphans. Like every Tristean not sheltered under the corporate wing of the Mission, they needed to eat, so they had to find ways to scrape money together. They were sometimes scavengers. Yoshi, their elder and leader (barely a teen himself) had a gifted eye with a slingshot. He liked to shoot down the drones.

They'd see the smoke of a crash and make for the horizon. This time: Yoshi halted them because of the wolves. The carnivorous bastards lurked in the trees. Wolves, mean looking wolves. These five or six timber wolves, big hundred pounders with ragged coats, lurked in the forest line in the darkening night. They might pick up the scent of people even this far away, no doubt, but Yoshi had night vision goggles. He could watch their movements. The second oldest, Toad, stood next to him. Toad asked for the goggles. Yoshi did not hand them over. He was the leader, and it amused people to see a fierce, little Japanese adolescent leading the pack of white surfer kids from the beach.

Yoshi stayed up all night watching through the goggles. Morning showed the wolves gone. He gathered up the sleeping younger kids. An hour later, the gang of four walked up to the big entrance gate.

"What kind of church is it?" Toad asked. He could read the word over the gate. CHURCH.

Yoshi could read, too. "It's not a church," he said.

There were white pillars pocked with bullet holes. Toad felt the place was full of ghosts—lots of ghosts but not ghosts with faces of people—a great thundering rush of ghosts—here—then there—then gone. There was a Guild truck crashed into one of the pillars. The truck had taken the worst of that collision. Yoshi investigated the empty cab, as they walked through the gates.

"Does everyone remember the parts we're looking for?" he asked.

The drone had taken off the top of one of the twin hypodermic steeples of the compound. A great scorching took what few gray shingles remained on the roof. Yoshi wondered how the building itself did not burn to the ground. He moved towards the crater. The younger kids were already stomping down tall grass to get a closer look.

Yoshi started small. The buyer sat behind his counter with a smirk on his chubby face. He was a middle-aged guy, black hair gone about 60% gray, and he wore a sprinter pilot's silver suit with the sleeves cut off. His bare arms had patches of what looked like acid burns all up and down. The walls of his pod had capacitors pinned up systematically, by color or size or usage, and they looked like a thousand beetles tacked in a collector's case. Yoshi pulled the downed drone's satellite antenna from his bag. The buyer whistled as if impressed, and Yoshi squinted at him to see if he was being mocked. The other boys, sufficiently trained by now, stood still behind him, arms folded or hands in pockets. They said nothing.

"Were you the first on the scene of a crash?"

"I shot it down," Yoshi said.

"Bull shit."

"I shot it with a sling shot. We followed it five miles."

The buyer looked at the antenna, but shook his head no.

"Do you have the motherboard?"

Yoshi pulled that from his bag.

"I need twenty-five hundred for this."

He showed the buyer the motherboard.

"May I inspect it? It's no good if it's cooked."

"Okay."

The buyer put the motherboard on the glass display case in front of him. He whistled again.

"What?"

"Charlie, come over here."

An old man got slowly up from a small table in the corner where he was soldering wires coming out of some antique device. Charlie had long gray hair and a red, wind burnt face.

"What have ya got, Markus?"

"Death and destruction," the buyer said. He pointed to a faint DD etched on the motherboard. "This little guy shot down a Defense drone."

"Did he?"

"With a fucking sling shot."

"Shit, boy," Charlie said. "How high was it?"

Yoshi smiled. He felt happy that a sale was coming. They liked him. They would buy.

"It was maybe a hundred feet off the ground."

"Nice."

"We can't buy this," Markus said. "We would get nabbed the second we tried to sell it upline. You should take it into the desert, wipe your prints off and bury it."

"Come on," Yoshi said. "You're trying to talk down my price."

"Nope," Markus said. "It's worth way more than twenty-five hundred. I'd give you five if I could fence it. But I can't."

"What about this?" Yoshi said, and he pulled out of the bag a thing that looked like a rain drop the size of his fist. He hefted it before handing it over. It was heavy. Markus whistled again. It was an ultra-wide-angle, fish-eye lens, and it didn't have a scratch on it.

"That's a real beauty," Charlie said.

"Yeah," Markus agreed. "That's a beauty. We can do something with that."

Chapter Eight

Cash back in their pockets now, Yoshi paid the fish man. They bought fish to eat, but they also had this amazing arrangement with him: $50 per head to ride in the truck, back and forth between the cities. Travel was dangerous these days. It was cold in there with the ice, but it was safe, and the truck was sent through every checkpoint with no questions asked. Yoshi was happy to be back at the beach with some money in his pocket. The rest of the gang was happy, too. They liked coming home to the white coral sand, the big horizon, the gemstone blue of the ocean.

"What's that stink, Yoshi?" Beetle asked.

"I don't know."

"It hurts my eyes."

Beetle was their small one, named for the shiny, black helmet of his terrible haircut. Yoshi was overwhelmed by the stink, too, an acrid, deadly air of burned plastic.

Yoshi needed a toilet. He loved using the fancy restrooms in the tall buildings across the boulevard from the sea wall. He looked that way and saw a large family crossing the road with their carts and bags and the long poles of their tents. Others came behind them, trucking the same. The police had decreed that they could return. They looked exhausted. God knows where they sheltered from the storm.

For miles of the boulevard's sidewalk, robotic laborers swept white sand off the edge of the sea wall back onto the beach. They pushed huge piles of it off the street. They were polite and moved aside from the stairways to the beach to let people pass. They nodded when folks thanked them and then returned to their work. Yoshi always found it creepy when they nodded those blank, featureless, silver faces.

"Watch the kids, Toad. I'm going to take a leak."

"Okay, go."

Yoshi sprinted across the boulevard and disappeared into a bank. When he did, the other kids sprang into action and went after one of the sweeping laborers. This was called taking the wrong initiative. That's what Yoshi said later anyhow. Toad was first to the curb and began pushing sand back into the street. He shouted hello to the nearest robot, and it looked at him. The robot did not seem to understand the strange behavior. Further down the curb, little Beetle pushed another pile of sand into the street, and gimpy Flat Tire, the last to arrive, did the same. Toad watched to see if Yoshi was coming back yet.

"Oh no!" Beetle taunted. "We're making a big mess! Clean it up! Clean it up!"

The robot stepped off the curb and started with its shovel.

"Down here, too!" Flat Tire shouted. "Down here, there's a worse mess!"

The robot stopped and looked at him. Somewhere in its computations, it decided this was correct and headed in Flat Tire's direction. The robot swerved too far into the boulevard, and, when it did, a bus crushed it. The boys cheered. The laborer broke into pieces. The head went flying.

"Get the head! Get the head! Get the head!"
Toad shouted. They were all laughing uncontrollably.

The head bounced into traffic. The bus driver was irate. He could not get the door of his bus open. Some part from the robot's shoulder had jammed it shut. He banged on the windows and made obscene gestures to the kids who all laughed. Damage to a laborer always set off a silent distress alarm that would swiftly bring the police. Time was short.

Yoshi was coming from the other side of the street. He put together what was happening and bent to scoop up the head as it rolled to him. That was a thousand in cash, he thought, and he found his disappointment could be bought off. He dodged a motorcycle that never even slowed down for the accident scene and herded the kids towards the beach. The police would come without sirens, so they could appear from anywhere any time.

"Let's go," Yoshi said. "I have it. Let's go."

Down the stairs and onto the sand, they went. Yoshi led them along the concave ocean side of the wall. It was curved enough to be almost a tunnel. He carried Flat Tire in his arms. He ran about 40% speed, so the kids could keep up. They passed murals of yellow fish and blue dolphins and green turtles. They passed murals of black rotors dropping bombs on bodies painted blood red. He was just starting to relax when he turned and saw several police come down the stairs to the sand. They had their guns drawn. They looked around wildly. One of the officers moved and revealed the bus driver standing beside him. The bus driver pointed at Yoshi, and all the police began to run towards him.

Chapter Nine

Piper submitted to the blindfold and the hideous full-body search, but she wasn't dumb enough to let on that she recognized the awful scent of the scorpionweed. She knew that Gun Club's bunker was in Daphne. As the blindfold came off, she caught a glimpse of the Slow Sun in the west. The tunnel door closed. Her escort wheeled the motorcycle down the tunnel's slope. Piper brushed off her clothes and followed. Her feeling was hopeful. Meeting Gun Club was always terrifying, but today she had good news to share. Gun Club would be pleased. Today, Piper would be the favorite child at the small table.

The old elevator barely fit two people and a motorcycle. They went down. The roof of the bunker was concrete twenty feet thick. When the elevator stopped, they exited and passed through a huge, steel door. Unicorn Park, the lettering on the door said, a play on Einhorn, which was Gun Club's family name. Piper was frisked again at the sentry post, but the sentry was kind. He did not cop any free feels. She made her way down the long corridor, passing dozens of small rooms and cubicles filled with the royal attendants. As she neared a turn in the passage, she heard Rocky, Gun Club's dog, sniffing his way towards her. He had his head down, and he was onto something. He sounded like he was trying to inhale the entire planet.

Rocky was a Miniature Schnauzer, black-and-silver, with an old man's eyebrows and a thick, yellowing beard. When he saw Piper, he barked and jumped and put his paws on her thighs. He wanted kisses, but she scratched the top of his head, and that was good enough. He went back to his sniffing.

Gun Club was in the tea room with his wife, Roux, and some of his inner circle. He listened intently to whatever Roux was saying, and she talked with a glowing, joyful, humorous face until she saw Piper pass by the glass wall. She couldn't hide her disgust. She pushed her red hair back behind her ears and looked at her tea cup. People called her the Red Unicorn. Never to her face, but that's what they called her.

The conference room table was a pentagon with a chair at each side. Piper sat in the one seat with no name card. It was a cozy room, considering all the deadly plots that hatched there. A wide trophy case like something from an American high school was filled with models of shiny, black rotors. The acoustic foam soundproofing of the walls and ceiling looked like pillows on which you could rest your dreaming head. Piper looked at the paper agenda on the table.

Flight Security Report
Colorado Report
Security Update
Special

Gun Club and his secretaries came into the room. He hadn't shaved, which was not unusual, but it made him look grayer, older than he was. He had prominent ears like all men with buzz cut hair. He had a faux humility about him. He tried to express sincerity in speech by raising his eyebrows, and this always caused the furrow in his forehead to deepen and redden.

His dress was somewhere below Tristean business casual. On Earth, they used to call it golf attire. He had a white collared shirt with the collar open under a fleece jacket of forest green. He came right over to Piper and warmly shook her hand.

"Hello, blue eyes," he said.

"Boss."

Frost, the CFO, came in. On his way to light up the video screen on the wall, he showed Piper a thumbs-up. His eyes pled for a good sign. Piper replied with a thumbs-up of her own, and the CFO was visibly relieved. When the screen came on, it was filled with the chubby, jovial face of Gun Club's brother, Leo.

"Who's that at the table, Jack?" Leo asked without any sort of greeting.

"This is Piper," Gun Club said. "I'm looking forward to her report today."

"Me, too," Leo Einhorn said. "I like Piper."

After Gun Club took his seat, everyone else did the same. He pushed a button on the table, and second video screen (to the right of Leo's face) turned on. This showed a data feed that always surprised and mystified Piper. It was a real time run chart that somehow connected to Gun Club's mood. She couldn't figure out how it worked. In the upper left corner of the screen was an image of mountains, the Flatirons of the Mission's corporate logo. Above the chart itself, in letters that changed colors with the circumstances, were the words Humble Jack's Misery Index. When the chart moved, especially in an upward direction, it was hard to keep your eyes off it. The genius of the thing as a tool of terror was that once he had turned it on, Gun Club acted as if it didn't exist.

"Let's get started," Gun Club said. "Frost, you can take it away."

"Thank you, Boss," the CFO said, nodding. "I'll begin with the good news of the quarter's flight safety report."

"Where'd you get that necklace?" Leo asked suddenly.

Frost stopped, and Gun Club turned his seat to look at his brother. He laughed.

"What?"

"That necklace, Piper," Leo said. "It's pretty."

She grabbed at the silver chain. From it hung drops of amethyst, ruby and peridot. Though she spent a long time picking it out while dressing, she'd forgotten all about it.

"Thank you."

"How fucking high def is our camera?" Gun Club asked. "Do you have a control? Are you zooming on our guest?"

"I'm sorry," Leo said. His smirk said he wasn't sorry. "Proceed, Mr. Frost."

"Don't interrupt again."

Frost frowned at Leo Einhorn and began again.

"The flight safety situation has improved. For the rolling quarter, we now have less than one half of a fatality per million flights. I've sent you all a copy of the report."

"That sounds good," Gun Club said. "Is it good?"

"It's better," said the man to the Gun Club's left. He was Dr. Wasser, Gun Club's personal physician, father-in-law and mentor. He was a mathematician. Dr. Wasser was red-headed and nearly blind. He wore glasses with the thickest lenses Piper had ever seen.

"We continue to see high numbers of near-misses," Frost said.

"Same reason?"

"Yes," Frost said. "Pilot in command error. Civilian pilots continue to ignore the true time. Those who have not converted continue to use the Fast Time."

"Idiots," Leo said.

"Yes," Gun Club agreed.

"Why don't you strip their licenses?" Leo asked.

"No," Dr. Wasser said. "Keep the conversion movement going. It's working."

"I agree with Red," Gun Club said. "Any objections?"

Piper looked to the screen, but Leo shook his head.

"Okay, then, little brother. Tell us about Colorado."

"It's just gorgeous, Jack. We've had snow this week."

"Snow?" Gun Club said, stunned. "Are you fucking with me?"

Leo beamed.

"No, sir. Hand to God. It snowed."

"Where? On the peaks?"

"All over. It's melted in Boulder, but there was a lot."

"Jesus," Gun Club said. "Here I am, and there it snows. Nobody tell Roux. She won't be happy we missed it to be here in a bunker."

Gun Club's mood was improving, Piper saw, watching the Humble Jack Misery Index. She had personally never experienced snow except in photos and movies.

"How are things there otherwise?"

"Quiet."

"How quiet?"

"We haven't had a soul come off the desert in weeks. Western border is quiet, too."

"Anyone trying to leave?" Dr. Wasser asked. Gun Club looked at him with a funny expression.

"What do you mean by trying to leave?"

"Trying to go back," Dr. Wasser said. "Back into the desert."

"No, Red," Leo said.

"What have you heard, Red?" Gun Club asked. He leaned back in his chair and touched the front of his own hair, the one long bit that was sun-bleached and was combed forward. "Rumors?"

"I've heard nothing. Merely curious."

The suspicion that his father-in-law was hiding something turned Humble Jack's Misery Index sharply up. The lettering went pink. Piper looked around to see who noticed. Nobody let on.

"What else, Leo?"

"Everyone's wondering when you're coming home."

"I haven't decided."

"How's the ship?"

"It's good. Should be tip top for the return."

"Anything else on Colorado?" Frost asked. There was nothing else, so he put a check mark on his agenda.

"Let's talk about serious business, then," Gun Club said. He pulled his chair close to the table and sat up straight. The two old generals opposite Piper at the table were ready to report. These were Messmaker (Commandant of the Marine Corps), and Justice Brand (Head of the Court). Old Earthlings both. They looked like a pair of ancient turtles. They'd been appointed by the previous Chair of the Mission, Jack and Leo's father. Old but still capable. Piper had seen Justice Brand in action in a court room. Capable was the right word for both men.

"General Brand, what are the police saying about the stadium fire?" Gun Club asked.

"Everything we hoped," Brand said. "They are looking for the suspects we suggested. They have no other suspects. They'll find the wanted men soon, possibly today."

"Good," Gun Club said. "Good, good, good."

"I can't believe you burned down the new fucking stadium."

Everyone turned to look at Leo on the screen. Piper watched the Index. It moved and jumped and turned red.

"We've talked about this, Leo. Many times."

"I did vote against the idea," Leo said. "Damn shame."

"Your vote was noted."

"It was excessive, and you know it."

"It was necessary."

"It was excessive," Leo said. "Wouldn't you agree, Red?"

"Oh," Dr. Wasser answered. "I don't know about that."

"What do you think, Piper? Were you shocked?" Leo asked.

Leo was putting everyone else's head on the chopping block. He was just naturally antagonistic, ready since birth for combat with everything that came before him, he liked to poke and jab, especially his older brother's plans. Piper liked that about Leo, but she did not want to be put under a spotlight she didn't personally control.

"It feels like history in the making," she said, taking no side. She hoped this was language Gun Club might like in his king-like arrogance. She had no sense of the desert outside, but she imagined, in that very moment, lizards crawling above them.

"Everything is falling into place," Gun Club said. "I'm sorry that I torched what in your mind is the wrong symbol. Everybody else's sacred cow to the abattoir, but not Leo's."

"It's just excessive is all I'm saying."

"Again, everything is falling into place. Operation Trojan Horse is running. It's galloping."

"Oh, just move on then."

"You sure woke up on the wrong side of the bed today," Gun Club said. "Everything okay?"

"I'm depressed that things have come to this," Leo said, and Piper thought he looked and sounded sincere.

"Leo, that's why I have you at home where the war has already been won."

Piper noticed that when Gun Club delivered an insult, his mood improved. Leo said nothing to this, so the meeting continued. Piper looked at the paper agenda then back at Leo's pink, chubby face on the screen.

"General Messmaker and I spoke briefly this morning about the impending apprehension of our friend, Serge Ville de Paix," Gun Club said. "The Marines have had eyes on him a few times in the last 48 hours. Anything new, General?"

"No update since this morning."

"Capture order remains, am I correct?" Dr. Wasser asked. You haven't changed that?"

"You are correct," Messmaker replied. The doctor wiped his glasses with a cloth.

"His force of bodyguards is growing," Gun Club said. "It will be tough without some additional help from the people."

"Tough to get him alive you mean?"

"Yes, right."

"What about the hangings?" Dr. Wasser asked. For the first time, Piper thought Gun Club might show a crack, but, no, he was swift. He changed the subject.

"This all brings us around to the reason I call you together. Yesterday, Piper sent me a text, Piper what should I call it, a beautiful text?"

"All the pretty girls get Humble Jack's personal mobile number."

"That's far from true, Leo. Anyhow, I sent Piper on a special errand, and her report simply said, 'Errand completed.' Short and sweet. Tell everyone what you meant."

Piper stood up from her chair.

"All right if I show rather than tell?"

"By all means."

She took a few steps back from her chair then removed a small cylinder from her pocket. It looked like a tube of lipstick. She opened this and a silver fog of nanobots jumped to the screen on the wall opposite the screen showing Leo's face. Images appeared. They showed, one at a time, POV recordings of Piper's flea bots jumping onto Colonel Endling and his assistant, POV shots of the two men entering the South American embassy and talking to the Ambassador, then live cam video of several locations inside the embassy.

"Was that Colonel Endling?" Red Wasser asked.

"Yes," Gun Club answered.

"That's pretty high profile."

"Yes."

"Who is he?" Leo asked.

"He used to be a big deal here at the Mission," Gun Club said. "Back when Father was managing the second and third waves of settlements on Triste."

"He's the perfect choice," Red Wasser said. "Perfect."

"I agree. Happy accident."

"What are those, bugs?" General Brand asked.

"Surveillance micro bots," Piper said.

"Oh."

"Tell them the fun part," Gun Club said with a smile.

"Well," she said. "I've rigged them all with incendiary devices."

"Shit," General Brand said.

"Walking, crawling bombs," Gun Club said. "They got in there as simply as you saw on that footage."

"We'll all be dining in there tomorrow evening," General Brand said. "Right?"

"Yes," Gun Club said. "Worry not. I trust Piper completely. Besides, she owes me this favor. She figured out exactly where we need to sit to be safe. We'll have a close-up view of the fireworks."

There was uneasy laughter all around. The best laid plans, Piper thought, and though the table's uneasiness was contagious, she was confident since she was the plan's chief agent.

"Jack, I hope you know I'll think of you fondly at my coronation as Chair of the Mission after you're blown up."

As the nanobots began to return to her tube, and the images evaporated, that last line of the Leo's stayed with her. She tuned out the chatter of details that didn't concern her. If Gun Club died, would her enormous debt be erased? Would it follow her still? She was the kind of person who tracked the hint of a possibility to its bitter end. What would happen if Gun Club Jack Einhorn, violent King of the Galaxy, died? Could he die? Definitely.

But she lived by the ethical axiom that actions have consequences, and she simply couldn't imagine it.

After the meeting ended, Gun Club kept Piper behind for a private word. He spoke softly, which she took as a bad sign.

"You fucked up one detail, Piper."

"What?"

"Quince is alive," Gun Club said. "He's alive. Did he see your face?"

"No. He may have been able to tell I'm a woman, you know, by my build. But that's it."

"All right then," Gun Club said. "Lay low tomorrow. Events will accelerate."

Chapter Ten

The Map Room was locked. It was strange to see it closed. Sleeper never beat the Colonel to the office. Since he was an employee of the Colonel's and not the Mission directly, his thumb scan couldn't open the door. He plopped down in a lobby chair. After a moment, he felt a low rumble and saw the windows vibrating, so he looked out. Three black hyperotors circled the beach like a wheel turning around the hub of a fourth. This one hovered over a cluster of white tents. It was too far to see what was happening on the ground. Beyond the action, the crystalline blue of the sea bellied up and down, up and down to the horizon.

He imagined the police standing at the sea wall and watching, too, knowing, as people had begun to say openly, that the police in Radium Beach were no longer the police. Air power was police power, and the Marines owned it along with the heaviest guns. At nine o'clock, the arthritic, abrasive Mrs. Lascaux shuffled off the elevator.

"Oh, boy," she said. "Old man's not here?"

"He's not here."

"That's not like him."

"Maybe he's sick."

"He doesn't get sick," she said. She opened the door. Mrs. L walked ten city blocks on her bad feet to get to work, so a priority on arrival was soaking her toes. After putting down her lunch bag and fussing with the vase of white flowers on her desk, she sat down to the chore of removing her shoes and socks. She did this with extravagant sighs.

"How's Tubby?" Sleeper asked.

"Driving me crazy," she said.

Leonid "Tubby" Lascaux was a great hill giant of a man. He started growing a beard the day he retired from the Space Port, and now his beard stretched past his big pot belly to his waist. He was one of Sleeper's favorite people. He and Mrs. L had matching honey bee tattoos on their forearms.

Mrs. L didn't like to admit how bad her toes hurt. Her two ingrown nails—big toe on each foot—had taken a turn for the very worst. Even so, she refused to give up—even for a day—her morning walk. She'd run warm tap water and pour it into a clear, plastic storage bin, an oblong cube 29" L x 18" W x 6" H. This could hold about 35 quarts without spilling—after taking the feet into account, that is—and, even though she had wide feet, both could fit in at the same time. She'd test the water with her right index finger then submerge the two terrible toes. Sleeper left her, so she could have some privacy.

He pored over some old scroll maps. He liked looking at the set of maps drawn to track the progress of the city's growth. The great leap began early in the century. Radium Beach had always had the attraction of the beautiful, natural beaches, but the explosion came when Wolfgang Einhorn opened the city's Space Port to civilian traffic in '08. Ring roads spread out until the Space Port looked, on maps, as it does now, a blank spot in the center not unlike the inner zone of a tick's bite.

Looking these over, Sleeper always felt a temptation to grab a blue crayon and color the sea.

Mrs. Lascaux's desk phone rang. It was the Colonel.

"The old man wants to speak to you," she said.

"Good morning," Sleeper said.

"Sebastian, how are you?"

"I'm fine. How about you?"

"I'm feeling a little silly," the Colonel said. "I'm in the lobby at the Aurora Hotel. I had the sense I was being followed this morning. Two cars took several turns with me in traffic. So, I ducked in here."

"That sounds not so silly to me."

"It *is* silly, I'm afraid. I'm going to hang out here for a bit and drink a coffee. I'll see you in a couple of hours. All right?"

"All right."

"Good. Can I talk with Laverna again?"

He handed the phone back and listened as the Colonel asked Mrs. L to follow up with the coders on the latest updates to his search project map. Sleeper realized the morning's delay would give him a chance to fulfill the promise he'd yesterday made to Hugo Hidalgo.

"I'll be back shortly," he told Mrs. L. "I have to deliver a letter."

Chapter Eleven

When they reached the drooling mouth of the flood control pipe, Yoshi pushed the other kids inside. They complained of the darkness and the water soaking their shoes, but Yoshi scolded them and pushed harder. This was safety. He asked Toad to go further in, all the way to the hatch. There, Toad started to bang for someone to open it. Yoshi got down on one knee and readied his slingshot. Little Flat Tire crouched behind him. Somewhere in the dark, Beetle smacked the robotic laborer's detached head with his palm.

"This thing is fucking awesome."

"Shut up," Yoshi said.

The bald police sergeant stood at the pipe's mouth, squinting to see anything. The cops were all lit by the sunlight, and from the darkness of the pipe, they looked like a movie about men who pace compulsively. Yoshi knew they were afraid of Serge. Everyone was afraid of Serge. So, they were undecided. They might not come in. Then again, they had numbers. They just might.

"Come out and talk. We just want to *talk* to you."

That was bullshit. The sergeant's baton talked enough. The baton in his hand talked of humorless, homicidal punishment. Would the police zap children? Oh, yes, they would.

Toad banged and banged on the hatch. There was little or no sympathy from the crowd of beach folk who began to gather. Curiosity, there was some, and Yoshi saw people he knew, people who would share nighttime fires with an orphaned child, but they all now had the crossed arms of disapproval. The bus driver was out there, too, stewing and pacing. The hesitation of the police officers was driving him crazy.

"Come out and bring back that equipment you stole. There's no trouble."

"I'm afraid of that man there," Yoshi said.

"Don't be afraid. Who do you mean?"

"The bus driver," Yoshi said. "He looks mean."

"Oh, don't be silly," the bald sergeant said. "Harry, come here. Talk to this boy."

Yoshi adjusted the extension of his slingshot. His palm was sweaty on the wooden handle, but he was steady. His hand did not shake. When the driver stepped into unobstructed view, Yoshi launched a small rock. It hit the driver's earlobe, which just plain disappeared in a spray of blood. He screamed, and, in a confused panic, he and the cops all hit the sand. They rolled to get out of the line of fire.

"Who's out there?" a voice from inside the hatch.

"It's Toad!" Toad yelled.

His name echoed down the pipe's length.   The wheel on the inside of the hatch turned, and the old iron protested with an irritable sound. When it opened, Serge's brown face appeared. His mouth made an O of mock surprise. Three of his bodyguards jostled with each other at the opening, checking the danger.

"Hello, boys," Serge Ville de Paix said.

"Can we come in? The cops are out there."

"Shit, yes you can, but hurry," Serge said.

They climbed through the hatch one at a time, and Serge slammed it shut and locked it.

"We got to move. Come on."

The passage they stepped into was red brick. The crown was round, and the whole thing looked like somebody's throat with supports coming down mid-tunnel like an infinite progression of uvulae. They passed these one after another with no turnings, so that Yoshi knew they had passed under the boulevard and under shops and sidewalks of the Radium Beach business district.

"Where can we go?" he asked Serge.

"Ray's kitchen."

"Okay."

Rayuela's place was set up in the back rooms of the Book Cellar. The entire group—-kids, Serge, five bodyguards-—climbed an iron ladder and emerged from a manhole cover across the street from the bookstore. As they crossed the street, a drone flew overhead and arrested their attention. It trailed smoke behind it, and, indeed, a small, orange fire burned on its right wing. It disappeared behind a row of tall buildings, so they continued to the Book Cellar.

One had to descend from the street to enter the Book Cellar. A pink neon arrow pointed the way. So, they went down again, down narrow, winding wooden stairs. The store owner, Gennady, was stationed at the checkout counter, paging through an English language version of The Great Soviet Encyclopedia. Somebody had used a small knife or razor blade to cut some pages out of the volume he was holding.

Gennady nodded. Serge took a key from his pocket and unlocked a wooden door. Inside, Rayuela carried one end of a long table, as one of her volunteers took the other. They were restoring the kitchen to its normal state. Rayuela wore an orange t-shirt the same color as the paint on the kitchen's walls. She saw Serge with the kids and shook her head, but he went right through anyway.

Serge had a weakness for Rayuela's furies. He loved her heart of gold and her long, wild curls, but, more than anything, he loved her wrath. She was amazingly alive. The curls bobbed and whipped, as she pounded around the room, slamming drawers and clanging pans. She had hazel eyes that flashed a dragon green when she got going. The four orphans sat at the table with him. They ate from enormous bowls of corn chowder.

"How did you know the cops didn't have a gun to Toad's head at the hatch?" Yoshi asked.

"I was aware of everything happening out there."

"How?"

"Don't worry about that."

"We're lucky you heard us."

"Very lucky, child."

"Thank you."

"Yes. Sure."

In the back of the room, a cook dressed in stained white stood in the stairway to the back alley. He had the door open. As he smoked, he alternated between blowing smoke to the alley and turning his eye back to Serge and the kids. Serge knew he was harmless, but he didn't like the open door.

"Go over and tell him to shut that door."

One of his bodyguards got up and made a show of adjusting the shoulder strap of his Kalashnikov. He slowly walked over and said something to the cook. The cook snuffed out his cigarette on the bottom of his shoe. They shut the door.

Serge's mind raced. There were too many things to do, too many people to reach. He needed to locate a dozen scattered partisans, and it was urgent that he share news. It was even more urgent that he learn news. He flipped through his red leather-bound notebook. He had three pages of notes for today, in code, and he was so tired he could barely decipher them. He closed the book and tried to talk to Ray when she slowed long enough to grab. She would not face him except to give him dirty looks. It warmed his heart.

"How many did you have here last night?"

"We had sixty people shelter here," she said.

"Sixty people in this room?"

"Yes. Sixty."

Serge whistled.

"Like sardines in a pressure cooker," he said.

"We had a good night," Ray said. "All fed. All slept."

"Except you, of course."

She shrugged her shoulders.

"Were any of my people here?"

"None that I know."

"Okay, darling. What do you need? What can I do?"

"What are those boys doing? After they eat, will they go?"

"They had some trouble with the police."

"Shit, Serge."

"They're just kids."

"I can't have the police pounding on my door."

"There will be no police."

"Serge."

When he smiled, Serge was irresistible and knew it. He was Afro-Guyanese, child of European Space Port workers who came to Triste in the second great migration before the worst times on Earth. Nobody quite knew if his accent was sincere. It came and went, and when he talked with it, he was charming, so nobody pursed the question very far.

With the timing of a clever stage manager, somebody came stomping down the steps and knocked on the door. The cook was leaning against the wall with his eyes closed, and the sound maybe woke him up. He moved to the door, but three bodyguards stopped him and pushed him away. Ray looked at Serge and threw her hands up in the air.

Serge was so strong. When the door opened, the man showed him a blue envelope, but instead of taking it, he grabbed the man by the shirt collar and dragged him into the room. The man said something about Rayuela and showed the blue envelope again. Toad had a deep feeling the letter contained bad news. The bodyguards checked the man for weapons and sat him down in a chair. Serge began to pepper him with questions.

"Who are you? What's this letter?"

"My name is Sebastian Sleeper. Hugo asked me to deliver this envelope. I don't know what it is."

"Hugo."

"Hugo Hidalgo."

"Yah, I know who you mean. He's a two-faced piece of shit."

"Give me the letter, Serge," Ray said.

"No, I don't like it."

"Give it to me."

He handed over the envelope, and she took it to her messy desk hidden behind a half-wall. She sliced it with a letter opener and sat down. Toad stared at Mr. Sleeper.

Serge said, "Look now. I don't like that you're gonna make my lady upset. We're gonna have to talk."

Toad could not stop staring. He sensed that Mr. Sleeper *knew*. He knew about the tunnels, the world beneath the world where children could find parents and a new life, the place Toad and Yoshi had heard legends about and desperately wanted to find. The place was in Mr. Sleeper's thoughts.

Toad leaned to Yoshi's ear and said, "He knows."

"You sure about that, Toady?" Yoshi asked.

"Yeah."

Ray came back with a disgusted look on her face. She pulled her hair back and clipped it up. Serge put his hand out. He wanted to read the letter, but she didn't give it up.

"Hugo says I should leave the city. The Marines have been waiting to arrest you, but the waiting is over now. They know about us. I will be arrested, too."

"What else?"

"Nothing else."

"Let me see it."

All the friendliness drained out of Serge's face. He turned to Mr. Sleeper.

"Now, who the fuck are you who knows Hugo and can move freely from Hugo to here?"

Chapter Twelve

Piper loved her new baby. He was her best design. She thought there should be a million copies. Standing on his six legs, he fit on the whorl of her thumbprint. He had the body of a worker ant—head, thorax and abdomen—-with the addition of two beautiful silver wings, shaped like scimitars, as long plus a half as the rest of him. She watched the magnification on her monitor, as she played with his wings with a pair of tweezers.

On another screen that her nanobots formed on her wall, the state dinner at the South American Embassy had reached the main course. She felt oddly detached from her anxiety. Gun Club had taken the detonator and its great burden from her hands. She would see a flash before signal loss. She went to her hammock in the corner of the lab and climbed in. From there, she could rock and still see the screen clearly enough.

The lab's card reader chirped, and this sound was followed by the awkward bump of a shoulder trying to push open the door. Piper had thrown the bolt. The card reader alone wouldn't work.

"Shit," she said. She'd forgotten the janitor.

The card reader chirped again.

"Oh, hold on," she called out. She turned off her screen on the wall, and it evaporated. The silver cloud of bots trailed after her like an emanation from her soul. Her bare feet felt cold on the white, tile floor as she crossed the room. She unlocked the door.

"Hey, Piper," Bear, the old janitor said. "You never lock that door. Are you changing your clothes in here?"

"You caught me."

"How ya doing?"

"Tired, Bear. I'll be over here in my hammock."

"Okay."

The lab was immaculate. Bear did his thing anyway. Piper gently rocked in the hammock, as he emptied trash baskets and pushed the broom around. She kept one leg curled under her and pushed off the cold floor with her left foot.

Bear was a good guy. Piper liked him. He lived with his family in the Five Mile Thumb section of the city. This was a rocky peninsula with small cottages that got flattened every few years whenever an epic storm rampaged along the coast. When asked why he didn't move from the Thumb after the fourth or, maybe, the fifth lost home, Bear said he loved the spot, and he loved owning his own piece of the Tristean ground, and so that was that. He was a huge soccer fan.

"Can you believe it about the stadium?" he asked.

Piper had practiced repose for this question.

"So sad," she said with a frown.

"Very sad. Those god damned terrorists."

Bear exited. She locked the bolt and went for her lipstick tube of bots. Before she reached it, Bear knocked on the door. She opened it.

"I heard the bolt again," he said. "Is everything okay?"

"Yes," she said. "I'm working on some new tech. I need absolute privacy."

He gave her a look.

"Just scream if you need help."

"Ha ha, thanks bud."

When he was gone, she got the screen up on the wall. Fuck, fuck, fuck, she muttered. There was no signal from any of her bots at the Embassy.

She'd missed it.

Chapter Thirteen

It was not like the rotors needed more menace, but Gun Club paid an artist to paint pale stripes on their black tails—-and he was good, that artist—-until the rotors resembled California Kingsnakes that could fly. This came after the production test pilots delivered an accepted rotor to the finishing hangar. The studious devotion of the painter at work was the only thing Leo Einhorn found interesting in the whole long, stupid process. His brother had left him with the unpleasant chore of managing the production of five rotors per week—-he threatened to raise that number to six—-and Leo hated it.

He waved to the painter and headed for the open end of the hangar. His bodyguard sat cleaning his handgun in the passenger seat of Leo's convertible. *Off we go into the wild blue yonder*, Leo mumbled to himself, looking at the perfect sky. The sunshine loved the Jaguar's green curves. It glanced, too, off Bruce Burden's silver gun.

"What a day," Leo said.

"True, boss," Burden said. "They don't make 'em much better than this."

"I'm going to jump on over to the Mission for a few minutes. Want to stay here?"

"No, I'll tag along," Burden said.

The Mission complex stood at the far end of the campus. Leo got a kick out of pushing his Jaguar to 150 mph on the long straight runways. The car was lovingly engineered and handled the abuse. Burden always double-checked his seat belt and thought to himself that it wasn't a bodyguard the boss needed. It was a great pastime in the upper floors of the Mission buildings to watch the green car zip back and forth with no purpose and to imagine the poor young man hanging on for life in the passenger seat. There was always some suspense that Leo, with a murderous or suicidal impulse, might fail to brake and continue to accelerate and drive straight up the gray stone mountains encircling the campus.

He cared too much for the Jaguar for that. As they approached the Mission, he slowed at the security perimeter. The two sentries there saluted.

"Top of the morning," Leo said.

"Good morning, Mr. Einhorn."

"Is Jim Apostle in his office?"

"No, Mr. Einhorn, he's with the bones in the Beer Garden this morning."

"Thank you," Leo replied. "We're off for a hike, Bruce."

He parked the car at the southern tip of the southernmost runway, and they set out on foot. To the southwest, Pike's Peak's white head and shoulders rose above the red stone and soil, the trees, the lesser hills and mountains.

Burden never spoke first, so when the boss was thoughtful, they walked in silence. Where they could, they followed old city roads, but this was not always possible. Park land was fiercely, densely overgrown. They took paths closest to those old roads.

Finally, Leo said, "I need to banish Iris from the bunker."

Feeling awkward, Burden said, "Is that right?"

"Yes. I kept her out of my suite last night. I spoke to her through the locked door, but she didn't believe a word I said about her banishment."

Indeed, this was true. Leo told everyone that Iris was his friend, but friend was not the correct word. When she knocked at his door the previous night, he did not open it as usual. He tried to break the habit of always opening it.

"I don't want to see you," he said.

"But I came all the way over here," she said.

"I'm sorry."

"You're just kidding. I know it. I know you."

"Your new prices are too high."

"You have another girl in there?"

"What do your other clients say about the new prices?"

"You're always talking about my other clients."

"Well?"

"Open the door."

He opened the peep hole. Her plunging, sheer gold dress left her shoulders bare, revealing her flawless dark skin. She fingered a diamond earring Leo had never seen before.

"Where did you get those earrings?"

"Open the door."

"Who gave those to you?"

"Open up."

He never gave in even as she lowered the front of her dress to show him the heavenly valley of her décolletage. Leo knew he did not have a strong will power, but troubled sleep and ceaseless, dark thoughts had taken away his desire.

He walked for eight miles, and Burden kept pace a few strides behind him. They passed hundreds of red sandstone formations. Here and there, they saw abandoned stores or tourist information huts, but they saw no other souls about. Leo thought this odd. He said so.

"Do you know what day it is, boss?"

"Friday."

"Yes, but in the old world's reckoning?"

"I'm afraid not."

"It's Good Friday."

"Imagine that."

They reached the pale tablets that read *Garden of the Gods*. Pike's Peak was dead ahead now, and its white top reached up as if striving to raise the horizon to meet the sun.

"How much further from here, boss?"

"It's not far. The bone field is less than a mile."

They walked on. Their shoes had a pink dust now, and the very look of that made Burden choke a little with thirst. He wanted to complain, but Leo's mood was unpredictable.

This James Apostle, who was the Chief Science Officer of the Mission, was a person Burden met once before. He was tall and wiry and tan, the very picture of astronaut health, and when they walked up, he was on his knees brushing soil from a stone embedded in the earth. The brush moved slowly and carefully as if he was sifting for priceless gold dust.

"Greetings, Jim," Leo said.

Jim Apostle stood immediately and shook Leo's hand.

To Burden, he said, "Please watch your step, young man."

Burden pictured a happy vision of shooting the man in the kneecap. He crossed his arms.

"Something new here, Jim?"

"No, sadly," Apostle said. He had pink dust in his gray hair and a yellow pencil stuck behind his ear. "I thought we might find a fossil in this dig here, but there's nothing I can see. Come over here."

He walked them to a huge, white tent with sides sealed all the way down. There was a hiss when he zipped open the door. In the middle of the space was a wide, deep hole.

"This is the Stegosaurus?" Leo asked.

"Yes, indeed," Apostle replied. "Have you been out to see it before?"

"No, but I've heard all about it from my brother."

"Oh, yes, Jack is quite fond of her."

"Don't tell anyone, but he's going to add a dinosaur to the corporate seal."

"How marvelous!"

"But, really, don't tell anyone."

"I swear I won't."

Burden peered down into the pit and saw the birdlike skull of the creature. It was small, but the spine was long, and the famous dermal plates looked impressive. The bones were laid out with care in an approximation of their connected shape.

"She's bigger than your car, boss," he said to Leo. "How old is she?"

"She's 150 million years old, give or take."

"Give or take?"

"It's too soon for us to tell for sure."

The wind picked up, and the tent seemed to breathe in and out with its gusts. The red dust of the encroaching desert pelted the vinyl of its walls.

"You hear that wind?" Apostle asked.

"Yes."

"Ages of that and the never-ending drought are what uncovered this dinosaur."

"Amazing," Burden said.

Leo couldn't take it any longer. He interrupted.

"I'd like to talk to you about someone you know quite well, Jim," Leo said. "That's why we came out here today."

"Certainly."

"What can you tell me about Colonel Endling?"

"Well, he and your father did not get along."

Apostle laughed and wiped his hands on his brown pants, expecting Leo to say well, who did, but he stopped chuckling when he saw that Leo had not joined in.

"I was so young then. Shooting guns with my brother."

"But you didn't get the nickname."

"Gun Club. Ha. No, I didn't."

There was a pause as the wind slapped the tent.

"It's important for me to know more about him, Colonel Endling, I mean."

"He was part of my inner circle. I leaned on him a great deal when I joined the Mission and took over the settlement of Triste. Do you know him at all?"

"No, I don't know him from Adam."

"Okay, then, well, he's old now, over 70, I'd guess. He's retired. He's a true polymath. He was a problem solver when we had disputes in the settlement neighborhoods. He also holds patents for some of the fuel valves on the first-generation sprinters we used in the early days. Also, I'm sure you know he became something of a genius detective in his later years."

"Oh, the gold heist."

"Yes, he solved that case and others. He has strange intuitions for such things."

"Is he a loyal person?"

"Yes. If there's a more loyal person in my organization, I don't know him."

"Tell me more."

"He's a lifelong bachelor. When you meet him, his eyes give you an impression of sadness. He came from Omaha. His father died young, an engineer... blown up working the LNG pipeline."

"No family then?"

"Any from Omaha are long dead."

"Thank you, Jim."

"May I ask what your interest is in him?"

"No," Leo said. "No, you may not."

Leo didn't say a word in the Jaguar for the length of the ride back to Boulder. The city was thronged with walkers on this beautiful day. Those who recognized the Jaguar turned to stare or wave, but Leo ignored them and sped along to the ranch and bunker. Burden saw him to his suite and waited for his own relief on the bench in the hallway.

A message waited for Leo. It was marked Top Secret. He touched the button on the wall to activate the player and saw Roux's face. It was a mess of mascara that had run all the way to her jaw line. She'd been crying, clearly, but why? Her words were brief for all their shocking content.

Roux said, "My father is dead. Jack has lost his arm, and his face is burned. He's in the ICU. There has been an evil bomb attack. I'm taking control. Await next update in two hours."

Leo sat down on the bean bag chair at his feet. He fell into it, really, and fall was the only thing he could do. He felt heavy and helpless so many miles-—infinitely many miles—-from the disaster. He held his head, but then had a clear, anxious thought. Did Roux know of the plot? She spoke as if she did not. Now Leo felt even heavier helplessness with the members of the board there on Triste with Roux, and any one of them could break at any time and tell her the truth.

Chapter Fourteen

(Courtroom filled to capacity)

COURT OFFICER: Jury entering.

THE CLERK: Treason and assassination trial continued. All parties are present. The jury is seated.

THE COURT: Sir.

MR. GLISSANT: The defense calls Leonid Lascaux.

L-E-O-N-I-D L-A-S-C-A-U-X, called as a character witness by and on behalf of The Defendant at the trial, having been first duly sworn, testified as follows.

COURT OFFICER: Sir, watch your step there.

THE COURT: You're a big one. Are you going to fit into my witness box okay, sir?

LASCAUX: Barely, but I think so, Your Honor.

THE COURT: Wow, you have a deep voice. You don't need to get quite so close to the microphone. That's better. If you don't understand a question, let me know, and it will be made clearer. If an objection is made to a question, I will tell you whether to answer it. Your witness, Mr. Glissant, sir.

Mr. GLISSANT: Thank you, Judge.

DIRECT EXAMINATION BY MR. GLISSANT:

Q   Sir, how old are you?

A   I am sixty-five years old, sir.

Q   And can you please state for the members of the jury your educational background?

A   I have a master's degree in Aerospace Engineering from the École Polytechnique de Montréal.

Q   And you are presently retired from working?

A   That is correct. I worked for the Space Port for three decades.

Q   Do you know Colonel Edward Endling?

A   Yes, I do.

Q   Do you see Colonel Endling in court?

A   Yes, that's him (indicating).

Q   How do you know Colonel Endling?

A   My wife Laverna has been his employee for twenty years. The day I met the Colonel, twenty years ago, we both recognized each other from passing in the corridors at the Space Port. We became friends.

Q   Would it be fair to say you have had many intimate conversations with Colonel Endling?

A   Yes, that would be fair.

Q   Was it in Colonel Endling's nature to speak about politics?

MR. RHINE: Objection to that. Speculative.

THE COURT: Sustained.

Mr. GLISSANT: I'll re-phrase.

Q   Did Colonel Endling ever speak to you about politics?

A   Yes, he did. Often.

Q   What political subjects did you have the occasion to discuss?

A   Things related to his role in the Mission, bureaucratic red tape type things.

Q   Did Colonel Endling ever express any feelings of revolutionary fervor with you?

A   No, sir.

Q   Did Colonel Endling ever discuss The Guild with you?

A   No, sir.

Q   Did Colonel Endling ever disparage, in your presence, Wolfgang Einhorn, Jack Einhorn, Roux Einhorn, Leo Einhorn or any other member of the Einhorn family?

A   Never.

Q   Did you speak with or see Colonel Endling after April 13th of this year?

A   Yes, sir.

Q   Please describe the occasion of this meeting.

A   The elevator in the Mission Building was broken, so I helped Laverna up the stairs. She has very bad joints and feet. In the Map Room, I spoke with the Colonel briefly.

Q   Did he seem calm and peaceful at the time of this meeting?

A   Yes.

Q   Did Colonel Endling ever discuss with you a plot to destroy the South American Embassy and assassinate the Chairman or any member of the Einhorn family?

A   No, sir.

Q   Has Colonel Endling ever discussed bomb making in your presence, even jokingly?

A   Never.

Q   To your knowledge, does Colonel Endling have a reputation for peacefulness among the friends and acquaintances that you share with him?

A   Yes. He's a peaceful man, a great man. Everyone in this room knows it.

MR. GLISSANT: No further questions, your honor.

THE COURT: Your witness, Mr. Rhine.

MR. RHINE: Nothing.

THE COURT: Thank you, sir. You're excused.

Chapter Fifteen

They passed the library, the city hall, the flat face of the police station. Each was the color of some strong stone. Through every ocean storm, the buildings looked like they would last forever. When water drops have worn the stones of Troy. That was a line from somewhere.

They turned down an alley. Black fire escapes went up from the street. The apartments were stacked six high with window boxes covered in vines or flowers. Friendly neighbors had strung wires across the alley. From these dangled flags and pennants and paper lanterns. Sebastian Sleeper and Serge Ville de Paix walked down the alley. Each awaited a phone call (Sleeper for word from the Colonel, Serge for news on Rayuela's progress getting out of the city). The gang of four orphans trailed behind them. Serge stopped at the glass storefront of an electronics boutique.

"Listen, Sebastian, I enjoyed talking with you these last few days. I only have a few moments before the pulse comes. But listen to me. This is going to be a bad time for a man like you, a man with no commitments."

"I heard the same thing from the other side."

"Hugo."

"Yes."

"He's a snake."

"So, you say."

"Listen. Okay? Any of us would just snap our fingers if that was all it took to knock things down and start over. Okay? The need for Chairmen? Done. The time for Chairmen ruling with a tiny group of sycophants? Done. The time for Chairman to hoard the money and decide who gets paid and who doesn't? Done. We tell him. But this Chairman is not like his father. This Chairman sits up all night long with one terrible thought, and he draws pictures of stick figure kings hanging from the gallows. The king is him, you get it?"

"That is an odd way to call on the fates."

Serge bent his tall frame and had a laugh at that. "Listen. Sebastian."

"I'm listening."

"No, listen."

There was no mistaking the sound of the rotors even far in the distance. It was the thunder of the storm you knew you were caught in. With a sudden pop, all the devices in the boutique's display window went dark. Sleeper looked at his phone: dead.

"This is a bad day, Sebastian. Watch out."

Serge ducked into the shop. Looking left in the direction they'd come, Sleeper could see white boats of the Navy near the ocean's shocking blue horizon. The kids swarmed him.

"Why are you looking at me like that?"

"You know about the tunnels," Toad accused him. He looked to the small face. He must've given away his own surprise.

"He can read minds," Yoshi said. "Just a little."

"I'm sorry, what did you say? I can't hear you."

They made way for a loud, armored vehicle moving slowly down the alley. It barely fit. Sleeper and the kids had to flatten themselves against the glass. The eight-wheeled thing was low and equipped with a mine plow that looked like a shark's mouth with two rows of harrowing tines. There were markings of the Einhorn engineers on the side of the vehicle. One door was open. Two medics sat inside with their hands on their knees. They had caps and coveralls of sky blue and nervous looks on their faces. Two hyperotor gunships flew quickly overhead in the direction of the beach. As far as Sleeper knew, there were no mines on the beach. What was happening?

"Wait here," he said.

The kids smirked at this.

The AFV moved out of the alley, across Ocean Boulevard and down a cement ramp onto the beach. Others of the same kind rolled down other ramps. The two rotors circled the beach. That was common enough and caused no alarm, but, sensing what was about to unfold, some police officers stood and blocked the AFV from approaching the nearest tents.

"Yo, what the fuck?" one cop yelled with his hands in the air. "Stop this thing."

The machine lurched forward. The blunt vertex of the plow's triangular blade bumped him hard and he stumbled backwards, grabbing his gun. What happened next was so immediate Sleeper could not even process the implications let alone a single coherent thought about the actions that led up to it.

The officer was shot by automatic weapon fire from inside the AFV. He fell dead, and his two colleagues were likewise shot dead on the spot. The AFV backed up and then pushed sand over the bodies. It turned to steer past the mound and moved toward the white tents of the beach folk.

"Bring out Serge Ville de Paix," a Marine's amplified voice demanded. Along the beach, this was repeated not by echoes but by other Marines in other machines.

This triggered no response. Men and women moved among the tents, but no one came forward. A hypothetical driver—-one with a hypothetical non-electric car—-driving north along Ocean Blvd just then could have looked right at this violent event or looked left to see Sleeper frozen in a spot halfway across the road. Along the sea wall, robotic laborers stood still in the postures they'd held when the pulse came.

"Bring out Serge Ville de Paix," the amplified voice repeated. "End this. Bring him out."

Sleeper broke from his spell—-a charitable person might say his lifelong spell, but that remains to be seen—-and he ran back towards the electronics boutique. He caught himself and stopped. Would he draw attention and bring the Marines directly down on Serge's head? He heard another short burst of gunfire. His guts were so cold, he thought he was shot. But it was fear he felt. When a formation of ten black gunships came screaming along the beach, he started moving again. He gathered the children, and he took them to the Mission Building.

They found Mrs. Lascaux on the 30th floor observation deck. She'd left a note on the Map Room door that the roof access was open. Some Mission officials were also up there, watching the beach in grim silence.

"What's happening?" Sleeper asked.

"Look."

One of the armored fighting vehicles was burning, and, in slow arcs, Molotov cocktails soared and burst in bright explosions against the armor of others. Still, the terrible work of the Marines continued. The plows drove along the beach, tearing up the white tents, small wooden sheds and stone cooking circles before them. They moved as if in mindless, childish revenge at some insult. A stream of people exited the beach and flooded the Ocean Blvd.

"Why are they doing this?" Sleeper asked.

"Did you hear the edict today?" Mrs. Lascaux replied.

"Oh my god, no, what did she say?"

"Roux Einhorn declared herself Queen. She read a list of names," Mrs. Lascaux said. "Any citizen who aids or abets the escape or hiding of any person on her list forfeits all rights and citizenship."

"They are looking for Serge Ville de Paix down there."

"Yes, but Sebastian..."

"What?"

"Your name is on the list."

Chapter Sixteen — Piper's Story

The two arrests were as polite as anyone could ask. In the new days of his paranoia, Colonel Endling had started wearing a sun hat to cover his bright white hair. Not much of a disguise, he knew. He was surprised it was not police who came for him. He was sitting on a bench near the fountain in Timekeeper's Square when Marines in desertcolored helmets approached and walked him away in handcuffs.

In another part of town, Piper stayed home and waited for the inevitable knock on her door. It came as she was cleaning her insect terrarium. She was flattered that General Messmaker, the chief Marine himself, was there when she opened the door. He had some burns on his cheek. "If you're wise, you'll remain silent at all times. That way, you might avoid a death sentence."

"Why the advice?" she asked.

"Starting now," he said.

Colonel Endling was already in his cell when they brought Piper in. He sat on the bunk with his back straight against the wall. His face was in shadow, but his crossed legs were in the weak light of the second dawn coming in the frosted window. Piper couldn't tell if he was looking at her or not.

"Do you recognize me, Colonel?" she asked.

"Yeah," he said. "I recognize you."

Colonel Endling on his bunk was thinking of the momentum of events. He tried to look a few moves ahead, but it was useless. It wasn't chess. It was a game he didn't know. The rules made no sense. He felt the real wildness of chance.

"I can hear you grinding your gears," she teased. "You won't think a way out."

"Believe me, I know."

"What have they told you?" Piper asked.

"Treason, murder, assassination. Penalty of death. One day to prepare for trial."

"Same for me."

"Same for you?"

"I'm the Gun Club's bomb girl."

He frowned and said nothing. There was a clanging of iron doors far away on some other floor. Filthy floors, disgusting walls posted with hideous scrawling.

"They've put us together here," Piper said. "We're free to talk. I can tell you the entire conspiracy. That means tomorrow will be for show only."

"Yes, it's starting to make sense. Undercover spies started following me a week before the bombing. So, let me guess. I was a Trojan horse who didn't know he was a horse, and you double-crossed the Chairman."

"He had it coming."

"Well, I don't think I had it coming."

"That's fair."

"What's your real name?"

"Piper."

"Piper."

"Yes."

"Piper."

"It sounds funny when you say it."

"Why me?"

"You were convenient. You're known. That will bring extra buzz tomorrow."

"I'm surprised your head is not on a spike right now."

She swallowed. All her bravery was sinking like something heavy at the edge of a swamp. It never had any solid ground. In the way of all would-be optimists, she just assumed she'd have a trial and get a jail sentence. She prepared herself for that. Her only regret was that the Humble Gun Club Jack might live. Maimed and ugly and humiliated and weakened, he might live.

"I think the Queen is struggling," Piper said.

"No, that sounds funny. Queen."

"She doesn't know what to do."

"I wouldn't count on that, Piper."

"She's a weak person. She has a lazy mind."

"No," he said, shaking his head. "No, no, no."

Piper laughed.

"If they offer you Texas tomorrow, you should take it."

"Texas," she said as if she'd never heard of the place.

An officer of the court came stomping down the row of cells and handed each of them their own red file folder. Piper's was twice as thick as Colonel Endling's.

"The evidence against you tomorrow. Law says you get it."

He stomped away.

"Ah, the litany of my crimes," Piper said, as the Colonel opened his own folder. He flipped through fake documents and false affidavits; however, the prosecutors had real pictures of him in the Embassy with Hugo. They were all innocent moments, but the lying context they'd found made him look guilty. One capture of him standing at a window with his hand high above his head could be talked into being evidence of planting a bomb. That's where the blast had come from. He closed the folder.

"So, Piper, what's your story?"

She laughed.

"You want bullets to use against me?"

"No. Honest curiosity."

"Bullshit."

"No bullshit."

"You must be filled with rage."

"I'm frustrated," he said. "Yes."

Piper's mind raced. She was troubled by the worry that the heavy lock of her cell would clang open and Captain Quince of the Redemption Rock police—-who Colonel Endling said he knew-—would walk in with a hammer to bludgeon her skull.

"I'm a free agent," she said.

"Oh, now there's some bullshit."

"Well, no," she said. "I'm for hire. Look through my file here. In my case tomorrow, they have the luxury that these things are true."

"So, Gun Club paid you?"

"He paid me nothing."

Colonel Endling was silent, considering.

"Help me understand."

Piper gave an abridged version of her story. Her father owed the last Chairman, Wolfgang Einhorn, Gun Club's father, an immense debt, an old, infinite debt. An unpayable debt.

Piper's grandfather was a hard, wiry man from Utah named William Sestina. Many of the Earth's most vicious men survived the great dying off from the ocean pestilence and the drought that followed. Sestina was one of them. His wife passed, but he and his four sons thrived like weeds in the new world for craven opportunists. With some associates, he took control of a massive copper mine, guarded it and made it produce again after years of dormancy.

At that time, Wolfgang Einhorn with his private, mercenary army—-no longer needed for the defunct government's wars—-and his fleet of black hyperotors had installed himself in Boulder as a city lord. He had been convincing other strongmen and regional councils throughout the West that the nation needed a philosopher king to lead its rebuilding, to form a corporate council (later named The Mission) and chair it, and that he, Wolfgang Einhorn, was that man.

What was fateful—-as far as Piper is concerned-—was that Wolfgang and the newly formed Mission in Colorado Springs needed great quantities of copper wire. They knew rumors of Sestina's success in Utah, so Wolfgang and two thousand soldiers traveled to negotiate the first link in a supply chain. In a dust storm created by the trucks and rotors of the army of visitors, Sestina and his twenty armed men greeted Wolfgang at the mine's perimeter fence. What happened is not debated. The self-styled philosopher king was a fair man, and he met Piper's grandfather with every intention for their co-prosperity.

With his blond, spiky hair covered in dust and his eyes nearly closed against the blowing grit, he asked for a tour of the mine. The fence gate opened for them. It was an enormous open-pit mine. It looked like an amphitheater and, from the sky, like a sketch of an octopus with miles of conveyor belts running away like tentacles. Wolfgang, the manufacturer, was impressed with the operation, and he said so to William Sestina.

"This is fantastic. How many men work here?"

Sestina hesitated. Some forty men at that moment worked machines or monitored the ore on the conveyor belts.

"We have a rotation of near a hundred."

Wolfgang sensed a lie. He grew more suspicious when he toured sweltering, wooden barracks with cots ready for many multiples of a hundred men. Wolfgang poked around at piles of old comic books littered throughout.

"We have plans for more capacity," Sestina explained. "You should see the ore processing sheds. We haven't touched our capacity--"

Wolfgang stopped him.

"Why do these barracks have locks on the outside?"

Sestina and his followers were disarmed and, at gunpoint, one son was forced to reveal a hidden bulkhead that led to underground storage rooms. The sight of near a thousand slaves walking single file out of the dark space-—the space that smelled and attracted flies like an army's makeshift field latrine-—into sunlight was depressingly cinematic, and that is the last thing that Sestina saw before he was hanged from the highest, strongest branch of a nearby Juniper tree.

"You should have armed them all when you saw us coming," Wolfgang said.

"Please spare my sons," Sestina begged, as Wolfgang kicked out the cot beneath his feet. He did spare the sons. One of these young men was Piper's father. Wolfgang told the sons their father had incurred a debt that would pass down from generation to generation it was so large.

In fact, when Piper last saw Humble Gun Club Jack Einhorn and his jumping Misery Index, she asked about her own inherited debt, the nightmare that had fallen upon her as if from the sky.

"When I do this for you, will the debt finally be cleared?"

Gun Club who kept detailed ledgers of everything ever owed to his father shook his head.

"Almost," he said.

Chapter Seventeen

In the Map Room, we find Sebastian Sleeper perplexed by the onslaught of four children. He moved about, packing his belongings in his knapsack. Beetle wanted candy, and he kept talking about candy, where was the candy? You said there was candy here. It was for Flat Tire who was exhausted and crabby. Flat Tire looked at Sleeper with burning, red eyes.

"Over there, I told you," Sleeper said, waving his hand.

Beetle found the mini fridge.

"In here?"

"In there."

Beetle came back with chocolates wrapped in silver foil. Flat Tire's face filled with dumb joy. He took a silver chocolate and stood himself at the drafting desk where Toad was drawing a dinosaur with a crayon.

"Tell me the truth," Yoshi said. "You think this thing is real?"

Sleeper came over to the table where Yoshi had the map spread out.

"These squares with the red flags, see them?"

"Yeah."

"Those are the zones the Colonel has searched. Many with me. No evidence yet. Nothing."

"That's not everywhere."

"Right. Many of these lots on Embassy Row, all this white, we have not searched."

"That's where he thinks it is."

"Right. Tell me how you kids heard of the tunnels."

Yoshi's black hair was slicked back with grease. He looked almost a man, but he didn't have a hint of stubble on his face. Funny little believer, Sleeper thought. And he's keeping these other kids alive.

"Everyone knows the story."

"I guess so."

"We met a guy who told us it's true."

"Who was that?" Sleeper asked.

"Erdapfel."

Sleeper laughed.

"The true time pusher?"

Erdapfel was the worst kook of the entire strange bunch of true time salesmen. Those pushers got stipends and incentives from the Mission to convert everyone to the correct reckoning of time. They carried ledgers of the converted and those who refused. If you were not in the book and you wanted them to go away quickly, you could show them a watch or device set to the true time. Erdapfel spun mystic gibberish about why Gun Club wanted everyone on the true time.

"That guy is nuts."

"He put us to work as scouts and paid us," Yoshi said.

"He never sounded nuts to me," Toad said. "Everything made sense."

"What else did he tell you?"

"He's never seen the tunnel himself," Yoshi replied.

"It's near water," Toad said.

"He never said that," Yoshi corrected.

"No," Toad said. "I said that."

Mrs. Lascaux returned from the roof.

"I think it's high time you left, Sebastian. It's getting worse out there. You need to get away."

How could he get to Redemption Rock? Without a Marines flight, he had few options. The checkpoints would all be on highest alert and maybe even sealed off. Could he disappear into Radium Beach? He doubted it. Somebody would turn him in for the reward.

"The fish truck," Toad said.

They mixed with the crowds on the fish pier. The navy had forced all fishing boats to port. There were people walking all over the pier, pointing at rusted boats, bumping shoulders with each other, it was all a disordered mess. Drones flew overhead, so Sleeper braced himself against some ruthless hand grabbing the back of his neck. The ocean remained a fierce blue. When they reached the end of the pier, Sleeper stopped to look out at it. Yoshi kept going, and he found the friendly comrade, Manny, pushing a hand cart stacked with dead fish.

"You know the score, Yoshi," Manny said. He leaned on the handle of his cart. "Fifty bucks a head, and an extra hundred for the big guy."

"Can I owe it to you?" Yoshi asked. "You know I am good for it."

Manny frowned.

What a new form of thinking, Sebastian Sleeper thought, this constant scanning of every encountered face for signs of recognition or betrayal. He recalled the time he was driving his car in Dreaming Back Lake and hit an animal that darted out in front of him. For months, the trauma left him painfully vigilant; his eyes couldn't rest a moment when he drove. Funny how the mind overcomes that eventually and forgets, but now he remembered it; his body remembered it because it was being asked to do it again. That woman over there with her back to the pier's railing? She watched him and wondered about the gang of four children for just too long. Any thoughts about the strong-arm politics behind what was happening to him-—what was happening on the beach, what was happening in the sky—-these thoughts were pushed out.

Manny had a truck, and it wasn't far. As Sleeper walked back down the fish pier, he looked around him. He didn't see a tail, but how would he even know? Those people are pros.

Manny opened the box truck's rear door. It was frigid inside. It stank of death. A pile of dead, silver fish sloped up towards the front of the truck. He threw the fish, one at a time, from his cart onto the pile. There was room for Sleeper and the gang of four, but just barely.

"Wait inside," Manny said. "I have one more cart to load."

The kids jumped right up, but Sleeper looked all around before climbing in.

Manny closed and latched the door. It seemed they waited a long time, nobody saying anything, just looking at each other without really seeing, feeling at the cold fish, then laughing. Finally, a man's voice.

"Is this the truck?" the voice said. "I think I saw it was this truck."

"Yeah, that's the one," maybe Manny's voice maybe not. "Thanks, buddy. Here you go."

The door opened, and it was Manny. He tossed in more fish. Something disgusting—-some inner part or organ of a fish—-glistened on the steel floor.

"Do the fish move around when the trucking is moving?"

"Every time he stops," Yoshi said.

"Oh god."

"Did you bring a change of clothes?"

A conversation in the cold darkness.

"What else did Erdapfel tell you about the tunnel?"

"There's a door."

"What's beyond the door?"

"No idea," Yoshi said.

"Water," Toad said.

"Water?"

"Maybe."

The truck stopped.

"Too soon," Yoshi said.

"Men with guns," Toad said. "Motorcycles."

Sleeper sat upright and tried to prepare himself. He heard some motorcycle engines.

"Opening up," Manny warned, and he banged on the door twice with his fist. The daylight was shocking after two hours in the dark. Three bearded white men in shorts and sandals pointed big pistols at Sleeper and the orphans.

"You got to pay your toll," Manny said. "They tell me today's toll day."

Sleeper searched him for a sign he was in on the extortion, but Manny was a face of stone.

"How much?"

"Two thousand."

"Shut the fuck up," Yoshi said. The guns all turned on him.

"No, boy, calm down. Two thousand."

"We don't have that much," Sleeper said.

"How much you got?"

"You know," Sleeper said. "This is some tiresome middle management bullshit."

"Excuse me? See these guns?"

"You guys work for Serge?"

The three bandits looked at each other. They lowered the guns.

"I was just with Serge. We all were. Just today."

"Where?"

"At the beach."

"You want us to waive the toll."

"Yeah. Hell yeah."

"No, man. You need to contribute to the cause. How much you got?"

"I have a hundred," Sleeper said.

"Not enough."

The guns came up again.

Flat scrub lands stretched out in all directions from the road. There was nothing to see. No other vehicles, no birds, nothing. Of all the places on this sad planet to get rid of a body and four little ones, this had to be among the best.

"We have something here," Yoshi said. He began to un-cinch a knapsack.

"Wait wait wait," a gun to his head.

The seeming leader of the bandits took the sack and removed from it the silver sphere of the robotic laborer's head. He rubbed his hand on the shiny skull as if it were some crystal ball. The dead eyes of the thing reflected the glare of the sun.

"Oh, boy, look at this," the lead bandit said, disappearing around the corner of the truck. The other bandits held their guns on Yoshi. When a motorcycle roared to life, they chased after.

"Those are not Serge's guys," Manny said, as the motorcycles burned the road at incredible speed. "Watch out."

"How do you know?"

"Gun Club's motorcycle gang patrols this road," Manny said. "But thankfully those guys are bandits pretending to be part of that gang. Lucky day. You could be dead."

"Shit."

They walked Embassy Row as far as they could go. Hugo's building was an enormous crime scene closed off by barriers and fencing. Where the bomb had exploded, there was a big black hole. Floors below had melted glass that had solidified in blurry shapes like dull, clear teeth.

"Anything here?" Yoshi asked Toad.

Toad closed his eyes, then shook his head. They walked back in the direction they'd come. Pretty young women with parasols passed them. They glanced at Sleeper but showed no recognition. Near the Icelandic Embassy, Toad stopped, and they looked at the fancy grounds. The singer was out there in the distance, working on a large water sprinkler with a wrench.

"Do you think that pond can be drained?" Toad asked.

"You feel something there?" Yoshi asked.

"Maybe."

The kids all slipped through the black iron bars of the fence, as Sleeper looked for a way he could climb over it. Here is where I get arrested, he told himself. Oh, just great, this is the moment.

Chapter Eighteen

The staging of the trials was meticulous. This was a surprise to nobody. Colonel Endling knew when he saw several techs fussing over their cameras before the judge entered. There would be no justice at play. He and Piper were each given an hour to present their own defenses, and they were each allowed to call one character witness. Colonel Endling called his old friend Tubby Lascaux to testify on his behalf. Piper waived this farce altogether. And farce the whole thing was.

During his explanation of the conspiracy against him, the Colonel was subjected to constant, ridiculing laughter from the citizens in the courtroom. There was honest-to-god hissing. A man in a gray business suit walked the pews of the gallery and whipped up this laughter, and the camera techs zoomed on the laughing faces. The only drama came at sentencing. Piper and the Colonel sat beside their appointed defender at the defense table. They stood to face the judge when he came in with his verdicts (both guilty) and the sentences.

"Colonel Endling," the judge said from the bench.

"Your honor."

"Death or Texas?"

"Texas," he said without hesitation.

"So be it," the judge said, "I sentence you to banishment to Texas for the term of your natural life."

There was disappointment in the gallery.

"Miss Sestina."

"Your honor," Piper said.

"This was a hard one for me. The Queen gave me latitude to sentence you as I saw just. That's a heavy burden. You have betrayed royal love and the justice of our society in a way I did not imagine possible. You deserve death, in my opinion, but I believe in our sentencing system here on Triste. So, I will ask your choice. Death or Texas?"

Piper looked at the Colonel, then she said, "Texas."

The next transport to Earth was two weeks later. The evening of the departure found the Colonel, Piper and Tubby Lascaux* in shackles in the Chapel of Our Lady of Good Voyage. They all three wore brown jumpsuits. The brown reminded Colonel Endling of his own dead father's uniform from the natural gas pipeline so many decades past. He recalled a park bench, that uniform, and, beneath the park bench, a red cola can with a white polar bear on it.

In adjoining rows, the three convicts could talk freely, but this wasn't much of a place for talk. Tubby in his rage mumbled to himself. He hadn't cooled off in two weeks' time. Piper was silent, and the Colonel was silent, too, as he looked at the chapel's stained-glass windows. There was an image of Earth, destination of the travelers who came to this chapel, the blue and brown planet, surrounded by the darkest imaginable blue of deep space. Left of that, the next window showed the hokey eight signs of Triste's Zodiac. Left of that one, there was Saint Augustine, gold-hatted with gold scepter, looking down at a copy of his City of God. And, straight ahead, behind the altar and receiving the light of the setting Slow Sun was the Assumption of Mary, done after Titian, the Colonel realized, the dark body of a hovering God above Mary as she rose to be assumed body and soul into heavenly glory. The blood red of her tunic led the eyes upward to her destiny, but other details gave the impression that it was not up that mattered. God was coming down from the sky, down on the heads of the faithful below.

"Tubby, forgive me for asking," Colonel Endling said. "Are you strong enough to break these plastic shackles?"

"You flatter me with your question," Tubby said. "I am not strong enough. Been testing that."

Tubby used his nose to scratch an itch on the honey bee tattoo on his forearm. He was thinking of Laverna and their goodbye, which, rather than being sad and tearful, was angry and silent. Tubby's response was ever to hurt anyone who upset his wife. He was known to literally crack skulls. And this was in his plans, his long-term thinking the Colonel had advised him to cultivate now. As the Slow Sun set, the chapel grew dimmer and the quiet was peaceful. Not as dangerous as going to sea in a ship was today's interstellar voyage, but it was no guarantee.

"I've never been to Earth," Piper said.

"That surprises me," Colonel Endling replied.

"Got the inoculation?" Tubby asked.

"No," she said. "Never."

"You might get hassled about that," Colonel Endling said. "You'll have to take care of that."

An altar boy lit candles at a small shrine in a transept of the chapel. The Marines guarding the convicts sat quietly at a distance and left them alone, but they sat up straight when they heard the squeak of a wheel and a man's coughing. Colonel Endling turned to look behind him, and he saw the Queen coming down the aisle. She was pushing a wheel chair, and in this chair sat the wreck of Humble Gun Club Jack Einhorn.

"I saw you admiring the windows," Gun Club said in a low voice. "Two point five million dollars. That's what they cost. Glass blower from Dreaming Back Lake. Probably worth a lot more now. Maybe three point five or four."

"The Assumption is a beauty," Colonel Endling said.

"Isn't it though."

Gun Club was missing his right arm. His left didn't look like much use either. He kept his left hand in his lap and did all gesturing with his head and eyes. He was very thin, and his head was shaven from the hospital. He looked like an entirely different man.

"The three of you can relax. I mean you no harm today."

The Queen rolled him closer to them. She said nothing. Her eyes, though. They were killers.

"Piper," Gun Club said. "Look what you've done to me."

Piper chewed her cheek.

"I've come to say bon voyage," Gun Club said. "The fleet will project you as far out of sight as possible, and this is good, but I will not stop thinking of you."

"I—"

She didn't know what to say. It was a strange situation. She would have to live with herself after all. She believed we must mean what we say.

"I feel like the Wizard of Oz," Gun Club interrupted. "I have one thing for each of you before you go. No ruby slippers, but, I feel it all the same."

Queen Roux rolled her eyes at this.

"Firstly, Mr. Lascaux," Gun Club began. "Your involvement in this is unfortunate. Hold onto this envelope here. Roux, please give it to him."

The Queen walked over and stuffed the envelope into the breast pocket of Tubby's brown jump suit.

"The administrators in Abilene hand out daily calorie rations based on body mass. They will try to cheat you and short change you. The letter will get you your fair share."

"How generous," Tubby said with a scoffing snort.

"You just wait," Gun Club said. "You'll thank me."

"Doubtful."

"Piper, we have something special for you."

The Queen came forward, and Piper panicked when she saw what looked like a large, homemade pistol. She carried it barrel-down like a confident gunfighter. No harm, they said. No harm. But it was just a jet injector.

"I hope this hurts as much as I think it will," Queen Roux said, as she put the device against Piper's upper arm and pulled the trigger. It popped, and Piper closed her eyes.

"I can't have you die a lousy week into your sentence."

"That leaves just one," the Queen said.

"Yes, that leaves you, Colonel Endling," Gun Club said. "Has anyone informed you of who has made himself Head Prisoner in Abilene?"

"No," the Colonel said.

He looked at Tubby, but Tubby shrugged.

"Our mutual friend," Gun Club said.

The Queen approached with a photo and handed it over when the Colonel reached out with his shackled hands. He looked at the photo. The ugly, expanded cranium was unmistakable.

"He's there?"

"Yes. He looks the same just a bit older, no?"

"It's been a long time."

"He remembers you."

"Of course."

"He's looking forward to the reunion."

And here I imagined the long trip would be dull, the Colonel thought. The Big Brain was a character he never expected to see again despite the Brain's own insistence that they would. Gun Club looked mighty pleased with himself underneath the physical pain and weakness he presented.

"This will be goodbye, then," he said. "Adieu and adios."

"We'll be back," Piper said defiantly.

Gun Club laughed, but the Queen answered this.

"You won't see the end of the year," Roux said. "You won't. This is a death sentence deferred."

Roux pushed Jack down the center aisle that divided the nave. They exited the chapel without another word. The brief, strange, gauche quality of this meeting did not sit well with Piper. It was not Jack's way to hold a meeting with no purpose, a meeting from which he'd gain nothing. She began to suspect there was something more than a vaccine shot into her arm. That injection hurt like a bitch. She'd have the star-shaped scar now. She wanted to rub the spot, but the shackles made it impossible.

As they waited to board the transport ark, the Colonel tried to bargain with himself about his expectations. Earth was origin and future—-his own, he meant—-but he would not be seeing the oceanic Nebraska grasslands last seen twenty-five years ago. He and his two companions would be dropped in Texas, the notorious heart of the American desert, the worst place in the geographical imagination of any long-time resident of Triste. And yet, somehow, as his mind worked on a plan, he could not elude hope.

* On leaving the courthouse after testifying, Tubby was arrested, jailed and given a speedy trial of his own.

PART TWO

Chapter One

Morning, the abandoned airfield. The sky was violet. Milt Waxman was out early. It wasn't quite abandoned, then, he thought, plus he wasn't alone out there what with all the kangaroo rats bouncing all over the place. He liked getting out early before the boss got up with his big skull and loud-mouthed, non-stop bitching. The surface of the sewage lagoon reflected the little light the sky gave, but everything else-—tall antennae, emergency escape hatch, intake and exhaust towers, and the gaping mouth of the launch silo itself-— looked dark and dead. He was a tall, thin, depressed man.

The rodents were there, yes, hopping with what looked like uncontrollable joy. Waxman had a flame thrower strapped to his back, and he was charged with incinerating any of the rats that fell into the silo. He hated this. It was enough to make him hate life itself. The kangaroo rats were not smart enough to stay away from the silo, or they could not remember brothers and sisters who fell in. They were just dumb animals. He prayed for them, but every morning was the same. He kept a pocket full of rubber bands that he fired at the rats when he had the chance to scare them away from their infernal deaths.

He approached the mouth of the silo with tender steps. He'd have to peek over the edge to see if any rats had fallen in during the night. As he approached, he pointed his ear to listen. Nothing he could hear, but when he turned his flashlight down the throat of the silo, he saw black eyes shining.

"Shit," he said, his hope defeated again.

He completed a full walking circle of the silo, deliberating. The concrete hole was exactly wide enough to fit a sprinter, and it was deep. What to do, what to do. There was no way to extract the rats without opening the escape hatch and climbing down there, and he didn't have the key, couldn't get the key without some embarrassing begging over at Maintenance.

Waxman had just about decided to suffer the embarrassment when a junk car roared to life at the far end of the airfield, breaking the morning's quiet. The one working headlight came on, and Waxman felt sick to his stomach. The Brain was on his way over in the rusted police car he'd gotten to run for a quarter mile at a time. The fucking fiend himself. Ugly, big-headed, unnatural good old boy fiend.

The police car made a direct line for Waxman and the silo. The Brain opened the driver door and climbed out. The kangaroo rats above ground had scattered with the headlight.

"You're up early," Waxman said.

"Osprey told me we have special prisoners arriving today."

"Special, huh? Who?"

"Never mind. How are things going over here? I have a ton of shit to do."

"Another day in Paradise, as they say."

"Must be a clean morning. I didn't see your torch going. I trust you haven't needed it."

"Right, boss."

"Let me see your flashlight."

Waxman handed over the light, but instead of following its beam, he pretended to watch something on the purple horizon.

"Oh, you fucking lying weakling," the Brain said.

"What?" playing dumb.

"The bottom is literally hopping with rats."

"Are you kidding me?" slowly walking over to look.

"Don't be stupid," the Brain said. "Don't even."

"I can't do it," Waxman whined. "I don't have it in me."

"This is very simple, Milty. You flick the switch, strafe for a minute, then flick the switch off. Done."

"You left out the murder of little innocent animals part."

"Are you fucking with me, Milty?"

"No."

The Brain turned his body abruptly such that he bumped Waxman slightly off-balance. Waxman teetered on the edge of the silo's lip, but he caught his balance.

"Where is this coming from, Milt?" the Brain asked. He pushed the warm-up button on the flamethrower. It hissed, and Waxman smelled the gas.

"It's not right."

"I wish I had a fucking movie camera right now," the Brain said. A blotchy birthmark came to life on the side of his neck. He pretended to be a movie man from ancient days with a crank camera, and he slowly walked closer and closer to Waxman as if running a slow zoom on his stricken face.

"I wish I had a fucking movie camera right now. I'd film you saying these stupid fucking things and play it back so you could see your fucking face when you talk. Are you a god damn idiot? What is your fucking problem?"

The Brain threw up his freckled hands. The invisible camera must have evaporated. Waxman said nothing. The flamethrower chirped to say it was fully warmed. The Brain grabbed the grip, making sure to turn the igniter away from himself.

"Give me this thing," he said. "Balls. God damn balls. I do not have time for this." Waxman looked down into the silo, but the flashlight was out.

Colonel Endling and Tubby Lascaux shuffled like zombies off the yellow bus and onto the pavement. The sun wasn't quite up. The sky was a fading purple, and in the remaining gloom, they were shocked to see, far down a runway, a bright finger of fire reach out from a flamethrower. It was so strangely unexpected they shrugged it off. More shuffling bodies bumped them from behind, so they moved on to the building where the herd was headed.

Piper climbed off the women's bus and looked around. A long time ago, this was Dyess Air Force Base, home of Global Strike Command, Eight Air Force, 7th Bomb Wing. Abilene, Texas. Earth.

"Come this way to be processed," said a bald man in civilian clothes. He held open the door of the small building. What with the flamethrower, that word "processed" could mean anything, Piper thought. Everyone inside the building was in civilian dress, too. In fact, since leaving the ark in the dark of the night, the only person she'd seen in official uniform was the bus driver. There were no guards, no weapons.

Two lines formed for the check-in—-men & women—-and they moved quickly.

"What are you good at?" Tubby Lascaux was asked by the slender man completing his forms.

"I'm an aerospace engineer," Tubby said.

"Mechanical, right, that's good. Come over here, please."

There was a scale behind the desk. Tubby stood on it, and due to his enormous size, a small crowd gathered around to see. The scale's digital display didn't show weight but rather a four-digit number that was the prisoner's assigned daily ration of calories. The red numbers showed 2100, and a groan went up among the watchers.

"Jesus Christ on a popsicle stick," somebody said.

"We don't see many that high," the slender man said. "Like ever." He handed Tubby a silver poker chip that had the number etched on it. "Wait in that room behind me for the Warden."

Colonel Endling was already seated on a folding chair in the room. Tubby stood next to him, and when Piper came over to sit near them, Tubby put his hand on her forehead to stop her approach. "Go somewhere else, free agent," he said.

She looked up at his big face. She looked at Colonel Endling, but he looked away, so she stood in a corner apart from the rest of the prisoners.

"What's this gonna be, Colonel?" Tubby asked. "Orientation?"

"Yup."

There were about thirty prisoners in the room, finally. Every one of them was groggy and quiet, and those seated were slouched or leaned way back. Some sat up straight at the sound of the rotor outside. Others seemed not to care or notice. After five minutes, a man in a brown cowboy hat and safety goggles entered flanked by two Marines in full battledress. The man in the hat was old and leathered by the sun.

"Morning, folks, my name's Osprey, I'm the Warden of Texas. This prison here."

He scanned the faces in the room.

"I don't see any familiar faces today. I'll give you the short lay of the land. Listen up cuz I don't repeat myself, and you're not likely to see me again anyhow. Statistically speaking, half of you won't survive the first month. If you listen up now you might. You just might."

The Colonel felt a terrific headache coming on. He rubbed his eyes. The stress of the interstellar flight was rough on an elderly person. He was depressed at the thought there might be no aspirin again ever. Osprey the Warden continued.

"You are presently in west-central Texas. You're in a prison that has no fences and no walls. You won't see many guards around here, but know there are indeed guards. You are free to move about. If it has been some time since you visited the United States, or if you've never been here, you should know we are surrounded by nearly two million square miles of hot desert pavement. That is half of the area of this nation. You will know it as soon as the sun is up. The coasts are poisoned. Do not go there. Mexico is poisoned. Do not go there. You will learn the rules of this prison from your fellow prisoners. If you violate any of my posted commandments, you will be shot or sent to Mexico where you will die. We will give you a five-gallon jug of water on your way out of this room. If you stick around Abilene and dedicate yourself to your work assignment, you will be fed a daily ration of calories. I'm sorry, but I don't take questions. God be with you."

Osprey and the Marines exited the room, and the rotor was gone as quickly as it came. A door was opened to the daylight outside. The wind had picked up and grit pelted everything.

"This way for your water jugs."

The prisoners lined up again and filed out. Piper dragged her heavy jug, leaving a line in the dirt behind her. The Colonel walked out into the wind with Tubby behind him. Tubby had his water jug in one hand and the Colonel's jug in the other, managing easily. Tubby turned to the man who'd processed him. The man worked at his own teeth with a toothpick.

"Where do we sleep?" he asked.

The man shrugged, but then he pointed.

"The town's that way."

Chapter Two

"I've been waiting for you."

The voice startled them all. One minute he was way over there, and the next he was right on top of them, talking and smiling down at their faces. Sleeper and Yoshi were on their hands and knees on the green grass, inspecting the small stone dam that kept the pond from running away to the lower acres. Caught with no prepared story, Sleeper blushed. Yoshi stood and got ready to run.

"Something's kinda fishy, no?" the Icelandic Singer said.

Yoshi and Sleeper looked at each other. The Singer held his nose against an unpleasant smell.

"Oh, yes, ha ha," Sleeper said. "Fish truck."

"This is not the place. Come. Come with me," the Singer said. He had long hair tied back in a ponytail. It was blond but dirty from his work in the soil. He turned back to them when they did not follow.

"I've been waiting for you," he repeated. "This is the way to the water house."

"What makes you think you know why we are here?" Sleeper asked. He stood still, unwilling to follow.

"The door," the Singer said. "Yes? The door?"

Toad rushed after him, and that was enough for Yoshi. Sleeper looked around. He felt about as dumb as he'd ever felt in his life. The grass stains on the knees of his khaki pants looked ridiculous. Beetle followed the Singer, too. This is the dumbest thing, Sleeper thought. The dumbest. I'm going to have to pacify four crying children. He scooped up little Flat Tire, and they all crossed the long green lawn at a trotting pace.

The water house was a pale limestone brick thing sheltered by a copse of black poplars. The building had no corners. It looked like a misplaced castle turret with a dome top like a planetarium. There were no windows and just one silver door.

"This source irrigates all of my flowers and hedges," the Singer said as he worked his key in the lock. "And the green, green grass, of course."

Inside, there was a tangle of black pipes coming up from the floor and heading out in all directions.

"Come inside, come inside."

He lit a lantern and looked them over.

"Oh, yes, it's you all right."

"Do you know us?" Yoshi asked.

"Not in so many words."

"What is this place?"

"This is the water house."

"Bunch of pipes," Flat Tire said. "Bunch of stupid pipes."

The Singer pointed.

"Those are the stairs down."

"What's down there?" Sleeper asked, throwing suspicion into his voice. "What is it?"

"The door."

"Where does it go?" Yoshi asked.

If Sleeper should have learned by now to anticipate a trap—-and anyone would agree he should have-—he was not sensing any trap now. He was a wanted fugitive. He should've felt a thrill of anxiety starting at the bottom of his feet, but there was nothing like that. He wanted to see what would happen.

"I've never opened the door. It was there before this parcel of land was developed. My predecessors, the former singers, built the stairs and this enclosure. Go ahead now."

He gestured to the stairs, and the gang of four began to descend. Sleeper took the offered lantern and followed. The stairs were heavy old blocks of unpolished granite. Black pipes made up the walls left and right, and water sloshed loudly up and down in them. They got to the bottom. The door was set in a wall of natural rock. It was old wood, dark and oily wood, and the handle or knob was missing. They could see the outline where the handle had been and the holes from which screws had been ripped out or just rotted out. Big black water pipes went into the wall to the right of the door. The door's only real feature was its knocker. This was a bronze owl with sleepy eyes and a big ring hanging from its beak.

"Why would they have a knocker?" Yoshi asked.

"Yes, strange," Sleeper said.

He put his finger in one of the screw holes and tried to get a hold he could use to pull the door open, but it was too heavy for that. He curled his finger through the owl's bronze ring and pulled. The door loudly objected, but he felt it give, and a second yank moved it an inch. He yanked until the flesh around his knuckle purpled. This will take all day, he thought. He took a break. He felt sad suddenly, as the Colonel's face appeared in his mind. The Colonel would have been tickled by this moment before the door. Sleeper had no way of knowing if the old guy was still alive.

"Let me see if the gardener has any tools upstairs."

He ran ups the steps and called out at the half way mark: "Do you have a crow bar?"

But he heard only his own voice echoing back from the pipes. The Icelandic Singer was gone. Sleeper went outside and looked around. He saw nothing but empty green land. He headed back for the stairs and saw, as if anticipated by a helpful hand, a long-handled garden fork leaning against the wall. He brought this back down the stairs and gave Yoshi a turn at prying the door.

With a big grin, Yoshi said thanks and went to work. By slow centimeters, the door came open. It was dark inside. Sleeper brought the lantern over, and they could see it was a tunnel dug out of the stone just as the astronaute Souci claimed in his diary.

"Well," Sleeper said. "Well well well."

"Let's go," Yoshi said.

"Let's be cautious."

They entered. Sleeper led the way with the lantern. Yoshi came next, followed by Toad, Beetle and Flat Tire. As trite as it sounds, the air of the tunnel was like a tomb; the perfect stillness was disturbed by their passing through. No worms, though, no bugs, just generations of dust that kicked up a bit with their footsteps.

"My head is swimming," Toad said.

They all stopped.

"Are you okay?"

"Yeah," Toad said. "Everything just feels confusing."

Sleeper felt his forehead: normal. Cool even.

"Maybe you should go out and sit on the stairs."

"No way."

"All right."

They walked for what seemed over a mile. If the tunnel sloped either up or down, it was subtle, imperceptible. Sleeper imagined, as Colonel Endling mused aloud on occasion, what Souci thought as he came down this same long hallway. It wasn't so easy to walk in the boots of that brave solo artist who traveled light years to the allegedly empty planet. His shock must've been overwhelming.

Eventually, the little crew came to the end of the tunnel. The walls on each side had rooms cut out, and the rooms had iron bars like jail cells. There was nothing in the cells. No old cots, no chairs, no anything.

"Let's stay out of there," Sleeper said. "These cells are spooking me."

"What are they for?"

"I don't know."

He brought the lantern to the end of the tunnel where there was another door. This one was gray steel. There was a metal handle, and stenciled in black letters, at eye level, was the word SOURCE. He reached out and knocked on the door. The echo made the other side sound cavernous.

"Try the handle," Yoshi said.

"Yeah?"

"No, don't," Flat Tire said. "Don't."

"Why not?"

"I'm afraid."

Yoshi made a face. He stalked up and tried the handle. It turned. He pulled open the door and asked for the lantern. There was a shimmering waterfall inside the room. With the weak light, they could not see past it. They could not see the extent of the room either. The room was carved out of rock like the tunnel, and big pipes ran along the ceiling and down to feed in the water behind the cataract. When Yoshi pulled the light away, the water shone black like new patent leather shoes or automobile chrome or the fold of a satiny black flower petal. It was so smooth and perfect, it glimmered like a mirror.

The kids approached the water, marveling at their own reflections since it was not boys looking back but owls. They moved their arms and dreamy owls flapped wings. Sleeper had no reflection at all in the water. Even when he leaned in and held the light close, there was nothing. Not even his own human face. The boys were amused with each other and laughed.

"Some trick here," Sleeper said, thinking the images were projected. He looked around nervously. "Owls. That explains the door. Funny trick."

There was little way to explore the room without stepping into the waterfall. The shelf of stone surrounding it was narrow and rounded, and it offered little foothold.

"It's so cool," Yoshi said. "I mean like weird."

"Yeah, and the joke is on me."

"So, what do we do now?" Yoshi asked.

Everyone looked to Toad for guidance.

"We have to explore this."

"We're not dressed for that, Toad," Sleeper objected.

"It might wash off the fish stink," Beetle said.

"Good point," Sleeper said. He reached out and mussed Beetle's helmet of hair. He sat down and removed his socks and shoes. He turned his face to his shoulder, and, wow, yes, he reeked of dead fish. When he dipped his first toe into the waterfall and stepped down on a surprisingly slimy and slippery pool bottom, he had a flashback to a childhood memory, a leech stuck between his toes that he did not notice for hours, a leech that grew enormous on his blood and that his father removed by pouring salt on it until it curled up dead. But, wait, was that the Colonel's story that he'd heard. Yes, that was not his own story. Funny.

They all stepped through the sheet of falling water. Flat Tire rode on Yoshi's back. The water slowly deepened until it was waist high on Sleeper. As they moved out from the edge, the lantern revealed more of the Source Room. The dome ceiling looked perfectly round and smooth. What tool was used to make it? This was inconceivable. When the water reached his navel, Sleeper began to feel very silly. He felt ridiculous though not embarrassed by it or angry. Just ridiculous. His easygoing bemusement ended when they reached an abrupt drop off and all of them slipped under the water. The lantern went under, and Sleeper dropped it. Eyes open in the dark water, he watched the light go away in slow motion, and he realized it was going away in a weak current he hadn't before noticed, and Flat Tire was caught in this current, too, and before he could surface to breathe, or stop his own feet from slipping, he was also caught in it and moving, and the strength was growing. It was immense, the strength, they were being swallowed, and Sleeper was turned ass over tea kettle and blacked out.

Yoshi woke on a sand beach. A young man and a young woman, each in black rimmed glasses, watched him, as he sat up. He looked around and saw the other orphans sitting up, too. Beyond the sand of the narrow beach, a green lawn ran up to the back of a mansion of golden brick.

"There are four of you?" the young woman asked. She came over with towels.

"No," Yoshi said. "Five."

He looked around.

"We're traveling with a man named Sebastian. Where are we?"

"You're in Dreaming Back Lake," the young woman said. "I'm Maggie. This is Julian. This here is the lake. Did you come through the door?"

"Yes," Yoshi said, struggling to stand. "We need to go back in and get Sebastian."

"I'm sorry," Maggie said with genuine feeling. "The door only goes one way. Julian and I have been here for years, waiting for someone, anyone, to come through it."

Chapter Three

He woke on a sand beach. When he touched the painful spot on the top of his head, his fingers came away covered in blood. It was a glorious day. The Fast Sun was shining on the pretty blue lake. He felt a small grief at feeling so wretched on such a day. He sat, hugging his knees, looking at the lake for several minutes before it occurred to him to wonder how he'd come to be there. He stood and looked around him.

What had happened to Flat Tire? Did Yoshi save him? Where were they all? He climbed off the beach onto some dead brown grass and walked towards the remains of a bombed-out house of golden brick. Weeds and small shrubs grew between the charred, split bricks and through cracks in the foundation. He looked back at the lake. It glimmered like a thing that would never stop. If the boys were drowned in that water—-no, that was not a reality he could handle. He put it out of his mind.

The drones had touched this neighborhood more than most that Sleeper had witnessed. Across from the house of golden bricks was a playground with a charred tank at rest before a tall slide that was toppled into a bomb crater. He walked down to the water's edge to drink from his cupped hands. He kept his eyes averted, fearing he'd see small bodies floating to shore. Sadness or horror or panic, the feeling testing itself out in him, was beat down by the pain in his head. He only wanted water and some clarity of mind.

His mobile device was dead, dashing his hopes of using GPS to confirm where he was. Somewhere in the restricted zone deep down Embassy Row, he guessed. He began walking and followed street signs pointing the way to: HISTORIC DISTRICT. The houses grew larger and more elaborately decorated as he went along. He didn't see any people out. In the yard of one house, he saw a pack of dogs, but after staring for a while, he realized it was a pack of coyotes.

Though he didn't know it, there were people around. They watched him from inside their homes, as he turned himself around, shook his head no and ran back to the lake. His eyes were filled with tears. He shouted hello at the lake, and it echoed back. He scanned the rocky shoreline, but he saw no sign of anyone. He began a search, but he quickly realized that, as clear as the lake was all the way to its bottom, he could not do it alone. It was too vast.

He sat on the beach with his head in his hands. The sand was hot beneath him. I am lost, he thought. He picked up a shell, and he was considering its coils when he heard a sandy shuffling behind him.

"Are you okay, friend? Has someone assaulted you?"

Sleeper wiped his eyes and turned around.

"You've got blood all down your neck and shoulders."

It was an old lady with an eye patch on her right eye beneath her glasses.

"Have you seen four boys?"

"Not recently," a weak, half-committed smile.

"Do you live nearby? Have you seen any boys wandering?"

"No," the lady said. "Not recently."

"You live here?"

"Just down the street. I've lived all my life in Dreaming Back Lake."

Sleeper's jaw dropped.

"Is that where I am?"

"Yes," the stranger said. "Now the war is over, we've all come back. Well, most of us. Some don't have a home to come back to."

She waved at the house of blasted brick.

"Those poor folks. Drone operator mistook the place for an enemy safe house."

"I'm so confused."

"You look like you've had a bump on the head."

"Yes."

"Bad one. You need a doctor."

"I was in Redemption Rock when I hit my head. I don't have any idea how I got here."

"That's a long way from here."

She came closer and looked him over.

"You don't look like a soldier. Did you fight in the war?"

"No," he said. "And that's a strange way to put it. Nobody has been calling things a war."

She stared at him with her good eye. The pines around the lake swayed in a gust of hot wind, and Sleeper caught a glimpse of what he thought was a drone high up in the atmosphere. He lost track of it in the sun.

"Maybe you hit your head harder than you think."

"I was traveling with four boys. We've been separated, but I think I'm in the wrong town altogether to get back with them."

"That's a tough one."

"Yes, sure is."

"The old hospital in town was destroyed, but there's a private company, Emergency Care. You should go there."

He touched his bloody scalp.

"I could walk there with you."

"All right."

They walked slowly, following the same route the HISTORIC DISTRICT signs pointed out. There was a great reconstruction underway. In the town's central square, engineering bots were everywhere, working in devoted, studious coordination. Steel beams and big plates of glass were moved easily and confidently. The security roadblock Sleeper knew from his last visit had been converted to a food vendor, and the white smoke of sausages grilling wafted up from there. This was so encouraging to see, and the smell stirred something alive in him. Through no conscious act of his own, his feet steered him towards the food. The onions frying on a big steel pan made his mouth water.

He tried to hand a vendor damp cash from his pocket.

"Oh, no," the man said. "Not that kind."

The woman with the eye patch paid. He was about to take a big bite of a sausage sandwich when a large display screen on the side of a bank branch caught his attention. In striking high definition (on half the screen) was the hideous, stridently narcissistic Queen's Misery Index. The screen's other half showed High Days in the History of the Queen's Mood.

Queen. The word made no sense to him.

"I'm sorry," Sleeper said. "I never asked your name."

"Maggie Trout."

"You've been awfully friendly, Maggie, and kind to me."

The montage running on the wall of the Denver Bank was downright strange. Gun Club Jack Einhorn was hardly a public persona. It seemed off. There was footage of Roux on the day of their wedding, her red hair pinned up elaborately. She looked beautiful. She beamed at the groom. There was also footage of Jack's Chairman Day. He smiled, but he looked surprisingly humbled by the spectacle. There was hiking in the Rockies, high up above the tree line, and a young son, one of the little Einhorn boys, hiking, too, and splashing in a mountain river.

The montage ended with a clip that took Sleeper's breath away. A pair of skin-headed Marines led a brown man up a set of wooden stairs to a platform. The man was handcuffed, but the cuffs were removed at the top of the stairs. When the camera gained focus, Sleeper saw the platform was a gallows, and the man was Serge Ville de Paix. Serge bit his lip nervously before the shot ended, and the montage looped back to its beginning.

"Oh, Jesus," Sleeper said.

"You okay, friend?"

"When did this happen?"

"What?"

"That hanging."

"Ah, must be near three years now," Maggie replied.

"What?"

"We should go over here to this bench and have a talk," Maggie said. "Let's talk about some things."

Chapter Four

Ladybug got his nickname from the jacket he wore every day, the red jacket with the black spots. He hated the name, but he pretended to like it, so he could fall in with the ball busting games they played in the boss' circle of cronies. Today, he was walking down Bishop Road, carrying Waxman's flamethrower on his back. Waxman had run off or disappeared, and the boss said his replacement was living in a garage on Bishop Road. Go find him. He didn't say which garage was the problem.

The day was blazing hot, and Ladybug walked through a wide-open space. The sky was enormous. There was no way the burning sun would hide or go away. He passed Debbie Cadabra who was walking in the opposite direction. They knew each other. He waved. Debbie raised an eyebrow at the flamethrower, but then she smiled and waved back.

What had happened to Waxman? That was a strange thing. Debbie was manslaughter, and Ladybug was grand larceny, over 75 counts brought before the judge. He couldn't help himself, and those were just the cases they caught him on.

The Brain surrounded himself with thieves. The way he looked at systems and power, well, he saw power as reversible and the way to reverse it was to steal pieces of it one by one. He wasn't wrong, as events from his life continually bore out. Within six months of arrival in Texas, he'd become Head Prisoner, a position of extreme convenience and one not gotten by the kissing of warden ass. Ladybug didn't go in for the political stuff himself, but he liked when the boss sent him out to cause some trouble and steal shit.

"Hey, wait, Debbie," he called, turning back to her.

"What?"

"Have you seen two new arrivals living in a garage? Know which house?"

"Yes, keep going another quarter mile. A white ranch house falling down. Long driveway."

"Thank you, Debbie."

He walked along until he came to the driveway. He looked back and saw Debbie's slender form crossing a giant heat mirage. She moved slowly like some dumb, reckless child on a sheet of thin ice, but that was impossible except for back in the days when ice was a thing in Texas. A long time ago. This made him think of Waxman again. What had Waxman decided? Was he out there in that heat doing something mortally stupid?

The garage door was closed, so they were in there or not. Obviously, he told himself. And only one way to find out. He walked up the driveway and put his ear to the garage door. He thought he heard a socket wrench cranking, so he knocked and said, "Hello?"

"Who's that now?" an elderly sounding voice.

"I'm looking for Leonid Lascaux."

"Who's asking for him?"

"Prison Works Administration."

The garage door began to rise. The old man, the Colonel from the Mission, was seated on a wooden stool, cranking a socket to adjust something on a heavy-duty bicycle. Lascaux pulled a rope that, via pulley, made the door go up. He tied it off. He was just huge. He crossed his arms, and a muscle in his forearm flexed, causing a tattoo of a bee that he had there to warp its shape.

"What do you want?"

"I'm here to do two things," Ladybug said. "And I'll tell you what those two things are."

"Go ahead."

"Well, first, I'm here to give you your work assignment."

"Oh, really," Tubby laughed. "Both of us?"

"No, no, just you."

"Ah, even better. What have you got for me?"

"Well, this," Ladybug said, holding out the flamethrower's nozzle. "I can explain it."

"You better."

"The Sprinter Corps can use your support."

"What's it for?"

"Well, it's entry level."

"What's the flamethrower for?"

Ladybug felt the Colonel's eyes upon him, sizing him up.

"When you accept," Ladybug said, nervously. He hadn't expected Lascaux to be so big and muscular. "When you accept your job assignment, I can validate your calorie chip."

The garage was cool and dry. They had two cots. Not a bad set-up, Ladybug thought.

"What do you need me to burn?"

"Oh, stray wildlife that disrupts sprinter launch silos."

"That sounds vicious."

"No, no, no, it's not."

"You want me to incinerate some rodents or birds or something, but that's not vicious?"

"It's only entry level."

Tubby looked at Colonel Endling who nodded.

"Hand it over, then. Here's my chip."

They made the exchange, and Ladybug took a mobile device from the pocket of his shorts. He scanned the chip's surface, and the device chirped. He whistled.

"Twenty-one hundred calories. Oh, boy."

By means of a clever double version of the Tenkai Palm, Ladybug swapped Lascaux's 2,100-unit chip for a 1,600-unit chip before handing it back. If either the Colonel or Lascaux noticed, they didn't give it away. Ladybug had practiced the trick so many thousands of times and pulled it off so many scores of times without getting caught that he was confident. Confident despite his general nervousness around these two, the giant and the VIP. Over the years, one chip swap after another, Ladybug had grown his original daily calorie intake from 950 to, now, by huge leap, 2,100.

"So, what am I gonna burn? When do I start?"

"It would be ideal if you could meet me at Dyess, on the airfield, at dawn."

"When?"

"Tomorrow."

Tubby laughed.

"Is that a problem?"

"What happens if I change my mind about this job?"

"No calories."

"Figured."

"You going to change your mind?"

"No."

"Good," Ladybug said. "Oh, hey by the way what are the bikes for? You planning to leave Abilene?"

"No."

It was Colonel Endling who spoke this time. Ladybug noted the fact of that. It was a tell, he thought. When he was gone, Tubby pulled the garage door shut. With only the light of the side window, the space returned to its dusky feeling.

"So, Piper and I have jobs now," Tubby said. "Why are they avoiding you?"

"I'm sure he's making me wait to think about it just as I thought about it the entire length of our flight from Triste."

"Should we consider changing our plan?"

"I don't think so."

"Okay, good. I agree."

"Wanna give these babies a test ride?"

"Yes!"

The bicycles were silver with black seats and black tires, identical, so they had to raise Tubby's seat considerably. Colonel Endling had a slow time getting the pedals going, but once he'd built some momentum on the open road, he flew along joyously. No dust wind today, and the sky was cloudless blue to the horizon in any direction on the flatlands. "This is some kind of prison," he shouted to Tubby, as they raced, pumping their legs and laughing.

Chapter Five

The free apples were not free, and the bananas, same. They came with strings attached—-strings in the form of answering questions-—and, now that they took a break, Yoshi watched while Julian and Maggie set up their scientific instruments along the lake. It was just after First Dawn. The lake was silver with a smear of pink like the sky's pink. Feeding dragonflies buzzed the air above the water, and here and there they kissed the surface only to pull back as if having second thoughts about an eternity dipped in pewter.

Yoshi found Maggie and Julian totally strange. In the night and all morning, they talked of square waves and demons and somebody's cat that was both alive and dead. It made his head hurt, but he was afraid to say so or ask his own questions. Maggie also kept talking about the Royal Engineers. She clearly kept calling Gun Club "King Jack," and that Yoshi intended to ask about. There was something special about the lake. Julian was wildly excited about the measurement on one of his gray boxes. He showed it to Maggie, and they hugged. During the embrace, Maggie's phone began to ring. She looked at the screen, frowned, and answered.

"Complaint line," she said, cheerfully.

Yoshi watched Julian walk away from her. Julian went back to the instrument with the exciting data. Then, he turned around and looked at the lake.

"Yes, yes," Maggie said. "If you're in town, stop by and let me look at it. Yes, Julian is here, too."

She ended the call and turned to Yoshi.

"Are your buddies awake yet?"

"I should check on them."

Unlike Yoshi, who was a troubled sleeper, Beetle, Toad and Flat Tire slept like the dead. They were snoring under blankets on the deep soft red carpet of a room on the third floor of Maggie and Julian's brick house. Yoshi kicked Toad's foot that peeked out from the cover of the blanket.

"You awake?"

"What? What? What?"

"Sun is coming up. Get your ass off the floor."

"Can we stay here?"

"For now, yes."

"That's good, Yoshi," Toad said, pleading with his tone for Yoshi to agree.

"I think it's good," Yoshi allowed. "I want to know exactly what this place is though."

"What about the train?"

"The train. Yeah."

"What about it?"

"I don't know, Toadie."

They explored the house. It was old and dusty, and the dust was unusual by the antiseptic Tristean standards of the homes Yoshi had been inside. Long hallways between rooms had floors of blonde wood and images of trees on the walls. They were forests of white-skinned trees Yoshi didn't know the names of. Some hallways had runners that muted footsteps, and at the end of one, Yoshi stopped at a triptych of windows that looked out upon the grounds and the lake. The rising sun and some wind on the lake gave glittering ripples that looked like a golden, godly fingerprint, whorls and all.

Maggie and Julian insisted they had not seen Sebastian Sleeper. That was sad and hard to believe. Yoshi had no reason to mistrust them, but he also had no good basis to put faith in them, and that was a thing he was slow to do.

He found Toad climbing the shelf in a big library room. There was a fireplace and shelves that went from floor to ceiling. In the center of the floor, resting on an old lectern was a book opened to a certain page near its middle. Only if a spotlight shined down on it would it be more obvious that it was put there to catch attention. *The Devil's Dictionary* by Ambrose Bierce, it was called.

A magnifying glass was set over the following entry:

PROOF, n.

Evidence having a shade more of plausibility than of unlikelihood. The testimony of two credible witnesses as opposed to that of one.

What the fuck, he thought, but just then an extremely loud doorbell rang under their feet. Toad fell off the shelf. Yoshi trotted to the triptych windows and saw Maggie coming towards the house and waving.

"Well, hello, stranger," she said to somebody on the porch.

The door opened, and a man came in.

"Yes, he's here," Maggie said. "He's down by the lake."

"Good," said a deep, male voice. "Erdapfel and I would like to speak with him today. Important matter. Most important."

"Is Mr. Erdapfel in town, too?"

"Yes, he is."

"Okay, cool," Maggie said. Yoshi heard her footsteps on the stairs. The visitor, too. "Let's go up to my workshop and look at your clock. 'Interference,' you said?"

Erdapfel, Yoshi whispered. Now that could not be a coincidence. Erdapfel did work for Maggie's agency, but, come on, what were the chances he would show up the very day the kids went through the tunnel he told them about. Yoshi blew air through his nose, a mocking laugh. He strolled down the hallway and found the doorway to Maggie's workshop. She looked up from her work.

"Hello, Yoshi, meet Mr. Sly."

"Hi, there," Mr. Sly said.

Yoshi shook his hand, as Toad, Beetle and Flat Tire came to fill the doorway. Mr. Sly had gray hair and a wolf smile with what seemed more than the normal number of teeth.

"Hullo."

"Where are you boys from?" Mr. Sly asked. "My territory has been the Lake for ten years. Don't think I've seen you before."

Maggie said, "Radium Beach."

"We live on the beach."

"On the beach?" Mr. Sly said with a big grin for Maggie. "You live on the beach?"

"Yes. Tent folk."

"I don't think the police let people sleep overnight on the beach. Are you telling a story maybe?"

"No, no, ask Mr. Erdapfel when you see him."

"Oh, you know him?"

"We do."

Maggie's phone rang loudly.

"Hi, Julian," she said. "Oh my god. Hold on."

She ended the call.

"Julian says the clocks down by the lake are going crazy."

"How about mine?" asked Mr. Sly.

Maggie turned the face of the atomic clock so they all could see. On the screen, a Venn diagram showing four sets of symbols and numbers was pulsing like a heart. The closed curves grew and shrank with no predictable pattern.

"Something's out of joint," Mr. Sly said, as Maggie rushed to the window.

Chapter Six

Iris knew she distracted Leo, passing, in her silver dress, through the threshold's columns of white light, but she was not kind enough to stop. She'd make a Princess, Dollfuss thought. Dollfuss was there on business, on loan from the Risk Department at the Mission, and he grew impatient. Leo chewed on an anxious thought. It was as clear on his face as the distraction. As for himself, Dollfuss felt a little paralyzed by formality. It had been beaten into him for so long. Leo Einhorn was not a stiff like the people around him, but there Dollfuss was, acting like one of the stiffs.

Leo sat back in a heavy bean bag chair that sighed when shifted his weight. Those columns of light could look like real stone columns, Dollfuss thought, but they could not be or, anyway, you'd have to touch one to find out. In the corners of the room were other lights. These were red lights, not an emergency red, not a stop signal, they were softer and dreamy, but they gave the room a strange mood.

"What's on your mind, Boss?"

"Oh, this and that."

Iris sat on the floor, her bare legs crossed, shiny dress hiking up her thighs. She was looking at the cover of one of Leo's vinyl music recordings.

"Play me the mother song again," she said.

"Later."

Leo turned to look at Dollfuss.

"You've been right about everything so far."

"I'm always right," Dollfuss said. "I study probabilities."

"You're the risk guru. That's what they told me."

"That's right."

"My brother's military operation seems high risk. Do you have an opinion?"

"Ah, yes, of course."

"And?"

"He seems to have supreme numerical and technological superiority."

"Meaning?"

"Meaning, with all due respect, I don't see the risk."

"I disagree. This mistake has been made before."

Dollfuss grimaced.

"Maybe I don't have all of the information."

Leo snorted.

"Feel free to speak your mind when you're with me."

"Can she—-"

"Oh."

Leo stood and approached Iris. He gestured with an arrogant toss of his head. She exited to the adjoining bedroom.

"I don't need any horseshit about asymmetric warfare. My brother is acting stupidly."

"That's not the word I'd...."

"He has never been sensible. Smart, yes. But always running into danger."

"Help me understand what you see as the risk."

"The reaction. It always comes. Assassination."

"That's a risk very close to home. For you, too. Look close to home for the biggest risk."

"You mean the bedroom there?"

"Closer."

Leo's attention drifted off. Dollfuss looked at himself in one of the room's tall mirrors. He looked like a Jesuit, all in black, except no collar. He held a glass of white wine in his hand and swished it, making little tides of gold.

"The risk…. that's to say nothing of the murder, what's wrong about the killing, all the killing," Leo said before drifting off again. He paced around the room. When he passed close by, Dollfuss caught a glimpse of something that, on top of the wine, made him blush. The Einhorns all got stuck with nicknames, and one of Leo's most notorious was Lord of the Rings. He had a leakage problem. Every time he urinated, he'd have leakage after, and he'd walk around with rings of wetness on the crotch of his khaki pants. Why he didn't wear dark pants was a question, but nobody close to him dared suggest it.

"My father didn't consider the communal and private spaces of his own cities as sites for violence."

"Your father was a wise Chairman, thankfully for all."

"Better Chair than father. Look at his sons."

"He was suited to the pressures he faced. Today, these are different. The mode of survival is different."

"Oh, don't be a politician."

"You won't get me to talk down the Chairman."

"What? You think I'm testing you?"

Dollfuss held out his hands, palms up. His smile said: "Give me a break." Leo laughed.

"All right."

"I sense, Boss, we haven't touched on the subject you asked me here to discuss. Is that fair?"

"Yes."

"Should I guess it?"

"Go for it."

"The Map of the Go-Betweens."

"Impressive."

"I know you've been asking about it, and that you're interested in scientific things."

"Is there progress?"

Dollfuss considered his reply.

"There's been a lot of speculation and theory. I think the team has moved on from the question of the coordinates."

Leo rubbed his chin. He sat in his bean bag chair. Dollfuss sipped his wine.

"Do they think it's settled?" Leo asked.

"No, but the coordinates have been set aside."

"For the so-called Seasonal Theory?"

"Yes."

"I don't understand that."

"It's a simple concept. The challenge is trying to establish any sort of pattern to the appearance of the Go-Betweens. There doesn't seem to be one, a pattern, I mean."

Iris closed the door to the bedroom. Leo looked in that direction for a long time.

"The Chairman has his own map," he finally said.

"Who is writing the code for him?" Dollfuss asked.

"He is."

"Really."

This was news. Dollfuss felt like a spy, suddenly thrilled to know a secret and tallying the points of prestige it might be worth. But it was a silly thing to know, and he smiled smugly.

"Have you seen this map?" he asked.

"Yes."

"And what do you think of it?"

"I'd wager that when the advisors at the Mission see it, they will adopt it as their own."

Leo clapped once for punctuation and stood up. Dollfuss checked his pink baby face for a joke. None.

"I should be getting back, Boss, if that pleases you."

"Yes, sure," Leo replied. "Except one more thing."

"Anything."

"At the Mission, did you know this Colonel Endling?"

Here it was. The question he hoped to avoid.

"We worked on a few projects together."

"He's here now. What did you think of him then?"

"He always seemed like the kind of man who lives forever."

When the guru was gone, and Burden the bodyguard had locked up the chambers, Leo entered his bedroom. Iris was on the balcony in the sunshine. It was windy. There was snow again on Pike's Peak. The wind made the mountain look like a powder puff that had been clapped. That white spray against the sky's blue, what a miracle, Leo thought.

"Can a person climb up there?" Iris asked.

"Not in that dress."

She turned and played with the shoulder strap. "Can they though?"

"Yes, sure. It's very cold at the top."

"How cold?"

"Below zero."

"Stop it."

"Below zero," he whispered, biting her ear.

She didn't lean into this, and he noticed, so he stepped away. He sighed.

"I'm going away for a few days," he said.

"Why?"

"I have some things to do in the southern sector."

"I'll miss you."

"Bruce Burden will be locking you out again."

Chapter Seven

With the state of emergency lifted by a new
decree by the new Queen, the high-speed trains ran
again between the outer cities and the capital. Sebastian
Sleeper used a rare, anonymous cash card to buy a
ticket. Along with some advice, Maggie Trout had given
him the card. Stay away from Radium Beach, she
warned. He considered that, both on his own and when
she said it. He considered it, but there he went.

His cubicle on the train had a small monitor that
showed the Humble Jack's Misery Index, and this
monitor could not be turned off. He looked and looked
for a switch or plug. Fear like a worm was now a
permanent crawler in his gut. It was something like a full
day since he'd seen Yoshi, Toad and the two little ones.
What Maggie Trout said, full of conviction, was that it
had been 30 years since she'd seen them. The scenery
rushed by Sleeper's window so quickly (at 700 KPH), so
inhumanly, unimaginably quickly those landscapes went
into the past. Ponds were just flashes of mirror light, and
dying desert trees, leafless, looked like black arms
reaching for heaven. These were there before him then
gone.

He held his breath, expecting the police to come
down the train car. Each moment this didn't happen
cranked up his anxiety as he bargained with whomever
or whatever for just a little more. The train hugged the
shore and slowed down as it passed the sprawling
shanty towns on the edge of the capital. There was fog
coming in from the sea. People walked the beach, mostly

alone or in pairs. The train passed a yellow bulldozer with SLUM CLEARANCE stenciled on its rear end. The machine was at rest by the side of the tracks, rusting maybe. Hopefully, Sleeper said to himself. Hopefully forever. A shadow passed his cubicle with a breeze of air, and Sleeper jumped, but it was only a passenger walking to the toilet. The train slowed further, approaching the city proper. Near the station, they crossed the Bridge of Mars, and Sleeper saw a shining brass plaque on a stone pedestal. Honoring those lost in the Battle of the Bridge of Mars, he read. What battle was that?

On the station platform, there were three Marines with AK-47s, but they were relaxed, smoking and laughing, not on high alert. Sleeper walked right past them. He looked back over his shoulder in fear of being noticed, but the Marines went on joking. In their helmets, they looked gruesomely happy. Sleeper sighed. He seemed to be camouflaged within the anonymity of the crowd. In the concourse, the huge weather radar display warned of an ocean storm. Three hours, the sign read. Three hours, two minutes, 47 seconds. He moved towards the escalator, or, rather, he was moved by the mass of walkers heading that way like a river rapid compelled by the sheer force of gravity and momentum. The escalator moved the crowd up to street level and dumped them out into daylight.

He stood in the familiar hallway, looking at his own apartment door. The tile floor was the same. So was the fake, plastic tree by the elevator. But the door was different. The tarnished brass lock was gone, and a shiny silver lock was in its place. Sleeper tried his key, but it did not fit. He took an annoyed, heavy step back then stepped to again and knocked. There were no footsteps or voices, but, after half a minute, the sliding panel of the peephole opened audibly. A woman cleared her throat.

"Who's that?" she asked.

"What are you doing in my apartment?"

"What?" she said. "I think you have the wrong door."

He heard the doorscope unit shutting.

"No," he said, loudly. "This is my apartment, but you changed the lock."

"I bought this place last year. Leave me alone."

"You bought it from Tito."

"Right."

"This is my place. Tito didn't own it."

"I have the deed."

"Shit," he said. "Shit. This is so wrong."

"If you're the last owner you better get out of here before I call the police. I know who you are."

Elevator back down to the street. The wind blew strong, and it had salty sea in it. Dark clouds moved inland overhead. The sky was truly chaotic. Great cliffs of thundercloud crashed together. No rain yet, but it felt imminent. He didn't have time to go to Tito's office and still accomplish what he wanted before the storm hit. Tito would have to wait. In Cathedral Square, before the face of the wide, squatting stone church, the farmer's market was as busy as a disturbed hive. Sleeper took a seat at a sidewalk café, people watching and waiting. If he wanted one of the true time lunatics, he just needed to wait for them to find him. He lamented not being able to change out of his filthy, stinking clothes. He wondered if his personal stink might offend others sitting by him at the café.

A pretty, Laotian girl he knew from the beach walked by, carrying a box of vegetables from the farmer's market. Her name was Cookie. She looked at him funny and smiled before hurrying away. Green trees swayed in the wind. Down the line of tables, the vendors were slowly conceding it was time to pack up. Piles of strawberries, carrots, lemons, limes, blueberries, radishes, plums made a rainbow, and he felt a small disappointment to see the colors go.

As the café crowd began to thin out, Sleeper finally saw one of the true time evangelists approach with his atomic clock in the familiar backpack. Sleeper did not recognize the man. When he accosted a couple at a nearby table, the couple waved him off, so he came over to Sleeper.

"Sit down, friend," Sleeper said, offering a chair.
"Thank you."
"Can I buy you a coffee?"
He looked up at the sky, shrugged.
"Sure thing. Thank you."
"What's your name?"
"I'm John Coldspell."
This Coldspell was an old, white man with a bulbous nose and a wooly gray hairline that had retreated to the back of his freckled skull. His plump

nose had a vivid blue vein that Sleeper could not resist looking at. The waiter came over, and they ordered coffee.

"And what's your name?"

"Sebastian."

"What time do you have?" Coldspell asked. He undid the clasps on his backpack. Sleeper looked at his watch. He'd set it to local time for just this moment.

"Half past three."

Coldspell pulled out a red ledger book.

"Sebastian, do you know my business?"

"Yes, I do."

"Have you ever considered following the true time?"

"I'm ready to do that today," Sleeper said.

"Well, now. Right here I have the clock. Hold on. Might I peek at your watch?"

Sleeper reached his arm across the table.

"You're making this easy for me," Coldspell said with a smile. "I don't even have to use my gimmick."

They did have gimmicks, too, corny and repetitive, and they caused Sleeper much second-hand embarrassment over the years. Out of the bag, the clock caused the table to vibrate a little bit. When the waiter arrived with the coffee, he rolled his eyes. Sleeper smiled at him, and he left.

"Do you know Mr. Erdapfel?" Sleeper asked.

"Yes, yes, of course. Great guy. Sad case."

"What do you mean?"

"He's very sick," Coldspell said. "He's dying."

"I'd like to see him. "Where could I find him?"

"He's in a hospice not far from here. I could take you."

"I'd appreciate that."

"Okay."

Coldspell turned the clock to show Sleeper the time.

"Set your watch to that."

The plants in Erdapfel's room were dead. They were too long unwatered. He complained that his days in hospice were endless. He'd watch the Slow Sun move across his room. He didn't believe the clock moved some days, so he would track the sun to prove the hours passed. Thank the Lord, he could still sleep. He hadn't visited that circle of Hell.

He was asleep in a chair when the nurse knocked on the door and announced Sebastian Sleeper's visit.

"Who's this?" Erdapfel asked before closing his eyes again.

"Your friend, Sebastian," the nurse said. She left.

"Sebastian?" opening one eye. "I've seen you before, but I don't think we are friends, are we?"

He had been destroyed by his disease, Sleeper thought, looking him over. Absolutely ravished.

"We have friends in common."

"Is that so?"

"Yes. I need your help. Or they do. I think you can help them." Erdapfel sat up straight. He fussed with the collar of his robe and grumbled. He scratched at his weak stubble.

"Look at me. I can't do much except talk."

"Talk to me. Tell me what you told Yoshi about the tunnel."

"I talk about that with a lot of people. It's my thing."

"You remember the four young boys?"

"Yeah."

"We went through that tunnel together."

"Where was it?"

"Beneath the grounds of the Icelandic Embassy."

"Huh. And what happened?"

"What happened? I think you know part of it. The kids disappeared, and I woke up this morning at Dreaming Back Lake."

Erdapfel was quiet, thinking about this.

"I seem to have lost two years," Sleeper said.

"That's puzzling," Erdapfel said. "There must be a fork."

"A fork?"

"A fork in the throat."

Erdapfel winced as if in terrible pain, and he closed his eyes. The room was spare. A cross on the wall. A bedside table had a pitcher of water and a glass, half empty.

"I've reached acceptance stage, but this pain is awful."

"I'm sorry."

"It's in my bones now."

"Do you need the nurse?"

"No. It's okay."

"Are you sure?"

"Yes," Erdapfel said. "Thank you."

"So, please tell me what you know, and assume I know nothing, because other than what I experienced, I know nothing."

"All right. I can talk some, but now I must adjust my thinking. I'm confused now."

"Maybe we can figure it out together."

"Hmm, maybe," Erdapfel said, his voice trailing off. Sleeper poured him some water when he nodded at the pitcher.

"This will sound strange, or make it sound like my mind is strange, but I always thought the boys were recurring boys, that Yoshi was a recurring Yoshi I met twice in my life."

"But that makes no sense."

"It isn't true, so the sense of it means nothing now."

"Go on."

"Are you familiar with the astrophysical theory of wormholes?"

"Yes. Some."

"Turns out there's a bug in spacetime, not a feature, mind you, but a bug, that opens up go-betweens like wormholes."

"How do you know this?"

"The Einhorns," Erdapfel said. "Gun Club knows, and they have always known. Gun Club travels through the go-betweens all the time. Souci the explorer went through a go-between, and they have known ever since."

"Same one we did, I think."

"Yes."

"Crazy."

"How do you feel? You look like Hell."

Look who's talking, Sleeper thought, but he caught a glimpse of himself in a mirror on the wall, and he was shocked. He was such a mess.

"Headache."

"Any strangeness?"

"No."

"Huh."

"Can I go back through?"

"Natural question," Erdapfel said. "I have no idea."

"Explain to me the recurring boys. That puzzles me."

"First time we met, we spoke only briefly. They knew my name, but our meeting was... interrupted."

The storm with great blowing and spitting and rattling the windows announced its own arrival. Erdapfel had nothing more for him, so Sleeper left. He walked as fast as he could against the wind. The beach was deserted. The sea wall was mounted by a tall fence topped by razor wire with padlocked entrances. Sleeper sprinted to Rayuela's shelter, but it was boarded up with military police postings on the door. Stay out, per order of the law. The rain came down on his hopeless head. He was hopeless, yes, but not panicked. He ran for the only residence he knew nearby, and when he knocked on the door of the town house, the door opened, and Laverna Lascaux's face fell as if he were a ghost long banished from her life.

Chapter Eight

Piper followed Tubby every morning for three weeks, and he gave no indication he ever noticed. He rose early in the morning. The stars were bright and plentiful in the clear, black Texas sky. The first day, Piper woke when she heard the garage door going up. She was asleep under the glassless bay window of a nearby house. She was a light sleeper, and the noise was enough. She peeked out and saw the outline of Tubby Lascaux shuffling down the road. Piper loved the darkness. It was her element. The ability to see without being seen, to watch without being watched, to be on that end of the ceaseless exchange, brought her joy and comfort.

What she knew about Tubby was only the little Colonel Endling had told her or the few things Tubby himself grunted. He was an aerospace engineer in the old days. His father worked on oil rigs when Tubby was a youth, up and down the coasts of Texas, California, and Alaska. He attended something like twenty different elementary schools before the family settled in Montreal. He'd been a giant from birth, and his size was the defining characteristic of his life. His shuffling along the pavement, the sound of it, you'd think a horse was coming.

Piper was getting used to the Earth, its awful heat and 104% of Triste's gravity. She was constantly exhausted. She rubbed her eyes and yawned, as she followed Tubby the first morning. He went all the way to the Air Force Base. She got paranoid around the base.

She couldn't always tell the Marines from the prisoners. There was no consistency to who got to wear the uniform legally and who was just an impersonator. She loitered at the perimeter fence as Tubby went out on the tarmac and was greeted by someone. Within a few moments, Tubby wielded a flamethrower and lit up the darkness with bright fire. Afraid to be called out for snooping, Piper ducked down. She kept watching. "Fucking disgusting," Tubby's deep voice carried for miles. There was small laughter then Tubby's voice again.

That was the so-called Brain out there with him, she presumed. The Brain was obsessed with incinerating the rodents. He personally micromanaged it. Done right, the job took a few hours. At sun up the first day, Tubby was done, and Piper followed him to the company store where he would cash in his calorie chip for the day.

As she watched him get onto the line with the others with prison jobs, her mind wandered. She had a vague idea to go to Utah to see the lands her family came from, the Great Salt Lake, the infamous mine. She had vicarious memories from her father's stories of red, stone canyons and flower-filled grass valleys in the mountains. None of the images added up to anything like a vivid picture. They were not memories, she sometimes had to tell herself. Not her own. More like fairy tales. Well, not quite fairy tales either. Tubby reached the head of the line and disappeared inside the company store. He was not inside very long. The prisoners queued at the door scattered when Tubby came out carrying a smaller man in a red jacket. The man was sweating heavily. Tubby held him by the waist band of his pants.

Piper could not believe her eyes. She looked around, guilty at spying and nervous about this confrontation. When the shouting began, the crickets in her vicinity stopped chirping. Despite his animosity towards her personally (and his short fuse, she had to admit), Piper thought of Tubby as a decent man. She was genuinely surprised.

"Now I know why you were so friendly to me, Mr. Prison Administration," Tubby said, as Ladybug dangled three feet off the ground. "You little thief."

"Hold on a minute, Lascaux."

"Did you think I would forget my number or not notice?"

"No no no. Hold on."

"You stole my chip. Hand it over."

Piper began to worry about weapons, but the rest of the prisoners mostly smirked at the proceedings. One skinheaded man looked down and watched his own string of spit as it stretched out toward the ground before getting grabbed by the gritty wind and flying away.

"Here," Ladybug said. "What the fuck, dude."

He handed over the poker chip to Tubby.

"Ah ha. I knew it."

When Tubby went back inside the company store, Ladybug trotted off by himself in the direction of the airfield barracks. Piper waited in the brush nervously, and, sure enough, before Tubby came back out, two Marines arrived in a Jeep. They had pistols but no long guns. The Marines spoke to Tubby in low voices, inaudible to Piper. They used aggressive finger pointing, though, that she found particularly unpleasant.

"I have a letter from the Chair!" Tubby's voice rang out.

The Marines laughed and punched each other as if to say get a load of this guy, but they un-holstered their pistols when he said, "It's in my pocket."

There was a tense, indecisive moment, but they did allow Tubby to take out, slowly and easily and without any dumb movements, by its white envelope's corner, the letter from his pocket. The ranking Marine read it while the junior kept his gun on Tubby who stood there calmly with his arms at his sides. Then, rather suddenly and without returning the letter, they got in the Jeep and took off in the direction of the barracks.

Tubby shrugged.

"Well, that was a surprising reaction!" he said. Some of the other prisoners came over and clapped him on the shoulder.

The second morning was uneventful. Tubby could do his flame throwing and collect his calories at the company store, and nobody bothered him. On the third day, however, when he got to the company store, somebody had tacked up a dubious sign that a group of men stood reading.

DON'T TRUST LEONID LASCAUX, the sign said.
HE WRITES FAKE LETTERS FROM JACK EINHORN.
"Oh, that is some fucking bullshit," Tubby said.
"You know the Chairman personally, bro?"

"Met him," Tubby said. "The letter was just a guarantee of my daily ration. Turns out he was right when he said these fuckers would try to take it from me."

"Bro, that is some bullshit."

"It doesn't matter."

"Why not?"

But Tubby was walking away. He didn't give a damn about that stupid sign. He was curious about who made it, but about that, too, he didn't give a damn.

Things settled into a routine for Piper. She followed Tubby every morning to the airfield, the company store, and then back to the garage. Nothing happened for three weeks after the hanging of the insulting sign. Then, suddenly, one dark morning, when the garage door opened, Piper heard, instead of Tubby's shuffling feet, the sound of bicycle chains and gears shifting. She peered out and saw Tubby and Colonel Endling, with heavy packs and gallon water bottles, pedaling away into the darkness.

Chapter Nine

Around the black lake, the outlines of rocks and trees and spiky fauna seeped together. Julian had swum this lake in darkness. It was deep, and the bottom was as terrifying and unknowable as the universe's deepest secret. He imagined how a bioluminescent creature-—some blazing neon serpent, say—-could come swimming up and electrify the night. But no. Hardly. There were instead only things that would emerge from the water unseen, like speckled black salamanders or creepy dark blind limbless amphibians.

So, yeah, Julian stared at the two Frogmen, thinking how hard it must be to get into one of those rubber suits. Tight rubber suits with close-fitting wrists, all one piece from head to feet. A second skin. All midnight blue. Midnight blue masks, too, so the frogmen were faceless. It didn't register to him what he was looking at. He didn't see them until they were on top of him, dripping on the beach sand and high stepping with their flippers. They both wore huge, silver wristwatches with minute and hour hands that looked as big as plane propellers. He jumped when he saw their guns hugged close to their chests. Amphibious assault, he said to himself. Amphibious assault.

He took a step back and stumbled over one of his recorders. This set off an alarm at the house, and all the lights on the first floor came on.

"Hello," he said.

"Don't move."

"I won't."

"Why are you so damn clumsy?"

"Sorry, sorry."

"What is this place?"

"Well... uh... over there... that's my home."

"What's your name?"

"Julian Trout, PhD."

"And what's this lake?"

"This is Dreaming Back Lake."

"That is wild. What's that alarm?"

"Oh, that? The alarm goes off if these instruments here get disturbed. These here I tripped over."

"Need you to kill that."

Maggie appeared on the porch of the house. She was dressed in her pajamas. She tried to smooth her hair while squinting to see what was happening at the shore. Julian whistled to her, then shouted, "Can you turn off the horn, honey? Thank you."

Toad woke with a jolt at the alarm. The dark of the room closed around his neck, it felt like. There was light coming in the window but not the generous warm light of the fast sun. Something terrible was coming. He saw the inert lumps of Beetle and Flat Tire sleeping, but Yoshi was not in his bed. Toad got up. He knew Yoshi was attracted to danger. Yoshi was like pathologically attracted to danger. Something was going on? Yoshi would stick his nose in it. Risk was like an on switch for him. What Toad didn't know at this age was that his own special seeing included seeing ahead, and the guerilla superstar he saw in his dreams was his friend Yoshi all grown up.

The remnants of their late-night snacking were scattered around. They'd raided the big fridge downstairs. They'd found a whole drawer full of bananas. They couldn't get enough bananas. The peels and stub ends of the feast putrefied and oozed all over the room. Toad was afraid to step into the hallway. There was something vicious coming, maybe even already arrived, already in the house. He heard a shrill whistle then Maggie turned off the crazed sirens. Maggie sighed and slammed a door.

As if his eyes were closed, Toad had a vision of a million fish dying and floating silver bellies up to the surface of the lake. And he could smell it, too, a week of them floating in stagnant water, rotting in the sun. Without warning, he longed for a mother, an embrace from a mother, one of the women from the beach who fed him and laughed with him, or Maggie might be able to do it. He was so afraid. Where was that train Erdapfel so lovingly described? The train to the land with mothers and fathers who wanted children. Yoshi had stopped caring about the train. Toad kept returning obsessively to this point of the train, and he was annoying about it, but, well, he was heartbroken about it.

He hustled down the stairs, now, and saw Maggie on the porch. Yoshi had his hand on the door knob, considering joining her. The silence was even worse than the screaming alarms.

"Don't," Toad said in a whisper-shout. "Yoshi, don't."

Yoshi turned and frowned.

"What's up, Toadie?"

Yoshi had his hands balled in tight fists.

"What's out there?" Toad asked.

"More like who is out there?" Yoshi said. "But I don't know yet. Wait right here."

There was the bounty, right there on the porch, standing beside an adult woman. This capture would be easy as tit. There was the weak, uncoordinated scientist here on the beach and the woman on the porch. She didn't look like much. The target himself was known to travel with a pack of other, smaller children. The capture would be fine. Getting back was another question. Franzmann looked at his partner Dernier who nodded.

"Do you mind if we change into our dry clothes in your bathroom, Dr. Trout?" Franzmann said.

"Ah, well, it's the middle of the night, friends."

"We're on royal business," Dernier added. "The Queen would be in your debt."

On their backs, the frog suits had the yellow trident insignia of the royal navy. Julian caved. As the three men crossed the green lawn, the bounty disappeared into the house. The woman stood there on the porch and positioned herself in front of the door in such a way as to signal she would need to be dealt with if the visitors were going to get into the house. The woman crossed her arms when they got to the porch steps.

"What's going on?" she asked.

"These gentlemen just need to change into dry clothes," Julian said. "Just a couple of minutes, honey."

"It's the middle of the night, Julian," she said, frowning. "Did they just appear out of the lake in the middle of the night?"

"Yes, they did," Julian said.

Franzmann sensed the woman was in charge here since Julian made no movement towards the door.

"Shall we?" Dernier suggested.

"I don't think so," the woman said. She backed herself up until her rear end bumped the door. Her arms remained folded tightly across her breasts.

"Well now," Dernier said, and he stepped forward and smashed the woman in the eye with the butt end of his rifle.

Maggie's first thought on coming to was absurd. My name and photograph will be immortalized in the Radium Beach Eye Injury Registry. Like forever, she thought. Ophthalmologists will see me when skimming the database for similar cases. How ugly. How awful. The pain was so urgently unlike anything in her experience that she was certain the eye was a goner.

While still lying on the boards of the porch, she opened her good eye and saw the volcanic bowl that had erupted and formed the lake about a million years back. She saw Julian lying like herself just a few yards away. She got to her knees, and then, with difficulty, stood. She wasn't out long, she figured. Her head was ringing, and, upon entering the house and hearing not a sound, she thought the worst thoughts. The children dead. The intruders covered in their blood.

She stumbled around the first floor, crashing into pieces of furniture that she usually maneuvered around. Where were they? Why couldn't she hear any voices or footsteps?

She rushed back to Julian who was no longer prone. He had turned his head at least.

"Can you hear me, Julian?" she asked. "Can you hear me?"

He did not respond.

Back in the house, she finally heard feet above her on the second floor. She took the stairs up and found the intruders scanning the walls and floors with a thermal imaging device. They saw her coming and took defensive stances, but she put up her hands and stood still.

"Are there secret cellars in this house?" Franzmann asked.

"What?"

"Secret rooms or cellars? Places you've hidden people?"

"No," Maggie said. "No, there's a cellar. But it's not secret, and there is nobody hiding."

"You're a liar."

Fear and outrage grabbed her.

"No," she said. "No, it's the truth."

Dernier became extremely upset, but he did not want to show it in front of Franzmann. The target had been right there. Right there in front of them. What a lost, perfect chance. They stormed past her down the stairs. She took a moment to check the bedrooms. Bananas everywhere, but no sign of the children. Yoshi was resourceful, she knew, and very smart. She hoped they'd gotten outside.

"I'm not picking up anything," one of their voices came from deep in the cellar. "No heat signatures at all. Nothing so much as a mouse in here."

Maggie walked to the stairhead and pointed her ear to listen to what they were saying. There was a mirror across the room, but she didn't dare look at it.

"Do we need to grab all four of them?" one voice asked.

"No, just the target," said the other voice.

Maggie got brave.

"You know," she shouted down the stairs. "We work for Jack Einhorn. He's gonna hear of this. He's gonna know all about what you've done."

They said nothing to this. She heard the bulkhead door squeal open. That door led to the driveway, the driveway led down to the road, and across the road there was a grove of trees. She took the stairs down. Nothing was disturbed. On the concrete cellar floor, in hasty piles, they'd discarded their wetsuits. She followed out the bulkhead door. If Yoshi and the boys were running out there in the dark, she liked their chances. She was peering with the good eye in the direction of the road, when Julian called her name.

"Maggie!" he shouted. "Maggie!"

He came running up.

"You're okay," she said, looking him over. "Thank God."

"Maggie, look!"

Julian pointed at the lake. There were more Frogmen emerging from the water. Two, four. No, she saw six. Her heart sank. "What is happening, Julian?" she asked.

In the unpiercable darkness of the grove across the road—-Maggie didn't know this; she would never know this-—a pair of owl eyes stared at her. In silence, the owl had watched the armed pursuers pass beneath the tree branch it perched upon. There was another owl on a branch higher up, and two more deeper in the grove, silent also and as troubled by possibility as anyone waking from uneasy dreams.

Chapter Ten

Laverna Lascaux's rocking chair was a work of art. The rockers were of golden trumpet brass, and they were curved like the front of a sleigh all the way up to the leather arms braces. The back rest was brown leather, shiny and dimpled. The fretwork on the brass rockers was leafy, a golden leaf storm that Earth autumns once made, but which Triste's eternal summer never knew.

"Tubby built this chair for me," Mrs. Lascaux said. "He even did the metal work, real skilled stuff he just taught himself one afternoon." She unconsciously rubbed at the honey bee tattoo on her arm. The frown on her face might have been sadness or just her resting face. She had finished soaking the bad toes, and her ugly feet were flat on the floor. She rocked.

"Have you heard from Tubby?"

"Not a word," she replied. "Didn't really expect any."

"Yeah," Sleeper said. "I suppose that's about right."

The gusts of the typhoon were strong, and with every rattling noise or roar of the wind, Mrs. L winced and gripped the arms of her chair.

"I have to tell you, Sebastian, I let you in here, but I'm suspicious of you knocking on my door."

"Tell me why."

"Don't get me wrong cuz I always liked you."

Sleeper noted her use of the past tense.

"Tell me what's suspicious."

"Well, what the hell?" she began. "Why now? Why tonight?"

"The timing was out of my control. I went by a shelter I know, but it's shut down."

"Where have you been for the last two years?'

"I was in Dreaming Back Lake."

She gave him a funny look.

"That's not a place you can just hide out."

"In a way, though, you could say I did."

"It's been a long two years," Mrs. L sighed. "So long without my Tubby. I never imagined how loneliness could stretch out the days and weeks like this."

"I'm sorry. That's hard."

"It's hard since Tubby is all I ever had. We never had any kids. We worked, and we had each other. It fills me with rage, what happened."

"Me, too," Sleeper said.

She looked at him again, less friendly than he liked, though he knew, by nature, she didn't like to share the release of a gripe session she got rolling. She was jealous of this mode. She owned it.

"Are you still working?" he asked.

"A little bit."

"At the Mission HQ?"

"Yup."

"They know anything about the Colonel and Tubby? Any news at all?"

"Nothing," she said. "They talk to me. Map Room is never touched. I get visitors in there, but they never touch a map. Something big, some giga project is happening on the Discovery floor, but I don't know what it is."

Sleeper scratched his cheek. He had a feeling he knew exactly what the giga project was. A thunderclap outside-—a lightning strike right over the roof by the sound of it—-made Mrs. L jump.

"Did you see much of the war?" she asked.

"Not from close up. What was it like here?"

"Well," she began. "It was stories and propaganda and rumors and noise in the distance. The fighting in the city limits only lasted one day."

"One day?"

"One day, yes. It was a disaster for the insurgents."

"The battle on the Bridge of Mars."

"Right."

"What happened?"

"How do these things ever end? They were betrayed."

The bridge was both opportunity and challenge. Serge Ville de Paix woke that morning, clear-eyed and in the best possible mood. It made him decisive. He sat with his lieutenants at a picnic table on a cliff in Boreum Park. The Fast Sun was bright, and the ocean sparkled below them. In the haze of the distant north, they could just make out the works and cranes of the Northern Silo. It all looked black from this distance and faded in and out of clarity with the warm pulse of the day.

Serge asked the men if they could take the Bridge of Mars, and, counting that victory, the train station. This was a strategic goal for years since the station controlled tunnels that could move fighters without being spotted by Gun Club's deadly black flying machines. They said they believed they could. Next, he asked if they would. They said they would. These men were veterans of the most violent battles in Triste's history, and they were realists. Serge trusted them. They organized the fighters for a surprise assault on the train station, so bold and sudden the Marine forces patrolling would be shocked, and, since outnumbered, easily overwhelmed.

They waited three days. The morning agreed upon arrived. They acted. As quietly as they could, they trotted, armed, through the network of alleys that led to the bridge. Serge knew something was wrong as soon as he got there. He reached it with the advance group of fighters. The three Marines on the other side of the bridge twitched and fidgeted nervously.

Oh, something is up, Serge said to himself. We are fucked.

History makes a place for us that is all our own. This was one of those moments. He decided to halt the action and sacrifice himself for his men, so that they might escape, retreat and take to their hiding places in Radium Beach. He watched the Marines, and he was more and more sure of a trap, and just as he turned to announce the fall back, one of his snipers shot a Marine and killed him.

"No," Serge said, but two more shots rang out. The Marines fidgeted no more. Rebels need constant charges of enthusiasm, said Trotsky or somebody. The killings moved Serge's men to swift action, and he could not stop two dozen fighters climbing onto the smooth, silver train tracks of the Bridge of Mars. They went slowly to balance and avoid falling into the canal below. Slowly until there were fifty at least. They inched their way to the train station, and like Zeno's Achilles, they kept not quite getting there. Serge went along, too. His decisiveness returned just as a helmeted Marine popped up from behind the counter of the open-air Pretzel Hut attached to the train station. The soldier had a heavy caliber gun. It looked like an M2, and, after steadying the mount on the counter, he unloaded a thousand rounds in the direction of the bridge. It was a disaster, just like the old lady said.

"I saw some images," Mrs. L explained. "The dead lay all over the banks of the canal."

"But, Serge lived, no?"

"He was wounded and captured."

"Only to be hanged later."

"That's right."

She got it in her mind to soak the toes again in advance of some minor surgery she'd self-perform on a big toe nail, and she needed the nail softer. The feet in the bucket of water did not stop her rocking. She got right back to the rocking, closed her eyes and looked thoughtful. The storm continued but less furious. As Mrs. L rocked in silence, Sleeper went to a window and cranked the storm shutter open. Rivers of silt flowed in the street and choked the iron flood control drains.

"I knew him."

The old lady opened her eyes.

"Who?"

"Serge. I spent a few days with his people when I first became a fugitive."

She grunted in a way that could have been friendly or hostile. He couldn't tell.

"What happened to them?"

"What do you mean?" she asked.

"I saw the beach is all fenced in."

"Oh god," she said. "More rumors."

"What rumors?"

"Vicious rumors."

"What are they?"

She sighed heavily. Sleeper watched a man and a dog outside. They braved the storm, so the dog could relieve itself. The dog was outraged by the conditions and huddled close by its owner. Its dog piss went all over the man's legs, but the man didn't care. He just stared into the storm.

"They say that every person in the city who could not prove a permanent address was rounded up and taken to the burned-out stadium. They were locked in with the debris and melted plastic and left without food or anything to survive on except for rain water."

"Christ."

"People have been arrested for talking about it. Just taken away and jailed. Engineers and project managers at the HQ simply stopped showing up at the office, and it was known they'd talked of it in critical tones, and everyone knew what happened to them."

Sleeper took this like a punch. He slowly cranked the storm shutter until it was closed tight. He sat down on the floor.

"You can stay the night."

"Thank you, Laverna."

"But."

"But?"

"What will you do?"

"Oh…"

"In the light of day, you'll be noticed."

After she'd gone to bed, Sleeper searched the cabinets for alcohol, but she had none. She didn't touch the stuff. He stretched himself out on the floor, but his anxious emotions churned, and he started to grind his teeth. He got up and went into the bathroom. Laverna still had all of Tubby's things. Sleeper found the kit the big man used to groom his beard every five years. He looked at his dull brown hair in the mirror. He turned on an electric clipper. With a buzz, he began to shave his head.

Chapter Eleven

Leo Einhorn hadn't expected real police handcuffs. He hadn't asked. Just an innocent assumption, he told himself. Innocent and dumb. He'd pictured some plush, easygoing bondage cuffs. Here, though, he was locked into stainless steel. Rigid, solid bars. He had to laugh. Through the window, he saw Pike's Peak partly hidden by fog, and against the gray and white, curved like a whip about to crack, there was a bold rainbow.

Iris came back into the room. She wore a black bra. Nothing else. She approached the bed, walking slowly while reaching behind her for the bra's clasp. She couldn't get it. It wouldn't undo. She turned her back again.

"Come over here, I'll get it," Leo said.

"Will you?" she said over her bare shoulder. "Got some free hands, do you?" She smiled at him. He blushed a little. He was naked, and, if she looked at it long enough, his member would come to life.

"Be right back."

She exited the room again and left him alone with the rainbow and his thoughts. He'd risen early in the morning. He was dragged from sleep by an urgent transmission from his brother. Jack had executed a purge of his Marine Corps. Messmaker remained the head, but other leaders were purged. Something had happened that revealed the depth or the alarming shallows of loyalty to the family and the Mission. Leo frowned since his brother was asking him to test the loyalty of the men in Boulder, and he didn't feel up to that task. There was a compartment of his mind that did not instinctively screech against such arduous work, but usually that hidden reserve led him to places like these handcuffs. Thinking of laziness got him looking down at his own fat belly. It didn't look so bad lying on his back, but when Iris came back in she thought he was looking at something else and thinking of her thinking that gave him an erection. She grabbed it with her hand.

"It's warm," she said. "You should shave down here."

"All of it?"

"Yeah."

"You like hairless pets?"

She laughed and tried the bra clasp. Again, she failed.

"You are torturing me," he said.

"That's the idea."

The time for kings is not over, his brother defiantly declared. His security forces had picked up reports time and time again of insurgent slogans saying the time of Chairmen was done. The time of kings is done. The time of war lords will never be done, Leo thought. The time of murder and assassination. By the bed, an old, silver wind up clock ticked. Yes, it said, the time of assassination.

Leo desired Iris constantly, and he was ravished by her beauty, but he did not love her. That's what he told himself anyway. They were too much alike in their selfishness, their sort of pure selfishness, and he knew that in any relationship of two, only one person could be purely selfish, and that one simply had to be himself. She left the room again, but she quickly came back. The black bra was off. She had her left arm across her breasts, and in her right hand she held something shiny and silver. It was a long knife.

"You gonna shave me with that?" he laughed anxiously. His mouth went dry, he noticed, when he tried to lick his lips.

"I don't think I'll shave you," she said slyly.

She climbed onto the bed and straddled him. Her breasts were free now and inches from his face. He suddenly recalled the warning. Beware those closest to you. And the denial that she would be the one to betray him.

She brushed her breasts across his face.

"Isn't that what you wanted?" she asked when he did not react. "Or is there something else?"

She shifted her weight.

"This?" she asked, grinding her hips on his own.

"Or this?" she asked, showing him the knife's long blade.

"I want these cuffs off," he said humorlessly.

"And you haven't even asked me what I want."

"Are you going to kill me?" he asked, his eyes searching her. Maybe he was rushing to the end of things. He considered ways of grabbing her body with his legs, but then what would he do? Where would he go? Iris touched his armpit with the point of the knife.

"You're so tense now that Mr. Knife is here," she teased. "Your mood has completely turned."

Outside the window, the sky could seemingly do anything. Sick of the rainbow, the sun had burned it away, and any clouds, too, away to nothing.

Iris touched some of Leo's most tender, chubby parts with the knife, parts he was most embarrassed about, his womanly breasts he tried to hide with loose clothing. She teased him often about this, and he allowed that, but the knife was making him angry. He thought of biting her but stopped short when she held the knife to his throat as if she'd slice it.

"Want me to show you the real misery index?" she mocked. "One drop of blood at a time?"

"That's sharp," he said. "I can feel it."

"It's gonna be a fucking blood bath in here. The poor bed sheets," she said, and, with this, she bounced off him. She waltzed to the cabinet containing Leo's golden liquors. She unstopped a bottle and poured a drink.

"Blood of the gods, you meant," he said, nodding towards the bottles. She looked great, standing there nude in the daylight. She sipped the liquor. Leo began to lose some of his fear, but the new fear was that that was a mistake, and the horrific, epic stabbing was merely theatrically delayed.

"The would-be gods," she said, pointing the knife at him. She had a mouthful of liquor, and it dripped down her lower lip as she said this. His erection came back to life, and when she saw it, she dropped the knife, which stuck point first through the carpet into the floor. She climbed onto him.

"You're excited now."

"How about you unlock the cuffs?"

"Promise me something first."

"Anything."

"Give me a royal baby."

He grimaced.

"That?" he said. "No."

She climbed onto him and took what he didn't want to give.

Part Three

Out of Abilene, they went north, following US 83, a road that went from the submerged bottom point of Texas all the way to Canada. The word Canada, they quickly found, was an ethereal joke to most people in Abilene. You couldn't get there. You couldn't make it across the desert. It meant a lot to Tubby, Colonel Endling knew. They talked of it some, much of the understanding left unsaid, but there was a lot of time to think about the flukes of our birthplaces, the arbitrary connections to geography, an awful lot of time to think of these things when you're on the road.

It was a bright, sweltering day. The wind was sporadic. Now and then, Colonel Endling felt smacks of grit on his plastic painter's goggles. He pedaled his bicycle. They did not leave Abilene unobserved. In the weeks since the ark dropped them at Dyess AFB, they'd come to know the spies, faces if not names, silhouettes of spies in the windows of houses.

How could our two travelers be described at this moment of starting out? In terms of morale, this was the high point. Hopeful, determined. The Colonel had friends in Colorado Springs, and despite being told, like Lawrence in Arabia, that nobody could cross the Great American Desert without paying an enormous cost, especially an old man and a hugely fat companion, they set out thinking it was just a 700-mile bike ride.

"Something to be done," Tubby said, and he meant generally, and he meant as opposed to nothing. The Colonel was agreeable. He agreed.

"I'm sure I'm Sancho Panza," Tubby went on, as he pedaled. "But that doesn't mean I think you're Quixote, my friend."

Colonel Endling laughed.

"Oh, I am. Just look at these monstrous, giant horses."

He pointed to pump jacks still standing, their horse heads frozen in waiting attitudes, just hoping for someone to come along and command them to move. Tubby maintained a straight line with his even, steady pedaling. He only broke that when pieces of the blacktop were missing. The Colonel would get lost in thought in looking at the flat, khaki landscape. He saw hints of red earth, red stones, surprising reds, and he swerved all over. Utility poles, some with wires connecting them like long strands of drool, others wireless, stood along the road.

"They could get the power grid back up pretty easily if they wanted," Tubby said.

"Not here," the Colonel said. "Yes, they could, but that's against their interest."

Tubby's beard was filthy with dust. The Colonel imagined his own white hair was the same. He ran a hand through it. He felt grit, possibly small insects. He'd recommended Tubby shave the beard for the raw heat, but Tubby declined.

Further thoughts on starting out: they'd been warned by sympathetic voices to watch out for three things in the desert. These were gray wolves, Marine convoys and invitations to itinerant weddings. The first was the country's apex predator save for the second, and the third was a mystery that went unexplained except for sincere, smiling nods.

The Colonel knew the way. Though in earlier times he'd personally driven a dozen times from Dyess to Colorado Springs in an automobile, they brought along a map. Tubby kept it in his pocket. It was a bicycle map. It had little pictures of bison and cacti all over it. There would be a lot of uphill pedaling and the searing, consistent 50+ Celsius heat of day.

By noon of that first day, they reached the remnants of drought-annihilated orchards in Hawley. Beyond those withered trees was the start of one of the Regional cemeteries. It revealed itself if you knew what you were looking at. This was grassless land now, so the white of the small markers didn't stand out, but once you saw them, you couldn't not see them. Like extracted, perfect little teeth for square mile upon square mile. He'd known death had undone so many, but the attempts by state governors to stick to the commitment of burying everyone taken in the first wave of the ocean pestilence struck him as pathetic now, admirable but pathetic, because they had no idea what was coming.

"See the graves, Tub?"

"Where?"

"Off to the east."

Tubby squinted.

"That the Regional?"

"Yes."

Hawley, Texas and Great Barrington, Massachusetts and Hoopa, California and Winter Haven,

Florida and Walnut, Illinois. These are the names the Colonel could remember as Regional cemetery sites. There were many more he was forgetting. The grave stones went on forever. Small brick sheds for diggers' tools were out there too. Those were empty no doubt, having been stripped of any useful items by scrappy survivors or the Marines. Edgar Endling, the Colonel's father, in his amiable moods, told a graveyard joke every time the family car passed a cemetery. "People are just dying to get in there," he'd say, and, unlike many of his own jokes, he didn't chase a laugh. It wasn't that kind of joke, and maybe that was because the passage to god knows where wasn't that kind of thing.

They were quiet after passing the graves, neither Tubby nor Colonel Endling saying much. They pedaled into Anson, Texas. Armadillos skedaddled from the roadside at their approach. They passed a sign on a church roof that said JESUS SAVES. They passed black, painted silhouettes of mounted cowboys on the outer wall of a hardware store. People had lived here. The things they did, the Colonel thought, somebody took some hours to paint that cowboy scene, and here I am these years later, looking at it. At an unmarked fork in the road, they had to stop. Road signs gone, they both weren't sure. Before them was a field of soft, red earth.

"Let's rest here," the Colonel said. "We'll look over your map for a while."

"Sounds good."

They each had single-person bivouac tents, which they pitched on the red earth. After watering from the heavy skin Tubby carried over his shoulders and eating some granola, they sat by the openings of their tents. No fire needed with the unstoppable heat, and they worried about wolves anyhow.

At dark, Tubby said, "Oh, man, I'd forgotten what the moon could be like."

"Yeah, me, too."

It looked like a great bulb. You half-expected a brand name and wattage to be etched on it.

"Think there's people in these towns we're passing through?" Tubby asked. He gestured back at the highway.

"I expect not," the Colonel said. "There's little water. None really in this zone."

"Where might we see some, do you think?"

"Hard to say."

Some time passed, and they grew tired.

"Who do you think is still in Colorado Springs?" Tubby asked. "All the old lifers dead now?"

"Well, we can't guess who Gun Club has removed."

"Maxwell?"

"Probably."

"Oriente?"

"Probably."

They zipped the tents closed and slept. The wind picked up in the night, and the sound of grit and debris hitting the canvas was loud. They slept through it. The morning was hot. Colonel Endling could feel the early sun through the canvas of his tent. After stretching for a while, he called out to his travel companion.

"You awake?"

"Yes, sir."

"I'm getting up now."

The zipper of his tent would not move. He yanked on it, steadied himself with his free hand, and yanked some more. He peered at the slider, but it did not appear to be caught on the inside of the tent.

"Tubby, my zipper's stuck. Would you mind checking it?"

"Coming now."

The Colonel grabbed his hat while he waited.

"Well, that's odd."

"What?"

The zipper went up, and Tubby handed the Colonel a piece of fishing line.

"What's this?"

"This was affixed to your zipper."

The Colonel frowned. He emerged from the tent and looked around, trying to scan the bright horizons.

"Is this a prank, Tub? Having a little fun?"

"No, Colonel," now it was Tubby looking around.

"Well," the Colonel said, exhaling through his nose. "I wish it was, Tubby. This is worrying. You're telling the truth?"

"Nothing but."

"Did you hear anybody in the night?"

"Just the wind," Tubby said. "All night."

"Well, let's pack up. Eyes and ears open."

They packed the tents and got back on the bicycles. US 83 had long, amazing straightaways. They pedaled on these stretches, perfect for drag racing but racerless now, cutting across old, flat grazing lands gone to dust. In Hamlin, Texas the sky was immense. There were other kinds of sky in the distance, and they were headed towards clouds hanging low.

As part of Colonel Endling's long-stewing plan, they'd each saved half of their daily rations from the Dyess commissary and stored all of it for this trek. So, along with the tents, the water skins and each a long knife, they had food for a certain number of days. The number was debatable and probably a matter of will power. When they stopped for a noon meal in Hamlin, they both thought they saw a face appear and then duck down behind the glassless window of an old, red-roofed Dairy Queen.

"Did you see that?"

"Sure did," Tubby said.

"Let's check it out."

"Our merry prankster?"

"Quietly."

They drew their knives from their packs. The ice cream shop was stripped to nothing. There was no person inside, but a back exit was wide open. They looked out that door. Nobody.

"You saw it, right?" the Colonel asked. Tubby's eyes looked exhausted, as he imagined his own did, but Tubby nodded.

"Let's look around."

Across the street was a Shell station. Most of the buildings still standing in this ghost town were one story, tan or red brick, not quite real looking, more like a ghost town movie set. They were all stripped. No furniture, no supplies, just empty or filled with sand and dust. In a consignment shop, there was a white toilet, dry as a bone, with a kangaroo rat dead in the bowl. Tubby laughed hard at that.

They gave up on the prankster, put on their goggles and rode on. Far to the east, the Colonel thought he could see the curve of the planet. The desert looked to go on forever, they might as well have been in its dead-hearted center for all the different this southern reach was. He noticed Tubby kept looking behind them as if spooked by the idea of a follower.

Near Aspermont, they passed a blue Adopt a Highway sign. The side of the road in places rose taller than the road, the first real break from flat land. Sometimes little hills spilled into the road. They could see tracks through the spill where Marine Humvees or fighting vehicles had passed. These little opportunities for high ground made the Colonel worry about wolves. They pedaled on past another red-roofed DQ and over the Salt Fork Brazos River. This was a track of red mud intriguing enough to the Colonel in its wetness that they stopped and stared. The river of the arms of God. The Colonel thought he heard this on the wind until Tubby said "What?" He realized he'd whispered aloud.

They stopped and sat under the roof of a gazebo. They considered sleeping there in the open air for the night. "I think this was a picnic stop," Colonel Endling said. As they chewed on granola and sipped water carefully, it was as if the word picnic opened a poorly-healed wound in Tubby's chest.

His heart poured out.

"Do you think of Earth as home?" Tubby asked with a crack in his voice. "Or is it Triste?"

"Here," the Colonel said. "How about you?"

Tubby's eyes were red and watery. "I feel homeless. Utterly. I'm separated from the partner who makes any place home. And whatever once made this home is dead and gone."

He didn't sound bitter. He was deeply sad.

"How did you and Laverna meet?" the Colonel asked. "I don't think I ever heard that story."

"Yes, you have."

"No, I don't think so."

"Well, our two huge skulls collided. My fault, but how else could it have gone?"

"Oh, boy. The concussion of your love? Maybe that does sound familiar. Tell me again."

"It was one of those awful, embarrassing, painful team-building retreats from the early days of the Mission. Remember? They'd bring engineers and clerks and supply manufacturers together, people who would never otherwise be in the same room unless there was some big speech or Einhorn was visiting."

"Yeah, I organized some of those."

"One of those. We were both there, Laverna and me. We were on competing teams, both so terribly shy so that we volunteered to be our teams' runners rather than have to be the spokespeople."

"Shy? You two?"

"This was a long time ago."

"Yes."

"So, I don't even recall the problem or the question, but the objective was to be the first to run up to the white board and scrawl out the correct solution."

"Let me guess."

"Now, you have got to visualize this with me. Picture my Laverna. I wasn't going to let her win, but when she dropped her dry erase marker onto the carpet, I bent to help, and she bent, and wham."

"Wham."

"Forehead to forehead."

"And inseparable ever since..."

The sentiment wasn't even out of his mouth before the Colonel knew he'd said entirely the wrong thing. He grimaced. Tubby took it in stride, but he changed the subject.

"Doesn't it seem odd we have all this freedom?"

Colonel Endling scratched his stubbly cheek. He said, "Yes. They are confident we're weak. We're weak and won't do anything with the freedom."

"That seems stupid."

"Yeah, it sure does."

"Does Gun Club even think of us?"

"No, I doubt it," the Colonel said. "And you know what?"

"What?"

"That's what makes me hopeful."

That night, the wretched, dirty wind chased them into their tents after all. The morning was overpowering. The heat was intense, and the sun was like a pest that would not go away. They pedaled to Paducah and Childress and Estelline. They lunched and rested in

Estelline then rode through the oppressive afternoon to Memphis, Texas. Here, they left the road on foot to follow a deep scar in the red desert. This was the path, past mounds of plowed red earth, to an interstellar ark that lay at rest where its crash momentum ran out. The silver length of the ship was untarnished and gleamed blindingly in the sun. It was so bright, they ducked from the pain it gave their eyes. It was almost as if it warned them: do not touch. It was hard to say how long the ship had been there.

"Do you still have all the crash history memorized?" the Colonel asked.

"I think so," Tubby said, laughing. "Let's test me. See if we can find the identifiers."

The Mission's military arks did not bear a name on the exterior shell. The damage was limited, considering the crash, but the ship was upside down. This was disorienting as they entered by the air supply housing, Tubby first, Colonel Endling following, and found the ceiling at their feet. This was a visit of pure curiosity. What will we gain from this? The Colonel asked himself this question, but his curiosity was too strong.

It was hot inside. They feared dead bodies and vultures and maggots, but they didn't see or smell any. They passed through the lounge and mess area, and the tables and benches hung down above their heads.

"Think anybody walked away from this crash alive?"

"It's possible," the Colonel replied. "It looks possible."

Random things they noted: the captain's cabin was ransacked; the escape pods were intact; the cargo bay was empty; the main crew belted-seating area was in decent shape. There were no busted chairs or restraints. It's possible there'd been survivors.

In the science bay, they discovered something that took Colonel Endling's breath away. Tubby had just complained about the worsening heat and dead air when the Colonel bumped into something heavy in a dark corner. He stepped back, and, when his eyes fully adjusted, he saw Sebastian Sleeper's face looking at him. As if in utter shock, the eyes of the face were wide open. His body was dangling like a tarot deck's hanged man. His skull was cut open and brainless. Two identical doppelgangers were hanged the same way beside him.

"Holy shit," Tubby said when he saw.

The Colonel was speechless. He didn't know there'd been copies made of his prototype. He reached out and touched the face with his fingers. Tubby came closer and ducked down to look up into the empty skulls.

"What the fuck," he said. "What the fuck? They left the husks behind?"

"I might need to sit down," the Colonel said, and the next thing he knew he was being dragged out of the ship. Tubby had him by the armpits. He must've fainted. He looked around. He wanted a cool, shady place to nap. That was exactly the thing he wanted.

"You're not having a stroke on me, are you?" Tubby asked.

"No. No."

"You better fucking not."

The Colonel had little pride about such things, and he didn't easily get embarrassed. He plopped down in a triangle of shadow cast by the ship. Tubby gave him the water skin, and he immediately felt better. It was the heat, he told himself, the dangerous heat and not the rush of guilt and disappointment he felt when touching Sleeper's face. His loyal assistant.

"That was so dumb," Tubby said. "How dumb are we?"

"It's an oven in there."

They passed houses lonely in the middle of red dirt fields, boarded up and sheltered by clusters of strong trees, and they didn't bother stopping. They pedaled on beneath the gigantic sky. Gas stations. Auto parts stores. Abandoned trailer trucks. Railroad tracks peeking out of (or disappearing into) drifts of dust. It had been a civilization of vehicles; you couldn't deny that. They pedaled through some of the oldest settlements in all the Pan Handle and never stopped. In what seemed, in the dark, to be Clarendon, Texas, they braked and set up their tents at the base of a big grain silo. In spray paint, far above their heads, there was scrawled The Cross, the Only.

"I didn't know Texas had so many Dairy Queens," Tubby mused with a yawn, as he drifted off to sleep. "So many of them. I'm gonna dream about them."

The old man dreamt that night of the Pacific Ocean, the warm, deadly ocean so full of dead things and the never-expected disease. Was it really poisoned, or was it a myth? In his dream, he needed to find out, and he could fly, not very high, more like low-to-the-ground flight, but fast against the gritty wind blowing across Texas and New Mexico and Arizona and California. When he got to the Pacific, it was beautiful, so clear and blue like the troubled girl Piper's eyes, and it was clean and full of life, and, of course, the poison was a myth, and, of course, he woke up. He groaned. His head hurt.

Awake, he did not want to get up. He looked through the screen of his tent door at a long root in the sand. Living? Dead? How long had the thing waited for rain? The patience of that life was unfathomable. He followed the root's path with his eyes. It went past where his mountain bike was parked. It went under the grain elevator's bulk and disappeared. There must be potable water under the ground, he thought. Some feet below the surface. Look for healthy mesquite or brush and dig.

His eyes scanned back. The tires of his bicycle were flat. This didn't cause him to immediately move. His brain started ricocheting all over, but his body was old, tired and slow.

"Tubby, you awake?" he asked. There was no answer.

He crawled out of the tent. The morning was a brilliant violet. The clouds and distant western elevations, the earth and all the wind's ancient sculpture were bathed in the beautiful light. He left footprints of deeper color, a dark blue, as he walked to the bike. Tubby's bike was gone, and Tubby's knife was sticking out of the front tire of the Colonel's bike. He looked around. Tubby's tent was still set up, and his water skin was inside it.

The days when Colonel Endling loved a mystery like this one were in the past. Not the very distant past, of course, but the stress he felt coming on was exhausting. Thinking of the fishing line and the merry prankster, he started to grimace. Tubby came flying around the grain elevator on his bike, and he must've misread the grimace for a smile, because he grinned like a gigantic, happy child. In the violet light, the contrast between his grin and his wild beard made him look like Karl Marx, a lunatic Karl Marx. He braked and blew air from his lungs.

"Where you been?"

"I got inspired today. Went looking for something other than granola for breakfast."

"Without this?" the Colonel asked, pointing at the knife in his bike tire.

"What happened?"

Like a puddle on a hot, dry road, the smile on Tubby's face slowly but definitively vanished. The Colonel's head throbbed.

"Perfectly obvious what happened. Did you do this?"

He searched Tubby's reaction. He was looking more for a glimmer of insanity than treachery. Tubby threw his own bike to the ground.

"How could you think that?"

"Tubby, look. It's your knife, buddy."

"It wasn't like this when I left an hour ago. My bike was parked right next to yours."

"You can understand how I'm thinking about this, right? My tires not yours. My tent, not yours."

"Somebody is messing with us."

"Who?"

"Somebody from Abilene."

"The Brain."

Tubby chewed his lip.

"Could be," he said.

"Why not just cut my throat?"

Tubby looked sad. He was hurt.

"You trust me, right? We need to settle this fact right here and right now."

Like a big bubble gum bubble, an idea popped in the Colonel's mind. He did trust Tubby. It was as close to absolute as it could get, considering their new circumstances. What was murky was a grasp on the motivations of the prankster. They had so far detected nobody following them, but they were being followed, observed.

"I do, Tubby," the Colonel said. "No more doubt. I won't question you again."

"Good."

Tubby grabbed the knife, then he looked at the tires.

"These are fucked."

"Yeah."

"You can take my bike."

"No. I have an idea. We'll need to do some playacting. You up for that?"

"I think I can guess it, and, yes, let's do it."

The sun rose and struck the purple from the sky. It was so hot, it felt wrathful, a terrible day to set out on foot, but that is what they did. The Colonel walked ahead with his bike left behind, and his tent rolled up and strapped to his back. Tubby followed, wheeling the good bike. They assumed they were watched, and every hour or so, they came closer together and pretended to argue loudly and with deranged gestures.

The road now pointed northwest, so the sun was behind them through the early part of the day. Looking back, it was impossible to see if anyone followed.

The Colonel had a vivid memory of the Brain's arrest. He was colorful in his reaction, since he knew it was not the police who'd got him. The arresting officers locked him in a hot police car with the engine off. It was a blazing day. The Brain sat perfectly still, as if he wouldn't so much as sweat let alone suffer. The Colonel watched him out of the corner of his eye as he stood playing grab-ass with the cops.

A crowd of more cops arrived to join the congratulatory party. The officers circled the police car and pointed and did mock coquettish hand waves at the Brain. He showed no reaction, but the sweat had started. His face appeared to be melting. The Colonel knocked on the window and asked, "You okay?"

The Brain turned his large, misshapen head and sneered, but his eye was caught by something behind the Colonel, and his sneer turned to a frightful outrage. The Colonel turned and saw the bright shining pile of stolen gold coming his way. To the Brain, this looked like a sunrise out for a Sunday stroll. His eyes widened. When he was taunted with bars of the stuff, he hissed.

"Karma, you bastards," he said. "Karma."

Back in the even worse heat of Texas, the Colonel wondered would the Brain show himself or otherwise announce he was stalking them? They were still more than 50 miles from Amarillo. That was the next agreed upon rest spot, but without a bike, it would be impossible to reach in one day. This realization caused a sinking feeling in his guts. He considered the word "quixotic," which had been on his mind since starting out. Two men with some ideas in their heads, the younger trusting his elder, the elder with some crackpot ideas, the younger not flinching or twisting one bit, even now.

"What if Piper is the merry prankster?" Tubby'd asked about the fishing line. The Colonel kept pushing this idea away. He didn't want this to be real. He pushed hard against it.

The long straightaway before them was a lonely prospect. Amarillo was now a stretch. The Yellow Rose of Texas. The city sheltered a million Texans after the coast began to sink. Amarillo was a stretch, and Colorado Springs now seemed a fantasy. The Colonel stopped walking to re-apply his homemade sunscreen. He did it slowly, and this allowed Tubby to pass him.

"Should we leave the road?" Tubby asked, quietly.

"At dark, yes. We'll know when."

The day was long as all bad days are long. They walked and walked and walked. The ticking of the gears on Tubby's bike settled into a strange harmony with the sounds of darkling beetles. At dusk, the day cooled some, and the colors of the sky paled and hid behind the dark mesas to the west. More and more of the sky gave up its light until everything was fuzzy to the Colonel's old eyes, and a house emerged from the gloom, another lonely bleak house of the Staked Plain. It was a ranch. There should've been exhausted cowboys, but he supposed he and Tubby were the cowboys.

He left the road, and when he heard Tubby's feet and the ticking of the bike gears, he called out to him. They hustled into a half-collapsed barn. In the absolute darkness inside, before they could speak a single word to each other, the Colonel was tackled to the ground. He heard snarling right by his ear and smelled an animal and felt teeth on his hands. It was on him and tearing at his hands. He kept waving the hands and punching to keep the beast from his throat. He was under so much weight and pressure that he could not speak.

If the wolf knew Tubby was there, too, it gave no indication of defending itself, but it certainly found out about him when he picked it up and threw it against the wall of the barn. The bulk of the body hitting the desiccated wood made a loud, snapping sound. The wolf hit the ground and coughed twice. It stood uncertainly and coughed again, and then it bolted into the blind night.

"Jesus, are you hurt?" Tubby asked, standing over him.

"My hands are torn up."

"Shit, let's see them. Come outside."

Under the light of the risen moon, they inspected the cuts. They were wildly painful, but not so deep. The two men looked and listened for howls or the movements of packs. With their ears cocked so intently towards the infinite night, they both jumped when they heard a rifle shot. It was not so far away.

"What the fuck," Tubby said. They crept back to the barn. "What should we do?"

"We have to get moving," the Colonel said. "Let's go now. Quietly, quietly."

They stole out across the dim tableland. Tubby rested the bicycle on his shoulder to keep the gears from ticking. They went for at least an hour in silence.

"Do you need rest?" Tubby asked.

"Yes. Very soon."

Fear fills up a solitude, doubly one of such darkness that they couldn't see the sea of sand and rock before them, a land with no boundaries, an infinite dark place. They awaited each moment a sudden rifle crack at a distance that would signal death for one of the two of them.

When they stopped for rest, they took turns at wired, troubled sleep. The Colonel woke into a black, swarming anxiety attack shortly before morning. Tubby sat awake, looking around, horizon to horizon, scanning for movement.

"How are the bites?"

"Worse than I expected," the Colonel admitted, and it was true. The hands throbbed. He didn't like looking at the wounds. "See anything this morning?"

"Nothing."

When the sun began to rise, the Colonel could see nearby a cluster of trees that looked like black toilet brushes. He had a bad feeling about them. He stared.

"Anything in those trees, Tub?"

Tubby peered at them, too, but nothing seemed to move.

"Which way back to the road?" he asked.

A rifle shot from the direction of the trees answered the question.

"Move, let's move. Leave the bike."

They followed their own footprints back.

"He's forcing us back," the Colonel said. "We'll see when we get back to the road, we can return to Abilene unmolested."

"Cocksucker," Tubby said.

"Let's keep moving."

The sun was stronger than ever, straight in their faces as they moved eastward back to the highway. It was a massive sun, taking up more of the heavens than seemed possible. They fled on and on, apparently unpursued. Their fast walk was approximately 50% stumbling. They reached the ranch, the barn, and the road.

Like cartoon coyotes they tried to stop on the black top and skidded into the personal space of a man speaking to a dozen others in front of a big, shiny, green John Deere tractor. The tractor had behind it two matching shiny, green gravity wagons. The men all wore cowboy hats and, amazingly, tuxedos.

"Howdy," the leader said, clapping Tubby's dusty shoulder.

"Hi," was all Tubby could muster in his surprise.

Beyond the tractor, two young women in coral-colored bridesmaid dresses were bent over something on the far edge of the road. It was the wolf. It was shot dead.

"Are you real?" the Colonel asked.

"Definitely," the leader said. "I'm Junior Soucy."

He shook the Colonel's hand and held it up to look at the vicious bites.

"I think maybe you met this wolf here?"

"Yes, it attacked me."

"When?"

"Last night."

Soucy was a tall man. Not a giant like Tubby, but he was towering and lean. He was too tall for the tuxedo. He wore socks the color of his tractor.

"Where's yawls' guns at?"

"Oh, we don't have guns. Somebody is out there with a gun," Tubby said, gesturing. "I think... well, we think that man shot the wolf."

"Yikes."

The Colonel looked at all the tuxedos.

"So, you guys are dressed for..."

"A big party! Yeah!"

"A party."

"There's a wedding. You should come. Hop in."

Men and bridesmaids climbed into the two slant wagons. The wagons had been repurposed with plastic chairs for hauling travelers. Junior Soucy took the seat of the tractor and started the engine. The Colonel and

Tubby looked at each other, shrugged and climbed in the second wagon.

From the sky, the tent city looked like a spill of Lego bricks, the colors blue and green and white repeating and the interstate running through the spill like a lost river system, dried, unmoving and gray as death. The bomber came from the north, a dolphin-faced Super Hercules. The four Rolls Royce turboprop engines shook the ground. The plane was flying low and slow. It wasn't sneaking up on anybody.

There'd been new people to meet all around. After the long night of wedding revelry, the Colonel found one of the many doctors Junior Soucy introduced to him. The doc was hung over and fog-brained, but he happily examined the wolf bites. They both looked up when they heard the bomber, and, not wanting close haircuts, they naturally ducked. As it passed, the Colonel thought the plane might kiss its own shadow, its large phantom twin, but it kept on at the same altitude. From the rear of the plane, a black cloud like a murmuration of starlings poured down the lowered loading ramp.

The way the mind works: What is that? It doesn't look good. You should run. Quick as anything. Colonel Endling prepared himself, but nobody else moved. They watched the plane and its trailing black cloud with curiosity, but nobody ran.

"What's happening?" he asked the doctor.

"Oh, those come around occasionally," the doctor said.

"Occasionally?"

"Yes, when they're looking for someone."

"What is it?"

"A swarm of drones. They have facial recognition software. They take pictures. Then, they gather up and fly off again."

"Well, here they come."

They were small, maybe each a foot in wingspan, but together they massed into a cloud that could hide the sun. They flew coordinated and with speed, but any movements of the swarm had a slow grace as if the huge sky were water, and they were blackened blood dripped in. The swarm came towards the collection of tents. As if standing by to take a medicine, the Nomads (that's what the Colonel had come to call these people) stood still and waited. As if the swarm were one wide, shared perception, when the first drone locked on a human face, the others visibly changed and split into individual intensities. They dispersed but maintained their 3rd internal rule collectively: avoid collision with your neighbors.

They were astonishingly efficient. Within seconds, every visible human had been scanned. Colonel Endling felt his own special, fish-eyed friend coming close. He smiled at it, as it captured his face. Unlike the others, when it finished its task, it did not turn back to the swarm. It just hovered there, eyeing him with the big lens. When he took a few steps backwards, it followed. "Oh, lucky me," he said, and the doctor led him into a nearby yurt.

The drone followed right up to the door of the yurt. Doctor and Colonel crawled across some empty sleeping bags and out a little doggy door on the back side of the yurt. A second drone met them there, and when it took the Colonel's picture, it locked on and signaled to the original drone, which came over and joined it. They both hovered about a yard away.

"I've never seen them do this," the doctor said.

Tubby walked over with a gathering crowd of the curious. Junior Soucy, too.

"Want me to smash 'em?" Tubby asked.

"No, no, no," Junior Soucy said, quickly. "That will bring the rotors. These drones only have about 20 minutes of juice. Let's see what they do."

And he was right. The Colonel took a stroll through the long row of tents, followed the entire time by his double shadow. He was uptight about it, as if the drones were big bugs that might bite, so it seemed a long while, but, finally, after some minutes, the drones fell to the ground. The rest of the swarm was long gone. Tubby and Junior walked over and looked at the drones.

"They might still be recording. Don't touch."

"All right," Tubby said.

"Let's talk, Colonel Endling. Come to my tent."

In the yurt, Tubby and the Colonel sat together on a sleeping bag while Junior lay on another with his arms crossed behind his head.

"He's your muscle, huh?" Junior asked.

"He sure is," the Colonel said, laughing.

"What did you think of our wedding last night?"

They had cold milk at the wedding. That meant they had cows. Where they grazed the animals, the Colonel aimed to find out. How it coated his stomach, the cold glass of it. He couldn't stop thinking about it.

None of the many toasts involved milk unless it was human kindness, and there was plenty of that. Oaths and prayers, too, some that mentioned Old Testament serpents and some that praised or called for a new Enlightenment. The nuptials began after dark, and the Colonel was stiff and cautious, remembering the warnings in Abilene, the warnings about the traveling weddings. They were always short on specifics, the warnings. He began to see why. These people were wonderful.

The polyandry pattern was a puzzle. The Colonel was not exactly a social butterfly to begin with, but he was left pretty much speechless. The bride and her two husbands beamed. The officiant had a look of genuine joy as he performed the ceremony. After, there was drum music, and people danced in the light of torches. There was a big circle of light, a space that looked like nothing much more than a cleared area in a campground. And that's what it was. But it looked beautiful. Tubby danced, too. He drank wine and danced. Dancing was far beyond the Colonel's capacities, so he wandered around the tents in the darkness beyond the torch light.

There was singing and drums and laughter all night. Very late, the Colonel walked away from the noise of it and watched paper lanterns lit by candles in their bellies, as they floated away from the party. They moved slowly, like leisurely hot air balloons, that shape, too, and he was mesmerized by their passing before the starry sky. Many burned out before landing. They'd wink out and complete the journey unseen. One he watched, though, stayed lit and crashed into some brush, starting a fire. The brush was so dry it practically exploded, but it was out again in mere minutes after burning to ash. There was nothing around to catch, not even grass, but Colonel Endling worried about vulnerable buildings (ghost town or not, they were vulnerable) in this part of Amarillo.

He went back to the party and found Tubby.

"Those paper lanterns are gonna cause wildfires," he said.

Tubby looked up at the sky then back to his drink.

"Take a load off," he said.

"Oh, I'm fine."

"I mean a load off your mind, friend."

"I can't," Colonel Endling said.

Tubby sipped his wine.

"Can you believe these people?"

"No, they are something else," the Colonel said. "This is something else."

"I didn't know how nice it would be to see other people. No offense."

"I know what you mean."

"How's the hand?"

"All right. There's a whole bunch of doctors here."

"What's our next move?"

"We need to talk to Junior. Find out what their relationship is with Colorado Springs. I'm guessing it's bad based on how they talk about the Marines."

"Same story everywhere."

"Look at these fools," Colonel Endling laughed, pointing at dancers soaked in sweat. "They'll go all night."

"There's time, then, for another glass of wine."

Junior Soucy groaned as he stretched. He remained on his back on his sleeping bag.

"So, who are you two that the authorities would be interested in tracking you?"

"We're nobody."

Junior laughed at that.

"What?"

"Well, that's just honestly not believable."

"It's true."

"Here's the thing. They let everybody just walk right out of Abilene. Okay? But not you guys. You've had a gunman stalker and a locked drone."

The Colonel shifted his weight on the sleeping bag.

"I have some history with the Head Prisoner."

"Oh, he's a cock sucker. What kind of history?"

"Old history," the Colonel said. "I'm the reason he is here and not on Triste. I got him arrested."

"Oh, shit. That's not a hatchet any man is going to bury."

"Right."

"Except maybe in your skull," Tubby said.

"You should be safe from him if you stay with us. One man however well-armed isn't crazy enough."

"He's sneaky."

"Where are you headed?"

Colonel Endling felt there was nothing to lose in talking.

"I want to get to Colorado Springs. I have friends there. I want to see the Einhorns."

Junior sat up.

"Leo Einhorn? Why? He's a fat zero."

"I think he's more like his father the Chairman than his brother the Chairman. His brother must be dealt with."

"The Chairman the father was a zero, too."

"Hardly."

"He was supposed to give us rain and fertile soil."

"He saved us," the Colonel objected. "He gave us Triste."

"No," Junior said. "No, my father gave us Triste."

"Your father..."

"Gerard Souci," Junior said, modulating his voice to an exaggerated French accent. The Colonel gave him a long look.

"How?"

"How? What do you mean how?"

"The legend of his disappearance. He was childless. Never seen again. How are you here?"

"Sometimes legends are just legends, Colonel Endling."

"He came home."

"Yes."

"What happened?"

"Wolfgang Einhorn wanted certain things kept so secret that my father was hidden away."

"Against his will?"

"Quite."

Tubby shook his head and grumbled.

"What was so secret?"

"The go-betweens."

"Go-betweens?" the Colonel started. "Go-betweens with an S? As in plural?"

"Right."

"There are more than the Great Window we came through on the prison ship?"

"Yes."

The Colonel was silent as he processed this fact.

"The Fates are funny, huh?" Junior said. He wore a big, silver ring on his left hand, and with it he scratched under his chin where there was a patch of acne pimples.

"You must know who I am to say something like that," the Colonel said.

"Imagine I do or imagine I don't, what difference does it make to what you want to do?" Junior said. He looked at his silver ring to see if anything was on it after the scratching.

"What do you think of our plan?" Tubby asked.

"Don't like it. For your sakes, don't like it."

"Do you have anyone who could transport us there in a vehicle?" Tubby asked.

"You should stay with us for a while," Junior replied. "Get healed and fatten up."

"We need to hurry," the Colonel said.

"Why hurry?" Junior said. "Stay. There's another wedding tomorrow night. Stay."

So, they did. The next wedding was identical to the first. It was uncanny. Colonel Endling thought the night repeated.

"Are these the same people?" he asked Tubby.

"I can't tell," Tubby admitted.

The color scheme repeated. The coral-colored dresses looked perfect. They couldn't possibly have been worn two nights before, and yet. The wedding officiant wore the same genuine smile, it couldn't be the same ceremony, and yet. The cold steel bucket of milk came around, as it did the first night, and the Colonel accepted a glass. He drank it down fast. He knew he should savor it, drink it slowly, but it was such a delight, he gulped it down.

The Colonel wiped milk from his moustache.

"My children will have two Daddies," the bride said. The two grooms were close in age, brothers maybe, they looked alike, but it hadn't been explained. Colonel Endling thought of the honey bee, an example of polyandry in nature, but that made him think of Tubby's tattoo and, then, Laverna, and he didn't want to feel sad, so he pushed it away. A squadron of paper lanterns was launched. They moved slowly with a miraculous lightness, as if gravity was shut off. The bride and two grooms watched them. The officiant pointed to something in the sky, and they all laughed. When a dry, hot wind pushed the lanterns, the Colonel put down his milk glass and walked north, following and worrying about where they might land.

"The goddamn lanterns," he grumbled. "Damn reckless."

As he walked, the chafing of his inner thighs bothered him. The wolf bites seemed okay. He'd lost a sense of how long the chafing had been a bother. How many days had they been on the road? He no longer knew the exact number, and it was probably a fact now impossible to recover. He'd have to let go of that tug on his mind that wanted the exact reckoning. Not every mind gets preoccupied like mine, he thought. How many days until X? How many hours until we reach Y? How many weeks until I die? Days? Minutes? What's that in seconds? The counting and returning and counting and settling of these fractions of time felt like a sort of miserliness, and never (before now) did he wish for the annoying appearance of a true time pusher with his atomic clock.

Up ahead, something big was burning. He could smell smoke and see the glow long before he saw the flames. He passed a building with a mural on the side, twin clown faces, the ticket booth of an amusement park. One happy, one terribly sad, the clowns. DREAMLAND, the place was called. The park was in shambles, but you could tell what it was once. A tall, wooden roller coaster was burning. What remained of the lattice work burned way more intensely than he imagined would have happened this quickly from the lantern. He walked as close as he could with the heat. THE BEAST, the sign said. Paint on that sign was bubbling, and soon the name was no more.

"Are you married yet?" a voice directly behind him asked.

He was somehow not surprised. He knew the voice, and he'd known a voice was coming, and he'd known who it would be. He felt what had to be the end of a rifle barrel against his spine.

"Is this a stick up?" he asked.

"Do you know how many people I've killed here in Texas, Colonel Endling?" the Brain asked. "Any guesses? Is it a high or low number?"

"Zero. I don't think killing was ever your thing."

"Wrong. You don't know shit."

"Oh, pardon me."

"I usually like the flamethrower. Your friend Lascaux learned how to use it. I showed him."

"He told me."

"I'm sure he did."

"Did you light this fire?"

"Still a smart Colonel, I see."

"I knows a trap when I see one."

"I've been watching you for a long while."

"I know," Colonel Endling said. "Okay if I turn around?"

"Go ahead."

Tubby had warned him about the change, but, still, the face was shocking. The Brain's skin was covered in irregular bumps as if he'd been sprayed with plaster fireproofing that hardened there forever. The skull looked the same as ever, shaped as if it encased a gigantic brain. The Brain stood there with the gun pointed in the Colonel's direction, but with a carefree attitude. The gun might or might not go off, and the holder of the gun might or might not care if it did.

"Who's minding the store in Abilene?" the Colonel asked.

"I left that girl, Piper, in charge," the Brain said.

The free agent, the Colonel thought, but he was 90% certain this was a lie. He chewed his cheek viciously. This moment he considered for years had come.

"Are you gonna drag me back? My sentence didn't say I had to stay there."

The Brain laughed.

"Your sentence was a gift."

"A gift?"

"For me. The greatest gift. An answered prayer."

Behind his own back, the Colonel could hear the burning roller coaster collapsing. He felt the thump of heavy pieces hitting the ground.

"Well," he said. "Here I am."

"Here we are."

"What now?"

"What should I do with you? Are you useful?"

"That depends."

"Yeah?"

"Yeah... I mean... it depends. What do you want?"

"Not what you think... or not what I think you think..."

"Say more..."

"Violence against you, Colonel, against you personally, I could take or leave."

That was a second lie, the Colonel thought. He'd been pursued by a man 300 miles across the desert, the pursuer on foot, he believes, 300 miles across the unforgiving desert. That was beyond what a rational person could call revenge. That was deep longing after wild justice.

"If it's not what I think then what is it?"

The Brain threw his hands up. The gun slipped, but he caught it.

"Come on, old man!" he said disgustedly. "I want the gold back. I want all of it back."

"The gold."

"I want it back, and you are gonna help me get it back."

"You can't be serious."

A third lie. What kind of game was this?

"Don't be offended."

Now, the Colonel had to laugh. He said, "This sounds a little off."

"I want the gold back. G-O-L-D. All of it. I know every bar. I see it when I close my eyes. I've memorized the serial number on every bar."

"Can we move away from the fire?"

The ghosts in this place were child-sized and excitable. Despite the park's long abandonment, the act of arson was troubling Colonel Endling to his core.

"Okay. Let's walk."

They walked towards the darkness. The Brain kept a few paces to the rear with the rifle up.

"How am I going to help you?" Colonel Endling asked.

"You can make my crime disappear."

"Oh, really?"

"Yes, sir."

"How?"

"I have a plan. All those years ago, you framed me. You're so guilty about it. Don't worry. We'll combine our great intellects when we get to Boulder."

The Colonel sniffed, a sort of weak laugh of resignation. His shoulders drooped. He heard the Brain's footsteps stop. The Brain removed a shiny, silver object from his pants pocket. On this silver thing (it looked like a toy beetle from some novelty shop), there was a black button. The button clicked loudly when the Brain pressed it. He put it back in his pocket.

"Gonna make a run for it?"

"Me?"

"Yeah, you."

"No way. I was heading to Colorado anyhow."

The fire had to be attracting the attention of the wedding party. As the two men walked, the Colonel scanned the dark with his eyes. He could see exactly nothing. He kept shuffling along.

"Where are we going?"

"Keep going this way. They'll find my beacon."

They crossed blacktop then soil then blacktop again.

"Go north."

This was the major, divided, north-south highway. Route 87, the Colonel guessed. In the middle distance, invisible but audible, some wolves howled in a chorus. The fire had unsettled them. Colonel Endling heard the chorus and at least six distinct voices.

"You recovered from that attack?" the Brain asked.

"I'm okay."

"Almost not! I thought I was losing my chance when that wolf jumped you."

"Big teeth."

"I've seen some nasty things down here in Texas, boy."

"How many bullets do you have?"

"Plenty," the Brain said.

The walking in the dark... the rifle at his back... the raging flames... the agitated wolves... how had events narrowed to this? Colonel Endling began to imagine a visual for the shape of his life. A sine wave, maybe, a sine wave of lows and highs, but that wasn't it. It was something wide, a field of possibility that narrowed and narrowed to this point.

A black Jeep came rumbling down the highway from the north. The headlights were off. When the brakes screamed, and the Jeep stopped, the Brain spoke to someone through the passenger side window. Colonel Endling could not hear what was said. Now's the time to run, he thought, but he stayed put. The Brain walked back over.

"Got us a ride," he whispered. "Everything is going according to my P-L-A-N plan."

The Jeep left, catching the Colonel by surprise. He looked at the Brain for an explanation.

"Just wait."

Within five minutes, a hyperotor came, black as the night sky it emerged from. With the aid of a blinding light, it landed directly on the highway. When the disc cut out, a large Marine jumped out, and, with a gracious gesture, hailed the Colonel and the Brain to the cabin. They took off and flew north. Colonel Endling had a starboard side window. When they got in the air, he saw a great deal of activity to the northeast. There were cranes lit by spotlights, and big clouds of dust, and rotors coming and going with cargo dangling by cables.

"What's happening out there?"

"That's the nuclear bomb plant," the Brain said. "That's Project Resurrection."

"Are you shitting me?" he hissed. The Brain said nothing.

The rotor flew swiftly north over the ultra-flat landscape. They flew over tall, white silos that looked like temples in the brief flash of the rotor's sweeping lights. They passed over the northwest corner of Texas, then the border to New Mexico, land of enchantment, over volcanoes that last erupted 60,000 years ago, and quickly, next, over the border to Colorado. The first hint of sunrise changed the horizon to mountains, great heights where land and clouds might touch, and there were strictly-speaking no visible borders, not anymore, just the desert, the stony, dead desert that was not impressed with birds or helicopters or anything that could fly, only itself, though, well, maybe here was something, and even the rotor began to slow before it, there was something, stretching its length from southwest to northeast and cutting off Pueblo from the cities above it. It was the Chairman's security fence.

Part Four
Chapter One

They'd covered the Icelandic complex in paving stones. Where the waterworks housing had been there was a fountain, bubbling gloriously in the Fast Sunshine. Pedestrians strolled about, enjoying the mild day as if the loss of the dreamy, green garden world meant nothing to them. Sebastian Sleeper was disgusted. He bought some peanuts from a vendor cart. He cracked some open and ate the shells.

Peering into the fountain's waters revealed no solution to him. What would be useful? Jackhammer? Steam shovel? Some heavy-duty explosives? He needed none of these if he traveled by his mind, in through the suction filter at the bottom of the fountain's stone basin, down the suction pipe, turning at the elbow, down more pipe to the pump chamber, right into the centrifugal pump itself, listening to the weary, grinding work of its labor, finally into the source, the strange pool Toad dreamed about, it was the power or merely the cover for the power, but, in any case, the power was here, the go-between. He needed it.

What would happen to a body that died at exactly the moment it passed through a go-between?

The sadness that cloaked itself as fatigue inside him was replaced by a rage he felt like electricity in his arms and legs. He wanted to smash the fountain with his hands and feet. His skin-headed reflection looked funny to him. His scalp neither tanned nor burned in the sun. That was funny, too. He chewed on peanut shells, and, when he finished the small carton, he wanted more. For the first time in years, though, he thought about the consequence of the expense. When his money on his card ran out, how would he get more?

He sat on a stone bench. He was aware of every person in view, and he marked them all as possible informants. He nearly lost control of his composure when a bicycle cop pedaled into the scene. The police officer nodded at him as he wheeled by then completed a full circle around the fountain and stopped nearby. He stood his bicycle by its kickstand. Sleeper didn't know him by face, but his eyes stopped on the silver badge on the blue breast pocket of the cop's shirt. Quince, it said. So, Sleeper said to himself. Alive and well. He felt a chill and chewed his fingernails.

Another officer, younger than Quince and in a shiny helmet, rode over and stood up his own bike.

"What time are you quitting today?"

Quince squinted at the Fast Sun.

"Any minute now," he said. "You?"

"Same."

"Let's get some beers."

"Magic words."

When he saw he wasn't on the radar of these two gendarmes, Sleeper pushed his luck and decided to follow Quince. The nearest precinct was just two blocks away. Sleeper kept up enough to see the bike head that way. He waited outside the brick building until Quince came out in street clothes with three younger men all in civilian dress, too. Quince had dark gray hair with little threads of white like a slab of marble. He was striking, and women and men looked at him longingly as he passed on the sidewalk.

The four of them walked into The Belly of the Whale, their fraternal watering hole. Sleeper followed them. The place was jammed with police. He moved his way through the crowd that bottlenecked around tables, the two ends of the bar and the restrooms. The only place he could avoid the constant shouldering and shifting of bodies was against the wall, so when a space opened, he took it and stood beside a neon sign that buzzed. He looked up at the sign. He liked it. It was a piece of antique light sculpture. You didn't see too many of these on Triste. The tubes were bent in the shape of a flat-headed, angry, white whale. He looked around for Quince's gray hair.

"I am the noblest creature of the Earthsea," the whale said, so Sleeper looked at it and raised an eyebrow. He stared.

"What?" he said.

"A noble creature of noble gases," the whale said. Well, Sleeper heard it anyhow, though he was not quite sure he could claim accurately that the whale said it. He smacked his own forehead softly. Around him, the police were talking about a plague of home invasions. "It's so obvious," one said. "The beach. It's so obvious."

The whale's power supply was plugged into the wall just by Sleeper's own rear end. That's how I'd get in, he thought. A transformer was cleverly disguised by the whale's tale. Plug, transformer, electrode. He followed the snaky cable with his eyes. That's how I'd get in.

"Yes," the whale said. "Electrons, ions, collisions. Beautiful."

"What the hell am I saying?" Sleeper said, aloud. Nobody heard him. He looked at the whale. "I don't have time for this."

At First Dusk, half the crowd left. Quince was one of them. Sleeper followed him out the door. He wanted to ask the Captain some questions, maybe speak to him about his own looming arrest, the warrants against him, and Piper and what the police knew of the truth about Piper and all the consequences that came from Piper stabbing Quince on that fateful day.

It was a longer walk than Sleeper expected. Along brick sidewalks, past brick houses and shops, for a dozen city blocks, they walked. They crossed a border to a more suburban section of Redemption Rock. There were more trees, and the buildings were spread out. He watched Quince enter an apartment building, a long, one-story place in an old Spanish bungalow style. In the low light, Sleeper could easily hop a short fence and hide in some lilac trees in a courtyard in the rear of the property.

A light came on in one of the apartments. Sleeper could see right in. It was Quince all right. He stripped off his shirt and walked to his kitchen where he grabbed a green beer bottle from the fridge. Sleeper approved of his physique, and he saw the Captain's scars on his abdomen. The window was closed. Sleeper guessed that Quince turned on some music on a digital player in the kitchen. The face of the player glowed with purple light, but, outside, Sleeper couldn't hear it.

What was his plan? More following if Quince left the apartment? A night of watching him? Knock on his door and accost him? He pointed his ear at the lighted window and focused his mind on listening. He wanted to hear the music, but instead a foot stepped, and somebody leaned against the fence, causing the chain links to jangle loudly.

"What are you doing?" a man asked.

He was obese and leaned on the fence, grinning from his fat, red face. Sleeper froze. He didn't know what to say.

"Peeping Tom?" the main said. "What are you doing here?"

"Nothing," Sleeper said, looking for the easiest exit from the situation.

"That's a man in there, you know."

That last sentence echoed and repeated as Sleeper sprinted out of the neighborhood. His face burned. He imagined it as red as the fat man's.

He ran until second dawn, and, with the slow sun up, he realized he was exhausted. He'd rest then think of what to do about Quince. He walked fast back through the commercial district, past the once again filled Belly of the Whale, and all the way out Industrial Road to its end at the sewage treatment plant. The plant was plopped next to a small hospital. He'd never been this far down Industrial before. A chemical odor hid the stench of the sewage. There was a humming turbine sound that attracted his attention. He followed it until he found an unlocked gate in the plant's perimeter fence. He walked in and found the steel box he thought contained the humming turbine. It was the size of a huge man's coffin, and, whimsically (and without any real thought) he tried a door on the box, and, as in a dream that only goes happily, he found the door did open.

There was room inside. "Come inside," the turbine said to him, and, fearlessly, Sleeper climbed in, ducked under the turbine's housing and fell asleep.

He woke when the turbined stopped. Some system was resetting itself. He felt refreshed, so he opened the box door and stepped out. It was the middle of the night. Very dark. As he walked along the grass outside the plant's perimeter fence, he was surprised by a flashlight beam straight in his eyes. He blinked and saw that it was some medical person from the hospital, a woman, holding the light. She wore blue scrubs and had an ID badge dangling from a lanyard around her neck.

"You must come back in," she said.

"No, not me," he said. "You got the wrong—"

"That's an order, Marine," she said. She turned the light on his shaved head and injuries.

"I'm not a Marine," he said, catching on to her mistake. She grabbed him by the elbow, and he went along with her. As they went through the sliding doors of the hospital entrance, a sleek ambulance arrived and zipped around the corner of the building. It flashed red lights, but it moved silent as a ghost. Sleeper looked around at everything as they walked through the lobby. It was quiet. Dimmed lights. Night shift staff.

"Is this a psychiatric hospital?" he asked.

That stopped the doctor dead in her tracks. She came over and felt Sleeper's forehead.

"You feel okay?"

"I'm fine."

They walked again, following white corridors until they came to a ward known as REANIMATION. The doctor' badge opened the doors and revealed a narrow room with two rows of white beds. Most were occupied. Oh, no, Sleeper thought. I've walked into some sad army movie.

"Which is your bed?" the doctor asked.

"I don't know," Sleeper replied.

"Oh," the doctor furrowed her brow. She had brown hair, a plain face behind her eyeglasses. "You've got a bad bump on the head."

There was no life support in here. Sleeper wondered why the ward was called REANIMATION.

"Take this bed," the doctor said, pointing. "This one here."

"That's Chuck's bed," the man in the bed next to the empty one said. He had only one arm. "Oh. Right. Never mind. Never mind that I said that."

Sleeper sat on the edge of the bed, putting as little weight on it as he could. He didn't plan to stay long.

"Who is Chuck?" he asked the one-armed soldier.

"More like who the fuck are you, brother?"

Sleeper played dumb. He grabbed the top of his head.

"I don't remember."

"Well, that's not your bed, brother."

A legless man came down the row of beds, swinging himself from one to the next by his arms. He moved like an Olympic gymnast. His arms were hugely muscled. He landed on Chuck's bed.

"Take it easy, Pork Chop. Chuck is gone."

"Hi," Sleeper said.

"Hi. I'm Shorty," the legless man said. "What's your name?"

"I don't remember."

"Huh. I'll call you Nobody," Shorty said. "Just until you remember. I don't see a tattoo on you. You're not Rotor Battalion. What division are you from?"

"No clue."

"Huh. Wow. You're a full-fledged mystery man. Well then. Welcome to the ward. Hope you're like us. We all want revenge. We all want to kill Gun Club and his family. Are you like us? Do you want to kill the Gun Club and his family?"

Chapter Two

Leo Einhorn drove south. He was alone in the green Jaguar. The top was down, and the wind blew his hair straight back. He'd grown it longer for racing with the top down on sunny days just like this one. He wore goggles for the grit in the wind. Bruce Burden the bodyguard was normally with him every second of the day, but Leo had slipped the detail and driven off. Burden was in a black rotor a mile or so back, chewing his nails down to nothing. He and the crew had Leo both visually and by satellite, but he worried.

The Jaguar sped through towns that were classic speed traps many years ago, towns that a century ago had just one police officer, an officer whose only job was to ticket speeders on these very stretches of road. Today, the only limit on the green car's speed was Leo's own sense of danger, his notion that there might be parts of the road crumbling, spots where even the Marines' repair work might be old and failing.

He was driving to locate the would-be assassin, Piper. He would take her back to Colorado, not forcefully by any power invested in his own position, but by her own agreement. That was his hope. He thought of her every day. He would be disappointed if she didn't come voluntarily. He'd be less disappointed but disheartened still if she came to Colorado under the false impression it was less than voluntary. He could tell her it was voluntary, and she might say she knew it was voluntary, but if, in her heart, she felt it was compelled, how would he know that was the real secret of her heart?

Of the chores given by his brother, one Leo did not neglect was the review of the new prisoner intake forms that came from Texas. If he was going be honest with himself and the historical record, he'd have to admit he liked most of all to click through the photos from intake. There could be surprisingly pretty faces. He would let himself go into whimsical daydreams. He never acted on these, and that was the truth.

And so now, he'd been fully aware of Piper's arrest. He'd known the details about the trial and her sentence and, even, her pending transport, but, when that was delayed, he'd forgotten until those blue eyes appeared during his most recent click session. He asked for the complete, detailed version of her intake file. This was sent to his tablet, so he read it.

Name: Piper S—
Age: 30 (approximate)
Sex: F
Height: 5'7"
Weight: 125

Hair: Brown
Eyes: Blue
Security Group Threat: Max
Parole Eligibility Date: Not eligible
Judge: Apple
Offense(s): High Treason, Conspiracy, Murder, Attempted Murder, Terrorism

Historical Criminal Data

Prior Felonies: None
Prior Misdemeanors: None
Prior Escapes: N/A
Testing
IQ Screening: 120 (superior)
Recommendation for work: Work consistent with age and physical condition

Mental Health History
Psych Hospitalizations: No
Mental Health Treatment: No
Psychological Medications: None
Self-Destruction: Inconclusive
List of drugs used: Marijuana/LSD (self-reported)
Medical: Ms. S— complained of no medical problems.

Custody Issues
Co-defendants: Yes
Name: Endling, Edward
Name: Lascaux, Leonid
Recommendation: Maximum monitoring protocol

Family
Spouse: None
Children: None
Comments: Siblings (deceased) were long mandated to servitude of Einhorn family and Mission.
Imminent Threat

Is the offender currently demonstrating fixated/threatening behavior toward past or future victims? No.

That last question is thrilling, Leo thought. Indeed, Piper's file was red. It ought to have had flashing sirens. How much reliability was there in that "no" answer? Some, he guessed. Leo did love a thrill. That's why he had his own personal Risk Management guru coming to pester him every other day. He'd come to think of it as pestering, yes, even though he'd requested it.

Leaving Colorado, there was only desert and what you'd have to call not-desert. The Jaguar was the only green thing for miles. He passed a spill of boulders where some birds in shadow hid their eggs from the deadly sun. In his rear-view mirror: a blue mountain, a sign for Denver 200 miles. And behind the blue mountain even bigger mountains. He passed a sign that told him he was leaving the Mountain Time Zone. That was a strange relic from the past. He thought of how his father considered his biggest achievement was the universalizing of marked time. The true time.

Leo felt time was running out. This was a vague notion, but it was emotionally deep. It was like a film. There was no bomb on screen, but he could hear it ticking.

Somewhere in New Mexico, the black rotor that had been tailing him since Boulder passed him and landed on the highway. He could slide past it, and as he did, he showed his middle finger to Bruce Burden who pleaded with him with a distraught face through the rotor's windshield.

"Fuck you, Bruce," he shouted, as he watched the rotor in his rear-view mirror. It took off to play the game again and flew past him (again) before landing. This time, the pilot landed so the length of the rotor blocked the highway entirely. Leo had to stop. Burden got out of the rotor and approached the fancy, green racing machine. Leo wouldn't look at him. He stared at the long, black body of the rotor.

"We can't let you go into Texas un-protected, sir," Burden said. "I can't."

Leo stared at the rotor's weaponry. There were three belt-fed, gas-powered machine guns. 7,500 rounds per minute, and those bastards never failed, never had a part break. He could see the two un-guided rockets on the near side. And two laser-guided Hellfire missiles. God knows what else I can't see, he thought. Bombs. The pulse gun.

"What do you suggest, Bruce?"

"Let us plan a trip with armor and support."

"No."

"How about a flight with an extraction team?"

"No."

Leo looked at his bodyguard now. Bruce was exhausted. He was asking for a break here.

"Will you allow me to ride in the car with you?" he asked. "At least that?"

Leo was embarrassed. He turned red. Since he so strongly wanted to do this thing without any security and without any eyes on him, he felt it was shameful.

Now, he wanted to turn back. What was his plan anyway? He didn't even have one.

"I'm going to turn back," he said.

"Okay," Burden said with relief.

Leo turned the Jaguar around. His disappointment was cold in his belly, and his face still burned with shame. He drove north, and by the time he reached the mountains, he was roiling with self-hatred and aggression. He looked around for something to destroy.

Chapter Three

The Queen entered the room under her own power. Her head was heavily bandaged. She wore no makeup, and her striking red hair was hidden under what looked like a rugby player's scrum cap. She smiled weakly at Dr. Aztec, and at Apple, the technician at the large screen at the back of the room.

"Should I stand or sit?" she asked.

"Sit, please, Your Majesty," the doctor said. "By your husband there in that cozy chair. Perfect."

She sat and handed Jack a pill bottle.

"Hold this for me."

He read the bottle and made a face like it smelled awful.

"How are you feeling?" Dr. Aztec asked.

"Comme ci comme ça," the Queen said. "A bit detached."

"That's perfectly normal," Dr. Aztec said. He gestured at the pill bottle.

"Yes, it's powerful."

The wall opposite the large screen was glass from floor to ceiling. The setting Fast Sun was bright. The field of purple flowers outside stretched for miles. It was a soft carpet of peace and calm.

"How do those flowers make you feel?" Dr. Aztec asked. He held a thin tablet computer in his hand. This interfaced with the tablet that Apple held and the huge display screen and, lastly, the Queen's own brain.

"What are they called?" Queen Roux asked.

"Scorpionweed," Apple said.

The Queen frowned at that name, and, as she did, a pink line of light appeared on the wall.

"That's a harsh name," the Queen said.

Her husband clumsily fumbled the pill bottle in his one hand, and it hit the floor. The pink line on the display screen turned redder.

"Jack," the Queen said. "Give that to me."

The doctor and his technician smiled at each other.

"I'm seeing success, boys," Jack said.

Apple took off his round eyeglasses and rubbed them with a cloth from his pocket.

"Are the colors fixed?" the Queen asked.

"No," Dr. Aztec said. "They can be changed. We've assigned the same your husband has always used in the Index."

"I see," the Queen said.

"The people know them."

"Yes, right," Queen Roux said. "But we're shutting down his Index. That must be made clear. I'll want my own colors."

"We can work on that now, Your Majesty. Apple can do that now if it pleases you."

"It pleases me."

She'd worried the implant would be present in her thoughts, if not an actual impediment or barrier then at least a blot that could not be ignored. But that was pointless worry. Everything was so clear. Her thoughts, her emotions, what actions she knew were needed.

"Drop the pink," she said.

"Consider it done," Apple said, nervously.

"No," the Queen said. "Show me."

"Absolutely."

Apple worked some code on his tablet. After 90 seconds, he said he was done.

"Pink was a shade of anger?" she asked.

"Yes," Dr. Aztec said. "It's on that spectrum."

The Queen closed her eyes for a moment then opened them again. The screen was blank.

"Nothing?" she asked.

"Oh, my apologies," Apple said. "It's not publishing."

Jack had fallen asleep in his chair. The Queen looked him over. He had gained back some of his lost weight, but his injured side still looked like a dead thing. What was sweet in his nature, and she knew those things so well, the sweetness was visible now in his manner, and what was vicious in his capabilities, and she knew those powers, too, the viciousness appeared to have vanished. It was a sad trade, and the Queen didn't like it at all. The wall displayed blossoms of red like fireworks in a dark sky. Though they weren't random, they had nothing of the order of an Index.

"That's working now," Dr. Aztec said. "I've frozen the visual for you, Your Majesty."

She stood and walked slowly to the display. The filaments coming out of the center of each red burst looked like capillaries.

"I liked the bodied look of it," she said.

Dr. Aztec and Apple shared a glance.

"You know, none of my husband's stock market charts all up and down. That's not alive."

"I see what you mean," Dr. Aztec said. "Your husband's, of course, has the benefit of obviousness to anyone looking."

"We'll make this obvious," the Queen said.

Out the window, behind the darkening horizon, the Fast Sun was easing itself down like a spent, old man into a hot bath. The purple flowers disappeared into shadow. Jack woke suddenly with a gasp for air. There was a spot of drool on his red shirt. He had a mischievous twinkle in his eye.

"You know, Roux," he said. "When the neuroprosthetic was implanted, I asked Dr. Aztec to implant a second piece that receives rather than transmits. I can remotely control you now."

The display screen showed icy blue cracks of doubt.

"Tell me that's a joke," the Queen said, looking at the doctor. That placed Dr. Aztec in a tight spot. Would he contradict Gun Club? Who'd cut his head off first?

Jack waved his hand.

"Let's pretend for a second I'm not joking."

"Oh, please don't," the Queen sighed.

"No, no, no, follow me, honey. Follow me here. How great would it be? My will and your agile mind and body? There would be no stopping us."

"Let me tell you something," the Queen said with a smile.

"What?"

"I hate that idea."

Humble Jack laughed, but it hurt him to laugh, so he closed his eyes. On the display, the icy blue had gone green. The Queen moved to the window and looked out. The gloom had crept over everything now. All the flowers and Tumtum trees were hidden, and Daphne was covered in the false night before Second Dawn.

"I'm tired now," the Queen said.

"Okay, darling," Jack said. "More tomorrow?"

"Yes," she said. "Turn off that screen for now."

Apple shut it off. The Queen left, and when she was out of the room, the Chairman called the doctor and technician over.

"You have the miniature for me?" he asked.

Apple handed the Chairman a coin-sized device that was all screen. "Ha!" Jack laughed. "It's a mood ring!"

"Don't know what that is, sir," Apple admitted.

Dr. Aztec shrugged.

"It doesn't matter."

The device showed swirls of different greens, sea greens and parrot greens and mossy greens and billiard table greens, as the Queen made her way slowly to her apartments.

Chapter Four

Now it came to pass that Toad fell asleep and dreamt of a city. He called it the City of Peace. It was a city by the ocean with a long, white beach. In the dream, the city streets were jammed with people coming and going on foot. They seemed to move with the orderliness of boxes on a conveyor belt. As people left the streets, new people took their places, having come in a line that went beyond the city limits. The people cycled through again and again. He began to recognize faces when they passed a second or third time. Within the cycle was another cycle of people walking down stairs to a world beneath the world, a city below the streets, and likewise came people up sets of stairs to emerge to walk in the light of day and cycle again through the streets. When he woke, Toad told the dream to Yoshi. At the breakfast table, Yoshi wanted to hear it eight times in a row.

"What were their faces like?" Yoshi asked.

"Just regular people's faces."

"Like Moms and Dads?" Flat Tire asked. He was under the table, chasing a dropped green grape so Maggie's dog, Bruno, would not get it.

"Just people," Toad said.

"Happy or sad?" Yoshi asked.

"Not sure," Toad said. He used a crayon to draw a face on his napkin. Two eyes, a nose, and just a horizontal line for a mouth. Yoshi laughed.

"Okay, buddy."

Beetle didn't join the conversation as he sat devouring his fruit salad. Yoshi looked at him and thought he might need a new nickname. Beetle now sported a blue mohawk. His head no longer looked like a black helmet.

Maggie was in the cellar, tinkering in her new laboratory. After breakfast, the boys would be going on a mission for her. Yoshi had ground down her scruples into tiny particles. This sounds bad, but they both saw it as a good. Each day, she gave him a brief list of items she could use in the lab. The kids would go out and steal them. See, since the incident with the Frogmen, Maggie was banned from official work. The old house had been seized by the Frogmen who were turning it to shit. Maggie could not communicate with colleagues to share work or supply the new lab. Don't get caught was her only demand of the boys. She set up a new camp in the basement of an abandoned science building at the defunct Redemption Rock Community College.

They descended to the lab. At one end, Maggie had a lecture hall whiteboard and some chairs for the boys to sit facing it. She walked over from her instruments when they sat.

"Good morning," she said.

"Hi, Maggie," they said in chorus. In the shortest time, they'd grown quite attached to her.

"How was breakfast?"

"Tremendous!" Yoshi said.

"Good," Maggie said, looking at the younger boys who nodded. "Boys, I need a big piece today. "I'm reluctant. It's an important piece. I said big, but I meant big as in important. In reality, it's kinda small."

"What is it?" Toad asked.

Maggie drew a black square on the whiteboard. She then drew a dozen black squares about double the size of the first one in an approximate circle around the original square in the center. These she connected individually to the center square with spokes. She pointed with her marker.

"This here is a quantum clock."

"Got it," Yoshi said.

"I have one, but it's dead. They don't last long. The outer squares here are standard rubidium clocks. The spokes are the beams the quantum clock sends to fix the rubidium clocks to the True Time. The R-87 clocks wander like all clocks do. Without a new quantum clock, my work is useless and must stop. Any drift, even the tiniest yoctosecond of drift from any of my dozen R-87 clocks will lead to horrifying errors."

"Where can we get one?"

"Any of the True Time team captains will have one."

"How will we know them from the rest?"

Maggie handed Yoshi a vinyl binder with papers inside.

"Their pictures are in there," she said.

"Got it."

"But wait. There's one thing. They know who you boys are by now. You can't be seen."

Most of the time men lived in Dreaming Back Lake. And, of those who did, most lived in a claustral, bachelor community at the Saint Eligius Hotel. It was a famous building that pre-dated any other structure in the city. The lobby had a floor of smooth white stone. There were white stone walls topped by a magnificent cupola of azure glass. The cupola's pointed arch when lit by the LED lights behind it looked like a blue flame reaching up for the heavens.

The hotel's nearest neighbors were a bodega (to your left as you faced the hotel) and a private drone racing club (to your right). The boys went browsing in the bodega while Yoshi thought about what to do. They joined a small crowd around some faro tables near the back. Yoshi could pick out the time men from the others. They all had a harried look as if the constant thought chewed on them that there was something impossible yet imperative they ought to be doing.

Yoshi knew without having to be told, too, that the time captains were cut from an even deeper part of the cult. That worried him. They might be dangerous about parting with their personal quantum clocks. He had no shortage of ideas on the riskier side. Most involved the windows of the hotel's rooms, windows high up from the ground but nonetheless vulnerable, all having been left open to the warm breezes of the morning. There was one obvious way for him to enter one of those windows, but he did not want to expose his new talents to the world.

There was a race scheduled to begin soon at the drone park. All sorts of characters began to arrive.

Trucks pulled to the marked unloading zones before the entrance, and teams of young men hopped out to unload their drones and carry them into the club. The racers sported the blank masks of untouchable ultra-cool that Yoshi always found aggressive and irritating. They were young people from all over and mostly harmless as proved by the deference they showed to the off-duty Marines who came with their own drones to race. The young civilian men would rapidly move their trucks to less ideal parking spaces to make room for the soldiers' vehicles. The time men preferred faro to the races, but a few did walk from the hotel to the club to watch and wager.

Yoshi loitered outside the club a few minutes, wondering if he dared enter. If it was a question of daring himself, he'd do it. That wasn't the question. He was bothered that he had plans, lots of dumb plans, but he didn't have any single good plan. Forget the club, he thought. It was the hotel. What would he do? Fly up to an open window, drop into a room, and then do what?

"Fuck it," he said and soared.

He picked a moment with not a witness around, and by the grace of silent flight (one of the miraculous surprises of his new life) he landed on a top floor casement with only the click of a talon to record it. The room was unoccupied, but a screen on the wall showed a talking head that said, "In the last fiscal year, slightly more than 20,000 people died in Radium Beach."

Yoshi dropped into the room. It was spare, the room of a monk or somebody with a singular obsession. White stone walls like the lobby, a bed for one person, some plants getting light by the window. On one wall, there was a map of the occupant's territory. Tiny flags were tacked into neighborhoods that were friendly to the True Time. The areal density of flags in particular neighborhoods made the adoption of the True Time look, in 2D, like nothing other than a contagion. Back on his human feet, Yoshi checked around the room, but there were few items, and there was no quantum clock. He walked out. The hallway was white with runners of bright sapphire fabrics. He moved silently along the soft rugs, stopping to listen at each door. The rooms with no sound inside, he tried, and he found most the same as the first: maps on the wall, some plants, sometimes a sleeper in the bed. He found the stairs and headed down one level.

In the stairwell, he came across a sign that said SOURCE and pointed down. He stopped and stared at it. Could it be?

He took the steps two at a time, trying not to make too much noise. All the way down he went, down all 14 floors, until there were no more stairs. A sign at the bottom said SOURCE, and this one pointed him at another white hallway. He was one level below ground. He heard the noise of the hotel kitchen above him, as he walked to the end of the hallway and found a wooden door. It was a simple door, pale wood with a silver knob, and a large feather carved as a decoration. He turned the knob, and the door opened to white, stone steps leading down into darkness. He heard water cascading somewhere in that darkness.

"Oh, shit," he said. "Oh, shit. Oh, shit."

Thinking of his small friends Toad, Beetle and Flat Tire, he shut the door and leaned his back against it. Focus, he told himself. Focus, Yoshi. Focus on why you're here in this hotel right now. Can't leave the kids alone here.

The draw of immense possibility tugged at him like a powerful undertow. Where would that go-between go? Their last jump was disorienting and had taken several days for them all to adjust to, but he really wanted to jump again. He couldn't leave his friends. He started back up the stairs. As he passed the kitchen level, he heard a sneeze just beyond the door, so he picked up the pace. He looked back over his shoulder to see the door open. A security guard came out and saw him.

"Hey, what are you doing there, kid?"

His face was not unkind, and he looked like his own question truly puzzled him. Still, Yoshi flew with his new wings and headed for the upper floors.

"What the fuck?" the guard said. "What just happened?"

He stomped up the stairs with heavy echoes, as Yoshi flew way ahead of him. But there was a problem. Yoshi hadn't thought about door knobs. When he got to the top floor, he panicked and hit the wall. He hurt his wing. When he reverted, his left arm felt broken from the shoulder to the elbow.

"Just STOP, kid," the guard shouted. "STOP. Wait for me."

No chance, Yoshi thought. His heart was pounding. He got the top floor door open and ran through. He needed an open window again. He sprinted to get back to the room he'd first entered. He held his left arm, which throbbed as he ran. A building-wide alarm sounded as he neared the room. He opened the door, ducked in, closed the door behind him and found the room no longer empty. A time man was adding a flag to his wall map.

"Hello," the man said.

Yoshi looked to the window and back to the stranger's face.

Chapter Five

Here's how power worked in Texas. Every single person in the loose prison system knew his or her own standing in the hierarchy in relation to every other person. There were no exceptions. Things were tested, yes, but nobody was fooling themselves about where they stood. For Bruce Burden who operated near the top of the pyramid, this was extremely convenient.

Burden was a muscular man with a mean face. Nobody really knew how he came to be an enforcer for the Einhorn family. He told people he was from Louisiana or Mississippi or the Everglades, depending on the audience, but, really, he came from the ruins of Hartford, Connecticut. He grew up in a gang that murdered its way to control of the old Colt Manufacturing Company's factory west of the city. He owned a great deal of Colt merchandise, including several Colt Python revolvers he was always seen loading or holstering or polishing the silver barrels of when he had nothing else to do.

And, anyhow, to get back to the original point about Texas, Osprey was the warden. He was a powerful man, but he knew he was not at the apex of the pyramid. He could be tossed aside when no longer useful. He felt this keenly, as he sat at his desk with Burden opposite him, listening to Burden's disgusting request. He thought maybe he could fight Burden to a stalemate in an arm-wrestling match, but the man's forearms were impressive.

"So, Mr. Einhorn doesn't know about this, then," Osprey said. He took off his plastic goggles from his head and laid them on the desk.

"Right."

"And yet, it's authorized," Osprey said. "I'm confused."

"It's a surprise for him," Burden said.

"Authorized by whom?"

"By Yours Truly," Burden grinned.

Osprey's predicament was this: Burden's power was real without being official. He felt nauseous. "Maybe I should call Messmaker just to get an official blessing on her release."

"Already done," Burden said. His grin did not let up.

The request was disgusting but also risky. Burden could handle himself, surely, but still.

"She's the most dangerous person in Texas," Osprey said, more forthcoming about his own fears than he intended. He caught sight of his Chief Deputy, Waterling, who kept nervously walking past his office door and looking in. Piper belonged in Serratura, here where the warden's office was located, the lock up facility for people who committed crimes while already sentenced in Texas. That was the place for her. Not that she'd committed any crimes that Osprey knew about. He wanted to get away from Burden's grin. It was oppressive. He'd stall.

"Want a coffee?" he asked, getting up. He ducked into a small pantry off his office where there was a coffee machine.

"I don't touch that shit," Burden said. Burden's chair screeched across the bare wooden floor as he got up impatiently. He was a heavy stepper. Osprey listened to him walking around the room and stopping to look at the photographs on the walls. "Most dangerous person in Texas, pfft," Osprey heard him say under his breath.

"Hey, is this a photo of Brownsville?"

"Yes," Osprey said.

"Before your time?"

"Grandparents lived there. That's them on the sea wall."

"You're a good old Texas boy."

"Close enough," Osprey admitted. He returned, holding his mug. Burden was still putting on a show of grinning like a warm friend, but after being made to wait too long through the charade of the coffee, the grin had transformed into a painful grimace. He clapped his hands together.

"So, how do we make this happen?"

Thinking, I can't wash my hands of this, Osprey did exactly that. He called Waterling in to start the shit rolling. Waterling left without a question. Osprey sat at his desk filled with a combination of foreboding and disgust that was the worst feeling in the world.

Piper was standing beneath an enormous turbine rotor when they came for her. The thing was a true immovable object. 200 tons anyway. Her thin frame before its exaggerated blades made her look like a weed in the path of a push mower. So much larger than life, it looked like it would plow all of Texas, it looked like a deadly thing, not larger than life so much as against life, counter to living things, and she wanted to get it working again, back in its spot in the power plant, making electricity again. That's what people did: wanted things; repeated mistakes; lost a feel for history that didn't scar them personally. We do not learn our lessons.

She calculated she could get the plant running again with about four years of full-time labor, but there was no way she could move the 200-ton rotor. No way. How or why it got moved 1,500 meters from the plant... she really had no idea. It was weird. She dreamed of air conditioning. She was determined.

It was a hot day in Abilene. She saw the dust in the distance before the two vehicles came into sight. She'd stuck to a low profile, but there was no hiding completely. The spies and snitches knew who she was and where she was living. They knew she'd been tinkering around the old electricity plant. She watched the dust rising on the horizon. The wind gusted. A row of wind turbines could go out there in that flat, she mused. Why not? Power the whole fucking town, neighborhood by neighborhood.

It was Marines, of course, but some of the sloppy, fat ones who worked for the warden not Messmaker's killing squads. They knew they'd found her, knew it was her, but they scanned her fingerprints anyway. There were eight of them, four per vehicle, and they were more nervous than she was. My reputation precedes me, she was secretly proud to know.

"We need you to come to see the warden."

She saw that one of the Marines wore the arm patch for the bomb plant. Those fuckers' skulls glowed in the dark, she'd heard people claim. The unholy radiation in the plant was slowly turning their bodies to silvery glass. The rumors were comical but disturbing.

"What's the warden want?"

"He didn't say. Just that you come with us."

Piper was tense about the possibility of one of these men touching her, and the radiation thing just added a layer of revulsion to her feeling.

"You gonna cuff me?"

"Should we think that's necessary?"

"I would prefer no cuffs if it's all the same to you all. And, no, they're not necessary. I'm cool."

So, she rode in the back seat of one of the Jeeps with no cuffs on her wrists, but there was a Marine on either side of her, and their thick thighs pressed her in. She tried to wiggle and make herself small, but it was no use, and, preferring no thick thigh vis the other, she just suffered. She looked out at the flat land.

"Fucking wasteland out there, huh," she said.

The driver looked at her in the rearview mirror. He bit.

"Compared to what?"

"Oh, I don't know," she said. "Colorado?"

"Funny you should say that," the driver said. "Pretty fucking funny."

The Marine riding shotgun elbowed the driver.

"What's that mean?" she asked, but nobody said anything.

Their destination was, indeed, the warden's office, but it wasn't Warden Osprey sitting at the warden desk when they arrived. It was a big bag of muscles with a huge sidearm holstered on his hip. He grinned at Piper so unnaturally that her reaction was a nasty introduction.

"Who the fuck are you?"

"Bruce Burden," he said, standing up.

"You the new warden?"

"I'm not."

"They told me I was coming to see the warden."

"Lucky you that you're not. You're in for much more fun."

HARM, was all she thought. Then another four-letter word. She said nothing, and Burden sensed her fear. He tried to look less predatory.

"Leo Einhorn would like to see you," he said.

"Why?"

"Some of your expertise."

"Horse shit."

"I'm just an errand boy."

"But what does he want? What if I say no?"

"Uh... you can't."

The room closed in on her. The fat thugs who'd been arranged around the room now seemed right on top of her. She got angry. She felt her nostrils flare.

"I was sentenced to Texas. The judge didn't order torture or sex slavery or whatever you creeps have in mind for me."

"It's admirable that you of all people have such a high opinion of how the system of Tristean government works. You can't imagine that matters here or that anything other than the boss' prerogative matters here."

That shut her up. She looked around the room.

"Can we eat lunch before we get on the road?" a pudgy redhead asked Burden. "I'm starving."

Piper saw them all individually for the first time. The redhead. A couple of dark-haired guys who said they were twins and descended from people who'd escaped the destruction of Mexico. An older man with gray hair falling out in clumps all over his head. The heavy-gutted one with the bomb plant patch.

"Eat whatever you want," Burden said. "You're not coming with me."

Piper stared at him.

Some of the Serratura prisoners were released to outdoor exercise. Excited, loud voices came through the walls. It sounded like dozens or hundreds of people. Conceivably it was every prisoner in this place or maybe Osprey was in some dark basement this very moment whipping somebody or burning them or pulling out their fingernails. Piper could imagine a lot, and she wanted no part of Leo Einhorn and his desires. She was jealous of the heavy, steel file cabinet across the room. It didn't have to go to Colorado.

She sat in the shotgun seat of the black SUV, as Burden drove. Her fingers were steepled on her lap, locked in strange cuffs that Burden had brought along just for her, kinda like Chinese finger traps, but no amount of relaxing was going to get her free. She was really fucking pissed off. They rode in silence until Burden's satellite phone rang.

"I'm on an errand," he said. "I'll be back in a few hours."

He terminated the call.

"The wife," Piper said sarcastically.

"No."

"Husband?"

"Stop it."

By personal powers of restraint (or owing to his own nature she didn't know), he was not rubbing it in about the situation she was in. She knew the score, and she knew he knew she knew the score. This pissed her off even more. Her rage was boiling. She wanted to kick him in the balls.

They were following the route her two fellow prisoners, Colonel Endling and Tubby Lascaux, had taken on bike, northwest across Texas. She didn't know this, of course, but it was the only road the Marine Corps had restored to working order. They passed through a string of settlements and towns that human life had fled and not come back to. The wind threw gravel at the windshield of the SUV as if politely suggesting they turn back. There were different classes of desert, she began to see, different classes of desert within the one, single, all-encompassing desert, there were half-deserts where trees still lived, quasi deserts of man-made blacktop the sand covered and uncovered by mad whims, and real desert, this latter completely hostile and depressing, even the SUV's tires seeming to groan passing through it. There was occasional roadkill, armadillos usually, but she strained her neck to look when they passed a large, dead wolf on the edge of the road.

North of Amarillo, Burden took the vehicle off the highway, crossed the parallel lines of rail tracks and drove onto a flat land that slowly tilted down like a drained quarry. He parked in the middle of what used to be Rita Blanca Lake. He got out, and Piper watched him wave at military drones flying over. He got back in. He chewed a fingernail and spat it out.

"So, you're just an errand boy," she said. "The royal family has lots of those."

"Tons."

"How?"

"How what?"

"How can one family have all the power?"

"You're really asking?" Burden turned to look at her.

"Yes."

He sighed.

"There's an agreement for co-prosperity at the top."

"What the fuck does that mean?"

"The Chairman owns Messmaker. Hear that word choice? It's deliberate. He owns him."

"Money?"

"Lots of money."

"Of course."

"The Marines are loyal to that old bird. That dynamic, I don't get. But it's real."

"Yeah."

"So, one just follows the other. Like cold logic."

A voice streamed through static on Burden's satellite phone, and five minutes later, the voice streamed through clearly. "We're coming in." And with the voice came a black hyperotor out of the sky. It landed close to Burden's SUV, and as the sleds touched down, Piper began to hold her breath.

Chapter Six

The museum's wide staircase was a double helix, allowing visitors to descend from the top without ever meeting people ascending from the bottom. The youths from Serge's sophomore class all stopped at the magical spot everyone stopped at, peered over the railing, and looked down into the dim spiral. It went many stories down, like a deep-set eye of stone, and the railings, gilded by sunshine from the glass dome above, were like stripes of some energy burning through from another world.

Serge looked forward to this Earth exhibit ever since the first day of school when he saw it on the calendar. His teacher, Mr. Coldspell, was the chaperone, and he knew a lot about Earth, but he was silent as the docent talked her way down the spiral. The idea was to get to the bottom and visit each hall on the way back up. Serge looked over the railing again and saw a waterfall and a pool of water casting reflected light all over the place in the center of the spiral, way down on the bottom floor.

He felt almost no connection to Earth or its epochs on display here. He had some sense of its history but not with any feeling, even though he was born there. His foster parents wouldn't take him to the Earth exhibit for some reason he knew they were not coming clean about. So, today he was thrilled. They reached the bottom. The waterfall he'd seen spilled into a pond filled with goldfish that darted around like orange bullets and seemed frightened by any movement near their pool.

The docent explained that the bottom floor's exhibit hall was not yet open. The unlit marquee above its entrance said THE HALL OF TIME. There was a velvet rope across the entrance from which hung a sign that said, "Coming Soon (or previously)." A time travel joke, the docent said, and she got a couple of laughs.

"Are these Earth fish?" a girl asked.

"Why, yes!" the docent said. "You're so smart."

She was a pretty, young woman with nearly-white blond hair. There was something repellent about her persona, but Serge couldn't place his finger on what it was. All the docents were beauties; it must've been a prerequisite for hiring. The group followed her up one turn of the stairs to the second level. The young patrons heard a loud digital animal sound, and, as a group, they sprinted into the Hall of Dinosaurs.

"Do I have to stay with the group?" Serge asked.

"Yes, let's all stick together," Mr. Coldspell replied.

He reluctantly followed. He wanted to visit the Hall of Space Flight, and that was only one level above.

"The dinosaur bones here collected are not bones," the docent narrated. "These are fossils, body fossils actually. These are copies of the original bones made of rock, made by Mother Nature over the course of millions of years."

Behind glass, along one wall, there was an exhibit of a red pit with bones at the bottom. "Are those real?" a kid asked.

"Oh, yes," the docent said. "Brought here from Earth."

The bones told the shape of the creature. It looked as if a sandwich press had flattened it into the red sediment. The white face was horse-like, and the neck was bent into the shape of a question mark.

"Are there many dinosaurs in America?" a kid asked.

"They're extinct," Serge said. The docent looked at him.

"What's extinct?"

"All dead," Serge said.

"That's correct," the docent said, but her look did not approve of Serge's cavalier facts. Her smile curdled. Serge drifted away, and, while the group continued to listen to the presentation, he looked at the skeletons of a Tyrannosaurus and a Triceratops arranged side by side. The teeth on the Tyrannosaurus were incredible. Serge couldn't believe it. Nearby was a mural of these two beasts locked in mortal combat. The Tyrannosaurus chewed a foreleg of the Triceratops, but the belly of the big carnivore had bloody cuts from the horns of its foe. They were grim, red wounds. The T. rex was a dead man. Serge would've said impossible. He looked at it for a long time, lost in his thoughts.

"Time to move," Mr. Coldspell said, breaking the trance.

Serge caught up with the crowd at the entrance to the Hall of Space Flight. Before they were even in the room, the chromeshine of Souci's silver sprinter caught every eye. The ship was suspended by wires from the ceiling. Space travel was an everyday reality, at least as spectacle, for the people of Radium Beach, but this sprinter was something special, an artifact from the world's deep cabinet of curious lore.

"Commander Souci was the last person to launch into space from Kourou, where there was a European Space Agency spaceport. The port was closed after his launch, and French Guiana was completely depopulated only a few months later," the docent explained. Serge tuned her out until he heard: Guiana. His birthplace. Where he'd come from.

Bravery was a thing Serge brooded over all the time. He doubted his own. Not so much a physical question, he thought, but a moral one. Sure, he'd fly into deep space if someone taught him how. Or that jungle in the pictures of French Guiana (the palm trees looked strangely like Triste's own beach zone), he'd hack through there. It was other dangers he feared. Moments of weak heart, embarrassment, failure. Bad faith. Betrayal. He followed the crowd as it slowly moved up to the next level.

This hall was filled with old, paper books. The 4th Great Awakening, the exhibit was called, and that was a thing Serge had never heard of before. The books were mostly Bibles, some you could touch, some under the protection of glass cases. Deeper into the room, there was a wooden boat, but the room was narrow, and the crowd was pressing, so he'd have to wait to check it out. Near the center of the room, there was a big, black book on a marble pedestal, and a Chinese-looking man about 25-years-old was flipping through its pages. Serge stopped and looked over the man's shoulder.

He turned and looked at Serge.

"Oh, sorry, sir," Serge said.

"I don't mind," the man said. "You can look, too."

It was no Bible there on the pedestal. It was a book of names of people baptized during the ocean pestilence when Death, so long a regulator, descended to assert full dominion over the Earth of men. There were thousands and thousands of pages.

"Are you looking for somebody's name?" Serge asked.

"Well, sort of," the man replied. "I guess it would be a wild stroke of luck to find my family. Look how many pages there are and such tiny print."

"Sure is."

"Not to mention all these other fine people hoping to get a chance to look. I'm going to move along here. I'm Yoshi. What's your name?"

"Serge."

"Nice to meet you."

They both moved along like leaves fallen into a slow stream, as the crowd inched towards the wooden boat. They got closer and closer. Serge could hear the docent speaking.

"We now believe the pestilence came to the USA from Africa on this very boat. Our best forensic anthropologists agree."

This was a lie. Serge looked at Mr. Coldspell who also seemed puzzled. Some of the kids took a step back from the boat as if it were some boiling cauldron of infection. Yoshi had a smirk on his face. What's so funny, Serge thought. It wasn't funny. He was angry.

"This is probably another history you can enlighten for us," the docent said, nodding at Serge. Many faces turned to him. Oh, he thought. I'm black. I'm of African descent. I see. What the fuck? Mr. Coldspell intervened.

"This is false," he said. "How are you getting this wrong?"

The docent turned red.

"What's so fucking funny," Serge asked, as Yoshi led him away by the arm. "Hey, man, I'm really fucking mad. What's going on here?"

They threaded the throng of patrons. Serge followed closely behind Yoshi. The stranger seemed to have a sixth sense about where holes in the gridlock would open. They pushed through an unmarked door and found themselves in the Butterfly Room.

"I had to get your attention," Yoshi said. "I got that girl to say that. She believed it. I had to convince you I could do something like that, so I can explain how and show you how."

"What the fuck are you talking about?"

"It's very important."

Gibberish, Serge thought, throwing up his hands. But he liked Yoshi. He was going to listen, and five butterflies landed on this new acquaintance, and everything was dreamy and bright and extraordinary.

Chapter Seven

Tubby Lascaux searched for his friend for three days. On Day 1, he had lots of help. On Day 2, less help. On Day 3, no help. This was the fourth morning. When he asked for help again, he met dried out, hungover, red-eyes faces telling him no. No more. Not today. He understood. He wasn't hopeful himself. Not anymore. The people saying no considered his own mud-colored eyes and saw begging and disappointment. But they also saw a forgiving understanding.

The smoldering wreck of the roller coaster was a clue, but it led to nothing. Tubby walked around it and looked at it from several angles. They'd all smelled the smoke in the night and seen the firelight warming the bellies of some drifting night clouds. The travelers didn't panic. The lanterns and reckless burning of abandoned things was a ritual with them, but Colonel Endling wandering away from the party and not returning spooked them. They did not find a body.

Tubby considered three possible explanations.

(1) Some animal dragged off the body. A wolf. Possible.

(2) The desert stalker caught up with the Colonel in the dark and led him off somewhere. If it was, as they suspected, the Brain, that could be even worse than 1.

(3) Colonel Endling took off for reasons of his own and would not be back until he was ready.

Tubby ruled out the last option. He knew in his heart that Colonel Endling would tell him at least if he had something to do in private. They had a plan, and solo side missions had no part in the plan. Junior Soucy got him a new mountain bike. He rode it, searching, in widening gyres with the wedding tent as a center point, concentric circular motions that, aloft, a falcon might use to hunt. This was Day 4, and the day was closing in on what he'd told himself was quitting time, when a black vehicle blasted through Amarillo at over 100 MPH. It was going north. The windows were tinted black, so he couldn't see who was driving it, but the vehicle was in such a hurry that Tubby decided he would head north, too.

Chapter Eight

EXT. — BEACH — DAY

CAMERA looks down the length of a beach. Two figures walk side by side in the distance. The sand is white as paper. The sea and sky are the flawless blues of gemstones. CAMERA pans right to a seawall above the beach. Built into the stone is a fence topped by triple spirals of razor wire. CAMERA takes a new, wider angle of the beach to reveal that the two walkers are the only people on the beach.

CAMERA moves in close on both walkers. They are a man and woman, both public figures, ROUX, the red-headed QUEEN and GENERAL MESSMAKER, the chief of the Marines. The GENERAL is sweating in the 100-degree heat, but he's not nervous. In fact, in this moment, he gives the impression of never having been nervous about a thing in his life. Now and again, the QUEEN looks out to sea and raises a hand to shield her eyes from the Fast Sun.

CAMERA takes a sudden, wicked turn to check out what the QUEEN might be looking at. It zooms through the bright air until it is following behind seven black rotors flying in attack formation.

CUT TO:

SAME BEACH — SAME DAY BUT LATER

QUEEN and MESSMAKER are seated in wooden chairs on the sand. CAMERA holds as they talk.

QUEEN: It's happening, then?

MESSMAKER: Yes, Queen.

QUEEN: And the other matter, too?

MESSMAKER: Yes.

QUEEN: What's the probability of success?

CLOSE-UP of MESSMAKER scratching his face.

MESSMAKER: I'd say extremely high for the former and most certain for the latter.

CLOSE-UP of the QUEEN nodding.

QUEEN: These are radical changes.

MESSMAKER: Now is the time. Now is the very time to move on them. They've miscalculated their strength. Wildly so.

CLOSE-UP: QUEEN leans back and closes her eyes.

MESSMAKER: Are you feeling well?

QUEEN: Yes, fine. Just thinking of today's ceremony.

CAMERA pans to the sea. There are no rotors now just sun glitter on the water, a few white clouds in the blue sky.

CUT TO:

INT. — A LARGE, ELEGANT BALLROOM — EVENING

CAMERA moves with QUEEN as she walks around a stage. She has a tiny, silver microphone attached to her black dress. She reads from a scroll of paper. Behind her, on the stage, is a screen fifty feet wide. The changing colors of the screen cause the diamonds in the QUEEN'S crown to change with them.

QUEEN: I have a list of my new favorite things.

REVERSE SHOT to the crowd in the room, smiling faces of people at tables, all dressed in the finest Tristean evening wear. They all have looks of anticipation. The CHAIRMAN is at the table closest to the stage. He looks smugly happy.

CLOSE-UP and hold on QUEEN'S face.

QUEEN: We will return to the common use of the people in this room all our cities, our parks, our great beach. These are common goods spoiled.

REVERSE CAMERA SHOT to crowd again. A few people clap, but mostly the anticipation remains, the faces in a suspended state of waiting on good news.

CUT TO:

QUEEN walking the stage. She looks at her scroll.

QUEEN: So, here we go.

CAMERA walks with her on the stage.

QUEEN: The Workers' Party of Redemption Rock [pause for effect] all dead.

A gasp from someone off-camera.

QUEEN: Serge Ville de Paix, dead, hanged.

The chapters of the Guild in Radium Beach, Redemption Rock and Dreaming Back Lake, all dead. Masterson of the University of Triste, dead, hanged. Colonel Endling, Piper Sestina, and Leonid Lascaux of the assassination plot, as you all know, banished to Earth during my husband's period of weakness and abundant mercy. They will die, I promise.

CUT TO:

CLOSE-UP of HUMBLE JACK's face. He shakes his head. CAMERA slowly pulls back to reveal JACK is holding his hands up in surrender.

QUEEN: We've taken back our capital. The beach will re-open with the New Year. Fishing industries will resume. The settlements in Daphne will resume. And, now, I must explain the screen behind me. I'm sure you've all guessed by now.

CUT TO:

EXT. — DARKNESS — THAT MOMENT — DAPHNE

The sound of armored vehicles in the darkness. Suddenly, brilliant tracer fire from a heavy machine gun lights the scene. The gun is mounted atop a sand-colored AFV. The gun targets tall stone statues, behind which someone attempts return fire. Chips of stone fall, as the statues take a beating.

CUT TO:

INT. — A ROOM IN THE COLORADO BUNKER — DAY

This is the CHAIRMAN'S dream. He is playing chess with his brother, LEO. He maneuvers LEO into check, and LEO rages and sweeps the pieces violently off the board. They clatter around the room.

CUT TO:

INT. — DIM BEDROOM — NIGHT

CLOSE-UP on CHAIRMAN startling awake. The QUEEN'S red head on the pillow beside him. She wakes, and her hand touches the CHAIRMAN'S shoulder.

CUT TO:

INT. — THE BALLROOM AGAIN — AFTER THE QUEEN'S SPEECH

CAMERA follows QUEEN as she moves about the room. The CHAIRMAN follows behind with a bottle of champagne by the neck in his one hand. QUEEN walks slow to allow CHAIRMAN to keep up. They are refilling the glasses of their guests.

CAMERA follows QUEEN as she turns and, over her shoulder, sees what she sees, the screen behind the stage. It displays an oily liquid green with smooth golden ripples in it as if someone had tossed a golden coin into it.

CUT TO:

EXT. — DAPHNE — NIGHT —THE STATUES WE SAW EARLIER

Marines are dragging bodies from behind the statues a long way across rough, rocky, desert ground to a pit dug about ten feet deep and fifty feet wide. The bodies are tossed in, and when they've all been tossed in, more than two dozen, the pit is filled back in with the gravel that came out of it.

CUT TO:

INT. — BALLROOM AGAIN — STILL LATER

TWO SHOT. QUEEN in foreground, CHAIRMAN in background with MESSMAKER whispering in his ear. Since the days of her surgery, the QUEEN has been paranoid about the CHAIRMAN's intentions. She wants control of MESSMAKER, but she feels pressing for that control to be a delicate thing.

QUEEN fills the champagne glass of a young man in glasses (30ish) who bows and moves off.

Return to TWO SHOT with CHAIRMAN in background. MESSMAKER now talking to someone on his mobile, as the CHAIRMAN looks on. CAMERA follows QUEEN, as she moves across the space to them.

QUEEN: What's with the grim faces?

QUEEN jerks her thumb at MESSMAKER.

CHAIR: We lost 2 Marines in Daphne.

QUEEN: Two.

CHAIR: That's what I just said.

QUEEN: How many on the other side?

KING: Three hundred.

QUEEN: Well, that's wild success then.

CHAIR: There's more of them than we thought. The company was ambushed.

QUEEN: If we keep these ratios, I think we'll be okay, Jack.

CHAIR: No.

QUEEN: No?

CHAIR: If we keep these ratios, we three standing here will be the only people left.

Chapter Nine

"Maidens call it love-in-idleness."

She looked up from the white vase. Had the phrase touched her? It had reached her. Surely, it did that. She had her wild, dark curls pulled back tightly in a ponytail. The florist had his own long, blond hair tied back the same way. She noticed it. Very unusual for a male on Triste. He smiled at her. She looked back to the white and violet flowers.

"You like those?" he asked.

She hummed a response that did not commit.

"Excuse me one moment," he said and disappeared into a back room. As she browsed, the florist began to sign. And the green grass grows all around, all around, and the green grass grows all around. And the green grass grows all around, all around... His voice trailed off.

Rayuela moved about the shop. Other options did not interest her today. Roses, no. Lilies, no. Tulips, never. She returned to the pansies, white and cupid-shot with purple.

Love and idleness had no relation, she thought. The word love made her think of a holdfast or root system stronger than the spinning of the mad world.

The florist returned.

"It's funny," he said. "Humble Jack's Misery Index in my back office has gone dark."

Ray looked at her mobile.

"Here, too," she said.

"That never happens."

"Maybe he's dead," Ray said. She pocketed the mobile.

"I hope you'll pardon my intrusion," the florist said. "But a trick of my trade is to ask if you're buying flowers for an occasion?"

"Oh," she said. "Well... for a grave."

"I'm so sorry."

"Can I have three dozen of these?"

"Yes, of course. Straight away."

He began to work. She watched his deft hands, so gently swift and precise. He quickly had the flowers wrapped, and she was on the brick sidewalk again, heading for home. It was never supposed to leak. The location of Serge's grave was to remain a state secret. For obvious reasons, the authorities wanted all memory of Serge to be erased. But the secret did leak. Ray had no desire to create a shrine or continue the revolt, but she needed to visit him.

She walked to the safe house, and she set the flowers in jars of water by the partially-boarded up window where a little bit of sun came in.

She'd wait until dark but not so patiently. No, not idly. She descended to the basement where donations of food needed some sorting. One of the neighborhood's stray cats had squeezed its way through a flimsy window screen and into the basement. She found it by the wall below that window, trying to think itself a way back out. It was small, gray, scrawny. Torn between fear and wanting Ray's affection, it arched its back and danced a funny, tiptoe dance, as she reached for it. She opened a silver can of tuna fish and fed it, and it purred in her lap as she stroked its neck for a long time. At second dusk, she lifted the cat and pushed it through the window screen, and it ran off.

She waited until full dark. Arms full of pansies, she walked quickly to the site. She feared being followed, so her ears were alert for any sound. The urban center was far behind her. The neighborhoods gave way to forest, and the darkness engulfed her by the time she slowed her pace.

She had rehearsed this visit during daylight. From the road, the graves looked like green heavings of something the organics-rich soil was trying to expel from itself. The oldest graves were greenest. The newest (Serge's among them) were brown and looked like the work of heavy frost though Triste had not had frost in Ray's lifetime. If you didn't know these were graves, you might not be able to tell, but, once you knew, it was obvious. Twelve rows of twelve dead. One hundred forty-four. She'd known that multiplication table since kindergarten. Twelve by twelve. There were rows between, horizontal and vertical from her POV, approaching. She walked with care along these lines. She did not know which grave held her beloved, only that it was new. So, she walked the youngest rows and dropped a flower on each. There and there and there and there. She began to cry, but she kept on with it. A flower there and there and there and there. It was the purest cry of her life, uncontaminated by shame. Where was Serge now? Where his soul? His sweetness? His stubbornness? His overconfidence? His recklessness? His good energy? His overflowing love?

Chapter Ten

The Time Man wasn't surprised to see his door come flying open. He'd left it unlocked. But Yoshi was surprised to see him. Oh, sorry, sir, he said. I'm sorry. The alarm kept shrieking. Security guards ran up and down the white stone floors. The alarm drove Yoshi's thoughts to the window. It was still open. He looked at the Time Man who was calm and smiling at him.

"You're right on time."

"What?" Yoshi asked.

"You're right on time."

Yoshi squinted at the man. His skeptical face.

"Oh, I know that look. Relax," the man said. "Don't worry about the alarm. Reach over and lock that door. You're safe."

Yoshi locked the door. He looked more closely at the stranger. He was young (younger than 30 anyhow), and he was Japanese. When the man put his hands in the back pockets of his pants and rocked on his heels in a familiar way, Yoshi began to have an oceanic feeling inside.

"We have something pretty important to talk about."

"What is it?" Yoshi asked.

"Please sit down."

Yoshi sat on the small bed, and the man stayed where he was, rocking on his heels.

"I'm not a fan of suspense or witty banter, so I'll come right out with it. I'm you."

"You're me?"

"Yes, and you're me."

"What do you mean?"

"Exactly what you're feeling I mean."

Yoshi sighed. The sea swells calmed some.

"Why did you come to the Saint Eligius Hotel today?" the Time Man asked. Yoshi hesitated for a moment. To steal, he thought. He was afraid to say it.

"Maggie sent you on an errand," the man said.

"Yes."

"What for?"

"A quantum clock."

"Yes," the man said. "Good. And what did you find downstairs?"

"Well, something. I'm not sure."

"Really not sure, or you don't want to say?"

"A tunnel," Yoshi said.

"And that was familiar, right?"

"Yes."

"Why?"

"I've been through one like it."

"And has Maggie told you what it is?"

"Uh... kinda."

"But not in a satisfying way?'

"Right. She never answers my questions. I ask questions and get silence."

"Where did you come from via the tunnel?"

Yoshi considered this question for a while. He saw birds flying outside the window, rock pigeons that flew from the hotel's roof to some tall trees nearby. They flew back to the roof and then to the trees again. The screaming alarm was startling them to impatience.

"Not where," Yoshi said.

"No?"

"Not where simply. More like where and when."

"Very good. When?"

"About 30 years forward in time."

"Yes. Very good. Do you know what this is?"

The man pointed to the map on his wall.

"That's your territory. You're a True Time Man, spreading the adoption of the True Time. I know another one like you. Erdapfel. He has a map like that."

"Ah, well, I've fooled you just like the rest of them," the man said. "It does look like that type of map, and I have phony records to back this up if anyone ever checks. But watch this."

He detached the map from the wall and turned it around. The paper was extremely thin. When he hung it back up, reversed so the back side now faced out, there showed a faint, ghostly outline of the city and red from the flags on the front side came through like a trace of energy almost.

"These red zones are places I have strong reason to believe there are more go-betweens."

"Go-betweens?" Yoshi asked.

"Like below this hotel. There's a window beneath that pool, a spacetime window. Like a wormhole. You know what that is?"

"Yeah, Maggie taught me about wormholes."

"You and me, and Toad and Beetle and Flat Tire, we passed through a go-between."

"I still haven't recovered from that," Yoshi said. "My mind, I mean. You do look exactly like me."

The grown-up Yoshi laughed.

"I'm here to recruit you for a dangerous job, as I was recruited to the same dangerous job, sitting on that same bed, wearing that same t-shirt, those same shoes, filled by the same doubt."

"You were?"

"Yes, by another one of us. I was your age. He was mine. I was you. He was me. We are all us."

Now Yoshi laughed. The sea swells came back. He was probably too young to have any complex, rational thoughts about fate, but he felt something. The cycle that grown-up Yoshi had only hinted at, young Yoshi could think out through many iterations, and the momentum of that was like one of the big turbines that made electricity in Radium Beach. When those things got going, a single human hand could not reach out and stop them. That grabbing would pull you right into the rotation. But here he was feeling he'd already reached out and would always reach out.

"My map is pretty crude, as you can see."

"Sort of."

Grown-up Yoshi laughed. "You agree?"

Yoshi tried to be diplomatic. He said, "Well, I don't see that work getting you a job at the Mission."

"Exactly!"

The alarm finally cut out, and the hotel became quiet and still. The pigeons returned to the roof. The grown-up Yoshi filled two glasses with water from a pitcher and they both drank.

"I'm glad you mentioned the Mission. Gun Club has his own map, and it's very sophisticated. The scouts and engineers at the Mission built it for him. What it is, really, is a spacetime diagram. If you could just see the whole structure of time as I have you'd understand it. You'd have the perspective. The diagram projects where-when spacetime points. It's probabilistic."

"Where-when?"

"Just like it sounds and just like we discussed already. Where and when in spacetime. Where and when the go-betweens will open and the likelihood of where and when they open unto."

On grown-up Yoshi's desk was a To Do list with items crossed off, already done and past. The next item not yet crossed out said, "Conversation."

It would be struck out soon. Conversation. They were having it. Yoshi didn't fully understand, but he was ready to ask the question on the tip of his tongue.

"What do you need me to do?"

"You must meet follow the original Gun Club through the passage of one of the go-betweens. Call him Gun Club A. Meet him and force him to do a thing he won't want to do."

"That sounds impossible."

"No."

"Well, it does."

"It's not impossible."

"How do you know?"

"I've done it," the grown Yoshi said. "You must do it, and you will."

"What is the thing he won't want to do?"

"Give his map to you."

"Does he carry it around with him?" Yoshi asked. That sounded like a dumb thing to do if the Chairman did that.

"Yes and no."

"What do you mean?"

"Well," he began. "It's inserted under his skin somewhere. It's not a paper map like mine. We have limited intelligence about your worldline, but I suspect it's ported behind his ear."

Yoshi unconsciously grabbed the back of his own neck. He hated thinking of implants possibly going under his own skin. He'd been an orphan raised in a class where it wasn't a worry or even a remote possibility, but it gave him an awful chill.

"What makes you think he'll give me the map?"

"I'll tell you exactly what to say."

"How will I get it out?"

"Surgery."

"Oh my god."

"It's dangerous, Yoshi. He travels with guards. Come on, though, tell me you'll do it. I know you will. I know you will."

Yoshi looked at the window yet again. He could still spring away. He knew he could. That possibility waited there, and it was wide open. But he looked back to the other's eyes.

Chapter Eleven

That was a rare sight. Soldiers in the Canal District. Mr. Trafalgar walked out of his shop-—Wigs by Trafalgar—-slowly, he did everything slowly—-sometimes you'd have to visually line him up with a tree or other stationary object to be sure he was moving-— well, that was his ex-wife's complaint anyhow. He walked out of his shop and peered over the green hedge railing to the bottom level of the shopping complex. That was two levels down from his shop. The canal ran between, around, and under the retail buildings. On one of its grassy banks, two Royal Frogmen in black diving gear sat talking with about a dozen Marines in desert-colored kits.

It looked likely to Mr. Trafalgar that the Frogmen were getting ready to jump into the canal. Shoppers on the opposite bank, coming out of candy shops and watchmakers and shoe stores, had stopped to gawk at them. Some Canal District security guards, too, stood on the opposite bank, watching.

"What kind of gun is that?" one of the dry land Marines asked one of the Frogmen.

"It's an Einhorn Amphibious Rifle."

"What kind of ammo does it fire? Bolts?"

"Five and a half by 40-millimeter rounds."

"Get out. Under the water?"

"Yeah."

"Is it new?"

"No, we've had these for a while."

"I want to see this. Show us in the water."

The Frogman laughed.

"You want me to shoot up the stocked goldfish or what?"

Mr. Trafalgar found this talk disturbing. It was loud, too. The brutes weren't even trying to hide their dangerousness. Oh, he didn't like this at all. He walked back to his shop. No customers. He came back out. There was an owl perched on the hedge railing. What a day of strange sights. Birds came and went every day, but an owl? Mr. Trafalgar reached up and felt his own wig. Fine. Nothing to adjust. Just a nervous habit. He did that hundreds of times a day.

The owl seemed to be watching the soldiers. It was a majestic creature. Brown feathers and the white mask of a face that looked like something God didn't finish.

One of the Frogmen jumped into the canal. The water came up to his waist, and it moved swiftly. He stood still easily, but walking against the current would be easier said than done.

The gun was long and black.

"Somebody toss something in that will float."

The soldiers all looked around, and, ultimately, a hulking blond Marine heaved a trash barrel down the grassy bank into the water. The Frogman grabbed it and let it fill with water until it was bobbing and sort of sinking and slowly drifting away from him. Mr. Trafalgar looked to the Canal District security guard, and saw the man walking away, shaking his head. Not good., Mr. Trafalgar thought. Not good. He considered phoning the police.

The owl was gone. He hadn't noticed it take off, nor did he see the young Japanese man sneak up to take its place at the hedge railing. He looked down.

The Frogman held his gun under the water and opened fire on the trash barrel, which had drifted to maybe 50 feet away from him. The barrel bucked and sprayed water out of its new holes. The firing produced bubbles of smoke from the gun's nose, visible just below the surface of the clear water. And the thumping of the bullets on the body of the trash can was dull but deep.

"That gun is a motherfucker," the big blond soldier said.

There was grumbling from the crowd that had been watching all of this from the far bank of the canal. Some had backed away, but other shoppers with bags of boutique purchases had come over to see what was happening, so the crowd had grown. Nobody was prepared exactly when the Frogman launched a grenade from his gun—again, under the water, so who could have seen that coming? — and the barrel exploded. There was nothing dull about that. It was LOUD. Mr. Trafalgar wanted to run back into his shop. He watched the young Japanese man—he was a teenager, a boy, really—beside him. The boy was stoic. He didn't flinch from his spot. At each of the five levels of the hedge railings above the far bank of the canal, faces appeared. Many people spoke on mobiles. Someone had called the police. The officers showed up in pairs. Two first. Then four. Within five minutes, there were more police than soldiers on the scene. There was ugly potential in the air.

"What are you doing down there, buddy?" an officer asked the Frogman.

"Scram," was all the Frogman said.

"Oh, yeah?" the policeman said. "Fuck you. Come out of the water."

"I said, 'Scram.'"

"Do you have a permit to demonstrate that weapon here?"

"Are you deaf?"

"Answer me."

"I don't need a permit, you bitch."

"I'm going to arrest you."

The dozen soldiers on the near side of the canal stepped to the edge of the grassy bank and pointed their guns. The competent choreography of their synced movements was awesome and terrifying. The police all backed away from their side of the canal, hands up and now bargaining in a babel of voices. The second Frogman—-who was not in the water-—started laughing.

Mr. Trafalgar felt his own armpits. They were soaking wet. Just then, 20 more soldiers arrived on the march. They moved in a formation that encircled another diver in a wet suit and mask who hobbled along with them, barefooted. The new diver was a near-cripple. When the police saw this new platoon of soldiers, they made a swift exit from the area.

"That's Humble Jack Einhorn," the Japanese boy said.

"No," Mr. Trafalgar replied.

"It's him."

Mr. Trafalgar tried to get a better look, but the diver was shielded by his guards. The Marines continued their cordon of his person right to the edge of the canal. There, the Frogman on land helped lower him into the water. Then, the Frogman jumped in himself and put on his own mask. Mr. Trafalgar looked around. What was happening? So strange.

"That motherfucker grenade-bombed a trash barrel right here in the mall, and the police didn't do shit," the big blond Marine laughingly told one of the newcomers.

"That true, Dernier?"

The Frogman who'd demonstrated his Amphibious Rifle raised and waved a hand as if to dismiss the hilarious accusation. He was busy with other things. He checked the new diver's air supply and mask, and, satisfied, he bent down so the half-crippled man could hook his arm through the Frogman's arm like an old grandmother about to be ushered down the aisle to her seat at a wedding. Then, the two Frogmen leaned forward awkwardly, belly first, into the water, and, when they kicked up their feet behind them, it appeared they had on jet boots, and these propelled them forward against the current of the canal. They quickly vanished from sight.

Mr. Trafalgar walked back to his shop. He found a customer there, bald, a good prospect. As he strode forth to introduce himself, he noted that Humble Jack's Misery Index on the wall behind his display counter changed from cool blue to a sparkling silver. He turned back to look in the direction of the canal, and, just as he did so, the Japanese boy dove from the railing.

Chapter Twelve

The mosaic took up the entire floor of the Rec Room. If there were ten hands involved in making it, there were twenty. If there were twenty hands, there were forty. The colors were cool in the fast sun, warmer in the slow sun. Sleeper would get up while all the broken soldiers slept or tossed around in their beds. He liked to walk the perimeter of the mosaic, checking on the previous day's progress, seeing new parts, and looking for sections still incomplete.

Bergen the therapist was a clever one. She charged her patients a price in virtuous deeds to get the tiles they desired for the project. Pork Chop was a cynic. He thought the whole thing was stupid, and he said so. Shorty scolded him.

Sleeper wanted people like Shorty to be the future leaders of humanity. I used to be just like Pork Chop, Shorty told him. Then, I lost my legs, and I had to survive. One day at a time. It was hard, brother. Real hard. But, I'm alive, and, well, I just wanna help people be alive and well, too.

Our lives have incidents, and our stories seem to have arcs we can understand, but they also have a core, and Shorty's core was pure good. Not that he didn't still have that nasty streak about the Chairman. He wanted the Chairman dead. But whenever Sleeper asked him about this, Shorty said, "We have to wait for City of Peace to get here. We have to wait." They waited.

The mosaic was a system of rivers that flowed to a big, blue sea. Green meadows and rolling green hills were somebody's idea of Paradise far from Triste. The rivers were each a kind of blue, except for one, and they were named in black lettering.

Dr. Bergen insisted they name the rivers for values the soldiers believed in, and the choices had to be unanimous among them. PEACE was immediately chosen. And HEALTH. River of Peace. River of Health. Those were the two first, and the tile work of these rivers was already completed. HAPPINESS did not get even half of the votes it needed. Sleeper was surprised, but Shorty wasn't.

"That's a word that doesn't mean much," Shorty said.

Shorty would talk about killing the Einhorns but always with the caveat that they had to wait for City of Peace. Just wait for City of Peace. Sleeper found that staying in the hospital with his shaved head and false amnesia kept him out of the notice of the authorities—-he assumed he was still on the wanted list—-but Dr. Bergen was curious about him after she figured out he'd wandered in with no relation to the place.

She was a kind doctor. She communicated much without words. Via smiles or nods or raised eyebrows. She was no dummy either. Although she didn't come right out with an accusation, she knew what was up with the section of the mosaic that pictured a unicorn hunted by a group of wounded, broken Roman gladiators. Trouble-making. Venting. Mischief, she thought. So, let's call her innocent.

Sleeper asked that one of the rivers (just one) be silver, and he got the soldiers to agree without too many questions or objections. The idea sort of just came to him. Dr. Bergen ordered special tiles. She didn't have silver in the original set, and, when they arrived, she let Sleeper open the pack, and he saw they were all tiny mirrors. Even better than he expected. The silver river remained unnamed. The names that occurred to him were not appropriate for the project. The naming rules from the doctor called for concepts or ideas for the world they wanted to see. It was Utopian. And like any good Utopia, it was filled with possibility. Possibility intrigued them all. They didn't try the River of Possibility. That was somehow too sweeping, too ill-defined, too nebulous. But it had the spirit.

Nebulous was a word Pork Chop had picked up somewhere, Pork Chop the cynic, and he used it constantly as a criticism.

"I need to find an acrotomophiliac, brother," Shorty said one night when he caught Sleeper gazing at his stumps. The limbs were cut off mid-thigh, and Sleeper kept thinking the folds and tucks of skin looked like the faces of two manatees.

"What's that mean, Shorty?" Sleeper asked.

"Somebody who gets the hots for amputees."

"That's a thing?"

"Sure, it's a thing. Everything is a thing."

There was a stretch of hot, dry weather. One particularly scorching day, Sleeper took a tray of cold glasses of lemonade to the workers breaking their backs digging to bury some new wires at the power plant next door. This was a Bergen-approved good deed that would get him some silver mosaic tiles. The men thanked him for the drinks. Their glasses sweated and dripped.

"You ever let civilians on tours of the place?"

They looked at him funny.

"You a civilian, kid?"

"I just mean somebody who doesn't work there."

"Oh."

"You want to plant a bomb, kid?" a question that brought laughs all around.

"Just kinda fascinated," Sleeper said.

When the lemonade was gone, the conversation ended. They didn't let him into the plant.

"I'm gonna leave soon," Sleeper told Shorty that night.

"Before City of Peace comes?"

"Yes."

"You got to wait."

"No," Sleeper said, shaking his head. "This place is nothing but waiting. I thought you guys were serious."

"You should stay," Shorty said, calmly, without pleading.

"I won't. Not much longer."

"Let me consult with the boys."

Sleeper continued to earn mirrored, silver tiles and to place them on the river with no name. It grew as long as its blue cousins and as wide. Nobody else asked for the silver tiles. At times, groups of four or five soldiers would work sections of the mosaic together. The work was slow. The soldiers were industrious, but the work was slow. They just couldn't get the tiles fast enough. The good deeds took some time to finish, and there were only so many they could do in a day.

On a night Sleeper had given up on his new friend's regicidal ambitions, Shorty approached him and whispered: We're in. They gathered in the dark in the Rec Room. Shorty led the conversation, as he usually did, and, for once, even Pork Chop had a hopeful face.

"We can get out of here," Shorty said. "We can get out and start on all the things we want to do. But we need transport, and we need a place to go."

"Right," Sleeper said.

"Can you get us transport? Some of us can't just walk out of here."

"Yes," Sleeper said, lying through his teeth. He thought of the fish truck and got an idea.

"What about a place to sleep?" Shorty asked.

"Yeah, this place is exceedingly nice for that," Pork Chop said. "I don't really want to give up a bed and end up in some tent on the beach."

"None of us do, Porky," Shorty said. "Obviously."

"Well then let's come up with some real ideas."

Dr. Bergen came in then and turned on the light.

"What's up in here?" she asked.

"Heated discussion, Doc," Shorty said, taking his surprise in stride. "Debating the merits of naming a River of the Good Life."

"Again?"

"Yet again."

"In the dark?"

"In the dark."

Dr. Bergen walked closer. She looked at Sleeper even though it was Shorty talking.

"What do you think about the good life, mystery man?" Dr. Bergen asked him. "Are you voting for this one or against it?"

Sleeper shrugged. And that was a mistake. It revealed they were not being truthful about their nighttime gathering.

"You have no opinion on this weighty decision?"

"I'm still deciding."

"Well, what's the good life to you?"

"The good life... oh wow... huh."

Shorty jumped in to save him.

"He hasn't agreed to help us kill all the Einhorns if that's what you're worried about, Doc."

"That talk makes me nervous, Shorty. You know that."

She herded them back to their sleep ward, a slow process with all the lost limbs, but she was infinitely patient. Back in the dark, Shorty kept talking and plotting, but Sleeper tuned him out. In the morning, Sleeper brought a tray of lemonade to the power plant, but there were no workers outside. He looked back at the hospital, wondering if he was watched. Since there was never any order putting him in the hospital, there couldn't be one keeping him there. He walked right down the road. Walked past the hospital and on down the road. His big idea: The Colonel owned a vehicle, a tiny electric car. Sleeper figured it was worth checking on. It might still be in the Colonel's personally-owned parking spot. It was tiny, yes, but if Sleeper could get it moving, maybe they could clown car it.

The next morning, Sleeper got to the Colonel's house. It was a large condo in an upscale part of Nuclear Beach. The doors and windows were sealed with police tape. He didn't dare touch it. There was some sort of Royal Decree posted to the door, but two years of ocean storms had smeared all the ink, and it was unreadable. He wondered if the Colonel was alive or was he bones in some desert somewhere? Sleeper felt in his own bones the man was alive. This made him sad, so he began walking to where he knew the parking spot was located. The car was still there as if waiting for Colonel Endling to come along and start it up. Sleeper looked it over. The fast sun was hot overhead, and it glinted off the silver rims on the wheels. He thought the battery must be dead. He paced around the sidewalk. Other pedestrians looked at him, but did they see a man who'd just walked out of a rehab hospital and was about to steal a car? Maybe some of them. He laughed at himself.

At one time, as the Colonel's assistant, Sleeper could open and start this car with his thumbprint. There was no way the police would have neglected to... he reached out and grabbed the door handle. The locks all released. Amazing. He sat in the driver seat and put his thumb on the start button. The battery was good. The engine started. Incredible.

Since it had not moved in so many months, the tiny car pulling out from the curb caught the attention of a drone high in the sky. The drone was coded to notice changes in the fixed landscape of the city. So, it locked onto the car and left its surveillance routine. It followed and recorded the travel of the car out of Radium Beach, and the car's long drive to the soldiers' rehab hospital. It zoomed and recorded Sleeper's walk to the front entrance doors and the crowd of men who came back out and followed him to the car. By this time, a human technician in the Chairman's bunker in Daphne had alerted General Messmaker. The technician and the General watched the drone footage together, and as the General's mind began to piece together what was happening—-including the detail of Colonel Endling's license plate—-he picked up his mobile and placed a call to the hospital and asked for Dr. Bergen.

Part Five
Chapter One

Tubby no longer recognized his own shadow. Tall, yeah, but who was that slender thing? Laverna's eyes would pop out of her skull to see him now. His mother, too. She was dead, but imagine her surprise. She'd always known him fat. The sun just above the Sangre de Cristo range to the east threw his long shadow westwards. He'd left the highway, Route 25, the artery the Marines used—-the only working road north-—after passing through Trinidad. The road was too risky. He hadn't seen a drone for days, and, luckily, no sandstorms either. He kept the mountains directly to his right hand. He had in front of him now some difficult-looking terrain.

"What dunes these are, I think I know," he said aloud in a Robert Frost sing song.

He walked the valley between the dunes and the mountains. He'd come here with his father as a child. It was greener then. Like everywhere. His father liked Old West vacations, easy treks from Southern California or Texas where they lived when Dad worked on the oil rigs.

"How did so much sand end up in these mountains?" his father asked him in the form of a science puzzle. This had been solved way back in the 20th century, but Tubby didn't know that. He was only eight, but the future engineer was precocious, and his father pushed him.

The dunes were enormous. They were vast and hundreds of feet high, but they were dwarfed by the nearby peaks, which rose to almost three miles up above them. Tubby was quiet as he hiked with his father. Then, an idea would pop into his head.

"The desert was here first before the mountains?"

"Nice one. Promising idea. But no."

So long ago, Tubby thought. His father was long dead. Another time, another world.

The valley before him was blocked with sand. The dunes moved around, and, in the spot he now approached, a crawling pile of sand had devoured some tall pines. So much so that only the tips of the pines showed. Before he got himself ready to hike up the dunes, he looked at the mountains. One peak, the highest, was white with snow. There was some health-looking green forest.

"Life comes back," he said aloud. "It comes back if we don't eradicate it completely."

Oh, and that prompted another memory. There were bison back then, a farm of them in this very valley. His father told him they kept the males separated from each other, since they'd otherwise fight non-stop. They'd ram each other until the weaker of any pair was dead. He and Dad walked right up to the fence to look at them. "Not too close," Dad warned, pointing at the lightning bolt warning danger on a yellow sign.

Tubby strode up the sand. At the top of the dune, his calves cramped. He drank water from his skin. He saw ahead of him miles of more dunes. He walked for two hours, and, as it grew dark, he stopped to check out the black remains of a fire some previous traveler had left. He agreed this was a good place to stop and sat down. In the dark, having no light (and no wood for a fire), he had nothing to do except sit and think. With no pressing worry, he fell asleep quickly, head on his crossed arms like a hibernating bear.

At dawn, he woke and hiked again. He considered whether he had a plan worthy of his old friend, Colonel Endling. Nope. Of course not. He strode towards a confrontation, a confrontation unknown but bad, and he moved against Junior Soucy's advice. Junior said don't be stupid. The time was not the right time. Tubby got offended and said Colonel Endling had little time left. He set off alone.

"If you insist, then don't stay on the highway much past Trinidad. They'll shoot you."

So, here was Tubby, then, trekking the motherfucking five-hundred-foot-tall sand dunes. His father, another huge man, had been overwhelmed to do more than one dune. That was a rotten day in Tubby's memory. Not that he blamed his father. Walking the sand hills was like boot camp. No, more like boots in peanut butter, tremendous physical exertion.

He tried to be conservative with his water supply, but it was tough. He was parched in the sun. He passed more fire sites that day, a cluster of them along with piles of horse dung that told him a caravan had come through. He sat as the sun set red in the west, and he gawked at the arresting blue mountains like a religious pilgrim come at last to the holy place. In the dark, looking up at the bright constellations, he examined the state of his hopes. Hope, the engine of every confidence game and every self-con that ever was. As an analytic personality, he liked probabilities. When he calculated them, though, it was not pretty. He had dunes, mountains, desert ahead of him just to get to the King's Wall. There was no hedge for these bets.

As he lay there, chewing on this, a massive interstellar ark passed overhead, a Colorado → Triste shot, and it was one of the big ones, a migration ark, the largest class. The blue light came like the glow of one of heaven's stars dropped down for a closer look at the earth.

It was difficult to see the oval shape of the silver ship. It was like a giant torpedo, fatter though, more like a perfectly smooth and tailless zeppelin. Usually a migration ark was one-way, and they'd all gone to Triste, and the Colorado Springs silo couldn't support a ship this huge, but... well, maybe things had changed. Maybe things had changed.

What was moving that required a migration ship?
A population obviously.

The ship's light was visible for about two minutes. Then gone. Tubby closed his eyes and slept.

Pledged to the plain of sand, in the morning he hiked on. The dunes were not endless, so, eventually, he saw their taper and terminus in the distance. But it was more up and down, up and down, across an undulating, umber sea.

He could not stop gawking at the mountains. They stood beyond the mortal scale. They were for gods. They were jagged like the 80 teeth of an ancient Egyptian crocodile god, set in the Earth like a trap, an ambush for the remainder of unsuspecting mankind. Above them, the lonely, moody sky.

"This is the most beautiful place on two Earths," Tubby said. "God damn."

Off the dunes, the walking was easy. He moved faster, covering many miles by evening. He slept on flattened grass that night. When he woke before sunup the next morning, a man was standing over him, looking down and smiling. The man had a shepherd's crook over his right shoulder.

Tubby sprang to his feet. He suddenly towered over the man, reversing their initial interface.

"Who are you?"

"Lázaro," the man said, smiling. "¿Y tú?"

"Tubby Lascaux."

Lázaro pointed towards the mountains, and Tubby could see goats in the middle distance. Half a dozen. No. Seven. Eight. He was thrilled to see them.

"¿Queso de cabra?" Lázaro asked, pulling cheese from the sack he wore around his neck.

"Yes, thank you," Tubby said. "Gracias."

They sat down on the flattened grass. Lázaro put down his crook. He smiled.

"Do you speak English?"

"Un poco," Lázaro said. "A little bit."

"Are you Mexican?"

"No," Lázaro replied. He held his hands out to the eastern and western horizons. "San Luis Valley."

The goat cheese was plain, but Lázaro had a small, glass jar of honey. This Tubby found miraculous. This is a miracle, he thought, a fantasy dream.

"Thank you," he said. "Delicious."

"¿A dónde vas, Tubby?"

"Colorado Springs."

Lázaro's eyes opened wide.

"No."

"Yes."

"¿Estás loco o qué?"

Tubby laughed.

"Tubby!"

"What?"

"They will shoot you."

The frolicking goats saw their master was near and loped over. They were brown with patches of white and black on their faces. They encircled Tubby and, one at a time, sniffed his hands, mining for food. What do you have? Share it. Hand it over. Give me some. Give us some.

"Eres popular," Lázaro said, smiling warmly at his tribe.

Tubby said, "I don't think they will shoot me."

"Tubby!" Lázaro said. "You are... how do you say prisionero?"

"A prisoner. Yes."

"Prisoner. Sí. They will shoot you."

Hearing this again did not convince Tubby. Who would start the rumor that the authorities would shoot on sight anyone coming off the desert? The authorities, of course.

"I have a friend who needs my help."

"Always there is some friend in need."

"You have a family, Lázaro?"

"Before," Lázaro said. "Not now. Not anymore. Except..." and he pointed at the goats.

"I'm sorry. The pestilence?"

"Yes."

"I'm sorry."

Tubby didn't know what to do with his appreciation for the breakfast meal. He wanted to hike in the cooler temperatures of the morning. He wanted to get moving since the clock was moving. He needed to get to Colorado Springs to make something happen. And yet, he met this lonely, generous pastoralist in the middle of nowhere.

"How do you go?" Lázaro asked. "¿Por las montañas?"

"North to the end then east."

"Hmm," Lázaro said. "Sí. Más seguro."

They watched the goats sniffing the grass.

"Mi casa. My house. It's on the way. Come."

They walked for half the day due north. The house was a log cabin, solidly built-—thick, heavy, logs the color of a Kodiak bear—-and inside it had the smell of a home, the first Tubby had encountered since landing in Texas. It was tucked into a copse you couldn't say kept it hidden but did protect it from the harsh desert wind and dust.

"Come in, amigo."

The goats followed to the door but stopped, to a one, before the threshold. Lázaro left his crook by the door and immediately strode to a wash bowl filled with water. He splashed his face and rubbed his eyes. Brown water dripped back into the bowl. He grabbed a towel.

The cabin was two rooms. One large room contained kitchen, sitting room with table and chairs, some book shelves, the wash area. A small room contained Lázaro's bed.

"Aquí," he said, and then he opened an icebox in the kitchen. "Ice and snow from the mountain."

An icebox! A fog poured out of it.

"How do you say it? Snacks," Lázaro said, bending, his head vanishing into the fog. "Snacks for your long walk."

He pulled out every imaginable kind of goat cheese. Tubby examined the room. Lázaro had many books. He had some Catholic crosses on the wall. There was a painting of Jesus, prominently showing his sacred heart, the abyss of all virtues, the Savior ripping open his shirt to reveal it to the world. The heart gave off shards of light, and looked like Krypton exploding.

Lázaro offered rosemary and honey and what he called Moroccan Spice. Showing them one at a time then handing the handful at once and wishing Tubby good luck. He was sad to go. Sadness was a luxury, however, in the desert valley, and, after an hour of walking, he was thinking forward again of Colorado Springs and the danger that waited for him. Lázaro told him about the Hayden Pass road and how to look for it, the obvious signs long fallen to the tyranny of weeds and shrubs. When he came upon the road, it was as described. The road was rocky and overgrown and steep. Tubby's calves were strong from the dunes workout, but, still, he dragged like a tired dog. When he reached the flat zone called the summit, it was dark. He collapsed and fell asleep. It was a cold night at the elevation. He woke a few times, shivering.

The east's dawn astonished him. Through the V-shaped opening in the trees, he saw dark hills, furry and squat with purple mountains—-majesty, truly-—behind them. The furry hills were scarred by fire. As the morning light spread around him, he saw strange things he was glad he didn't encounter in the dead of night. He stood up and realized the sky and clouds were just beyond the reach of his stretched arm. All around the gravelly clearing, he saw fire pits. They were filled with bones. Large bones. Bones of large animals or was that a human leg bone? Although the sun was warming him, he shivered. He found a weird altar covered with wax candles and smooth, flat stones, and, he could hardly believe it, the corpse of a kangaroo rat. He stepped back. How could he not take that as some sort of personal omen? No wonder the mountain, so capable of hosting life, was not settled by anyone.

He knew the path to the eastern downslope, but he stumbled a bit on the fire pits and bones, and he got disoriented, and when he caught himself and straightened up, he was staring west across the San Luis Valley. The great flatland was decorated by ghostly circles and squares where great irrigation works once operated. So beautiful and not a soul out there, or, maybe, a herder of goats, but nobody else. He understood suddenly the Kingly impulse, the desire to own it all. He felt his heart drop and gathered his pack and his water skin and strode down from the summit.

US Route 50 out of Coaldale clung to the muddy bed of the Arkansas River like a snake chasing its own shadow. The road was abandoned and rock strewn. There were patches of pavement. Rusted sections of guardrail on the river side. He walked on the dirt between road and river, constantly scanning the sky ahead for drones. He passed the ruins of an old motel. The green vegetation devouring the place was heartening. Along the muddy river bed, things were especially green. In places shaded by tall rock hills, the river was more creek than mud, and, a few times, he stopped and splashed his face.

He rested and ate a meal of goat cheese inside an abandoned box car on a piece of track across the river. I'll just close my eyes for a moment, he said. He fell asleep in the darkness inside the car and slept for many hours. When he woke, it was dark night, and he heard voices, two people, a man and a woman, passing by along the highway. He held his breath. He had his knife, but what if they had guns?

He waited for daylight to start out again. It was a harshly bright day. The road curved as the river curved. It declined as the land declined. After turning one blind, rocky curve, Tubby had to stop dead for Colorado's massive wall rose before him on the horizon. It glimmered in the sun. One of the five wonders of the world after the world. The Glimmer Wall. It was bullet proof glass-clad polycarbonate, and no bomb yet brought against it proved powerful enough to breach it. It was a one-way mirror. They could see you. You couldn't see them. The weak spots were the gates, and that's where Tubby looked.

Chapter Two

SCENE

An austere room in the Einhorn Bunker, Boulder, CO. The walls are bloodless pastels without ornament. The only furniture: five bean bag chairs, presently occupied. No windows.

THE BRAIN: They call this the Green Room.

MAN: There's nothing green in here. That's stupid.

BRAIN: What's your name, pal?

MAN: Veruca.

BRAIN: Well, Veruca, they call it the Green Room, cuz we're going to have an audience with Leo Einhorn. It's like we're going on air in the old kind of TV studio.

VERUCA: Even dumber.

COLONEL ENDLING, clean shaven now and bathed, turns his head to look at VERUCA, as that frustrated man grumbles and fusses in his bean bag chair.

COLONEL: What's your business with the Einhorns?

Faintly, deep in the background, an alarm is sounding.

VERUCA: The city planners won't approve my charity.

COLONEL: Why not?

VERUCA: Don't like my business plan.

BRAIN: Probably sounds like a scam. Is it a scam?

VERUCA (who has heard this before): God damn it. It's not.

Enter FLATTERY, the Green Room's steward, through a previously locked door. The alarm is louder in the brief time the door is open.

BRAIN: Everything okay out there?

FLATTERY: Yes, why?

BRAIN: That alarm.

FLATTERY: That's nothing.

BRAIN: What times are we all slotted for, Mr. Flattery?

FLATTERY: Well, that depends.

BRAIN: Oh?

COLONEL: Upon what?

FLATTERY: It depends upon what time Himself rises from bed.

MAN (in a bean bag chair on the other side of the room): That could easily mean never.

FLATTERY: Caution, sir.

BRAIN: What's your name, comrade?

MAN: Mario.
BRAIN: Mario, what's your business here? We've heard from Veruca already.

MARIO: I will explain, but, first, why caution?

FLATTERY: Any one of you could be an informer.

With that, the steward left the room, locking the door from the outside with a loud click.

BRAIN: Ha! He knows how to make an exit.

The five people in the room look at each other, mistrust and suspicion boiling in their already anxious hearts. Looks turned to the Brain.

VERUCA: What's wrong with your face, man?

BRAIN: Chemical burns.

VERUCA: Huh.

BRAIN: Think that makes me an informant?

MARIO: Well, who are you?

VERUCA: Yeah, since we're hearing from everyone.

BRAIN: You don't know who I am? I'm crushed.

MARIO: Nope.

COLONEL: He's Head Prisoner.

VERUCA: Shit. Not an informant but a cop!

BRAIN: If you're all free citizens of Colorado, I have no power over you. In fact, it's the reverse.

COLONEL: In this room, that's meaningless, Brain.

MARIO: Who is he. Why is he in cuffs?

BRAIN: You don't recognize him either?

The Colonel falls under scrutiny.

MARIO: I don't know him.

VERUCA: Me neither.

MAN: That's Colonel Endling, the great traitor.

BRAIN: Indeed, it is. What's your name, my comrade?

MAN: Morningwood.

BRAIN: For real? Ha ha ha.

MORNINGWOOD: Yes.

FLATTERY enters through the door. He is followed by PIPER. PIPER and COLONEL make eye contact, but they do not speak.

BRAIN: Chair for the lady.

He rises. PIPER sits in the bean bag chair. The chair hisses. FLATTERY exits through the door.

MARIO: Room is filling up.

VERUCA: Busy day for Young Leo.

BRAIN (nodding at PIPER): Why are you here?

PIPER: No idea.

FLATTERY re-enters through the door, carrying a tray upon which sit glasses of ice water.

BRAIN: Who is up first, steward?

FLATTERY: The young lady.

BRAIN: And after her?

FLATTERY: To be determined.

BRAIN: But we're all here, right? Can't you slot us in?

FLATTERY: I would love to do that for you. Doesn't work that way.

FLATTERY exits through the door. THE BRAIN, who is the only one standing, hands out the glasses of water.

MORNINGWOOD: You seem anxious, friend.

THE BRAIN silently considers this.

BRAIN: I am.

VERUCA: I think we all are. Any of you meet Leo before?

MARIO: No.

MORNINGWOOD: Nope.

COLONEL: I have. Many years ago. He was a child.

VERUCA: How about you... uh... young lady?

PIPER: No. Never.

VERUCA: So, nobody knows what to expect.

COLONEL: He's a narcissist.

VERUCA: Meaning what?

COLONEL: Meaning adjust your expectations.

MARIO: A fuck to that, traitor.

THE COLONEL says nothing.

VERUCA: What's that alarm? It's not cutting off.

BRAIN: I wonder about that. Sounds like a fire drill.

FLATTERY enters. The alarm is louder as the door opens. FLATTERY carries in his arms a wooden box with knobs and dials on its face. He puts it on the floor about ten paces from the door. The box is brown. The knobs are silver. It is about the height of the steward's knee.

PIPER: What's that?

FLATTERY shrugs and leaves by the door. The lock clicks.

COLONEL: That's an old radio.

PIPER: How's it powered?

COLONEL: Old electrochemical cell batteries.

BRAIN: That's a bizarre item to just bring in and drop off with an idiotic shrug.

The conversation develops a lull. The eyes of the men in the room begin to settle on PIPER. How this dynamic always works.

BRAIN: Leo never did marry, did he?

MARIO: Forever in mourning, they say. His youthful love.

VERUCA: Have you seen that picture?

MARIO: Which?

VERUCA: Oh, young Leo in his mourning attire.

MARIO: Never seen it.

VERUCA pulls up the picture on his mobile device and hands it to MARIO. MARIO holds it in his large, beefy hands then passes it to PIPER. The picture moves around the room like the flu virus. In her bean bag chair, PIPER hugs her knees.

MORNINGWOOD: Feels strange for us all to be here, mixing and talking about our business.

MARIO: Yeah.

BRAIN: Kinda like cattle in a stockyard.

MORNINGWOOD: Gross analogy, but it's true.

BRAIN: If we're able to choose amongst ourselves who shall go first, it will be the COLONEL and me after the young lady.

MARIO: Why you?

VERUCA: Yeah, why you?

BRAIN: Seems best to me.

MARIO: Oh, seems best to you, huh?

VERUCA: It's a trick. Must not be best to go first. Best to go last, I bet. Insider like you knows these things.

BRAIN: No, you misread me.

COLONEL: Hope no one misjudges you by your cover, Brain.

BRAIN: That alarm.

Indeed, the alarm has continued to sound. It is almost lost in the background such is its steadiness and low quality. Some time passes in silence, then FLATTERY enters again.

FLATTERY: Sorry for the long wait, folks.

VERUCA: Is it better to go first or last?

FLATTERY: I'm sorry?

VERUCA: With Mr. Einhorn. Is it best to go last?

FLATTERY: He doesn't get this many supplicants on most days. It's hard to know. Do we need more water in here?

PIPER: I'll take some.

MARIO sighs. Loudly.

BRAIN: What is it, comrade?

MARIO: Story of my life. Wasting time waiting on some futile dream.

VERUCA: Deep.

BRAIN: Did you tell us what it is? Think you got interrupted.

THE COLONEL begins to pace. Like the rest, he hadn't anticipated this delay.

MARIO: I have a business proposal, too, for Leo. Relates to the water supply.

VERUCA: See the guards around the reservoir when we came in? That was shocking to see.

MARIO: Yeah.

MORNINGWOOD: You with the face. Hey.

BRAIN: What?

MORNINGWOOD: You ever get someone object strongly to you calling them "comrade?"

BRAIN: Because of my face, you mean?

MORNINGWOOD shrugs.

BRAIN: Not is so many words.

MORNINGWOOD: Must be a burden. Life with that face.

BRAIN: I'm ugly, but what I do have is charm.

MORNINGWOOD: Does the young lady agree?

PIPER looks over and smiles.

PIPER: Yes. He's got charm.

MORNINGWOOD frowns. THE BRAIN clearly likes this answer. He grins like he won something when the pacing COLONEL passes him.

MARIO: You know, that door being locked is odd. If any of us wanted to leave, guess what? We can't.

VERUCA: And no emergency pissing.

MARIO: Exactly.

As if on cue, the lock clicks. FLATTERY enters with a pitcher of water. PIPER hands him her glass.

PIPER: Thank you.

COLONEL (to FLATTERY): Do you have the time?

FLATTERY: Almost noon.

BRAIN: Oh. So, you do answer questions.

COLONEL: He out of bed yet?

FLATTERY (indecisively): Well, I have not seen him on the floor yet. I shouldn't even be saying that.

BRAIN: Company man. Good for you.

FLATTERY gives THE BRAIN a look. This is the first time he's shown annoyance. FLATTERY leaves the room and locks the door. The general conversation breaks into small groups, pairs. PIPER and COLONEL ENDLING walk to a corner. THE BRAIN hovers.

COLONEL: What are you doing here?

PIPER: I was sent for. A special order, you could say.

COLONEL: By Leo?

PIPER: No. He doesn't know. I'm a surprise gift.

COLONEL ENDLING'S face grows sad. He looks exhausted, and, with his wrists cuffed, pathetic. PIPER gestures at the cuffs.

PIPER: This is quite the reversal.

COLONEL: Tell me about it.
PIPER: Why'd he drag you here?

COLONEL: You know the story of his arrest?

PIPER: Yeah.

COLONEL: Well, he wants the gold back, and he's gonna try to talk his way into getting the gold back.

PIPER looks at THE BRAIN who is maybe listening while pretending not to listen.

PIPER: That's crazy.

COLONEL: Well. He is crazy. But there's a method to it. He'll get the gold.

MARIO: Hey, comrade. Can't we get some relief for your companion's handcuffs? I mean. Come on.

BRAIN (shrugging): Threw away the key.

PIPER (quietly): How'd you come in?

COLONEL: Rotor. You?

PIPER: Same.

The alarm increases in volume. This is because a second alarm, this one just outside the door of the Green Room, had joined it in screeching duet.

BRAIN: WHAT. THE. HELL.

MORNINGWOOD: This is a stupid way to arrange a society.

MARIO: Explain what you mean.

MORNINGWOOD: All of us here, having to line up to beg one man for graces to get things done.

VERUCA: Totally.

A ghost enters the room by walking straight through the locked door. Looking confused, it walks forward all the way to the footlights and stops. It is invisible to everyone on stage.

GHOST: I heard someone say, "What the hell," and now here I am. But how?

BRAIN: Where is Flattery now? How do we get him back?

GHOST: Beware those closest to you, the guru said. But I didn't catch his meaning. He told me exactly what would happen. But I didn't catch his meaning.

BRAIN: Something smells like blood.

MARIO: What does blood smell like?

BRAIN: Oh, you know, iron. Metal.

GHOST: That must be me he smells. My throat.

The alarms go silent.

VERUCA: There's blood coming under the door over here.

The men rush to the door. PIPER stands alone. The GHOST vanishes.

BRAIN: That's a lot of blood. Hello? Hello? Flattery?

MARIO: Hello? Anyone? Hello?

VERUCA pounds on the door with his fist. PIPER walks to the radio, switches it on.

RADIO: All citizens with valid tickets for Migration Flight Omega should prepare for Colorado Springs Orientation this evening. All citizens with valid tickets for

Migration Flight Omega should prepare for Colorado Springs Orientation this evening. All citizens with valid tickets for Migration Flight Omega should prepare for Colorado Springs Orientation this evening. All citizens with valid tickets for Migration Flight Omega should prepare for Colorado Springs Orientation this evening. Et cetera.

BRAIN (to THE COLONEL): Well, what the fuck does that mean?

COLONEL (looking worried): I don't know.

Chapter Three

Piper dismantled the radio. She straightened a coil from the tuning knob and picked open Colonel Endling's handcuffs. She picked the lock of the Green Room's door. The door opened out. They had to push hard. The pool of blood was from the bodyguard, Bruce Burden. He was dead and blocking the door. His throat had been cut. His big, shiny silver pistols, buttoned into his belt holsters, never saw action.

"Where's Flattery?" the Brain asked as if any of the Green Room crowd could tell him.

Piper hopped over the red puddle, but the men didn't bother. They tracked bloody footprints down the hallway. Expecting to run into guards, they went slowly. But they got all the way to the White Room without encountering anyone.

"It's a coup," the Colonel whispered.

That stopped the Brain like an emergency brake. He felt suddenly exposed, stripped of his status. Everyone stopped with him. The White Room was enormous. The white pillars that held up the ceiling made it impossible to see far into it from the doorway. All around, they saw famous paintings looted by the present Chairman's father after European civilization ended. The Colonel stared at the long wall holding Picasso's Guernica. The original. 25 feet wide. How did they get it across the ocean?

"Is anyone in here?" Piper asked.

They walked in. Broken wine bottles everywhere. More pools that looked like blood. Maybe wine. Maybe blood. Red stains not just on the floor, but on the walls, the pillars. They found Leo's throne-like chair, which, like a church altar, was two shallow steps up from the main floor. Leo lay on those shallow steps with knife wounds all over his body. The Colonel looked around in a panic.

"Julius fucking Caesar," the Brain said.

"We might get blamed for this," the Colonel said. "We shouldn't stay."

"Let's go," Mario said.

"Hang on a minute," the Brain demanded. He grabbed the Colonel by the arm. "Hang on just a minute. You hang on."

"Let go of me."

"Look at him," the Brain said, pointing at Leo. "This is fucking insane. What is happening?"

"I have no idea."

"That weird radio message," the Brain said. "Piece it together. You know everything, Ed."

"Let go of my arm."

"Is it really a coup?"

Piper knelt by Leo's body. The pool of blood was as enthralling as any poet ever said. The steps and the floor were polished marble, an element not to be slaked. The pool just sat there and grew. She watched it then she reached over and grabbed Leo's wrist. No pulse. She dropped his arm.

"If it was a coup, there'd be people holding this room," Mario said. "Anyhow, he's not the Chairman."

"Good point," the Colonel replied. He struggled to re-center his bearings. He'd expected to speak with Leo as the Brain made a fool of himself over the gold.

Leo would hear him out, hear reason, know that the Colonel had been framed. Now, that notion was dead. Still, he was a man ever dogged by hope. He thought of Colorado Springs. Possibility. Piper was thinking the same, the promise of what would happen there that very evening. She cracked her knuckle. Flattery came stumbling around the corner. His clothes looked orderly and neat, but his pant cuffs were splashed in blood.

"Did you do this?" the Brain shouted at him.

Flattery had been crying, but his face now showed him stuck at the denial stage of his grief.

"Get him up," Flattery said. "Sit him up. Medics are coming."

"He's dead."

"No."

"He's dead," the Brain insisted. "Look at his throat."

Flattery looked at the corpse, maybe really looked for the first time. He wobbled like he might fall over. The Colonel steadied him with a firm hand on the shoulder.

"Do you know who did it?"

"Oh," Flattery said, foggily. "Not their names. Three men. Wine drinkers. They were all drinking wine with Leo. Babysitters sent by the Queen."

"What the fuck?" the Brain blurted. "You sure?"

"Yes. Yes."

Flattery sighed. The Colonel and the Brain shared a look.

"Are there secret exits out of this building?" Piper asked.

"What?"

"How do we get out of here?"

"Yes. Right. Of course. Come. Come."

They took an elevator down from ground level to an employee locker room. Flattery continued to wobble, but he knew where he was going. "We'll have to go down to get out unseen. Down and under." They approached a room with metal detectors and AI bomb sniffers. "Wait here. I'll check for guards."

Flattery ducked in then quickly back out.

"There's nobody."

They followed the steward out, a strange and friable collective of supplicants who wanted nothing now except exit from the building. He led them to another employee wing, this time through a set of blast doors. Curved, concrete doors. 300 tons. "These doors take 10 hours to close."

Next, down a flight of stairs to emerge in a kitchen. It was empty of staff.

"These are the Messmaker family living quarters."

Empty, as they passed through. They took stairs another layer down and emerged in another kitchen. The Einhorn family living quarters, Flattery told them. He was a tour guide now, leading the first and last tour of the massive, suddenly tomb-like structure. They passed through further galleys and military officer living spaces never even furnished.

"What kind of attack did they expect?" the Brain asked aloud, and this caused Colonel Endling to think of the nuke facility in Texas. He shook his head at the stupidity of it all, the waste. Flattery stopped and put his hand on a door. A small door. Drink Me, Alice in Wonderland sized.

"Are any of you claustrophobic?"

None admitted they were. Flattery took a ring of keys from his pocket. He unlocked the door. Behind the door was a tunnel, a stone pipe.

"This," he said. "This is our way out."

There was a sound of moving air, a whistling as if there was strong wind at the other end. The Brain was looking around as if he had no intention of crawling into the tunnel.

"I wanna go make a mess on the Queen's pillow," he said. His ugly face contorted with mirth. But, he was serious. He let all the others climb in then closed the door on them and fled the room. The Colonel was relieved to hear his footfalls thumping away. As if that character was a nightmare receding in the early morning, as if all of this were the same.

The tunnel was a tight squeeze. It was slow going with Flattery in the lead, and, it was unnerving with the roaring sound of the wind. Like some beast awaited them, and they were its unsuspecting snacks. They saw brightness grow ahead. The Colonel watched his fellows drop from the tunnel into the brightness, one after another, ahead of him. He was surprised to find they were still inside the bunker. A large bright room. Not outdoors yet. The beastly sound came from a massive air intake system with a mouth that poured into the room.

"That was the easy part," Flattery said.

Soon, they were ducking under an even tighter space.

"These are base isolators," Piper said, pointing to a collection of giant black springs. "The entire bunker is supported here. Amazing."

"What's it for?" Mario asked.

"They suppress vibrations from an earthquake."

"Or a nuke," the Colonel added.

"I feel like a bug about to be squashed," Mario said. "What if somebody jumps up and down on the roof? Huh?"

Piper laughed at that. They had to crawl some more and squeeze between closely placed dampers. Heavy heavy metal, these things. "Is this a well-known exit?" the Colonel asked Flattery.

"Definitely not."

They came at last to another low door, barely tall enough for a small child. Flattery pulled the ring of keys from his pocket. He said there was a swimming pool inside. A water fall sprayed and bubbled at the far end.

Piper laughed again. "What?"

Colonel Endling noticed a brass plate on the door. SOURCE, it said.

"We'll have to walk the edge of the pool. Be careful you don't slip in."

"Thanks for the warning."

Piper turned to the Colonel.

"How far to Colorado Springs?" she asked.

"Oh," he said. "Say a hundred miles. A little less than that maybe." He scratched his chin and waited for Flattery to unlock the door.

Chapter Four

A rumor circulated about a mass grave discovery just outside the city. When Gun Club told the Queen about the rumor, she already knew. The warm color of the Queen's Misery Index did not fade or flicker for one second. She kissed her own fingers and touched them to her husband's lips.

"The rumor is true," she said. "This news, though, is not the worst our people will hear today."

"What do you mean?"

"The speechwriters will be here in a few minutes."

They were in the top floor suite of the Strand Hotel. The ocean today had whitecaps, but it was relatively peaceful. The fast sun was bright. The Queen looked at the now obsolete Eastern Silo, tall and shimmering in the distant heat.

"What speech?"

"I've given the cutoff order."

The Chairman coughed. He put his fist to his mouth out of rote politeness. The coughing continued.

"You're surprised?" she asked.

"Yes. You didn't ask me."

"Well."

"Is everyone getting out?"

"Everyone we want."

"Leo?"

The Queen walked across the room. Her red hair was growing back, but it was still the shorter length her husband preferred. He watched her.

"Leo won't be coming to Triste."

She looked over at him. Something in his eyes dimmed then quickly reset. He sat himself in a chair in a corner of the room as far from her as possible.

"I knew this day would come."

"Yes," the Queen said. "You did."

The speechwriters knocked and were let in.

There was a written order for History someday to find. The order was sent to General Messmaker, and he quickly executed its simple instructions. The Queen sundered Triste from Earth, the planet that was both its mother and its twin. Transit between the two planets would now be unlawful for the duration of the new Unlimited State of Emergency. Consider how shocking this was. A generation before, the largest human project ever undertaken was successfully carried out. A living piece of the world's people, a big one, left the dying planet and founded a new home. The colony thrived. The original home, the mother and twin, had people of its own still, survivors, projects, needful resources, metals not found on Triste, and travel back and forth was costly but necessary. So, the people thought.

The Queen's thinking was that it was now urgent that she stream a speech directly to the people via the Misery Index. This had never been done before. Jack always said that would break the mystery, so he was against it. But the Unlimited State of Emergency was based partly in fact, and she could make a persuasive case that the drastic sundering was the right move and would be temporary (though in her heart she knew it would not be).

Historians were not in the room with the Queen and her speechwriters. They get wearied enough, historians do, chasing facts without the torture of listening to propagandists.

They (the writers) wanted to make her sound like FDR. She wanted to sound like herself.

Words flew around the room like some bird. Not a dove. Some exacting, engineering type of bird.

Engaged in suppressing an insurrection against the Mission. Public safety demands. Your best interest. My concern is hard-headed but not hard-hearted. Cold, hard facts.

The Queen had so little poetry in her soul that the speechwriters despaired. The order would permanently cleave families that had members on both home worlds. It would crush spirits. Her cold style would add to this problem.

She knew this. About herself, about the situation. The sheen of her Misery Index was green like the head of a mallard. In moments like this, it turns out the Misery Index was no window into anything inside her. It was stage craft. She knew how to manipulate it. Her husband across the room watched her and thought about this. She could be plotting my death next, he thought, for all that Index shows me.

He was agitated. He wanted to take a petty revenge for Leo. He spent his time thinking about exactly how. Was he heartsick over his brother? No, he was not. Was he insulted? Yes. His thoughts drifted, and he saw an image of the rotor hangar in Colorado. Leo's one real job. Shipping the attack rotors. The Chairman grew angry. It was a good thing his Misery Index was decommissioned. He walked to the windows and looked at the ocean. The whitecaps pressed each other and pushed and tumbled like rival siblings. He put his hand on the glass and felt the heat of the fast sun.

"I am speaking to you tonight from the center of our city."

"I don't love that," the Queen said.

"I am speaking to you tonight from--"

"No."

"I am speaking to you tonight--"

"Yes. Go on."

Gun Club watched an LNG carrier move across the watery horizon. Orange. Enormous. If it stood up end to end, it would be the tallest building in Radium Beach. The huge spherical tanks for liquefied natural gas looked like eggs that some robber creature was taking away. The ship was accompanied by navy vessels and black attack rotors. Protection against the inevitable strike. What if one should explode? Even that far out, it would flatten the city like a barrage of atom bombs. He had fears. The Queen did not. Things would soon turn dark.

Chapter Five

Witnesses reported seeing an ugly man—-among the all-time ugliest, one said—-pushing a wheel barrow piled with bars of gold. This was right down Broadway and through the old campus of the university. Everyone was distracted by the news of the Queen's order, but the ugly man seemed to have an idea of exactly where he was headed.

"He was sunburnt to a crisp," a witness said. "Definitely Texas. Definitely a prisoner."

There was no sign of this ugly man on the campus when the MPs went looking.

"The gold was shiny. Recently polished for sure."

"Like a bucket full of sun."

The unlocked vault was a mystery for Tony Jones, the MP investigating Leo Einhorn's murder. The vault was just sitting there wide open. Coins, cash & jewels untouched. Some priceless deeds sat there, too, un-stolen. What was missing? Gold. That detail matched up with the report of the ugly man and his wheel barrow. Tony Jones asked the other MPs were they just gonna let this man walk away with that gold? A lot of gold apparently. What would the new order bring? What kind of economy? Would gold be worth anything? That unknown was troubling.

The vault door's hand wheel had five points like a starfish. Tony Jones spun the wheel as he stared into the vault, considering what to do. They had orders from Messmaker not to leave Boulder. What to do. What to do. Tony was a pragmatist. But that gold. Oh, that gold.

He typed his report on the contents of the vault. It was known to the Mission that the burglary and the murder were not connected, but the burglary sure was convenient for the narrative. What to do.

Chapter Six

The boys sat on the beach, waiting for Yoshi's return. They had nothing better to do. Just wait. Hope & wait. He told them he might be gone for a while. He had far to go, but he'd be getting a new map that would lead him back to them. Toad felt good about that. Every few weeks, the authorities would send a spy to Dreaming Back Lake. The spy would masquerade as a civilian from some respectable profession. They'd find a way to introduce themselves to Toad or Beetle or Flat Tire, and, inevitably, they'd ask a question about Yoshi. This week it was the limnologist. One morning, he appeared on the beach and started cutting open the body of a shark. Curiosity attracted a crowd. The boys kept their distance, but they could see and hear everything.

"Did that shark come out of the lake?"

"Sure did," the limnologist replied.

"No way!"

"Yes. It did. I caught it."

"With what? A fishing pole?"

"I trapped it."

"Where's your trap? Where's your boat?"

"All of the apparatus was taken away this morning."

The man split the shark's belly, and a shudder ran through the crowd of onlookers. Toad received a vision of sea urchins, squid, crabs, saw fish, rays, bony fishes, eels, porpoises. The souls of these fleeing the shark's soul.

"What did you find in there?"

The limnologist put his hands inside the shark. He yanked something out. Something big. There was a wet plop. "Oh Lord, a dead colleague," he said.

A lady gasped.

"Yours?"

"No," he said, pointing at the shark. "His."

Half of a smaller shark lay slicked in oils and blood on the sand.

"Are you an ichthyologist?"

"No."

"What then?"

"I'm a limnologist."

"What is that?"

"I study lakes mostly. I'm interested in what this shark ate for what it tells us about the lake."

"We didn't even know this lake had sharks."

"Yes, some. They are rare. They come jumping up the Fourberie River like salmon. We've tagged them all. Most of them is more accurate."

"That's the craziest thing I ever heard."

But Toad thought the man sounded legit. He now doubted his doubt. He closed his eyes and felt for the truth. It was tough. Something in the lake interfered. After several minutes, the crowd dispersed. The limnologist left the shark's corpse and came over to where the boys sat on the hot sand. Toad ground his teeth. He doubted his doubt of his doubt.

"What do you think of this lake?" the man asked.

"It's special," Beetle said.

"Yes, special. What's your name?"

"Beetle."

"And you?"

"Toad."

"And you, little friend?"

"Flat Tire."

"What do you mean by special?" Beetle asked, teasingly. Toad watched the man, but he merely smiled gently. A breeze kicked up, heavy with the scent of the ocean, meaning an intense storm was on the way. The wind came across the water, touching down every 20 meters like some giant, invisible ballerina skipping across a stage.

"It's a magical lake," the limnologist said. "Full of surprises."

"Like what?" Beetle asked.

"It's very old. Ancient."

"How old?" Toad asked.

"Evidence says 50 million years old."

"Wow."

"And it's very deep."

"How deep?"

"2,000 meters in its deepest spot."

"Impossible," Beetle said.

"It's also rich in biodiversity," the limnologist said. "Do you know that word?"

"I've heard that word," Toad said. "Earth doesn't have much of it."

"Yes, exactly. You're sharp."

"What are the big mysteries though?" Beetle asked.

"Well," the limnologist began. "Until two years ago, this was the world's clearest lake. You could see down to about 50 meters. Now look at it."

The boys did look, but they already knew the lake was murky as the Devil's secret heart.

"We have no idea what caused the change. No idea."

"Pollution."

"No."

Toad and Beetle both wondered if the scientist knew the real secret of Dreaming Back Lake. Toad was politely waiting for some kind of indication, but Beetle couldn't stop smirking. Toad wanted to pinch him.

"You boys aren't dressed for swimming. What are you doing here on the beach?"

"Eh."

"And shouldn't you be in school?" he asked with a twinkle in his eye that suggested solidarity with the truants of the world. Poor Beetle wanted to explode. Toad knew it was too much to ask a little kid to hold in a secret, to avoid spilling the beans, especially a secret like this one.

Maggie saved them from the school question. She came slowly walking down from the road.

"What's up, boys?" she said. "Hello, Chuck."

"Well, howdy, Maggie," Chuck, the limnologist, replied.

"Terrorizing our sharks again, I see."

"That's not the word I'd use."

"Murdering then."

"You of all people should have some sympathy, Maggie. It's science, Maggie. Our work."

"What's new with my lake?"

"Tons! Did you read my paper?"

"I don't read your papers, Chuck."

"You have to. Come on."

Maggie shrugged.

"Nothing new with my study," she lied.

"Uh huh," Chuck said. "All your activity suggests otherwise."

"Is that so?"

"That's what I'm hearing."

Maggie grew tight-lipped. Annoyed. Her bad eye twitched.

"Boys," she said. "Let's go get some breakfast."

They'd have to get far away from the dead shark before their appetites would return, and that's what they did. They walked the long strand to a shoreside café and sat down. From that distance, Chuck the limnologist was a stick figure moving about in a heat mirage, and Maggie wished he'd just evaporate.

As his friends waited for him, Yoshi walked the streets of a city he didn't know. He pursued Gun Club Jack and the two heavily-armed Frogmen. Yoshi carried no gun, no knife. He had no plan. He was sopping wet, and the rain showed no signs of stopping. It was dark. His feet, which felt heavy, squished along in water-logged shoes. He'd been surprised nobody met the Chairman when they emerged from the river; Gun Club was risking it, travelling with just two guards. The streets were well-lit by bright, yellow lamps. Water ran down the gutters on both sides, but the road was otherwise perfect. No potholes. No cracks. Serious people lived here. He'd walked about two miles, maybe a little more, when a civil defense siren began a panicked keening in the distance. Five minutes later, the water flow in the gutters doubled. Yoshi stepped onto the curb. The flow rose for a few minutes then subsided to its prior level. He walked on. This repeated itself five minutes later, this time with an even greater flow. Siren, flood, subside. Siren, flood, subside.

Long, sleek, silver cars drove by, careless of the water. He arrived at a busy intersection where men in yellow hazmat suits and respirator masks pushed the flood waters into storm drains using long water sweepers.

The siren sounded again, and the men in the yellow suits leaned on the handles of their wide, rubber brooms and waited for the next wave. The wave came, and the men studiously pushed it to the drains and flood control channels.

Yoshi approached one man.

"See two men and a cripple come through here?" he asked.

The man nodded. He pointed down one of the cross streets, and Yoshi followed his finger to a long string of yellow lamps. "Thank you," he said, bowing.

"You'll want to get a respirator," the worker said. "Get a respirator if you're gonna be out during the river's cresting."

"Oh. Yeah," Yoshi said. "Yeah. Thanks."

Yoshi moved on, down that cross street, subconsciously counting lamp poles and blooming, green trees. At another intersection, he stopped at one lamp pole, a curious one that had blue signs attached to it. The signs looked like old Earth mail envelopes.

QUITO 2856 mi.
LEEDS 4748 mi.

Those words meant nothing to him. He walked on. He jumped each time the civil defense siren screamed. It was growing louder. He was getting closer to it.

Yoshi remembered what he'd been told. Gun Club will be looking for a hospital, grown-up Yoshi had told him. If you lose track of him or get delayed, look for the hospital. Which hospital? Who knows.

He passed a sign pointing to River Road and a Waterfront Park. He did not want that direction. The respirators. My god. The hospital is the only thing the Chairman wants. Repairs for his body. His great want is our great advantage.

Walking on, Yoshi came to a cross street that was fully a river. He stopped at the edge of the swift water, and, as he did, a police airboat came along and pointed a bright, silver light on him. It was just a moment, though, and the airboat loudly continued its journey. He watched it and its spotlight sweep several city blocks before disappearing in the distance. He considered whether he should test the current with his foot. He felt indecisive, standing there, when suddenly he was hit by a realization. There were no Marines. Where am I? What city is this? He decided not to risk crossing the water.

He watched for hospital signs, as he turned 90 degrees and followed down the street the police had taken in their airboat. The rain poured down harder, so when he came to a crowded pub that was bright with neon signs, he went inside.

Nobody looked at him. He could pass for older than he was, especially with his soaking black hair plastered to his face. The pub buzzed with chatter. Yoshi sat at an open table and looked around. It was good to get out of the rain, but he was dripping all over the place and leaving a puddle on the floor. A server came over. She has dark hair and sunken eyes.

"No umbrella, chum?" she asked. Her nametag said Lucy.

"Forgot it."

"Forgot it!" Lucy laughed. "Forgot his umbrella. You're not from around here, are you?"

"Right."

"No umbrella in a Biblical flood. Poor you."

"Yeah. I'm wet."

"You're wet. Can I get you something?"

"Got soup?"

"Stew okay?"

"Okay."

Lucy brought a piping hot bowl. The warmth was great. He felt it as energy in his arms and legs. He hoped it would work against the strange heaviness he'd felt since climbing out of the river. Oh, man, he'd been in the river! And those respirators! He felt fine though. No problem with his breathing, no dizziness, no sickness. The heaviness was all.

When it came time to pay for the stew, he didn't panic though his pockets were empty. He picked a moment nobody was watching (so he thought), and he snuck out the door.

A block away, out on the street, he approached a police officer (a Japanese woman, what luck) who stood watching the traffic that zipped by between surges of the flooding.

"Can you tell me where the hospital is?" he asked her.

She looked him over.

"Are you hurt?"

"No. A friend is there. I'm from out of town."

The civil defense siren sounded. The officer looked back to the road in expectation. She seemed to forget him. The flood came through and subsided again.

Yoshi felt heavy. The ground seemed to be pulling at him.

"Still here?" the officer asked when she noticed him.

"The hospital?"

"Oh. Right. You're heading the right way. Keep going. If you come to the cemetery you've gone too far. I don't know how you'd miss it, but if you come to the cemetery then you've missed it."

"Thank you."

He felt her eyes in his back, as he walked away, but he didn't look back. The pattern of siren, flood, crossing repeated as Yoshi traveled block by block. Like he was stuck in a life-sized version of an ancient board game about the demigod of the deeps.

He was nearly run down by a water ambulance that came quickly through an intersection without its lights or sirens on. That would be one way to get to the hospital, he thought, when he stepped back to watch it. It was yellow. Amphibious. It rode wheels where the road was dry, moved like a boat in the flood waters. As if it were the signal to gain entry, the ambulance turned on its lights as it approached the hospital. The building was a palace of brightness, and it accepted the new light into itself. Yoshi followed, invisibly, in the vehicle's wake.

The immaculate, sterile, white light of the lobby was shocking after the storm gloom outside. He caught a glimpse of himself in the glass doors. His black hair looked like a sea urchin now, spiked all over in every direction. And, looking, you could tell he'd literally climbed out of the river. Still, nurses and ambulance drivers and patients smiled at him in a friendly way. He smiled back and moved about the Waiting Room without anyone stopping him.

He saw the Chairman, backed by his two big goons, talking to a nurse at the Triage Desk. After getting what had to be disappointing news—-although Yoshi was far away and could not hear—-they moved to Waiting Room chairs. Gun Club sat between the two goons and slumped his shoulders like a sulky child.

"Where-when are we that the Chairman can be told to wait?" Yoshi asked himself. Very strange.

Feeling heavy and tired, Yoshi fought to stay awake as they waited. He was surrounded by people in gruesome, torturous pain. A woman next to him comforted a small girl with a gauzy eye patch that oozed blood. Yoshi didn't know where to look.

One of the Frogmen approached the Triage nurse and handed her a plastic payment card from his pocket. She held it up in front of her face, looked at it for a long time, then shook her head no and handed it back. The Frogman sat back down next to Gun Club. The Chairman wore a serious face. Yoshi could see the very muscles working his frown.

Yoshi considered for a moment that none of the strangers in the room had the remotest idea that four people sitting amongst them had traveled through time. A sleeping giant, that secret. Outside, a flood surge brought a tree trunk to rest against the glass wall of the Waiting Room. It was long, branchless, worn smooth. Just as a man in a white doctor's coat began speaking with Gun Club, Yoshi felt a hand on his shoulder. When he turned, he saw it was Lucy from the pub. In the bright light of the hospital, her eyes looked better. Less sad. Not as sunken.   "Don't worry," she said immediately to disarm him. "I'm not after you."

"Did you follow me?"

"Yes," she said.

"Why?"

"No umbrella. No poncho. That gave you away."

"Gave what away?"

Yoshi tried to look at her and keep one eye on the doctor in white who was now leading Gun Club and his small goon squad to the elevator.

"What's your name?"

"Yoshi."

"Yes. That's exactly right," she said as if remembering something from a dream.

She noticed his preoccupation.

"Do you need to speak to that man?"

"Actually, yes."

Yoshi tried to stand up, but Lucy held his shoulder tightly. She had a good grip. He moved her hand and stood up. When he saw how close Gun Club was to the elevator, he tried to fly. He leaped forward and spread his arms wide open.

But he didn't fly.

He hit the floor lightly, capably, on eight legs.

Lucy screamed. Some men shouted.

He ran straight up the wall. His speed and agility were obscene, inhuman.

"Get that thing, Balthasar," a woman cried. "Kill it."

But Balthasar was frozen in his chair. His eyes, like the eyes of every other face in the room, followed the arachnid across the ceiling. Yoshi was now a kill machine. He moved by smooth hydraulics, and his fangs felt like the deadliest guns in the universe. Ready to fire. Ready to kill. He had dark thoughts. As rapid and straight as a bullet train, he sped to the elevator. He got in before the door closed, completely unnoticed by the occupants.

"Hey, you in the elevator!" Balthasar's wife shouted, but the door closed. Her warning was lost.

Yoshi hung onto the ceiling of the elevator. He found gravity to be no concern anymore. If he lost hold on his metamorphosis, though, he'd fall embarrassingly and dangerously on the people below.

The doctor was talking.

"Normally, there is a six-month wait list for the chamber, but since you have significant resources."

"Can you treat me today?" the Chairman asked.

"No," the doctor said. "Quite possibly tomorrow."

"Tomorrow. Good. That's good."

"I'll get you admitted for your injury. We have a room for you to sleep in tonight."

Sleep, but no rest. Gun Club talked in his sleep, as Yoshi dangled down, suspended by a silk thread, just above his face. "She's no imperial manager," Gun Club said "No, she is not."

As the endless rain lashed the window of the hospital room, the Chairman fell asleep counting the cells in the dropped ceiling. He didn't see any spider. The spider now inches from his face. It was dark enough that if he suddenly opened his eyes, he might not even see the spider.

The Frogmen sat in the hallway outside the room, taking turns resting, one awake, one asleep. Yoshi alighted from the thread onto the thick hair on the good side of Gun Club's head. Silently, swiftly. He moved down the head, across the pillow, along the length of the mattress and down to the floor. When Yoshi flipped on the light, Gun Club didn't immediately stir. Back in boyish shape, Yoshi sat down in a blue chair. He waited patiently, stretching his back and arms, recalling the words grown-up Yoshi had told him to say. Gun Club slowly woke.

Noticing the light finally, Jack sat straight up. He looked directly at Yoshi. He did not show surprise. It was as if all of this had happened before.

"Do you know me?" Yoshi asked.

"I do," Humble Gun Club Jack said. "Of course, I do."

"And why I am here?"

"Not to kill me."

"No?"

"No, it is to tell me some bullshit about how the treatment in this world won't heal my body."

Yoshi swallowed his shock.

"How?"

"You think you're the only one who has met another version of himself?"

Grown-up Yoshi had not prepared our present Yoshi for this. He stood up. As the reveal sank in, Gun Club looked at him with an expression of understanding sympathy. He almost looked kind.

"So, you're thinking, 'Now what,' aren't you?"

Yoshi said nothing. He stepped towards the bed.

"Strangle me? Some other kind of violence? Are you armed?"

"No."

"Why don't you have a seat? I'll tell you everything I know and everything that you know that is all wrong. Sit back in that chair. There is a lot you need to hear."

Yoshi sat.

"As you no doubt have figured out, killing me here and now won't end your mission or solve your problem."

"I'm not here to kill you."

"I know that. But..."

"I'm supposed to convince you."

"Never mind that. You need to understand one thing. My map shows me everything. It shows me every time, every space. Look there."

He pointed at the door, and Yoshi looked. At the bottom, struggling to squeeze through the tiny space, he could see the hairy legs of two big spiders.

"I control everything."

Chapter Eight

The tiny, silver car struggled. It moved steadily—-okay, steadily enough—-but it was clear to Sleeper, at the wheel, they were pushing their luck with the heavy load. The broken soldiers were squeezed into the car like jigsaw puzzle pieces, the tabs of good limbs pressed into the blanks of a comrade's missing limbs until the mess made a kind of sense. The good thing was they left behind nobody who wanted to come.

"You okay back there, Shorty?" Sleeper called out over the murmur of the passengers.

"I'm good, man."

Sleeper was concerned about the little guy's ability to breathe back there in the pile. He was a survivor, though. Sleeper had never met anyone like him.

Unbeknownst to our friends, their silver car was being followed by a drone and a small convoy of armored fighting vehicles. Rotors would've given the game away, General Messmaker said, as he gave the follow order. See what they are up to, he said. Follow them and report back.

The city skyline was fuzzy in the tiresome haze. Even the Mission HQ building, which on a bright day reflected everything as a better version of the world, looked humdrum as it grew on the horizon. When they got to Radium Beach's elevated inner ring road, the traffic stopped. Several cars back, the black AFVs stopped, too. Nobody could move.

"What's happening?" Shorty asked from the back.

"Total stop," Sleeper said to groans from the soldiers. "Weird. It never backs up here."

Maybe twenty cars ahead, Sleeper could see drivers out of their cars, looking down to lower levels of the interchange. "Let's get out," he said.

"What? Why?" Pork Chop protested. "No. Stay. The car is the way, boys."

Sleeper got out, leaving the car running. He walked to the road's left lane Jersey barrier and looked down past the crisscrossing ramps below them like so many strands of fettucine in a bowl. At the bottom, at ground level, there were people—men, women and children—marching in a massive crowd. Other people walked down ramps past the jammed cars to join them. Still others walked up the same ramps, waving to fellows above to come down.

Sleeper stood where he was, transfixed, trying to figure out what was going on. His comrades climbed out of the clown car.

"What is it?" Shorty asked, as he pommel horsed his legless body over.

"Looks like a demonstration or protest. Big one."

Pork Chop whistled when he looked down and saw the size of the crowd.

"Humid out here," Pork Chop said.

"Hot as balls," Shorty agreed.

Sweat was pouring off all of them.

"How long can we run the AC in the car without charging?" Pork Chop asked.

"Not sure."

"Leave it here then?" Shorty asked.

"Probably best," Sleeper said.

"Ah, shit," Pork Chop said, but he didn't fight when they all started moving—slowly, slowly—down the nearest ramp. Shorty climbed onto Sleeper for a piggyback ride. Sleeper felt the half man's incredible forearms under his chin.

The Marines that had followed the silver car set up a roadblock where they'd been forced to stop. A crew of five stayed with the vehicles. A dozen began to pursue our hobbling gang. The drone circled the interchange and kept its eye on the prey. Progress down the ramp was like a slow fire drill down the stairwell of an office building. Sleeper felt his own face running through the emotions on the faces of the people going down. Bewilderment, fear, anticipation. Discomfort in the heat. Shorty's weight was a burden.

In the sky, squadrons of Messmaker's drones circled the downtown like carrion birds. Whether they were armed or not, Sleeper couldn't tell. He imagined them hissing with evil. It was strange to him to feel the structure of the interchange moving with the weight of so many human footsteps rather than the rhythmic vibration of car after car after car. When they reached a section of ramp level with the tops of the green trees, Shorty reached out and pulled off a wide, green leaf. He fanned himself and Sleeper with it.

"Thanks, Shorty. That feels good."

"Any time, brother."

High above them, on the road they'd left behind, Marines stood at the Jersey barrier, looking down. One of them spit out what looked like the disgusting juice of his chewing tobacco, and when the juice landed on a protester, a second Marine smacked him on the helmet.

"Looks like the bad guys are checking things out."

"Where?" Shorty asked.

"Up top."

Shorty looked up. He grimaced.

"I know those guys. Those are not good guys."

"They don't seem to be on the street yet."

Shorty looked down. It was true. No Marines in sight on the street yet.

"I see police," Shorty said, as they finally reached the ground. "But are they—"

"They're with the protesters," Sleeper said.

It was true. The police they could see nearby stood and walked with the men and women of the crowd. Sleeper led the broken soldiers to a shady spot under a tree. Pork Chop leaned on the trunk. With them were Malory, Mort, Arthur, Lance. They all stood and sweated and looked to Shorty for some encouragement and guidance. Just as Sleeper noticed the Marines up top were now gone from the Jersey barrier, one of them grabbed him by the collar of his shirt.

"What are you soldiers doing with this robot?" the Marine said. He was helmetless, skin-headed. His tag said RIVERS. Shorty dropped to the ground and bravely came forward.

"What are you talking about?" he asked.

"We've been following you from your rehab hospital. This guy here is artificial, an honest-to-God, made-on-Earth android."

Sleeper didn't know whether to laugh or run. Mistaken identity, of course, yet why did he feel something like relief deep in the pit of his stomach?

Men and women walked by, giving Rivers a wide berth as they did. Sleeper noticed some. A man in a striped shirt. A woman with curly black hair in a dress the color of the sky. A man with a boy on his shoulders. The boy wore a red shirt; he was repeatedly photographed by protesters with mobile devices. A woman in a silver skirt and silver bra. Two men carrying the long pole of a galley tent from the beach settlement. Another two carrying another pole.

"Think you got the wrong party," Shorty said firmly.

"I don't think so, little man. What are you doing out here? And with him?"

"He's a friend of ours, a fellow Marine."

Rivers laughed.

"Oh yeah? Which division?"

Shorty looked up at Sleeper's face for the answer. Sleeper didn't see the look. He was seeing, over Rivers' shoulder, a crowd surge coming. He took a step back, behind the tree Pork Chop leaned against, and scooped up Shorty in his arms. Rivers clutched Sleeper's shirt collar and came along with them, but he was quickly lifted off his feet by the tidal bore of the human tsunami. Sleeper and Shorty got bumped to the ground, but they rolled out of the path of the crowd. They kept rolling, for safety, and stopped on the black stripes of shadow cast by the tree. They watched Rivers try to free himself from the crowd. Pork Chop was nowhere in sight. Malory, Mort, Arthur and Lance were gone, too.

"Shit," Shorty said. "Where'd they go?"

"The crowd. They must be over there somewhere."

"I don't see them."

"I can't see them either."

"Shit."

"Let's hang here a minute. The crowd looks indecisive."

It was a relief to have Rivers gone, even if temporarily, but Sleeper puzzled over what he'd said. He looked at his own hands. They looked like real hands. Mistaken identity? What about the strange machine dreams? The neon sign? The power plant? Sleeper could not explain those things.

Shorty gave no indication he had even a second thought about it as if it deserved no consideration or was so obvious he didn't need to be told. He was scanning the faces in the crowd, watching for his comrades to return. The crowd lost its energy of movement. Like a river dammed, the ripples of force propelling it slowed.

"Let's move west a few blocks."

"What about the guys?"

"We need to get somewhere we can see without being seen."

He scooped Shorty on his back and walked along the front of a bank branch. Inside, customers and bankers looked out at the protest as if from a lair.

The pack of Marines from the top of the interchange could be anywhere now.

"Where are we going?" Shorty asked.

"Just over here. Good spot."

They could not see the extent of the crowd. Sleeper didn't hear any voices amplified by megaphones or whatnot. There was no violence other than the rough-ups caused by sudden surges. With the police having joined the body of the protesters, and the Marines no yet on hand in large numbers, things were chaotic but not yet mayhem. This was all unprecedented in Sleeper's own memory. A crowd like this, a dense mass. Nearby, a True Time man was set up at a table with his book of converts and a pyramid of water bottles.

"You wanna get some water?" Sleeper asked Shorty.

"Yeah."

They waited in the short line at the table.

"Have you two converted to the True Time?"

"We have."

"Both in our book?"

"Indeed."

"Like a water?"

"Yes, please," Sleeper replied. "I'm Sebastian."

"Peter Loos," the time man said. They shook hands.

"What do you suppose this is all about?" Sleeper asked.

"History," Peter Loos said.

I've never seen anything like this," Sleeper said. "I've never seen anything like this on Triste."

Peter Loos looked at him when he repeated himself with the slight alteration.

"Have you been off-world?" he asked Sleeper.

"No," Sleeper said. "No no no. Didn't mean to imply that."

"Just wondered what you meant."

Things began to change as the Fast Sun set. The number of drones flitting around seemed to double or triple. Marines in black helmets and black body armor arrived with numbers. Shorty grew desperate as the neighborhood grew dark. He could no longer make out faces in the crowd. Sleeper decided to test an idea he had tucked into the back of his brain.

"Humble Jack will show up out of thin air any minute, huh?"

"Huh?"

"He'll just pop out of whatever time he's hiding out in."

"Who have you been talking to?" Loos asked.

"Erdapfel."

Loos raised an eyebrow.

"You knew the old man?"

"I met him," Sleeper said.

"What are you guys talking about?" Shorty asked.

"Erdapfel has an interesting theory. But he's wrong. Fundamentally wrong."

"How so?"

"You really want to talk about this here?"

"It's pretty important to me, but I understand if you don't want to talk about it."

"Why so important?"

"Well," Sleeper began. "It's because of things that have happened to me."

"You've been through one of the go-betweens?"

"Yes."

"Holy shit."

"What the hell are you guys talking about?" Shorty asked.

He tried to turn Sleeper's face to his own to get him to answer. A line had formed behind them.

"Here," Peter Loos said to Shorty. "Man my water station. You, come with me."

Sleeper dropped Shorty onto the chair on the staff side of the table. Then, he followed Peter Loos through the crowd to a side street near the bank again.

"Let's get right to it. You think the King moves through time, right?"

"Right."

"The ultimate weapon, right? The ability and will to manipulate events past and future."

"Well, I hadn't thought that far into it."

"Erdapfel is wrong. There are no wormholes per se."

"Well, but—"

"The travel is between worlds. Versions of the world. Naming the crossings go-betweens was brilliant entirely serendipitously. Stumbled upon."

Sleeper was silent. He touched his face.

"Here's the big reveal, kid. And this is the part that is original to me. And you won't believe it, but consider how perfectly matched the gravity here is. How close to perfectly matched. Damn near. Triste isn't another plant. Triste is Earth. It's an alternate Earth. It has its own history. But some of the history is stacked on top of an Earth history some of us are just beginning to suspect is below our feet, a world beneath the world."

"No."

"Yes."

He liked Erdapfel's version better. He could make sense of it. No. Loos was crazy. The two suns. Sleeper's own experience. It couldn't be true.

Chapter Nine

The green Jaguar was parked in a reserved spot at the Mission HQ in Colorado Springs. Piper made them all stop in their tracks when she spotted it.

She asked Flattery, "You know this car?"

"Of course."

"What's it doing here?"

Flattery shrugged. Colonel Endling could guess who it belonged to. He sweated in the heat radiating from the airfield's tarmac, but, at the same time, he could see snow on a peak to the west. It was amazing, and it cheered his heart to see it. There were just three other cars in the parking zone.

"Everyone got out of Dodge," Piper said.

"That's what it looks like," the Colonel agreed.

"We should go in," Piper said.

"Is that safe?" Flattery asked.

"Right through the front door," the Colonel said. The door was not locked. Through the glass, they saw an empty lobby. It looked blue then green then blue in the alternating LED light coming from the unmanned reception desk. Passing through the revolving door, the past came back to the Colonel. Years of work in this building. Years of planning and waiting, decades ago now. His body immediately recalled the stress. But also, the exhilaration of the enormous success.

His own picture was on the lobby's wall. He tried to quickly pass it, but Piper stopped him.

"Hey, look at this handsome face."

But it was other faces that held his attention, colleagues and friends he had not seen in a lifetime. Astronomers, engineers, biologists, electricians, the rocket scientists, the nuclear fuel geniuses. And there was Souci, the heroic one, Souci, the one who had so many secrets.

There had been a Bon Voyage ball, the night before the maiden emigration flight. The menu from the dinner was framed on the wall. He wondered could he remember the dishes without a hint from the menu? Certainly, there were black beans. Black beans were a massive Colorado crop in those sweltering days. Black beans in almost every meal. Black beans in tortillas and soups and salads and casseroles and bean burgers (he'd liked those). Black beans in rice and these so-called lasagnas and black beans straight up in a bowl until you couldn't stand the sight of them anymore.

"That's you, huh?" Flattery said. "What a big shot."

"That's me."

"Where do we go?" Piper asked. "Up?"

"Up. Yes. Up."

The elevators were out of commission.

"Stairs then?"

"Yup."

Colonel Endling was sure Jim Apostle would stay. He was a Mission lifer, promoted always by merit and so critical in getting the Mission through the dark years of failure. And the Colonel was right. Jim was waiting for them in the stairwell about ten floors up.

"Halloo. Who goes there?"

"Jesus, no elevators, Jim?"

"Ed Endling? Is that you?"

"Live in the flesh."

"Holy shit. Get up here."

Colonel Endling, Piper and Flattery climbed the ten flights. The Colonel reached out to shake Jim's hand, but the Director deflected his hand and grabbed him in a bear hug.

"You wear glasses now," the Colonel teased.

"Worst development of my life, my fading eyesight."

Jim led them into the Ops space. The layout looked mostly the same. The gear was newer. Aside from the glasses, Jim, too, looked largely the same. Older, but still fit and healthy.

"Y' all must be exhausted. Let's use the lounge. Where'd you come from?"

"Boulder."

"On foot?"

"On foot."

Jim gestured to the lounge sofas, and they each picked their own and dropped onto them with heavy, delighted groans. Jim sat in an arm chair and grinned at them all.

"What's with the Jaguar downstairs?" the Colonel asked.

"Somebody who had a ticket for Omega Flight drove down in that car and left it."

"Who?"

"Not sure. Nobody would admit to it."

"So, what happened?" Piper asked.

Jim sighed.

"What do you already know?"

"Imagine we know nothing," Colonel Endling said.

"The Queen issued a cut-off order. Permanent, it seems. We are to send no more flights, construct no more ships. We've had no communication from Triste since Omega Flight left."

"For what reason?" the Colonel asked.

"Fear of revolt, I guess."

"From what quarter?"

"The Queen is paranoid. She suspected Leo was building his own army here."

"Is the Chairman alive?" the Colonel asked.

"Last I heard? Yes."

The mountains outside looked like footage from a film or a fragment of a dream. And fleets of cloud behind them moved swiftly west to east.

"Only 38% of the ticket holders for Omega Flight showed up," Jim said. "I was surprised by that. Very surprised."

"My brother had one," Flattery said. "He didn't go."

"Can it possibly really be permanent?" the Colonel asked.

"I doubt it," Jim said. "They are still stripping resources. Or they were two days ago."

"Have all the soldiers gone?"

"From this base, yes. The rest, I don't know."

"Crazy."

"Leo is dead," Jim said.

"We saw his corpse," Piper said.

"What?"

"Long story," Colonel Endling explained. "This has all been a long, strange trip. We were in the bunker Green Room, waiting for an audience when it happened."

"Leo was foolish about risks."

The talk paused, and all three of the exhausted travelers noticed the lounge's refrigerator at the same time. The door handle was a shiny silver. They imagined what might be inside. Jim followed their eyes there.

"How about some eggs? Who's hungry?"

"Oh god please," Piper said.

Jim sprang into action at the electric stove.

"How do we like them?"

He whipped up a giant batch of scrambled. When the warm bowl landed in Piper's lap, she steepled her fingers and said, "I feel like I should pray to some higher power. Thank you."

"Enjoy."

Jim sat down to eat, too.

"So," the Colonel said. "What's going to happen now? Is anything being organized for new leadership?"

"Our work goes on, Ed," Jim replied.

"That's it?"

Jim didn't say anything more. He shrugged and smiled.

"What do you do when a line of tanks drives up here from Texas tomorrow, and the drivers say they're in charge now?"

"Ah, well, how likely is that?"

Colonel Endling shook his head.

"What were you just saying about fools and risk?"

Jim shrugged and smiled. His face said, "You got me."

"Did you know Souci has a son that leads a group of people down south of here?"

Jim Apostle looked confused.

"How?"

"You tell me. You didn't know?"

"No," Jim said, and the Colonel believed him. "You don't rest for a minute, do you, Ed?"

"Not much. Only when I collapse."

"Why don't you all get some sleep. Then, tonight, I have something to show you."

In the staff quarters, all three of them slept an entire day. Climbing out of the bed he'd spent the night a half a day in, his old bones and joints grumbling at him, the Colonel went looking for a clock. Looking out a window, he squinted at the bright afternoon and saw red rock formations, jagged like a ruinous, ancient wall in front of perfect, purple mountains.

He found Jim Apostle sipping a cup of tea, looking at the same view.

"Want a cup?" Jim asked.

"Please. Yes."

"You've been through a hell of a lot, Ed."

"A lot of bull shit. I don't usually talk like that, but there's no other way to put it."

"But you've pulled through it."

The Colonel shrugged.

"Pulled through to what, Jim? How do things stand now? We should be acting quickly to re-establish some democratic frameworks."

"We will."

"We can't wait, Jim."

"I've been thinking a lot since you arrived. We must get a reckoning of who is still here and then figure out how we are going to feed them all. If the Texas soldiers are gone, we can expect a large northward migration."

"Good. Yes. Good thinking."

Colonel Endling held his forehead with both hands.

"What's wrong?"

"I'm too old for this. Too exhausted."

"No, Ed. We will do this together."

The Colonel sighed.

"Oh, I almost forgot. I have something to show you. Come. Follow me."

Jim led him through his own office to one of the hallways connected to the Mission's superprocessing center. There was such a light crew on-site that just one tech managed the room that looked to the Colonel to be about four acres in size.

"Matt is here to basically monitor the air conditioning," Jim said. "Matt, this is Colonel Endling."

"Holy shit," young Matt said.

Jim laughed.

"The legend himself."

"Can I help with something?" young Matt asked.

"Nah," Jim said. "I'm just going to show him what we got from Operation Watershed."

"Okay."

"Operation Watershed?" the Colonel asked.

"So, before I boot this machine, let's catch up. It has been a long time since we talked about the Map Room in Radium Beach and your obsessive project."

"Yes. My disaster."

"Well, you were onto something deep. We successfully hacked Gun Club's own map. Which means basically we hacked his brain."

"Before or after his injury?"

"After. He didn't have any vulnerability until after."

The Colonel was not all the way on-board the train of understanding.

"What is it a map of?"

"What do you think? Got a guess?"

"Not a guess. Just a lot of fear suddenly, Jim. Are you gonna tell me about magic?"

"Well... let me show you what we grabbed."

At a tall work station, a wide monitor lit up. Jim touched the screen with his thumbprint and logged in. A file directory spiderwebbed to thousands of video files.

"One of our techs in Redemption Rock got close enough to use a spear MRI to hack him."

"A what?" the Colonel asked.

"It's a hacking tool for the visual cortex," Jim said. "It's not new per se, but it's gotten very fast in the last year or so."

"For hacking the visual cortex."

"It's exactly what it sounds like."

"Forgive me, but it sounds like Lizzie Borden."

"All right. Ha ha."

Piper coughed behind them.

"Um, you can hack brain activity patterns and decode them into signals and rebuild them if you have an ANN like I'm guessing Jim has here."

"Hello, Piper," Jim said. "Correct."

"What's ANN?" the Colonel asked.

"Artificial Neural Network."

"You're looking at it here," Jim said, gesturing with his long, tan fingers at the room. Piper's always-calculating eyes calculated. She strode to the work station.

"You got it to work?" she asked.

Jim played a video at random. It was extremely blurry, only the outlines of most objects were reconstructed except in moments when the visual field moved into a sudden bright spot. It looked like a stylized scene from an art film. Piper, though, was impressed.

"My god," she said.

Colonel Endling rubbed his eyes.

"His map?" he asked.

"Yes," Jim said. "His map. Gun Club has a build on top of his cervical vertebrae. It's not detachable in any way that wouldn't harm him gravely. We learned about it from a spy who got the scoop from Leo. It's a map of the go-betweens."

"A map of them? How?"

"It seems to be a map of his memories. But we need a bit more computing power to make what we got useful."

"How many go-betweens are there?"

"How high can you count? What's the biggest finite number you can think of?"

"What will the map be useful for?" the Colonel asked, feeling naïve and innocent.

Piper grinned. "Well, we gotta catch him, right?"

They rested for three days. Lots of sleep and food and conversation. Against what any reasonable person would call good judgment, Jim let Piper check out the hardware and the code for the ANN. She didn't violate his trust or hospitality. She simply read the code and smiled with joy at its elegant complexity.

On the third day, the Mission had an unexpected visitor. It was the day of the regular, weekly HQ morning assembly. Things were informal for the assembly compared to the Colonel's recollections of the old days. Jim sat on the edge of the stage in the HQ Auditorium as techs, engineers, pilots and staff slowly arrived. Probably sixty people showed up. He sipped from a cup of tea. He had his customary yellow pencil behind one ear. Colonel Endling, Piper and Flattery sat in the first row of seats, facing him.

"So," Jim began. "This is our first assembly since Omega Flight. We had out debrief sessions, but what questions to people have at this point?"

A great deal of throat-clearing and shifting-in-seats.

"What do we do now?" young Matt asked. He took off his thick, greasy looking eyeglasses and rubbed them with his shirt.

"We work. We carry on."

"With which projects?"

"I have a new one, an urgent project."

They all waited for him to explain.

"We need to complete a census. I was just talking about this with my friend, Ed Endling, the other night. We need to count how many people remain here in Colorado and document where they are living."

"Should we start up the postal service, too?" one of the pilots asked. He was dressed in black pants and the flashy silver shirt of his division. His question drew some laughs, but the faces were all sympathetic.

"It has been at least 20 years since we even attempted a census of the population."

It was at that moment that Iris walked into the Auditorium. Her pregnant belly came one step ahead of her. It was round and enormous and looked like it might burst at any moment and drown them all in a great flood of amniotic fluid.

"Who's that?" Piper whispered.

"Iris," Flattery said.

"Who?"

Iris walked down the center aisle of the Auditorium like a bride coming to a church altar.

"I think," she said. "I think maybe he's about to arrive."

Chapter Ten

"On the chessboard, lies and hypocrisy do not survive long. The creative combination lays bare the presumption of a lie; the merciless fact, culminating in a checkmate, contradicts the hypocrite."
- Emanuel Lasker

No less an authority than the 11th Encyclopedia Britannica says, "She is the most powerful piece on the board." Who is she? She is the Queen, of course. And yet, daring to contradict the famous encyclopedia, the game can continue without the Queen. A Queen lost does not lose all. We love games, and perhaps we love none more than those with stakes that carry life and death. Yoshi kept seeing Roux's face. And her red hair. He was confused. This vision wasn't his own. Gun Club mentioned her again and again in his rambling, philosophical talk. It was as if Gun Club himself was compelled by some outside agent to mention her in contexts that made no sense.

He was making big promises, the Chairman was. Yoshi supposed a Chairman was a class of person who could deliver on big promises, but this one was a scoundrel and a liar.

The rain kept on.

"This event has happened before," Gun Club said. "Many times. You and me. This conversation. This path. These words. Your doubts. Sometimes, I nearly convince you."

Yoshi's head swam.

They headed back towards the river, back into the night, away from the hospital's light, the four of them walking single file in the following order: Frogman, Yoshi, Gun Club, Frogman. The walk was Yoshi's chance to consider the Chair's offer. Come over to the right side of history, he said. Better yet, come over and we can change history. We can change it. We can make it good. We can save more people. You've been misled by Serge Ville de Paix and the others. Badly deceived. I can show you what absolute power can accomplish. It's a power of goodness.

Yoshi doubted it all. Every word. The river reflected the gloominess of the rain sky and the faithlessness of Gun Club's speech. When they got to the edge, they jumped in, one at a time, and the Frogmen each grabbed a diving buddy and swam toward the waterfall that emerged from the blinding rain.

When he opened his eyes, Yoshi's first waking thought was that something was very wrong. Something smelled FOUL. He sat up and realized the foul something was himself. He had a crazy thought that he was dead, and the stink was his own corpse. But, no. He was alive.

He was seated on old tiles, once-white tiles that had not been cleaned in years. He was only feet away from an open pool of sewage, or, maybe, it was a deep, wide-open latrine that would have tested even Dante's bottomless powers of nightmare imagination. The two Frogmen were fast asleep on the tile. Yoshi looked around and saw an open door. Wet footprints led to it. The Chairman, Yoshi thought. I'll follow.

"He's alone with no guards," the possibility thrilled him. Now was the chance. Now.

He should have been more cautious.

As he passed through, he noted the door said CELL BLOCK Y. The room was darker than the latrine and much larger he sensed by the air and the echo of his own footsteps. As his pupils adjusted to the dark, he began to realize he was standing in the wide, central opening of a panopticon. He froze. The wet footprints led directly to one of the cells, but the cell had a glass front and was dark, so he could not see inside. He walked to it and tapped on the glass.

"Hello?"

The building was circular. The cells occupied the outside of the circle, a single story only, but the ring was expansive. There had to be 200 cells or more.

"Hello?" he repeated and banged on the glass. Every cell was dark, so Yoshi could not tell if they were empty or occupied. He stepped away from the glass.

"Another one," said a voice from a cell to his right.

"Not another one. Really?" answered a second voice.

"Yes. He's right outside."

The voices sounded uncannily familiar. Yoshi walked the circle and tried to peer into the gloom of each cell, but he saw nothing but a reflection of himself and the cells behind him. Suddenly, there was a noise like somebody threw the lever of a circuit breaker. Yoshi turned around and saw the cell with the wet footprints was now backlit. He walked over to it. Gun Club's wet clothes were in a pile on the floor. A door leading out of the back of the cell to the outermost part of the ring was open.

"Don't go in there if she opens it," the first invisible voice said.

"He will. We always do," said the second voice.

As if to confirm this suspicion, Yoshi clawed at the edges of the glass, but there was no getting in.

"Why is there no watch tower?" he asked when he got frustrated with the glass.

"That's a question of will and consent and agency."

"What the fuck does that mean?"

"Can't tell you. You'll have to be shown."

"Shown what?" Yoshi threw his hands up.

"She will be along any minute."

"Who will?"

"You know who."

"You're very frustrating," Yoshi said.

"Yes," the voice said. "We are."

"She moves very fast."

Yoshi looked around.

"How will she come?"

"Doesn't matter. All the ways about here belong to her."

Yoshi walked back to the disgusting latrine pool. The Frogmen were still asleep. Maybe, he thought, one of them is dreaming all this strangeness. He walked away quietly to avoid waking them. He did another slow walk around the ring of cells. A prisoner seemed to rouse as he passed.

"Another one?" the prisoner said.

"Yes, another one," came a call from the other side.

"That's depressing."

You know the strange, almost extrasensory perception of another body's gravity that lets you know there's another person in the room? Yeah, that's a real thing. Yoshi sensed the Queen was nearby before she revealed herself. In the middle of his restless circling, he turned his head, and there she was.

He was not prepared for her freckles. In photos, she must've worn makeup or had them brushed out. They dotted the bridge of her nose and her cheeks below her eyes. Her red hair was tucked under a black diving hood. She wore a black wet suit, and she held a long, silver knife that looked extremely sharp.

"You're here already," she said.

Yoshi stared. She was beautiful.

"Are you going to stab me?"

"Probably not. The knife is for my own protection."

"Where'd the Chairman go?" Yoshi asked, pointing at the cell with the pile of wet clothes.

"He's resting."

"Where are the guards for this prison?"

"There are no guards," she said. She smirked prettily.

"Why did the Chairman lead me here?"

"Perfect. Now that is the question."

Yoshi guessed there was a cell with his name on it. He didn't suspect that all cells had his name, and that he was all prisoners. If he expected violence or a duel of some kind, a duel of wits, say, he figured he was bound to lose or find the game rigged against him in some demoralizing way. His errand had not gone as planned and foretold.

"So?"

"So, what?" the Queen asked.

"Why am I here?"

The Queen sighed.

"Are you going to lie to yourself already? You brought yourself here. You followed my husband. You tell me why."

"Curiosity."

"Bull shit."

"It's true."

"Lies are bad, Yoshi. This place is filled with liars."

He held his breath a moment, said nothing.

"I might as well show you," the Queen said. She closed her eyes, and all the cells in the panopticon lit up. In every cell, the occupant stood at the glass, looking out. Every face was Yoshi's own. His black hair. His body. His style of dress. Some had facial scars, and some had injuries, but there was no doubting each prisoner was one of Yoshi's doubles. It was like a house of mirrors. He gasped.

"This is a trick."

He approached the nearest cell. The Yoshi inside the glass said, "It's no trick."

"Are you real?"

"I am real."

Yoshi turned to the Queen. He said, "What have you done?"

She scoffed.

"It should be obvious. We started with one. He said no. We took a second. He said no. The loop has repeated. You can see how many times."

Don't listen to any of her bargaining," the nearest Prisoner Yoshi said. "That knife is nothing. You can take it from her."

The Queen closed her eyes again, and the glass front of an empty cell opened.

"Take my husband's offer, or there's the one for you."

"Your husband wants me as his apprentice, but why? There's nothing special about me."

"Come on."

"What?"

"He told me about your special powers of (oh, what's the word?) becoming."

"How's that—"

"I've had enough now," the Queen said angrily as if she suddenly had a skull-bursting headache. "Get in your cell."

"No."

"A man who says 'no.' You all say 'no,' you know."

Yoshi began to slide away from her.

"Get in the cell, or I'll gas the others."

He stopped.

"What?"

"Dead. I'll gas them right there in the cells. All of you."

"No no no. Don't do that."

"Don't bargain with her," the nearest Yoshi demanded. "Go. Take the knife. Get her."

"There's no actual gas," another Yoshi said.

The Queen laughed. "Let's see you test that one."

If there was no gas, Yoshi thought, well, that was one thing, but what if there was, and the prisoners despaired and wanted their despair to end? Horrifying. That's a paraphrase of his thoughts. Nothing that clear came to mind in his panic. He was chilled by the possibilities and what might happen.

"She'll keep bargaining," the nearby Yoshi said.

Moral decisions made in a panic are dicey. The evidence in front of him suggested there was no world-yet-found in which Yoshi and the Crown were friends.

"Keep looking," the Queen said. "Keep searching your soul. We can change the past. We can change it for good."

She was pleading with him now. A crack in her voice gave him a small bit of confidence. Thinking of a world in which he might agree to join these terrible royals made his head swim again. That's a world where what made him him was endangered. There was no continuity with his present mind, with what he knew of what she called his soul. He risked imagining himself necessary when it was clear the Queen was prepared to gas all of them. Right? Yet how had this many accumulated without gassing up to now? He decided to make a run for the knife. He turned, and, without warning, sprinted at her.

"Behind you," two prisoners shouted in unison before he'd taken three strides. The annular shape of the ring gave the prisoners a good vantage of the showdown. The Frogmen were up and running and about to fire rifles at him. He changed his path and dove, and, with a sort of maximum, numinous surprise, fell to the floor with a hard thud in the form of a dark stone. The Queen put her hands on her hips. The Frogmen skidded to a stop over him.

"Another stone," she said. "Throw it in the cell. Let's start over again. Go get Jack."

Chapter Eleven

The Brain thought he was clever, hiding out in the old, abandoned planetarium. But we're never as clever as we think. His presence was instantaneously found out. By sundown the first day, word had spread. Children came from all over, some from miles away, to see the man with the hidden gold. "Treasure," they said, or, "Treasure?" with a question mark, daydreaming of old, old stories. He was on alert for thieves every time a fist banged on the locked door. He got the projector working. The building was on the Mission grid, and some of the outlets still worked. The projector itself was a robotic, silver egg, but, in complete darkness, when turned on, it looked like a planet about the explode, bright energy escaping from a thousand tiny holes. Many of the kids who came for the gold would forget about it and stay for projections of the universe, expansive and starry and wondrous on the inside of the dome.

One child, who disapproved and sneered, endeared himself to the Brain as a kindred spirit. His name was Santiago. He was Central American. He was an adolescent, windburned and tanned by the restless American sun.

"We can just sit outside and look at the real stars," he scoffed. "Why all this?"

"If you shut up, watch and listen, maybe you will like it and learn something," said the Brain.

Santiago had the enormous scar of an amateur inoculation job on his left shoulder. The Brain asked if his parents were alive. He shook his head no.

"What happened to your face?"

The inevitable question, the eternal question.

"Chemical burn."

"Did it hurt?"

"What do you think?"

"Yeah."

"My father was a goldsmith," he told Santiago, who sat there and listened. "He was a masters' master, the one the other masters came to when they got stuck with a problem. He added leaf and detail work to religious items, paintings and icons, 99% of them Christian, during the 4th Great Awakening. That was a memorable time for me. My mother was a doctor, and she was an atheist, but my father dragged all of us to church every Sunday. His work was all over the inside of that church. We often sat by the Stations of the Cross. The haloes of the savior in those pieces were unmistakably Dad's fiery gold. I remember, same as my mother probably did, tuning out the words of the mass, the priest's tedious droning. Those haloes of fire, though. Kisses of agony.

So, I'm chasing something. Those kisses. I took some gold that does not properly belong to me. Yes, I'll show it to you later. My gold isn't just a legend. It's real, but I have it hidden. It's a test. What I've done, stealing this gold, is a test of what can be done, damn the consequences. That's what real power is. To be able to do anything, damn the consequences.

I expect to be arrested any day now.

Yes, my mother was a doctor. She died very early in the first wave of the ocean pestilence. She was too devoted to her patients, and she didn't protect herself. We lived in Sacramento, and we fled inland, as did everyone when the great dying began. My father and me. How we ended up in Colorado. Pure chance that he got sick, and I didn't. Pure chance that I lived.

Mom was keenly interested in Dad's work. She thought it was important. Much more important than her own. That's funny in hindsight, considering what happened to the world. She watched him work, always trying not to hover. She thought the work was magical. Maybe that's just the nature of gold. Something about it. That something.

She encouraged me to take it up, the gold work. I never did, but I watched him closely, too. By the time I was your age, I could do anything Dad could do with gold leaf."

"Is this why you stole it?" Santiago asked.

"Yes."

"Show me."

The Brain led Santiago to a locked room. He opened it up, and, to Santiago, it was like looking into a pirate's treasure cave. The room glowed golden as if lit by floodlights. In the center of the room was a long table covered in sketches and doodles. The drawings were of Christ, each one the same scene of Christ carrying the cross, and, Santiago noticed, though some had stylistic differences, in each one, Christ had a halo and feminine features and long feminine fingers.

"What are these?"

"Oh. Those are lousy. I can't draw."

"What are they for?"

"Oh," he hesitated. "I'm going to paint a figure on the ceiling."

"Why?"

"It will be my mark that I was here in this place before moving on."

"Oh, like vandalismo."

"Very like vandalism."

"That's funny."

"I support vandalism, as a personal rule," said the Brain.

"So, you'll put Jesus on the dome?"

"That's my idea."

"I can draw," Santiago said. "Can I help?"

So, he did help. The Brain had him sketch figures on large sheets of paper. They were extraordinary. Mannered and expressionistic, the Brain thought they were beautiful. Sort of a fog-brained-just-waking memory of a dreamed El Greco.

"What about painting?" the Brain asked. "Can you paint?"

"I can paint."

"I wonder if you could paint the same Jesus you sketched. Could you paint it on the ceiling?"

"Yes," he said. "Yes, I could."

The Brain had some ideas about working with the abnormal shape of the dome, and he got to work on it. The planetarium had gear and pieces of scaffolding for maintenance. It was covered in dust and cobwebs. There was not much weight to support, so he did his best with Santiago's help to rig a cruciform support system with two long arms of aluminum lattice beams bolted together. He oiled and got working an old winch to raise the system into place.

He sent Santiago on a mission to rummage through the campus for paint. The youth succeeded wildly and brought back a blue, an autumnal beaver color, and a pink.

"Very good," the Brain said, smiling.

He explained to Santiago how he would beat the gold into leaf, how he would sand and prepare the surface of the dome where they would work, how he'd clay the surface and etch it for the gold, how the gold halo would go on first then the rest of the painting. Santiago watched as he beat & quartered and beat & quartered the ribbons of gold. The Brain used his father's hammer, the hammer his father used for 40 years. It was heavy, strong, indestructible.

The scaffolding and ladders held when he climbed up to sand and prep the ceiling for their work. It took a long time, but he was in no rush. He enjoyed the work. The following day Santiago climbed the works to begin his outline. That was quicker. The Brain loved how it turned out, and he had just climbed the scaffold with his leaves of gold when Santiago shouted to him that there was a man at the door. The Brain froze to his core.

"Don't unlock the door," he shouted back.

"Too late," Santiago said.

The Brain turned his body around.

"Come down from there, you ugly bastard."

"No."

It was Leonid Lascaux, and he had murder in his eyes. Santiago stood several feet behind him and looked at the Brain for a sign of what to do.

"Come down. Now."

"Not a chance."

The giant man began to shake the foundational supports of the scaffolding. The Brain grabbed onto the flat toe board beneath his rear end. He thought of his gun. It was out of reach, but maybe—

"I'll shake you down, I swear."

"I'm not coming down."

Lascaux kicked at the scaffolding in frustration, and, whether it was his true intention or not, the whole thing crashed down. It was slow-motion destruction, and that saved the Brain from broken bones. He landed hard but rolled over and tried to stand up. Lascaux kindly helped him to his feet by grabbing his throat and yanking. He choked as his body fought the deprivation of oxygen. The giant released his grip but only to land a punch on the side of the Brain's strange skull. He fell to his knees.

"Santiago... there... behind those boxes... my gun."

Santiago and the giant looked at each other and both ran for the gun. The kid beat him, but only by a second, and Lascaux pushed him against the wall. It was a rifle. The kid swung it, as if he'd smite the big man with it, but too late, and two fists RIGHT LEFT knocked him down and out. Lascaux turned back to the Brain who sat cross-legged on the floor with a red egg growing on his skull.

"Where's my friend? What did you do to him?"

"Oh. Oh. Oh. The Colonel! Last time I saw him, he was at the Einhorn bunker. We were there together."

"You dragged him there from the desert?"

"Well... in a sense... as a figure of speech... dragged... yes."

"You're going to come with me now," Lascaux said. He grabbed the Brain by the throat again. "You're going to bring about a happy reunion. Come on."

The Brain looked up at the dome. He saw the incomplete, ghostly outline of the so-called Savior, untouched by gold, as likely never to be seen again as the continental migration of extinct butterflies, one of the joys of springtime in his own late youth in Colorado. Never to be seen again. So melancholy. So pointless a conclusion. But, he thought, there would be more domes. He trusted that Santiago, waking up, would be smart enough to lock up the gold. He walked out of the planetarium ahead of the shoves and kicks of the giant.

Chapter Twelve

In a happy breeze, trees look like they're telling a big story and waving their arms. By body English, the arms are drawing you in, luring you into the story. And the red poppies drowsily nodding are telling you don't be afraid of the story. It's your story. Your very own. Come in. Let yourself go.

From the bench on the train platform, Toad could see those red poppies on the far side of the tracks. They followed the tracks like a red pen's underlining as far as he could see into the distance. There were benches spaced five feet apart on the platform. Toad had one all to himself. To his right, on the next bench, Beetle was hanging down (impatient child) with his head nearly touching the ground and his feet planted for balance above him. And two down from the bench, Flat Tire sat by himself, hands in his lap and swinging his feet that did not reach the ground.

They were all amazed by the sudden and unexpected twist. After all this time and looking and searching and waiting. The funniest thing. The train had been looking for them, too. That's what the Icelandic guy said. He was over with the poppies right now. The train was due any time (or, no, not any "time," but it was due soon). The Icelandic guy had dirty hair, dirty hands, soil all over his clothes.

"The train is real?" Toad had asked.

"The train is real."

"Yoshi was wrong then. The train is real."

The fast sun shone bright.

"The train for kids who have no moms and dads," Flat Tire said to himself quietly, as he hummed and swung his feet.

The Icelandic guy whisked them away when Maggie wasn't looking. He said it was urgent and necessary that she not know about it.

"She's just holding you back."

He came to the platform, carrying three red poppies, one for each of the boys. He pinned a flower to Toad's shirt, then Beetle's shirt, then Flat Tire's shirt.

"Trains do two things," he said with a sly wink. "They move people, and they make people wait. This is the waiting part."

Toad fought the future disappointment he knew was possible. He had a good feeling about the Icelandic guy and what the Icelandic guy told them about the train. But, as the day wore on, doubts crept in. When the Icelandic guy said he was leaving to take a leak, disappeared around the corner of the station, and, then, never came back, Toad went looking for him. He was gone. Toad ran back to the train platform, fighting an attack of panicked embarrassment. He was about to cry and give up in despair when he heard a faint note—maybe a train whistle—in the distance. Then he heard it again, closer. A minute later, here came an old steam locomotive into the station, loud and dramatic, huffing like a marathon runner collapsing at the finish line. The train stopped with a painful exhalation. Relief.

Toad touched the flower pinned to his shirt. Beetle and Flat Tire both jumped and stood at attention. The passengers detraining looked bewildered, some groggy enough to rub their eyes, others smiling and stepping down with heavy luggage. They all had red poppies of their own.

From the caboose, a man stepping off—while putting on, first, a silver jacket, and, then, the black hat of a conductor—turned out to be none other than their Icelander.

"What?" Toad shouted. "How?"

"All aboard," the Icelander said with a wink.

"Us? Now?"

"All aboard now if you're coming."

The kids climbed onto the surprisingly ordinary train. Aside from its antique age, nothing about it seemed special. The seats were leather, worn by so many years of rear ends. They were all empty. Every row was empty. They chose seats. They sat together, plenty of room, the seat was big, and they were small. When the train began to depart, the Icelander passed through their car, and he waved, but, then, he left by the forward car. The trees waved outside the window, and the poppies lolled, and Toad thought he could even smell the flowers, but it was just the one pinned to his shirt, his ticket, a red flower for a ticket, and he was thinking that was silly when he fell asleep.

The sound of the rain woke them. It slapped the roof above them and ran in rivers down the windows of the train car. It was daytime still, but the rain clouds made it dark.

"Where are we?" Beetle asked, yawning.

"No idea," Toad replied. "Let's wait for the Icelander."

They waited, but he didn't come.

"Wait here," Toad said. He went forward to the next car in the train. It was empty. Forward of that car was the engine. He politely knocked on the cabin of the engine car and waited. Nothing. Silence. He knocked again and got nothing. He decided to walk the length of the train, and he caught Beetle and Flat Tire ins his wake, as he passed them. They walked eight cars to the caboose. Not a soul on board.

"What happened?" Flat Tire asked.

They jumped off the back of the caboose into the rain. It was steady rain, colder than Toad expected, and it made all the green grass outside a squishy sponge that drew puddles when you stepped on it. Between the rails of the track, too, huge puddles, small lakes almost, looked deep enough to hide shy, slumbering fish. The boys leaped the tracks and dashed to the shelter of an apple tree.

"Where are we?" Beetle asked.

"Look," Toad said, pointing.

Many yards away, but clear as day, the word CHURCH over the entrance gate to the big horse stadium. They knew that place. "Oh no, the wolves," Flat Tire said, his memory strong and correct. This was the place they'd seen wolves.

"Let's go back to the train," Beetle said. "This isn't the place, Toadie. Let's go back to the train. We'll be safer."

Toad said: "Hold on. I have a feeling this is the place."

"I'm scared," Beetle said.

"Me, too," said Flat Tire.

"It will be okay. Stick near me."

They rushed over to the horse stadium, past the white pillars pocked with bullet holes and the white truck crashed into one pillar. Inside, an orchard had sprung up in the tall, grassy middle. Though they didn't know the names, they walked under plum trees drooping with heavy fruit, and black cherry trees, and Elderberry trees, and mulberry trees, all healthy and dripping rainwater. They stopped under a huge plum tree in flower that looked like a purple thundercloud. Toad looked around and wiped rain from his face. He coughed.

"I don't see any wolves," he said.

"They are hiding."

"Watching us."

"Lurking."

"Yeah, they lurk," Beetle said. "That's the word. That's what Yoshi told me. They lurk."

They all turned to the tumbledown grandstands behind them. Where the scorched roof leaked, the seats below were anointed with rain. They scanned the huge structure. Whatever events happened here in the past must've been big. Toad thought about that, and he wondered why he no longer felt the ghosts, the ghosts of the horses.

"Let's go sit under the roof. There are dry sections."

With the rainstorm, it was dark beneath the overhang. And there were bugs under there, like the boys, seeking shelter from the endless deluge of drops from the sky. No mosquitoes, thankfully, but thousands of acrobatic stink bugs, and Toad hated those. They had to smack them out of the air, and not too hard, though, cuz of the stink if you squash one.

"Just keep moving. Keep going this way."

They went deeper into the gloom. As they approached the top of the lowest grandstand level, a flash of light surprised them.

It was a door opening unexpectedly, a rectangle of daylight. Just as quickly, the door closed.

"Let's check it out," Toad said. "But carefully."

They tiptoed up the stairs. Toad pushed the door open.

Sheets of rain smacked them in their faces. Through blurry eyes, Toad saw three young people running across the broken pavement of an empty parking lot. An uncanny feeling hit his belly. Even soaking, didn't he recognize a boy's blue mohawk? Wasn't that a familiar limp on the little one? Wasn't that his own awkward posture?

"Hey!" Toad shouted.

The boys in the parking lot froze. The Toad Double turned back and shouted: "Hey!"

It was a perfect echo.

"What is going on, Toadie?" Beetle asked. His young face, wet from the relentless rain, looked confused and troubled.

A woman and a man emerged from a thicket of lilacs. They came forward with their arms spread wide and gave big hugs to the Toad Double, Beetle Double and Double Flat Tire. Then, they all began to walk away, holding hands like a family. They looked back once to the open door where our friends stood with wide eyes and dropped jaws. But, then, they all walked on again, hand in hand.

"Let's get down there," Toad said. They sprinted back down the ramp of stairs, through the cloud of bothersome stink bugs and out into the rain. Toad in the lead, they sprinted around the corner of the building, out the gate and through a side fence to the parking lot.

"Hey, wait up," Toad said. "Wait wait wait for us."

It didn't take them long to catch up. As they got closer, strangely, the distance between them and their doubles grew. Like skittish animals, the doubles kept taking small, slow steps away. They didn't stop to greet the newcomers. They just looked at them without saying anything, and Toad did not have the words to describe the uncommon fright on the faces of the doubles. The woman and the man looked nervous, too, but they smiled.

"Hello, boys," the woman said. "What's this? Who are you?"

"I'm Toad."

"Of course, you are. How funny and weird. And that's Beetle, and he's Flat Tire."

"Right."

"But what is this? How?"

"We're us," Flat Tire burst in, crying. "Who are they?"

"This is quite a puzzle," the woman said. She looked from one Toad to the other.

"My name is Peach," she said, and she sort of waved hello.

"What a bunch of nouns we are," Double Toad said. He eyed the new boys with extreme suspicion.

"You don't have your Yoshi, either?" Toad asked, and his double nodded and smirked and turned over his palms to signify yeah that was correct.

"Let's all get out of this rain," Peach said. "Y 'all may be on the edge of tearing the fabric of the universe, but we can do that in a nice, dry place. Come on."

Her husband, Burn, stood nearby, scanning for wolves.

"Here they come," Burn shouted. A pack of wolves came charging, noisier than usual, looking starved and vicious. Everybody ran.

Chapter Thirteen

Crawly

Crawly was an informant for the Chairman's Justice. None of that Queen's Justice, he said. He was the Chairman's man. Forever, and who cares who knows it. The night of mass protests continued into the morning and showed no sign of letting up. Crawly was on edge. He was dreadfully nervous. He kept his fighting fish in a bowl by the front window, and he visited it over and over as an excuse to look out and see what was happening outside. Mostly nothing. He faced a stretch of beach far from the main action. He could see the fencing and the top of the sea wall.

He fed the fish its blood worms. Day after day, he gave blood to the carnivore. He drank a cup of chamomile tea to relax his anxiety. He sat at the small card table by the window, glancing at the fish bowl and absentmindedly sipping the tea, when he heard voices outside. He sped to the window and lifted one slat of his Venetian blind. Two dark men with bolt cutters worked on the fence above the sea wall. They cut a wide opening, and people began to jump through it to the sand below.

This made Crawly angry. He reached for his phone. "The vermin," he said.

He couldn't get through to the Marines barracks. No answer.

"Damn it."

He waited two minutes and tried again. Same result.

"Damn it."

He waited five minutes and tried again. No connection.

"Well, then, I'll just walk down to the barracks."

Yoshi

Yoshi the yo-yo, back and forth he went, from fascination with the absurdity of his situation to boredom, crushing boredom, then back again, wondering where they were located, all these prisoners, of which he now numbered himself one. Where was this prison? Nobody knew.

Every day, they heard what sounded like icebergs cracking far above their heads.

The day porter came in the mornings with a big tray of food. Yoshi learned after his first day that the food had to last until the following morning. The porter only came once per day. The porter would talk about food, expansively and enthusiastically, but you couldn't get him to talk about anything else.

"Where are we?" Yoshi asked. "Can you at least tell me that much? That's not much to ask."

Poker-faced, the porter shrugged, said nothing.

Yoshi could talk with the doubles in the cells to his immediate left and right. He called them Lefty and Righty in his mind. Since they were all sufficiently identical minds, he must have been Lefty to his own

Righty and Righty to his own Lefty. And on down the line. Or around the ring. That was better.

"How long have you been here?" he asked Lefty.

"400 days."

"What about the others?"

"Hard to say. Facts move around in here like the old game of telephone. Five years for some, I've heard. None more than five."

"Have any of us had any ideas about how to get out of here?" he asked Righty.

"Well," Righty said. "What happened to you happened to me, happened to all of us. I'm kind of hoping Fate will intervene."

"Fate?"

"Something."

"Something like what? Who?"

"On the outside, did you see the Icelandic Singer any time in the recent past?" Righty asked.

"I don't... uh... let me think."

Yoshi looked down at his feet and considered it. No. Definitely not. Not even proximity, he thought. But it gave him an idea.

Colonel Endling

Jim Apostle put Colonel Endling in charge of recruiting for The Mission. This was his area of expertise when he first joined the organization as a young man. The room he used for meetings was also the room with drafts of a new national Constitution spread all over. After a week of resting and cleaning himself up, he felt like himself again, and his striking looks made people want to talk to him as he walked around Colorado Springs. He liked to bring recruits into that room to see the nascent Constitution. It was impressive and made them feel important.

"I'll show you the room where we're working on the new Constitution," he told Daniel Fox, a polymath, mid-20's wunderkind (singer, writer, math whiz) from Steamboat Springs. He was handsome. Young. A face from a bygone Hollywood era.

"You're a writer. You'd probably be helpful."

Today, HQ was a busy hive of unfamiliar faces.

"What is the current Constitution like?" Daniel asked.

"There isn't one."

Colonel Endling opened the door. They found Iris in the room, changing baby Leone's diaper right on the table on top of the documents.

"Oh, Iris, what are you doing?" the Colonel said, mildly chastising her.

"I told her," said Piper who was sitting in a corner of the room unseen until she spoke up.

"Sorry," Iris said. "Emergency."

She finished the diaper, scooped up the baby and hurried out of the room. Daniel Fox looked at Piper, and Piper looked at Daniel Fox, and there was an instantaneous spark. The Colonel saw it happen. He practically heard it happen, a crackle of tension across wires of lust.

The Chairman Who Died

People kept on coming. You learned to feel a way out of the surges by a sort of combination of touching and hearing your way. There were areas of fewer bodies. There were areas of colliding bodies. Pressing bodies. Groups with the strength of enormous hydraulic presses. The work they could do, lifting and driving and forcing their fellows along paths narrow and wide, straight and branching, was, frankly, terrifying. This was the sixteenth day of uninterrupted protests.

The strikers broke for meals in an unofficial rotation. During these periods of relief, vendors would spring into place with carts or tables, selling anything they could to the strikers. Pictures of the Chairman Who Died, Wolfgang as he lived, preyed on nostalgia for a home and past far from the present. The Chairman standing in front of a deadly, black rotor as if posing for a sales brochure. But, also, the Chairman watching children plant trees in Colorado. The Chairman at the Mission, looking over a topographic map of Triste, putting his finger on a contour line, declaring where Daphne would be settled. The Chairman piloting a black rotor, this time with a more serious expression than the brochure glamor shot. A scandalous vendor had photos of the Chairman's funeral, shots many of us had never seen, his sons in black, downcast and vulnerable.

Just after the setting of the slow sun on Day 17, something surprising happened. The Queen's face appeared on every electronic screen in the Radium Beach protest zone. But not only there. Her image also showed up on every glass surface, every composite surface, every puddle. It was a strange, evil miracle. She spoke to the people from loudspeakers nobody knew existed in the city. The speakers rose from roofs and the tops of street lights like secret missile silos. Slow drones, too, hovered with speakers of their own. The Queen did not speak benevolently. She delivered an ultimatum.

"Our good faith has not been returned," she said. "My people, our good faith has not been returned. Ask yourself this question. What am I doing in this street with these anonymous strangers? This is a war-like posture. You should know that, threatened by a war-like posture, we will not hesitate to sacrifice our blood to cleanse the city... to cleanse this city of the infection that has led to this. You have six hours from now to go home. Six hours until the deadline will pass."

She stopped speaking. Her face vanished. It was replaced by three words of text that remained on all screens and surfaces: LEAVE OR DIE.

Tubby & The Brain

After he got in a few kicks, Tubby began to mellow. The Brain was overconfident—-he was always overconfident—-he didn't know that Tubby's personal deadly sin was wrath—-he didn't realize how much real danger he was in. With each kick, the Brain looked like he'd topple over. He was so top heavy with the oversize skull. He stumbled along the Denver-Boulder Turnpike. The road was a major Marine Corps artery, so it was well-maintained. It was bleached by oxidation, but it was smooth and level, as good as a road got for walking.

"Don't take us through Denver," the Brain advocated.

"Why not?"

"It's a big morgue. Not good. Take us wide around it. Very wide. That's what I would do."

They passed a rusted, yellow school bus. The glass of its windows had been shot out.

Tubby didn't answer the Brain's advice.

"Remember the flamethrowers down in Abilene?"

"How could I forget," Tubby said.

"I got those from bad people in Denver."

"I'm not afraid."

"You should be. Wolfgang abandoned the city for a reason."

They walked in shuffling silence. Eventually, the Denver skyline appeared on the horizon.

"Why didn't you steal a car?" the Brain complained. "My feet are hurting like crazy."

"I'm not like you. I don't live in Psycho Brain Cuckoo Land."

"Ah, this is the world for me, Lascaux. This destroyed world. This inhospitable world."

You thrive like a weed, Tubby thought, but he only sighed in reply.

"Maybe Denver's worst will find us on this road and light up both of us with flamethrowers, or, you know, maybe just you. I can talk my way out of anything."

"Not this," Tubby said.

They shuffled along in new silence, but the Brain could only abide quiet for about 30 seconds. He began to sing as they walked, softly at first, then louder, annoyingly louder when Tubby ignored him.

"No, I would not give you false hope on this strange and mournful day," the Brain sang. He dragged out the last word as DAAAAAAAAAAAAAAAY in the most obnoxious way.

"But the mother and child reunion is only a motion away—"

Tubby kicked again, aiming for his ass, but the Brain was waiting for it and caught Tubby's foot. He pulled and, like a wrestler, kicked out Tubby's plant foot, sending the huge man to the asphalt. He hit his head and saw stars. The Brain sprinted away. By the time Tubby stood up, he could see the little shit running towards the shell of the old NFL football stadium.

Piper & Daniel Sitting in a Tree

They were in love with the snow on the mountains. Just like everybody but also in their own way, since they looked at it together, and Daniel wanted Piper to see it, and Piper wanted to see it, because Daniel wanted her to. Coming by way of Texas, Tristeans didn't believe in the snow until they saw it with their own eyes. Daniel said something to Piper about the word autopsy, how it means seeing something with your own eyes. She didn't care about words in that way, but his eyelashes were so beautiful that she pretended she did.

She was alarmed. She hadn't felt a force of attraction like this in years. And that wasn't quite right. If it was an alarm going off, it wasn't a warning but a wake-up. And it had to be a strong pull to get her to throw on a mask of caring about something she found light and airy and a waste of time. She sighed, because she wanted to waste time with this new friend.

They followed a path that was not a path or maybe it was once a path, a real blazed trail that kind people maintained in some Long Ago. The trail followed the mud of a streambed. In the spring, a newborn stream had flowed here with ankle-deep runoff. They came to a clearing with bright sunlight and stopped to rest. Piper could smell berries. Raspberries? The scent caused a dull rumbling in her belly. She sat on a big, round rock. Next to her, on a small rock, a bumblebee rubbed its antennae with its fore legs. She admired it and worried for it when the large shadow of a bird darkened its space, followed by another shadow, they were violet-green swallows, she had no idea if they ate bees, but they seemed to be chasing each other anyhow.

Daniel Fox sat on some grass in the sun. He sat like a jackknife, and, stretched his hamstrings, grabbing his feet and bending. His face was pink from the hike. Enjoying the sun, he looked adorably youthful and dopey. Impulsively, Piper grabbed some mud from the streambed and flung it at him.

The mud hit his arm where he'd rolled up his sleeve to cool down. Some dripped off, but a big glob stuck there. He looked at Piper with mock hurt and dismay.

"Oh, really?" his smiling eyes said.

She smiled back at him, embarrassed at herself over how flirting never really changed. Daniel stood up and walked over to her. He pretended calm, but his eyes gave him away. He stood over her, looming at advantage, but disoriented by his surprise and the bright sun in his eyes.

"Are you ticklish?" he asked.

"Yes, but I won't say where."

He looked at her bare legs, and her smile told him he'd guessed right on the first try. He didn't tickle her. He got down on his knees and kissed her thigh. She grabbed handfuls of his brown hair, mostly to brace herself against the new feeling of voltage coursing up her spine. She liked how his lips felt on her skin. He moved steadily up, not too fast, just right, and as he got to the fabric of her shorts and kept pushing on, her heart raced, and she was struck by the strangeness of a destiny—-a pair of destinies really—-that brought them to this encounter.

[Editorial intrusion: For his part, Daniel's cock bulged in his pants. He thought if he stood up, Piper might laugh at his excitement. She would, however, find it soon enough].

"Your skin is making me crazy," he said.

"Don't stop."

He pulled her shorts down and patiently worked them past her bulky brown boots to get them off. He did the same with her underwear. The big boots stayed on.

"What are you two seeking here?" the hard, blue mountains asked them. Piper felt a mountain breeze on her belly as Daniel lifted her shirt. She grabbed at his bulging pants.

"Let me see it," she said. "Come on. Let me. Now."

Daniel undid his pants, and Piper reached inside. She was impatient now. Driven.

"O this is what I want," she said.

The penetration was brutish, intense and more painful than she expected. They both sort of stared at each other when it was done. The mountains looked down on them ("their far—slow—Violet Gaze"), and the breeze was now sharp on their sweating limbs and torsos.

"Keep going?" Daniel asked.

"Oh," she said. "Not right away..."

"The hike, I mean. Keep going or head back?"

She laughed. She looked at the blue sky and sat up to view the peaks nearby.

"Yeah," she said. "Keep going."

Sleeper

Sleeper saw the crowd crush developing. He had a good vantage from the top of the sea wall. He stood on the concrete and rested with his back against the fence. Shorty sat next to him. They both watched as soldiers fired tear gas canisters into a thick arm of the crowd about 1,500 meters away. That arm of the crowd had only two avenues of retreat from the gas. One was directly towards the sea wall. The other was perpendicular to that route, left or right, but both left & right had black, military AFVs blocking them.

"We have to get people out of this choke point," Sleeper said, smacking Shorty on the shoulder. Turns out, there was no time. "Move, you people! Move!" Sleeper shouted. "Hurry and move! Make room!"

Some heads turned to see what he was about. Those closest tried to move. The crowd's voice changed. That singular sound of wild alarm and affront came loud, rolling down the mass of bodies. Why can't I speak to it? Sleeper thought. Speak and calm it. He sensed he was now on a dismal shore. Shorty was already climbing the fence, yanking his body up with his incredible arms. Sleeper put a first hand on the fence. Just to be ready.

He looked back. Figures of language to describe the movement of the surge failed him. The crowd moved like a fluid, yes, absolutely, with the shear force coming from the rear, and the poor people in the front hit the sea wall very much like an ocean wave. Those who hit the wall first bore the brunt of all that force. When hands began to grab at his feet, Sleeper climbed the fence. He looked back and down and saw despairing faces, like souls in Dante looking up jealously at his safe position in a bark to safety. He cut his palms on the razor wire atop the fence, and the cuts weakened his grip, causing him to fall to the sand below. He hit his face hard on the sand. He wondered if he'd been knocked out, because when he opened his eyes, Shorty was standing on his stumps over him with a concerned look on his face.

"Daring young man," Shorty teased. "You okay?"

"Think so. Maybe."

"Sorry I wasn't there to catch you."

Shorty smiled with self-deprecation. Sleeper didn't notice. He'd developed a weird sort of face blindness from hitting his head. He recognized the little man's shape, and his voice, but his face? It was like some recognition chip in his brain was dead. He scrambled across the sand to the wall and peered over the top. The crush had eased. Strikers at the far end of the crowd ran towards the tear gas canisters and the soldiers beyond. Brave, he thought. Braver than me.

"Hey, check that out," Shorty said. Sleeper turned and saw a bonfire burning about a mile down the beach. It was a small fire, but it gave off a colossal tower of smoke.

Shorty climbed onto his back, and they began to walk.

"I can't see your face, man."

"That's because I'm behind you."

"No, I mean when I look at your face I see like the image inside a dull spoon."

"Weird."

"I know."

"Your head feel all right, bro?"

"Yeah."

"Weird."

They walked toward the bonfire. A group of men circled the fire. They all wore ventilator masks for the smoke. They were feeding wood to the fire. Sleeper watched a tall, black man with rope-like strands of hair moving around, joking with the other men in the circle. Their leader. There was no mistaking him, Sleeper thought, though he could not see his face. Serge. It had to be Serge. He bounced excitedly from foot to foot as he threw tablets into the fire. These burned to vivid black smoke. He chanted in the voice Sleeper recognized.

Off to prison you must go
You must go
You must go
Off to prison you must go
My fair lady

"Serge?" Sleeper shouted. "That you?"
The man took off his ventilator mask.
"Who me? You a cop?"
"Yeah you, Serge. What's happened? What's happening?"
"Not me, comrade."
"What? Why won't you—"
"Get over here. Hug time."
"What's happening? I don't understand."
"Big things. Big things. The biggest things."
"Can you be very, very specific?"
"Toss some pellets on the fire," he said, pouring from the abundance in his own hands into Sleeper's hands. Sleeper looked at them.
"It's like for that old Italian Papa. White smoke, pope. Black smoke, nope. No popes here. Black smoke means come for the revolution. My people will see it."
"Are they not already here?" Sleeper asked, pointing back to the streets of protest.
"We need more."

"Did you see how many people are there now?"

"Yes, comrade. I did. But the soldiers have not even begun to unleash their swarms. They are waiting. Very evil men. Something is coming."

These were days of mental anguish and confusion for Sleeper. He began to cry.

"What is it? What?"

"I saw video of you... captured and hanged."

"Not me."

"What?"

"This video. That video. Propaganda. Who was it?"

"Are you scamming me?"

"Never. Listen. Can you stay and feed this fire for me? I am late."

"Eh... okay?"

"Good stay here for now. I'll be back."

The man put on his ventilator mask and ran off into the smoke. Just like that, meaning and comprehension and available ground in the universe slipped away from Sleeper's fingers. In their place, pellets for the bonfire.

Yoshi's Big Idea

Although not obliged by the 8th Amendment of the Constitution of the former United States of America-—the amendment which banned cruel & unusual punishment-—the day porter sincerely stuck to the spirit of that old law when he prepared meals for the prisoners. His food would be nutritious and tasty. He knew everything Yoshi liked and would dazzle him in conversation.

"You like those cooked carrots with the honey-butter-cinnamon glaze."

"That's right," Yoshi said. His eyes widened. His mouth watered. "Those are amazing."

"I do those in a skillet once a month," the day porter said.

"I can't wait."

"Those carrots come from Daphne. I shouldn't tell you that."

Yoshi smiled, and it dawned on him that the day porter had been feeding his counterparts for five years. He knew everything about him from talks just like this one. Every day, still, Yoshi tried to keep him talking. He'd tickle an opening if he could.

"Ever get bananas?"

"You always ask that. They spoil too quickly. There's never a surplus from the military."

"I miss those."

"Sorry, they never come available."

The conversation was stopped by the strange, loud music of ice shifting above their heads. It was like a long, taut wire thrummed. The day porter looked up at the high ceiling.

"What is that?" Yoshi asked.

The day porter shrugged. In the pause, Yoshi seized some agency.

"I saw your assistant in here last night," he said.

"My assistant?"

"Yeah, the tall dude with the long, blond hair? The ponytail? He's in here all the time in the dark... I assumed he comes in and cleans up after hours."

"Huh."

The day porter left at that, and Yoshi waited for something to happen.

"That was an interesting move," Lefty said after overhearing the exchange.

"Yeah," Righty chimed in. "There's not been any night visitor. Brilliant. So obvious now. Why didn't we think of that?"

"Let's keep this to our little corner," Yoshi said.

"Of course."

"Absolutely."

"But... for the record?"

"I know," Yoshi said. "Circular jail. There aren't any corners."

The next morning, before lights up, Yoshi woke to the sound of something metallic tapping on the glass wall of his cell. He opened his eyes and saw Queen Roux in her black wet suit, standing before the cell with a long knife in her hand. She tapped on the glass again with the pointy end of the blade.

"Top of the morning to you," she said. The look on her face was stern but not unkindly, like a disappointed nanny. With hope dead in all the prisoners except Yoshi and his Lefty and Righty, the Queen's appearance caused no commotion. She yanked back her black diving hood. Her red hair came free. She put the knife between her knees, so she could gather her hair with a black elastic she'd had on her wrist. Yoshi couldn't stop looking at the knife.

"Tell me why I shouldn't take this big knife and… OFF WITH HIS HEAD?"

He took her joke as a joke—-or he wanted to, but—-

"You're going to cut my head off?"

"It's one sentence of many possible. I don't have to worry about trials. I don't have to worry about verdicts. I'm the Queen, you know?"

"Yeah," Yoshi said. "I get it."

The Queen pointed at the glass.

"What do you think of getting walled in?"

"What do I think of it?"

"Yeah, your situation. These walls."

The lights came up and revealed many, many walls. Or many walls were one wall. All a matter of perspective. The light behind them, the Yoshi shapes in each cell began to move about their morning routines. He had no feel for how this looked from above. No image of it since what loomed above was a mystery. Were they one prison or many? From the sky, one circle only or like a diagram of a methane molecule, four valence jails around a center, then four more around each valence now a center, then four more—-et cetera—-until the mind grew dizzy with armies of captive Yoshis.

"How do we usually answer?" he said to the Queen, but this was really for Lefty and Righty, a gallows joke, a lame one. He was feeling lame.

"O how depressing," the Queen said. She turned around and surveyed the enormous room.

"Why did you lie to the day porter?"

Yoshi said nothing.

"To get me to come here," the Queen said. "Okay, I'm here. But I have been wracking my brain, wondering what now? Here I am. What's your next move?"

Yoshi blushed. He felt tiny. Feeble.

"You think you can talk me into opening your cell?"

"Well, why not?"

The Queen laughed, a hiss from her pretty nose.

"I don't like underhanded dealing. I don't like secret hearts. I like open, trustworthy hearts."

His head filled with things to say, all, sadly, dishonest. He remembered his days—they were not so long ago—-on the beach where he could do anything by his wits alone. He was clever and could talk even street-smart people into doing things he needed done. The past was like a world beneath the world. Couldn't see into it, but you could maybe think your way into it. An alternate past, though?

An alternate past? What about it?

The Queen stared at him as if waiting for an answer to a question. Had he drifted off?

"Where were you just now, young Yoshi? With him?"

"Who? The Icelander?"

"No, no. Not the Icelander. My husband. Were you him?"

Yoshi had no idea what she meant.

"Like in my head?"

"Right. Exactly. That's it, isn't it?"

Two Frogmen emerged from a door at the far end of the room. They had mean-looking faces today. Angry faces as if personally offended by Yoshi's very existence. He didn't like those faces. He felt his stomach tighten. He decided to risk it.

"Yes," he said. "That's it."

The Queen's eyes lit up.

"Does he have some control over you, too?"

"Not control..."

"Oh, you have to come clean. This is the whole game."

"I'm ready," he said.

She pointed at his cell, and one of the Frogmen pointed a remote control. The cell door clicked.

The Dream of Technological Omniscience

This is power's dream—-even benevolent power's dream-—to knowingly—-and even benevolently—-direct every event. Does power sleep? Is this a sleep dream? No. It is a dream in the sense of aspiration. Omniscience would bring power boundless joy, mirth, gladness. Don't look for it in the old books of St. Anselm. Did he ever manage the interests of 10 million people? Interests not souls. Aquinas on God was more what the Chairman dreamt of. God sees all things together, simultaneously, not one thing then another thing. All things always & completely.

He strove for it. That joy, mirth, gladness? His Misery Index would be back, and it would be all greens. His striving was asymptotic. Omniscience-—practically speaking now-—didn't have to be infinite. But, there he was, striving. His recent losses in the political sphere, mostly those born of the Queen's diverse and numerous incompetencies, didn't make him bitter. They drove him harder.

He granted access to his personal lab in Daphne to just three people. Speck the technician worked in there with him every day, but most hours the Chairman was alone. In solitude, he followed the map. Many days, the required concentration was beyond him. He had a bed brought in, and he worked on restorative cat naps as a craftsman might, testing the optimum length. He somehow settled on 16 minutes. Since his injury, naps were preferable to long sleep anyway, and he often popped up refreshed and ready to delve.

His biggest problem—-of the problems he was aware of-—was the paranoia that gripped him when he began to doubt the very existence of time—-at least in the sense he'd know it all his life. His biggest problem he was not aware of—-omniscience!—- was that Piper and Daniel and Jim Apostle were working in the Colorado Mission on the spear MRI and Piper's ideas for improving it. How could they get it to work from farther away? The challenge and mortal danger of the spear MRI was somebody had to get real close to the King's body to strike with it. Piper had been thinking about nanobots, but that lab was out of commission for the foreseeable future.

Daniel was teaching himself how algorithms worked. Hourly, Piper—-who, as we know, easily got bored—-would invade his work station and his personal space. Her touches made him dizzy and broke his concentration. He'd look in her blue eyes and kiss her pretty mouth, and she'd sigh and slink away again. The artificial neural network, as they used it, and, because of the mind contents they'd stolen, was a deep time map. Apostle wanted to teach the ANN to read the Chairman's mind. To stream his mind, the stream of time. Daniel felt high half the time he listened to Apostle talk about it. The implications were magical. Theoretically possible, Apostle said to every objection. Theoretically possible.

"Is there enough processing power?" Daniel asked Piper.

"For that? Well... not yet," she said.

"Who is working on that problem?"

"I think maybe you will get recruited soon."

Each time they tightened the algorithms, Jim sat the team down in the viewing room to read the MRIs. "Let's run through File 1 from the beginning," Jim said. The viewer responded to his voice and began.

"What do we see versus what the AI sees and labels on the screen? Any errors?" he said, the same thing each time. The AI was getting smarter, making fewer errors in its analysis.

"Stop," Piper said, and the moving images stopped.

"That says 'road,' but it looks to me more like the bricks of a levee or other kind of embankment," she said. "Do you both agree? And is that a waterfall?"

"Go back 15 seconds," Jim said. "Play forward."

"Does that look like it could be water beyond the bricks? Piper asked.

"No confirmation bias allowed here," Jim said.

"Mark my observation," Piper said. The AI marked it.

Much of the imagery remained blurry. Sure, more of it became clear with each new set of convolutions. But it was iceberg theory here in terms of what could be used vs. what was suspected to be there. 85 X 10^9 neurons, she thought. How many convolutions to map that? It was a substantial number.

A minute later, the external HIPPO drive showed a spike, an unusual synaptic firing.

Jim stopped the video.

"What?" Daniel asked. "What was it?"

Jim looked at the readings on the HIPPO.

"Impossible," he said.

"What?"

"According to this, as we pull the signal out with the spear, Gun Club's brain is pulling some outside signal in."

"What?" Piper said. "Ours? Some feedback from the spear?"

"No," Jim said. "Not ours."

Chapter Fourteen

How these structures fall apart. Slowly. How nature takes over. Slowly. Steadily. Tubby entered the stadium through Gate 7. The Brain was either inside the stadium or not. He was either lying in ambush or not. Tubby walked slowly, keeping his footsteps quiet through the cracked concourse. The gray concourse. Walls and supports gray or veined with rust. Dead escalators. There was graffiti in places, shockingly good pictures or blocks of letters, like old time NYC artistry.

He pushed on and found access to the playing field. It was brown with green shrubs and ground cover with the flowers of Colorado blue columbine bursting out of it. Pale blue, white, yellow. Down on the field, it was like being inside a blue crater. The seats were largely intact, all blue save one stripe of faded red. He looked around and listened for any sound beyond the old, lonely wind. The Brain was hiding himself adeptly.

Tubby kicked at some shrubs, angry at his own stupidity, his dumb carelessness. He probably faked me out, he thought. "Don't take us into Denver," the asshole said. That's probably exactly where he went. Downtown. Tubby could see that city skyline from the parking lot. He stood on the flank of a fallen Bronco statue and scanned the horizon in all directions. "It's a morgue," the asshole said. The sentence rattled around in his skull in the Brain's tedious voice.

The wind picked up as he crossed the dried bed of the South Platte River and crossed the path of Route 25. Why didn't he just leave the asshole be? Move on and leave him behind? Two reasons—reasonable reasons, he thought—beyond the unreasonable rage he felt. Maybe the Brain was forming a posse right now and would hunt Tubby down. That was entirely possible and frightening. Tubby wanted to witness the Brain's comeuppance in the form of justice. He had abused his power too profoundly.

The former metropolis may have been a morgue, but Tubby soon found it was not empty. All street signs were gone, but he recognized 14th Street when he turned onto it. There were people out walking, and they gawked at him, as he passed. A stranger coming in off the desert. Not to be trusted.

On a building with a buffalo stenciled in black on its best remaining wall, he saw the following rude proclamation: THERE ARE EVIL WITCHES LIVING IN THE FOUR SEASONS.

That was too promising to ignore. He walked past buildings of brick. Gray brick, red brick, sandcolored brick. He walked past a forty-foot-tall blue bear that stood by the ruins of the convention center, looking proud, as if it had used its paws to smash out every single pane of glass.

When he got to the Four Seasons, he half-expected to find armed guards at the entrance to the lobby. There was nobody, so he feared booby traps. He stepped lightly through the marble lobby, his head swiveling around. He caught a glimpse of his own face in a bright, shining mirror and thought, "That looks nothing like me," but he only held the thought for a moment for two women came noisily walking down the MC Escher staircase that emptied into the lobby.

The Evil Witches, presumably. One was tall and blond. The other, short and bald.

"You're one of the prisoners from Texas," the bald woman said. She held a handgun at her side.

"This is true," Tubby said. "Don't shoot."

"What do you want?"

It was late afternoon now, and the slanting sunlight ducked below the second floor's haphazard window boarding and freed itself to shine brightly on the two women. They were older than he'd guessed by their voices.

"I'm looking for somebody."

"Who?"

"A man called The Brain."

They both laughed.

"Friend or foe?" the tall blond asked.

"Foe."

"Correct answer."

The bald woman put her gun into the waistband of her silver pants. She rubbed her nose.

"Let's see your shoulder. Show us your inoculation scare. Come up a few steps."

Tubby rolled up the sleeve of his left arm.

He said, "Think I could have grown this old and destroyed if I never got the inoculation?"

"Oh, Alice," the bald one said. "He's a self-deprecating humorist. Let's shoot him now and put him out of his misery."

"I don't know, Dorothy," the blond said. "Under all that dust and beard, he looks like a good guy."

"Both probably true," Tubby admitted. "Sad but true."

"Not many good guys left."

"What do you want with the Brain?" Alice asked.

"I want to bring him to justice."

"How noble."

"What makes you think he's in Denver?" Dorothy asked.

"We were just separated today over by the stadium."

"Damn," Alice said.

Humor flew from both of their faces.

"He's notorious around these parts I take it?"

"We've all been wounded by him in one way or another," Dorothy said. She rubbed her bald head as if the Brain was responsible somehow for that.

"Come on up. We'll give you some clean water. No charge. On the house."

It was a Bohemian apartment, even downright specifically 1960s USA hippie, Tubby thought. He saw peacock feathers in a vase, a Mandala tapestry with Vishnu in the dead center, the overgrown foliage of hanging plants in every corner of every room, a rainbow of scarves on the ceiling like a circus tent, lamp shades like flapper dresses, a blue guitar on the wall, a framed Esquire cover of John Lennon set on a tiny piano, a long bead necklace dangling from a wooden dresser knob.

Alice gave him a glass of water.

"Where are you from originally?" she asked.

"Montreal."

"The underground city! I knew tons of Montrealers in the time before the migration."

He drank the water and felt the cool cascade from his lips to his tongue and down the throat.

"Ah. Thank you," he said. "That's heavenly."

He put the glass down on a coaster on the piano and picked up the picture of John Lennon. The singer wore a big belt buckle and opaque eyeglasses. His arms crossed his midsection like he had a bellyache.

"There's a barrel of water in the loo if you'd like to wash up," Dorothy told him.

"Thanks. I think I will."

He went into the bathroom and before he even found the big water drum, the door closed and locked behind him.

"Hey, what's-—"

He stopped himself for he quickly realized there was a person thrashing around in the tub. He slid open the Beatles shower curtain and saw the Brain tied up in the tub. His hands were bound with silver electric tape. His mouth was sealed with the same. He was naked save for black socks that came halfway up his shins. His ankles were bound. He had a look of fear in his eyes before he even recognized it was Tubby locked in with him.

"There are evil witches living in the Four Seasons," Tubby mumbled aloud.

The Brain's eyes went wide and he nodded in total agreement. There was a window, but they were more than 30 floors up. Tubby thought of ramming down the door, but the women had guns. That was his second worst option. His worst option was to yank off the tape from the Brain's mouth, so, of course, that's exactly what he did.

Chapter Fifteen

The 400 trucks stood ready. Lieutenant Metzger owned the operation. He paced nervously as he waited for the go signal from Messmaker. His newly-promoted platoon Sergeant Flowers watched him and stood against a truck with his big arms folded. The truck sat with an empty cab. The driver, PFC Visceri, was in the alley nearby, shitting his brains out behind a garbage dumpster. Flowers smirked when Visceri came back.

"You moonlighting at a laxative-testing factory, Visceri?" Flowers asked. "What the fuck, man?"

"Sorry sorry sorry."

Metzger had a narrow view of where the sky met the sea. Blue upon blue. No storms in view. He walked to the truck where Flowers ragged Visceri through the window. All day long, these two went at it, Flowers giving it out, and Visceri taking it.

"Your butt empty now? Or you got more?" Flowers asked with a sneer.

"Hey, I got a problem. Have some sympathy."

"I'll put my foot in your ass... clear up that problem stat."

The trucks were all pulling flat-bed trailers loaded with modular, prefabricated, concrete walls, big Alaska barriers that stood 20-feet tall. Something had changed in the upper echelon of royal strategic thinking. The change in strategy had led to very specific plans. The new mission had to be conducted lightning fast if it was going to accomplish the Queen's goal, which was rapid surrender of the resistance.

There was some thick, black smoke Metzger didn't like the looks of coming from the beach. Beyond the smoke, navy boats arrived to form a blockade a few hundred years off-shore.

"You expect any armed resistance?" Flowers asked.

"I expect panic. So, who knows?"

"Any reports of weapons in the protest crowd?"

"Very few."

"That's good to hear."

"Yeah."

"Crazy, though, all this."

"What about it?"

"That things have come to this... walling off a small section of the city."

"The Queen knows what she is doing. Messmaker does anyhow."

"But, bud, once this wall goes up, it's never coming back down."

Metzger sighed. He felt this was true. He felt depressed. What were they about to do to their city?

Security drones arrived just as Messmaker's signal did. The engineers programmed them to watch the lines where the wall pieces would go. They used the municipal street grids, and the drone flights tightly followed the lines. They were amazing at such tasks, they lifted and rose like hopeful-hearted creatures, so different looking from what they were: engines of death.

"Okay, it's time," Metzger told Flowers. Flowers shouted the same to the next truck, and the message relayed down the line. The trucks came to life with the sputtering, COPD cough of old diesel engines. The soldiers put on their gas masks.

The area-denial weapon had been a complete success. Messmaker had authorized its release after protesters ran through and around the tear gas dispersals. The stink bomb—-similar in tactic to the Israeli "Skunk" but way more powerful and offensive-— was made with thioacetone and delivered by firefighting drone. The stuff was so unholy, they wouldn't even let Marines have a tiny whiff of it during basic training. Luckily, there was a land breeze. The drones sprayed the compound in seemingly frugal amounts. The liquid came out weakly like the last dribbles from a kid's summertime lawn sprinkler when the hose is shut off. Some of the protesters pointed and laughed. Within seconds, the malodorant reached them downwind and delivered shock and dread. None of the men and women in the already tense and anxious crowd had ever experienced anything like it.

Some of the old and vulnerable among the crowd fainted straight off and fell to the ground. Others bent over to vomit. The most fit made a run for the ocean and rubbed at their limbs and clothing as if trying to put out invisible flames. Within 10 minutes, every living human was cleared from the zones where the Alaska barriers would go up. The Queen's command became Messmaker's orders to build a security barrier to enclose a space 17 blocks wide and two blocks deep. Plus, the beach. The Queen had forfeited a 17-block wide chunk of the beach to make her point. The beach would have its own walls, left and right, straight down the sand to the water, the same Alaska barriers 20-feet tall.

The trucks moved forward. Behind them, mobile construction cranes, tested for this singular project, also moved forward. Then came the military engineers with levels and gas masks.

Sleeper was feeding smoke pellets into the bonfire when Shorty gasped for air beside him. "My God, what the fuck is that stench?" Shorty covered his face with his hands and, then, the sleeve of his shirt. Sleeper did not smell anything.

"What is it?"

"O God, you don't smell it?"

Shorty fell over and vomited onto the sand.

"What is it?"

"Some kind of chemical attack."

Shorty dragged himself toward the water.

"I have to get this off me, off my clothes, out of my hair. It's horrible."

Sleeper grabbed him by the armpits, took him to the water and dropped him there. Shorty grabbed handfuls of warm water and splashed himself. Others on the beach did the same. Meanwhile, holes had been cut in the sea wall fencing, and large numbers of protesters jumped onto the beach and ran to the water.

The cranes were loud. The 10+ ton barriers hitting the ground were loud. The streets shook for hundreds of feet around as the work began with the lifting and dropping of block after block. Metzger watched the operation, standing several meters away, holding his rifle and occasionally adjusting his gas mask when he felt tiny leaks of air and heard the soft hissing. Within a few hours, the construction began to look like a wall. Flowers drifted over.

"We're gonna have to burn these clothes, or the stink will come home with us."

"Yeah."

There were 40 small businesses inside the new walled zone. The owners had all been warned to secure their merchandise in the first days of the protests, but, realistically, those cafes, shops, and, even, two banks were lost.

"Nobody in our squads would loot, right?" Metzger asked, and he watched Flowers' face for a reaction. Just a twinkle in the sergeant's eye, he thought, but it could have been the glare from the gas mask. How many of those 40 shopkeepers, chefs or bankers would be on the wrong side of the wall? Impossible to know yet, but the drones would inventory the population with face scans as soon as the wall was done. The drones presently had no threats to report. The stink bomb had succeeded beyond anybody's wildest expectations.

At that very moment, as Metzger and Flowers talked about looting, Queen Roux watched a live feed of drone footage of the wall construction. She was in the bunker in Daphne, eating a delicious salad, but her Misery Index on the wall wore a gray color that showed she was worried something could go wrong at any moment. She was surprised when the door to the tea room opened and Rocky, the old black & silver dog, came bounding in, barking, followed by the Chairman and General Messmaker. Rocky sniffed around at her feet, looking for dropped food, and the two men sat down at the table. The Chairman groaned, as he always did after some walking. Messmaker played with the table's white table cloth. He was nervous.

"What's that on the screen?" Jack asked. Roux thought of his name and title, the title as altered as his body now. It was his father, Wolfgang, who insisted Chairman be always capital C in public usage. Capital M for Marines, too, that on Wolfgang's insistence.

"Drone footage."

"Of what?"

"Operation Drive Out Rubbish."

"Oh, it's happening now?"

She looked at Messmaker when Jack asked that. He damn well knew. Something was up. Jack was making a move.

"Roux. My love. This was very stupid. I have corrected the General's thinking. We can't stop it now, but I've lost confidence in you."

The Chairman held a silver remote control in his hand. He pressed a button, and the Queen's Misery Index went blank. She felt it, too. She felt a loss. Across the city and in Redemption Rock and in Dreaming Back Lake, screens showing the Queen's mood went blank.

"Tell me, Jack, exactly what was very stupid?"

She put down her fork and folded her hands.

"You're losing the people," Jack said, his temper rising. "You've lost the people."

"I own the people," the Queen said.

"Not anymore," Jack said. He slammed his fist on the table, and, as he raised it to slam it again, the Queen grabbed her fork, leaped across the table and stabbed him in the throat. It went deep, and she twisted it. Blood spurted. The Chairman struggled and grabbed at the fork. His face went ghostly. The General knocked the Chairman over in his chair, and Jack landed on his back. The force of the fall knocked out whatever strength he had left.

Her husband died, but the Queen did not die of grief. She clapped her bloody hands and shrieked.

No storms for three days. The palm trees didn't move. The fronds were bright green, wide, healthy. Shorty noticed all the sea birds had fled the stink bomb and had still not returned. It was a long three days. There were no ambulances, no supplies, no medicines for the sickened. We need City of Peace to come, he told himself. It was bad. Yes, it was bad, but there was no dog-like resignation in the people. They cared for one another.

His buddy Sleeper had fallen apart. Well, in the metaphorical sense. Not literally. Shorty wasn't about to tell anyone Sleeper was an android, but folks would figure it out soon enough. Sleeper's eyes were deteriorating, so he spent most of his time in a tent, keeping them closed. The eyes that is.

There were gunboats off the coast. Nobody could leave that way by swim or raft or whatever. Why should any of us be surprised, he asked. The royals were evil people.

Pork Chop never turned up. Lucky him, if he's on the other side of the wall, Shorty hoped. He grabbed his own dog tags and looked at them. Shiny silver. Still wearing them without a thought why.

NOBLE, JJ. O NEG. XXX-XX-XXXX. USMC S CATHOLIC.

Drones came in swarms. Not constantly, but he hadn't reckoned the pattern of their timing. They scanned faces. Anybody who hid their face got plagued as if by fleas or aggressive flies on a corpse.

City of Peace, where are you?

There was one man stalking up and down the beach who bitched and moaned and could not remain calm. His name was Crawly, and he kept saying he got caught on the wrong side of the wall. He had vomit on his shirt that he refused to wash out. Crawly screamed when the Time Men tried to recruit him for one of their sneaky patrols to check on the progress of the wall.

There was only one gate, the Time Men said. The soldiers appeared to have stacked pallets of bottled water on the other side of the gate. Who knows what they had planned?

Shorty grinned at the drones when they flew into his personal space. And he flipped them the bird. "That's for Gun Club," he'd say. "I'm gonna kill him." Little did any of them know, the Chairman was already murdered. He was already dead.

On the fourth day, the first death occurred. A young woman named Cali developed a fever on Day 3 that skyrocketed in the night. She died shortly after the fast sun rose. A group of women carried her body to the gate in the wall. The Marines there were prepared to repel just about anything, but not this. They gave them women a case of water bottles and took Cali's body without any explanation of what they'd do with her. When the furious women raged and began to throw the water bottles one at a time over the 20-foot wall, the firefighting drones came back, and everybody ran.

"Any word from Pork Chop?" Sleeper asked. He lay in the white tent with a cloth over his eyes.

"No, brother. He hasn't turned up."

"Would you mind wetting this cloth for me?"

Shorty dragged himself to the water. He dipped the rag, wrung the water out, dipped it again. He turned and looked at the reduced landscape of the beach, the city's signature attraction, part of its founding history and its name. It had become this? He gave the wet rag back to Sleeper who was effusively grateful. Shorty sat with him for a long time, neither of them saying much, enjoying the company, listening to the activity in the other white tents around them.

On the fifth day, the wind changed. Everyone felt it at the same time. La Ruine, premonition of an ocean storm. It would be followed by a purple sky in the time between the setting of the fast sun and the rising of the slow sun. The people on the beach waited for the purple sky, and when they saw it, they got to work preparing for the monsoon. Shorty heard determined voices, and the sound of temporary camps rapidly dismantling in the purple, false eventide.

One legless and one eyeless, Shorty and Sleeper went together to one of the beach shops that had been relieved of its locks and security measures and turned into a shelter for the monsoon. The Time Men refused to allow things to fall into chaos. They measured the square footage and calculated the capacity of each standing building inside the wall. Shorty and Sleeper ended up inside a t-shirt shop.

"Be glad you can't see, bro," Shorty said.

"Why?"

"Some ugly beach gear in here. Ug-lee. Wow."

"Well, thanks, Shorty. I feel blessed."

"I was hoping the queue would work out for us to get placed in the taffy shop. Oh well."

"Mmm. I love that shop. Been going there for years..."

The storm came in the deadest, darkest part of the night. Shorty woke to the sound of beach sand flung at the shop's hurricane shutters. He had a pillow of soft hoodies rolled up under his head. He turned to the front of the store. People crouched at the door, trying to peek out.

There was no power. No lights. So, there was nothing at all to see. Occasionally, a thump on the shutters, a fleshy sort of thump, made Shorty start.

"That's a fish," Sleeper said without opening his eyes. "I know that sound."

"So weird!" Shorty said. He went back to his pillow and rested his head. When the storm intensified, it sounded like an animal screaming, but no living thing could scream for that long. Shorty fell asleep, listening to that and hoping the city's drains could handle the surge.

Outside, an ill-advised last recon flight for a squad of drones got caught in the hysterical winds. The drones flew over the shore's palm trees that writhed as if stricken by grief or outrage at all the vicious, unnecessary pain. They rose like desperate prayers shot heavenward, and they were knocked back down, denied, by the strong hand of the storm. They tumbled, and their glass eyes sent back images of gray nothingness save for blue sparks when they crashed to the concrete of the boardwalk.

One drone caught a ride on a strong gust and went up instead of down and exploded in a quick, bright fireball against the mirror glass of the Mission HQ building.

The Queen wasn't watching these feeds. She had her eyes, ears and interest focused on the screen that showed her the surgical room two floors below her in the Daphne bunker. In the center of this theater, the robotic surgeons were implanting the King's map port behind young Yoshi's ear. A human doctor observed in the room and spoke to the Queen.

"They use a GPS-like navigation, Your Majesty. Highest precision. They follow my pre-operative blueprint exactly."

Yoshi lay on his side in the middle of it all, wide awake. He felt nothing, and he could not move. Above him, the swiveling power booms moved about, handling their tasks with competence. They interacted with each other with the symbiotic grace of bulls & matadors. One arm, the camera. One arm, the light. One arm, the surgeon. The fourth moved tubes and cables and wires and anything that could get in the way of the others.

The floor was washed in a pleasant blue light Yoshi liked. The blue was easy on his eyes. He felt peaceful. The time for fear had come and gone. His mind was stuck in a groove though. He had first thought it ironic that this was the way he'd fulfill the fateful errand that grown-up Yoshi had sent him on. Meet the Chairman and get his map. But there was no irony to destiny. Destiny was destiny. To call it ironic was either too small or too large a vision. But it was ironic, right? He was stuck in a groove. He found he didn't care for irony. In five or six hours he'd be able to move his arms and legs again. He'd get up off the table. He'd move around this big room. He couldn't see what would happen next. Not yet.

But this was the first day of a new world, a new life, and the last day of the old world, the old life, and these were the same world. The same life.

TO BE CONTINUED IN VOLUME TWO: CITY OF PEACE.

CPSIA information can be obtained
at www.ICGtesting.com
Printed in the USA
LVHW041504141019
634126LV00001B/133/P